# NIGHTWALKER

Defeated, Darclan passed the red, insubstantial form of the nightwalker and knelt by the bed. He kissed Sara, but her dead lips remained motionless. He ran his hands along her face, searching for some sign of life. This could not be his last memory of her—not this cold, bitter silence . . .

"I grow bored, Darclan. Stand aside; you have lost."

The nightwalker reached out for Sara. When Darclan snarled and struck out, his hand passed through the wraithlike body, and the nightwalker laughed. "Come, you should know better. We are already bound, this one and I.

"I have tasted her blood."

The walker touched Sara's cheek and she stiffened beneath his insubstantial fingers. Even this much response she had not given Darclan . . .

By Michelle Sagara
*Published by Ballantine Books:*

INTO THE DARK LANDS
CHILDREN OF THE BLOOD

# CHILDREN OF THE BLOOD

## Book Two of *The Sundered*

## Michelle M. Sagara

A Del Rey Book

BALLANTINE BOOKS • NEW YORK

A Del Rey Book
Published by Ballantine Books
Copyright © 1992 by Michelle Sagara

All rights reserved under International and Pan-American Copyright Conventions. Published in the United States of America by Ballantine Books, a division of Random House, Inc., New York, and simultaneously in Canada by Random House of Canada Limited, Toronto.

Library of Congress Catalog Card Number: 91-92388

ISBN 0-345-37621-8

Manufactured in the United States of America

First Edition: June 1992

# prologue

*Time had become the strangest of enemies.*

It still could not change Stefanos; its long fingers could find no purchase in his immortal features. But few indeed were the Servants who chose to dwell so completely within the mortal world, and he was First among them.

He spread his hands and gestured sharply. His room, lighted with torches and a central fire, turned a deep shade of crimson.

*Time.*

Only once had he ever felt constrained by it. A bitter smile touched his lips. He had paid the price to be free of that constraint, but he knew time now as an enemy. He saw its march in the faces that surrounded him; saw its seasons turn and change them, eventually laying them low.

Impatient, he gestured again.

As ever, the map unfurled before him, its red lines spreading like velvet flame to occupy the space before him. Every city, every hill, every valley, bore the signature of his power.

He frowned. All save one.

Dagothrin, last of the Lernari strongholds, still defied both his army and his Servants. It shone white and brilliant, standing out in sharp relief against the red that surrounded it.

*Lady, was this your hope?*

He gestured again, a smile touching the pale contours of his lips in the red shadows.

Much had changed in him, enough that he could appreciate the work and the power that had gone into the fortification of Dagothrin's cursed walls. The Lady of Elliath had long since been destroyed—but in this, she lived on. He wondered if her power had been diminished by this task; certainly no word of it had reached his ears, or the ears of his spies.

1

Some hint of noise filtered through even the thick stone walls, ceasing its shuffle as it reached the single door. He frowned, surveying the white.

"Enter," he said.

The door behind his shadowed back swung open.

"Lord."

*Ah. Vellen.*

He heard the swirl of robes that spoke of homage; the high priest was bowing. He listened for the soft touch of forehead to stone before turning to speak. "High Priest."

The man rose, his face a careful study of neutrality. Stefanos had seen enough of humanity to know what it concealed, and against his will he felt a wild impatience. He held it; he had long since learned how.

"Your report?"

The blue eyes turned, and a smile touched the man's pale lips. Stefanos frowned for a moment and then nodded. Vellen had only just succeeded to the title of high priest of the Greater Cabal, and with him, several of his contemporaries had joined the ranks of the Karnari. Vellen was young; perhaps the youngest that had yet achieved First among the Karnari, but he understood power well.

Never mind. It had been centuries since the Church had commanded any respect or attention from the Empire's Lord, and he would not waste more time on their circumstances now.

"We have received word, Lord." Vellen pulled a slightly battered scroll from the folds of his robe. "From Dagothrin."

Stefanos took the scroll in hand and unraveled it slowly and deliberately. His fingers tightened perceptibly, adding creases to the worn vellum.

"Duke Jordan?"

"Yes, Lord." Vellen's smile smoothed itself away until only his eyes contained it. "Three months hence, he will allow us access to Dagothrin."

"The king?"

"Will not trouble us. Nor will his heirs."

"And in return?"

"He wishes governorship of the city. The Church will support this."

Stefanos did not like the edge in the young Malanthi's voice, but he passed over it; the news that he had delivered merited no less.

*Three months.* Time. He felt it, implacable, immovable. *Three months . . .* He looked again at the trace of black against cream; studied the crumbling seal. His eyes saw, for a moment, the preternatural green of the walls of Dagothrin, with the Lady's promise writ large: *No army from without shall destroy thee.*

*Lady,* he thought, as he set the scroll aside, *it was foolish of you to depend upon the consistency of so gray and weak a people. It was only a matter of . . . time.*

"Very well," he murmured, turning away from the High Priest. "Mobilize the army in Verdann."

"At your command, Lord."

"And High Priest?"

"Lord?"

"Tell them that I ride with them."

Vellen was still for a moment.

"Go."

"Yes, Lord."

Stefanos waited until the door clicked and began to gesture anew. Strands of red moved forward, encircling the white of Dagothrin.

*Lady, the battle is over.*

His hands shook; it surprised him.

With a quick, curt gesture he sent the map away. The red lingered a moment, and then it was lost to the comfort of shadow.

*Sarillorn. Sara. Soon . . .*

# chapter
# one

*Nobody can just do what they want to do, son. That isn't the* way the line works.

Darin glared at the closed door of his small room.

Easy for them to say. When they wanted to send him to his room, they sent him to his room. But when he wanted to leave, he couldn't. It was very clear to him.

"The king," he murmured to the bare walls, "*is* stupid. And that's that." He walked over to his desk and dragged the chair across the floor loudly.

History. History was the other thing that was stupid. The boy sat down, thunking his feet loudly against the floor and hoping it irritated his father.

*It's already happened.* He pulled out his new slate, which had replaced the third one he'd dropped, and picked up a wedge of chalk. *And everyone's dead.*

"Why," he said aloud, "can't we talk about what we're *going* to do instead of what everyone else's already done?"

No one answered, which was better than what usually happened when he asked this perfectly reasonable question. Very dutifully he began to inscribe seven names. Seven lines. And only Culverne remained.

*Doesn't that tell you something?*

He frowned as the Grandmother's question reverberated in the near-empty room. His mother had once told him that not all of the Line Culverne patriarchs or matriarchs had chosen to teach, and further, that he should be honored to sit in a class given by the line's leader herself. Hah. He couldn't understand why the Grandmother was always so grouchy—his own grandmother never was.

Unbidden, her words sounded again in his mind. *The Lady*

4

*of Elliath was the greatest power that the lines possessed. With her loss, much of our defense was lost also. But worse still was the loss of the Gifting. The Bright Heart was weakened, and we cannot now recover what was taken. Darin!*

Great, he thought, as he shoved the slate away. I can't even be alone in peace.

*Bright Heart's blood, boy! Can you not pay attention for even a minute? Corvas, shutter those windows.*

Darin stood and began to pace the room, wearing tracks in the wood, as his mother often said. He knew that history was important. But why must he spend so many hours studying things that had gone before? Why couldn't they do something instead of just talking?

His eyes lighted upon the large window that was centered in the outer wall. Smooth, old wood framed two worn shutters. Flecks of gray paint had peeled away with Darin's impatient help, and the latch had been twice broken. A third time, and his father promised the latch would be strung with something other than metal.

Yes, the king *was* stupid for disowning Darin's hero—everyone knew it, except maybe teachers and parents. Darin thought of the prince of thieves and smiled. Renar was not a tall man, at least not according to the stories. Remembering this, Darin stood up on his toes almost proudly and undid the latch. He took some care with it, even though he knew his hero wouldn't have. Renar wouldn't be sent to his rooms to study, either, and that was probably as much of the Bright Heart's blessing as anyone was likely to get in this life.

The shutters creaked open an inch at a time as Darin held his breath. His heart was thumping loudly in his chest as he spun around to look suspiciously at the closed door.

They hadn't noticed. He smiled, every inch the noble thief, and then tried to pull himself up onto the window ledge. Of course Renar could probably do it more smoothly, but he had years of practice. Trembling slightly, Darin gripped the window's frame and hoped that it wouldn't give out.

*Hooks,* he thought, as he stared down at the darkened grass. *And grappling irons. And ropes. That's what I need.*

Just how had the window gotten so high up?

Darin managed a strained giggle that the gentle breeze blew away. With a high little whoop he cast off from the window ledge. Dark blades of grass rushed up to meet him. His slippered feet hit the ground first, quickly followed by his knees,

his hands, and his left cheek. Dirt clung to his tangled, pale hair
as he got unsteadily to his feet.

*Where to now?* he thought, glancing furtively over his shoulder at the lights of the fire-room. The orange glow flickering
through the shutter cracks told him clearly that his parents were
still awake. Probably talking about something boring or silly,
too.

Under cover of night, the house looked somehow larger, a
squat, flat rectangle that covered the small horizon he could see.
A momentary pang caught him. *How am I going to get back in?*

*Easy,* he lied. *I'll just wait until the fire's gone out and I'll
sneak past them.* He had a vague idea that it wouldn't work, but
he could worry about it later. Right now he had something more
important to do. He had made his escape, but in order fully to
redeem himself, there was still a small business matter to take
care of. He got quickly to his feet and began to crouch in the
shadows as he loped toward the scum of the Empire, his sometimes—former—best friend, Kerren. If it weren't for Kerren
tackling him just when the lesson bells had gone off, he wouldn't
have been late for the Grandmother's class. She wouldn't have
been angry, and he wouldn't have been sent to his room to "make
up" for lessons he'd missed. Kerren was going to pay for that.

The winding pathway that had been built between the houses
of the line's settlement was a lot less smooth and flat than it
seemed during daylight. Longer, too. He stumbled several times,
but managed not to curse too loudly. He passed the houses of
the priests and initiates, counting them off one by one. Numbers
and counting were something he had always been good at when
they were worth the bother.

The fourth time he stubbed his toe, he decided that he would
need to sneak leathers into his room for such secret excursions
as this; slippers were too painful.

Then even that trivial thought was pushed aside; he'd passed
the last of the priest's houses and was entering the more modest
dwellings of the line servers. There, flat, squat, and small, was
the house that he sought.

Fire ebbed low in the room nearest him; Kerren's parents were
also probably awake. A bad sign, this, but if he was very careful
and quiet, he wouldn't attract their attention. His hand touched
the dry, solid wood of the outer wall, and he began to creep
along it.

He couldn't wait to see Kerren's face.

The shutters of Kerren's window were just within reach. Darin pushed at them experimentally. They were latched. No one was there to see his face fall in the shadows.

Now what?

He frowned, pushed a little harder, and got the same results. *Lock picks. I need lock picks. Renar would have lock picks.* Of course, he would also have a plan on the rare occasion that he was caught unprepared. *I need a plan.*

He sat down heavily beneath the closed window. His small brow furrowed as he put his face in his hands in an unconscious mimicry of his mother. He sat that way for a few minutes and then suddenly looked up. With a gleeful smile, he made his way back to the path and began to scrounge around for the rocks that had troubled his toes. It wasn't hard to find one, and in the darkness he didn't notice the dust and dirt that attached itself to his nightdress.

He scrambled around the house, stopped outside of Kerren's window, and launched the rock. It gave a loud, dull thud against the shutter and fell to the ground. After a few minutes of disgusted waiting, Darin picked the rock up again and gripped its rough edges firmly. He threw it, it hit, and it bounced.

*Come on, Kerren—can you sleep through anything?*

He bent to retrieve the rock again and dropped it suddenly as the creak of a shutter alerted him to the presence of his intended victim.

With an impish smile, he crouched beneath the window as the shutters passed outward over his upturned face.

"Hello?"

"Hah!" Darin sprung up and grabbed the hand that Kerren was resting against the window frame. "Got you at last, vile fiend of the Empire!"

Kerren let out a shriek of surprise and pulled back.

"You idiot!" Darin hissed, his own shock grounding him suddenly in the real world.

"Is that you, Darin?" The words were faint and trembling, with just a hint of annoyance.

"Who else? Did you have to scream? Your parents'll probably be here any minute. Quick, give me hand up—I'll hide under the bed."

"What are you doing here?"

"Catching you—and paying you back for this afternoon."

"Cheat!"

"Cheat, nothing! You waited for the lesson bells on purpose!" Darin grabbed the window ledge firmly and tried to pull himself up. Unfortunately, his strength was matched well by his size, and he slid down again. "Now quick, help me up."

"I don't see why I should."

"Kerren?" A third voice entered the conversation, older and feminine.

"Dark Heart, Darin, look what you've done!" The smaller argument was forgotten as Kerren, larger and stronger, grabbed Darin's hands. "Hurry up!" He gave a hard yank, and Darin muffled a squeal as his chest was dragged across the window ledge.

"Quick, get under the bed!"

Darin nodded, gulped, and began to crawl along the floor.

"Kerren?"

"It was nothing, Mother," Kerren shouted loudly. "I just— I had a nightmare, that's all. Go back to sleep, everything's fine. Really. Nothing's wrong."

*You idiot*, Darin thought; he had almost made the bed. *You couldn't just keep quiet and act normal.*

"Kerren." The door swung open. Kerren's mother stood framed by wood as she held a flickering lamp high. It shone down on the peppered length of her hair, bringing her cheeks and the lines around her mouth into gentle relief. "Just what is going on here?"

Darin would have had a hard time imagining the plump, friendly woman he knew so well wearing such a frown. He tried to make himself smaller as he looked at the distance between himself and the safety of the underside of Kerren's bed.

He wilted visibly as Kerren threw a guilty look in his direction. The light that suddenly flooded his back might have been magical given the effect that it had.

"What's this?"

He got slowly to his feet as Helna approached him, swinging the lamp gently to and fro.

"Or should I have known?"

"Hi, Helna." Darin kept his voice as meek and friendly as possible.

"I should have known." She shook her head, the frown fading just a touch around the corners of her mouth. Darin knew he wasn't safe yet. "Do you have any idea what time it is, young man?"

"No, why?"

"Yes, you do, Darin. You don't normally wear a nightdress

early in the evening. And what's that you've got on your feet? Slippers?''

*Why are you asking if you already know the answer?* Darin thought. He was wise enough not to say it out loud, for though it was a perfectly reasonable question, it always had the worst possible effect on adults.

''And don't think,'' Helna said to her son as he sidled toward the wall, ''that I've finished with you yet, either. Darin's a troublemaker, all right, but he's his mother's problem. I wish I could say the same of you.''

''Helna?''

*Oh, great.* Darin thought. *Just what we need. Another one of them.*

It was just one of those evenings. Jerrald rambled into view, wearing a night robe that his broad shoulders strained against. He was carpenter and blacksmith to the small enclave, but given his size, Darin was always certain that he'd have made a better warrior.

''What's this?''

Helna turned to face her husband with a sigh. ''More of the same.''

He raised an eyebrow, which was difficult considering he only really had one dark line of hair across the upper ridge of his eyes. ''Kerren, have you been troubling your poor mother?''

Kerren gazed awkwardly down at the ground. After a moment he murmured a word of assent and hung his head.

Helna looked at him. ''Aye, that he has.'' Her lips gentled again, this time into a smile. ''But not near as much as young Darin here's troubling his.''

''Darin?'' Jerrald's broad grin was much less reluctant than his wife's. ''That'd explain a whole lot. What're you doing here at this time of night, boy?''

''Pretending to be Renar,'' Kerren said, with just a hint of spite in his voice.

Darin shot him a dirty look. ''Was not. And anyway, I'm better at it than you.''

''Yeah? Well, I didn't notice you escaping when the bells rang!''

''Well, if you had to learn anything, maybe you would've!''

''Boys!'' Helna's voice rang out.

''Pretending to be Renar, eh?'' Jerrald said. ''Ah, well. Helna?''

She frowned. ''Jerrald, I swear you're getting far too lenient

in your old age. If Hanset had ever done anything like this, you'd
have had him in stocks."

Jerrald shrugged ruefully. "Aye, lass. But maybe at that age,
I was little more than a boy myself, and you little more than a
slip of girl. Come, love. They're boys, they'll be what they are.
And there's worse to imitate in the world than the thieving
prince."

Kerren relaxed. When his father called his mother "lass,"
things usually went for the better.

Nor was tonight to be any exception. Helna shook her head,
a soft blush warming the lines of her face. "Lass, is it?" Jerrald
held out one arm, and she walked slowly into his embrace, her
eyes on his face alone. "I swear, Jerrald, there's a reason why
Kerren's more of a handful than any of the rest of his brothers
or sisters."

"Maybe he has more of youth in him than we can remember." He kissed his wife gently on the forehead, then turned
back to the boys. "But still, that doesn't mean you're to stay
here, Darin. Your folks are like to worry."

The relief that Darin felt instantly faded when he thought of
his own parents. They weren't likely to be nearly as forgiving
or understanding. Then again, he might just be able to sneak
past them and back to his room. After all, they couldn't worry
over something they didn't know about.

He nodded. "Thank you, sir, ma'am."

He started to walk toward the window, and Jerrald's har-
rumph made him stop.

"The door, Darin."

"Oh." Darkness hid his blush as he made his way round
Kerren's parents.

That was when the earth started to shake.

Darin reached for the door frame as Helna was thrown against
her husband. He heard clearly her sharp exclamation as she
endeavored to cling to the lamp; in a wooden house, accidents
with flame could be fatal.

"Heart's blood!" Jerrald stormed to the window. "What was
that?"

Kerren scurried over to his mother's still figure, and Darin
found himself doing the same. Neither of them could see the
window that Jerrald all but blocked; neither cared. Helna put an
arm around her son's shoulder; both of them were shaking. Such
sounds never came to the enclave, either by day or night. And
the fact that it was night made it more ominous.

Silent, the three watched Jerrald's back as he pulled away from the window.

"Bright Heart," he said, each word so soft it barely carried at all. He could not tear his eyes away from the outside world.

"Jerrald? Jerrald, what is it?"

Kerren had never heard his mother's voice sound like that.

"Dad," he whispered, "what's out there?"

"Fire." There was no comfort or warmth in the single word the large man uttered.

Darin could not even speak. Something was wrong; something worse than fire. He could feel it slicing into his skin—a cold, clear danger.

The screaming started, the high, thin sound streaming in the open window to shrill past even Jerrald's wide chest. The fire, if fire it was, crackled loudly. Darin was certain he heard thunder's voice, but it was close, too close.

Helna looked down at him, the lamp beginning to falter. She touched the deathly chill of his skin, and she paled herself. For Darin was of the lines, and the blood of the Bright Heart shuddered within him. Only now did she fully realize this.

"Bright Heart," she said, a dearth of hope in her voice.

Jerrald turned away from the window, blanching. He offered no explanation as he straightened out. "Quick now, Helna. We've got to leave—I think I see soldiers!'

She closed her eyes, shook herself, and nodded. "Get your boots, Kerren. Darin, you'll have to make do with what you're wearing. Darin!"

Shaking, he looked up to see a terrible knowledge writ large in the lines of her face. She shoved him out of the room; he felt Kerren jostle against him.

Jerrald squeezed past them in the narrow hall.

"Jerr, where are you going?"

The smith wheeled back to his wife. "Take the boys, lass," he murmured. His eyes were as flat as hers. "I've—I've things to do here."

She shook her head, dazed, and he kissed her once, fiercely. Her hands reached for the front of his night robe. "Jerrald . . ."

He pressed one large finger against her near-white lips, and a smile touched the corner of his mouth. "The Bridge of the Beyond, dear heart. Go, and quickly."

Still she hesitated.

"Helna . . ." He looked down at Kerren and Darin, both too confused and too frightened even to speak. "They need you."

These words had the desired effect. She set the lamp down; there would be no use for it now. Her plump arms encircled the two children almost fiercely.

"I love you, Jerrald," she whispered, although there was no need to say it.

He stood against the wall and she ushered the children toward the door, and toward the waiting darkness.

# chapter
# two

*Fire burned red against the darkness of cloudy sky. Stefanos* watched, only occasionally raising his hands to add fuel to it. The earth had done its work at his behest; the temple of Culverne lay in shards so sharp they might have been glass. It had not been an easy magic, to move the ground itself, but he had been unwilling to approach the last of these temples by dint of mere physical force alone. The tremors had long since stilled, but he felt them in the smoke-laden breeze.

He felt unaccountably weary on the eve of victory. The black and red backs of his Swords spread out thickly between the burning buildings. They moved like noisy shadows; he caught the occasional laugh or shout, whether of pain or triumph mattered not. The end was clearly in sight.

His vision caught the flickering lights of Lernari power as the city's few defenders moved among red embers. They almost seemed unclothed to him; they were very, very weak. Had it been so long?

*Ah,* he thought, as four lights went out. *Soon, soon . . .* His claws curved inward to touch the chill of his palms. Tonight, this last night, he wore no disguise. This was his only gesture of respect for an enemy that had long eluded him. He stood, black and white against the horizon, his pale lips and pale teeth glinting gently, although with frown or with smile, not even he could be certain.

His magery had destroyed those dwellings that the Lernari had taken for their own; his vision had separated the servers' dwellings from the masters'.

A long, loud scream ebbed up in the heat of the night, faded into a whimper, and then into silence. That voice would never break silence again. The laughter of Swords took up where it left off.

"Lord."

He turned to look down at Vellen, resplendent in his mortal robes. The high priest was pale, as the First, but his hair was gold, his eyes blue, and his expression so much more definite. The high, red collar of his office framed him perfectly.

"It is almost over."

"Yes," Stefanos said, and turned his gaze back toward where the last of the light was dying.

Vellen barked an order, and another priest came forward, hands holding an ebony box. Vellen took it, opened it, and looked almost reverently down the fine edge of a black blade.

"We consecrate this ground tonight."

Stefanos said nothing. Here and there voices still erupted, passing over the clash of metal and the crackle of preternatural flame.

Many times had he seen such an end; many times had he been the instrument of it. Unbidden, the thought of her returned to him, her fire and light strong enough to be felt against even his best effort. Upon such a night as this had his course been decided.

"None of the Lernari," he said, suddenly and coldly.

"Pardon, Lord?"

"None of the Lernari." Stefanos stepped forward. "Gather their servants if you wish, and sacrifice those that you choose from among them. But the Lernari are to be given swift passage to the beyond that they seek."

Vellen opened his mouth to speak, and then clamped his lips down firmly over the words that he had been about to say. He looked at the First Servant, Lord of the Empire, and saw the nightmare of children: nightwalker, devourer of souls. Almost against his will, he shivered. For although he and all the rest of the Karnari had always known in truth what the Lord was, they had never seen it until now.

Still, it was hard not to feel anger at this unwarranted interference. The Church had its own laws, and not even the Lord of the Empire could contradict them on whim. Nor had he ever tried, in living memory. Vellen started to speak, and again thought the better of it; the time to confront this Lord was not upon the field of battle, and not without the power of God behind him. When he returned to the capital, however, he would bespeak the Dark Heart; perhaps this once he would receive a solid answer. He nodded, and his anger grew at the subtle play of smile around the First Servant's lips.

Soon the swords brought the wounded and the whole, dragging them toward the gentle hilltop upon which the Servant stood. Stefanos watched the faces of the prisoners. Some stared at him in open fear, some in confusion, and some with a hatred that time would do nothing to ease.

*Nightwalker.* He heard the murmur as it passed between adults and children. Here or there a child gripped the skirted thigh of a mother or the robe of a father. Tears fell, mingling with blood and silence. They gathered before him, these cattle, these mortals, as they had done only once before.

"Is this all?" Vellen said, his voice steady.

"Yes, Karnar."

"The rest?"

The Sword smiled grimly. "None escaped the watch on the perimeter."

"Good." Vellen echoed the soldier's smile. "Ready the army, then, for the ceremony. Secure the city."

The man saluted once, crisply, and walked away.

Kerren held his mother's dress, his grip too tight to be dislodged easily. He was large for his age, and at any other time he would have stood aside, fearing to look too much like a baby. Nor did Darin notice this, for his fingers held the other side of Helna's fine-spun nightgown.

Only the woman cried, her tears silent. She looked around from side to side, knowing that she would not see her husband here, but hoping nonetheless. Her arms still clutched the two children as she stood witness to the fall of Culverne. They had done their best to run, and failing at that, had done their best to hide. The screams and the fighting had provided no cover for them, and they had been brought back at sword point, traversing the growing graveyard of Lernari and servers alike.

Kerren looked up at his mother, and she pulled him more tightly to her. Darin looked at the Servant. The nightwalker stood so close, an emblem of the Dark Heart. But here, unlike in history books and upon tapestries, there was no Bright Heart to defy him.

The fire was still burning; if Darin looked hard enough he could see the flickering outline of the house that had been his. He said nothing; did not even look around at the gathered crowd. He knew he would not see his family here.

An icy hand gripped his heart too tightly for sorrow.

This creature was the horrible wrongness that he had felt. No nightmare, no daydream, no story, could have prepared him for it.

Death walked among them all.

Stefanos surveyed the crowd with growing disinterest. He saw their fear, but did not allow himself to feel it. These were, as the others who toiled within his empire, beneath his notice, beneath contempt.

"Lord." Vellen bowed low. "Should you wish it, you may preside over the ceremonies." In his hands he held the knife of the Karnari. There was no warmth in the words, but Stefanos expected none. He was tempted to accept the high priest's offer, if only to discomfort the mortal, but decided against it.

"You may continue."

Vellen nodded smoothly, a sure sign that the knife was proffered for the sake of formality alone.

*Did I travel this far and wait this long to suffer the presumption of a priest?* It had been long since the luxury of thwarting the Church had been his; but the time had come for many things, and here, perhaps for the first time in centuries, he could relax.

One dark claw shot out and caught Vellen's pale hand before the priest could begin his benediction. The susurrus of muted whispers echoed around his back; the Swords were surprised. He could feel them join him as he studied Vellen's face. Anger was there; so intense an anger that for a moment Vellen could not help but let it show. For anyone else, such an offence merited death at the least; Stefanos knew it and allowed his smile to show the knowledge clearly.

"Perhaps, High Priest, I shall accept your offer after all."

All anger vanished as the Servant released the priest. They stood matching wills for minutes in the sudden silence. The blood of the Dark Heart stirred as blue eyes met red-tinged black.

It was Vellen who broke away first; this, Stefanos had expected. What surprised him was the mien of the priest as he bowed smoothly. Power recognized power. But there was grace in the acknowledgment; grace and no hint of the bluster or fear that had marked any other encounter that Stefanos had chosen.

"Lord."

"High Priest." *A pity, Vellen, that you are merely half blood. You might have otherwise proved a worthy opponent.*

The black of obsidian shivered in his palm as Vellen passed the dagger to him. Stefanos looked down at it. His lips curled over his teeth. In any other heart, this legendary blade might invoke fear. His head rose, and he gazed out at the gathered crowd of slaves. He did not need the dagger; it was an emblem of a lesser power. With barely concealed contempt, he laid it aside.

"Will you choose?" Vellen asked, an edge in his voice as the symbol was put aside unblooded.

"Indeed."

The shadow began to walk. It descended the grassy hill that had been trampled by the feet of hundreds of soldiers. It advanced upon the cowed and silent throng. As if they were water, the people standing near Darin, toward the front of the crowd, pulled back in a wave. The boy felt Helna's grip grow stronger as she pulled him back as well. He followed her wordless direction without realizing it. If the shadow walked, it would find him. That conviction grew in him until he could not contain it; he trembled visibly.

Helna would risk no words, not here. But she tried to calm Darin by drawing him yet further into the meager shelter of her arms. In silence, they waited.

Everyone had heard the stories of the priests and their dark communion with the Heart that none ever named. They knew what the dagger meant, and what the man in black-traced red had intended. He was not their fear.

No, their fear came to them in icy shadow, carrying a darkness too deep for the night, and too final. Even the children were silent as he began to walk among them.

This close, it was harder. Stefanos' red eyes trailed across the faces of gathered servants. If they could, he knew they would bolt like a panicked herd. With the Swords on the perimeter, however, they chose instead the guise of rabbits; they stood straight and still, moving very little, as if movement alone could catch his attention. Thus had they stood, Sarillorn at their head, too many mortal years ago. And he had chosen to live each one of those years alone.

He saw her then, as he often saw her, a trace of green light warming the lines of her body, hands clenched tightly at her side, chin tilted up in defiance and resignation both. She stepped forward, a human ghost, and he stopped before the memory of her hands could pass through him.

*Sara.*

For lives such as these, she had bargained away her own. He wondered if she had been aware that he'd had no intention of living up to his word once he'd taken what he desired. He had never asked.

But he had chosen to play the game, and it had grown, in short hours, beyond either's understanding. For a moment he ached at the haunting.

*Sara. It is over. The war is at end. You always desired peace.*

He shook himself and walked further into the crowd, seeing other faces, another time.

And then he stopped.

The air carried just the faintest hint of wrongness here, a trace of what had been. He looked back at the high priest and then shook his head; time had weakened the half bloods, and Vellen's power alone was not enough to detect this. But he was First; in him the power of the Awakening flowed undiminished.

Perhaps one of the Lernari had fathered a bastard among the servers. In times past, such a thing would have been unlikely, but mortal blood had weakened the light as well.


Darin's eyes grew wide as the nightwalker suddenly gestured. A red haze shimmered around him, deeper and darker than the red of his eyes. In panic, he raised his arms, hands flying futilely in the air. Helna gasped and reached out to grab them.

Too late.

The nightwalker turned, his gaze falling on Darin.

"So," he said softly, and began to walk, his gait as measured and precise as before. But this time he did not walk at random. People moved to grant him passage; anything else was death.

He came to a stop in front of Darin, and his black claws reached out.

Darin gave a little gasp as they enfolded his chin. They were cold; he had not imagined that anything so red could be so icy.

"What is your name, child?"

"D-Darin."

The claw tightened. "You will learn," the nightwalker said softly, "that you are a slave now. You have no name."

Darin said nothing.

"You." The nightwalker spoke to Helna now, relieving Darin from the pressure of his eyes. "Is this child yours?"

"Yes." There was no hesitation. She trembled, that was all.
"The father?"

"Dead." Her voice grew weaker as she felt Kerren's sudden
lurch. She held on to him as if he were life, and he was wise
enough to say nothing.

"Dead." The nightwalker smiled. Then he drew his free
hand back and slammed it into the side of the woman's face.
She collapsed, pulling the other—man? boy?—with her. "That
was not the question I asked." He waited for a moment, but she
had been silenced; he would get no answers there.

Darin stood alone, without Helna to anchor him. His blue
eyes were wide beneath the pale glow of his hair. He saw, out
of the corner of his eye, Kerren struggling to tend to his mother.
He might have helped, but he could not move; his face was still
locked within the nightwalker's grip.

"And you, boy, how do you come here?"

Darin said nothing.

Stefanos smiled, but it was an odd smile. Once before, he
had encountered a Lernari alone among the slaves. And once
before, he had spared that life.

*The lines*, he thought, pressing his claws deeper into fair skin
until they drew blood, *must perish. They stood between us, as
they must not stand between us again.*

He raised one hand again, a perfunctory gesture.

She stopped him, or the memory of her. Her pale face, framed
by auburn, highlighted by green, looking up at him in silent pain
and pleading. Six times in the past he had looked through the
memory. Too much had been at stake, too much arrayed against
the armies he had led. But this seventh . . .

He looked at Darin as if seeing him for the first time. A small,
frightened boy, mortal in seeming and carriage, stared back. He
could not judge the age well; human children had not been a
concern of his, or an area in which study seemed useful. The
boy was short, thin, his face so angular that were it not for the
softness of youth, it would be sharp. And his eyes were blue and
blinking.

*For such as these, Sarillorn, you gave me your life.*

He lowered his hand.

*Let us start again as we started in the beginning. These lives
are yours, let them fare as they will in our Empire.*

Without another word, he turned and walked to where the
high priest still waited.

"There will be no ceremony," he said softly.

Not even Vellen had enough control not to blanch. "No ceremony, Lord?"

"Not unless one of your number cares to volunteer."

Vellen said nothing, but after a tense moment, he nodded. He retrieved the dagger, staring down at it as if its unblooded presence accused him. In anger and in silence he ran his thumb along its edge, giving it the blood that it claimed as its right.

Stefanos began to leave, then turned back to stare at the crowd once again. The child, too small to stand above the head of the newly acquired, was lost to sight.

"And High Priest?"

"Lord."

"One among those—a fair-haired young boy in the fourth rank—I shall claim for my household."

"Do you wish to take him now?"

He thought for a moment, then shook his head. "No. He cannot travel as I do. I shall trust him to the care of your house for the moment." He had no need to say more.

"The others, Lord?"

"As usual. But claim them or no, High Priest, their blood does not grace this field."

"Lord."

Stefanos turned, and the battlefield faded into gray. It was over. He could almost rest. The castle that he'd constructed was half-full now; a few more months and the tapestries he had ordered would be complete. The slaves he had gathered thus far would, he felt, be appropriate, and the grounds, except for one area, were well tended.

Only one thing was missing. And now he could begin the last task of drawing her into the new world. His world.


It was no longer dark.

Darin looked up at the open sky and started to get to his feet. Chains rankled at his arms, pulling him firmly into the real world. In silence, he looked at his hands. They were damp and cold; rain had come in the night, and very few of the prisoners had any recourse but to endure it.

Helna was nowhere in sight. They had dragged her body away shortly after the nightwalker had departed. A few of the other women and men were also gone, and Darin thought they, too, might be dead, if the screams he had heard in the night were any indication.

*Dead.*

He closed his eyes and shuddered, curling in on himself. The screams were still close, and he desperately prayed that he would not join the ones who had uttered them so pathetically.

"Darin?"

He froze for a moment and then relaxed; the voice was a familiar, quiet one. Turning his head slowly to the left—he had to move slowly, in case they noticed—he met Kerren's eyes.

They stared at each other in silence.

Shakily, Darin reached out as far as his chains would let him. Kerren did the same until their fingers touched. Each boy tried to draw strength from the contact, but neither really knew how.

They were fed some hours later, then dragged to their feet and across to where two large tents had been set up. A few more of the servants disappeared at the feeding; the old and the injured. Darin wanted to know where they were going, but he couldn't ask. He didn't want to do anything to attract attention.

Later he might realize just how lucky he had been. All of the priests and initiates of Line Culverne, along with their children, lay dead by fire or sword. Not one had escaped. All of the servers of the line knew who he was, and the older and wiser knew that his survival was by chance and not by any darker purpose—but none of these people came forward or tried to bargain with this information.

Now, though, he could only see his loss. Any time he looked to the east, he could see the blackened remains of buildings. He wondered how his father and mother had died. Did they have any warning? Did they have the time to arm themselves or draw upon God's power?

Had they thought about him at all?

He thought of them often in the next few days.

But he didn't cry.

Vellen looked out upon the gathered array of slaves. They were women and children for the most part, with a few men who'd been caught unawares. Dirt stained their faces and hands, where visible, but the rains had kept their smell from becoming too odious.

This part of a battle he sometimes enjoyed, but today it felt empty. The trampled green of open hill annoyed him, unblessed as it was by the blood of those who had dared to stand against his God. Worse was the absence of any who had been his true enemy. Although he had ordered many of their corpses brought up to line the city walls, it was, for his personal sense of victory, a hollow gesture.

Still, they had won. The cursed walls of Dagothrin had finally been opened to allow his chosen their entrance. And what better trophy of victory than these? Alive, and soon to be branded, they would adorn his house and remind all those within of the absolute will of the Dark Heart. The pathetic beating of the Bright One had finally been stilled; no more would he suffer the call of weakness from afar.

"This one." The high priest had chosen to wear his informal garb; black, red-bordered robes with a hint of metallic copper embroidered through them in a pattern of a broken circle, drawn tight by a long red sash. They were new; he had ordered them made in anticipation of his victory.

The Swords moved forward and yanked a young woman to her feet. She glared balefully up at them, but said nothing as they led her off to one of the tents.

Vellen continued to look at the gathered crowd. It had grown in number with the fall and surrender of Dagothrin, but not nearly as much as he would have liked. Still, the duke had busied himself, retaining the governorship of the newly won province and accommodating the Church until a formal structure could be built.

Ah. "That man; the larger one."

The Swords nodded and went forward again, approaching the man with only the slightest evidence of caution. Nor had they much to fear. He went with them, showing more docility than the girl had. Those that had caused too much trouble in the beginning had been killed out of hand, sometimes quickly, sometimes slowly—but always in plain sight.

Darin watched as the high priest walked along the perimeter of the gathered slaves. He shrunk in on himself, trying desperately to look smaller than he already was.

"Her. The pregnant one. Bring her here."

Darin followed the Swords' path through the crowd, and saw the foremost among them grab a young woman by her wrist manacles and drag her to her feet. Peggy. From where he stood, he could see that she'd been crying. He wondered if she had stopped at all in the last four days.

They brought her to the feet of the high priest and then forced her back to her knees.

"You. How many children have you borne?"

She choked out a reply that was too weak for Darin to catch.

The high priest raised an eyebrow and then gave a bored nod to one of his men. A mailed glove rose and fell almost lightly against Peggy's face. She jerked to the side, her chains still held by another Sword.

"How many?"

"N-none."

The Priest repeated his nod, the Sword his slap.

"None, lord."

"This is your first, then. How long did it take you to catch?"

At any other time, Peggy's ears would have burned at the question. She gulped, but before the Sword could slap her bleeding mouth again, she answered.

"I was—was married for a month, lord."

"A month?" The high priest nodded. "Take her, then."

He looked away, the slave already forgotten, and continued to choose his portion.

Darin counted thirty-four. He lost count after that because the Swords came for him. Kerren looked up, choked, and looked away as they dragged Darin out of his life.

Darin looked back to see the strained fear across his best friend's pale features. He wanted to speak, to say something. Without thinking, he reached back, but the chains caught and held him as surely as the Swords did.

There was no Renar here; no thieving prince to rescue them or to mete out the fate that the high priest had earned. Darin tried not to drag his feet against the wet dirt as the Swords brought him to stand before Vellen.

"Boy."

Darin looked up to meet the gaze of the high priest. The older man's eyes were blue and icy, and the corners of his thin lips turned slightly down in a frown. Darin began to shake. He couldn't help it. Although he didn't know what he had done, he knew that something had angered this man, and his life depended on the Karnar's good grace. He waited for the high priest to speak.

"Who was that other boy?"

Darin shrank back, and the grips on his arms tightened.

"A—a friend."

"Of yours, child?" Vellen spoke smoothly, softly.

"Y-yes, lord."

"I see." The annoyance ebbed away, and the edges of the lips turned up in a smile that was somehow far worse. The high priest turned to two Swords. "Take that one as well."

Darin's heart sank as Kerren was dragged forward to join him. Kerren smiled shakily in a way that told Darin he was happier to be here than to be left behind. It was a smile that would haunt later.

In a silence punctuated by the clink of chains, they walked away from what remained of the only home they had known.

Later that night they became as Vellen had envisioned them.

They were woken from sleep by the Swords; the high priest did not seem to keep normal soldiers in his command.

"Come along," an older man said, his expression a trifle bored. "We'll be moving in a two-day, and the lot of you will have to be ready by then."

Darin was quick to wake, and silent besides. Kerren was not quite so lucky. He'd slept poorly the first three nights, even compared to the rest of the slaves, and the crisis that had come upon them did not make him easier to wake. He moaned slightly and tried to turn over when a Sword shook him harshly by the shoulder.

"Is he all right?" a guard at the back asked.

"Right enough. He'd better be," the Sword replied, and aimed a swift kick at the young boy's ribs. Kerren's cry of pain forced the transition between the world of dream and the world of nightmare. His eyes shot open and he swung around, his lips trembling.

"Mother?"

A Sword laughed. It was a hideous sound, but Darin knew from the teaching stories that the Malanthi could make anything ugly. He bit his lip as the Sword's foot connected once more with Kerren's rib cage.

"Enough, Callum. It's the high priest's right, not ours."

"Aye," the man replied, just a tinge of regret in his voice. "True enough." He reached down and yanked Kerren to his feet. "You've cost us time, boy. Believe that we'll take it out of you if you don't smarten up."

Darin wanted to speak. He didn't. Instead, he waited until Kerren was close enough to touch and held out his hand as inconspicuously as possible. Kerren didn't usually notice subtle things, but he noticed this, and his own hand snaked out quickly.

Kerren had always been strong; once or twice, when they'd played a game of hand-grip, he'd crushed Darin's fingers hard enough to numb them, and his parents had come out to break up the ensuing squabble. Not tonight. Darin felt the cold prickle start up the side of his right hand, but he didn't pull away. He could see, by the light of the campfires, that Kerren was crying.

He didn't expect Kerren to be as careful as he himself had managed to be; Kerren had never, ever been that. But he felt his own throat constrict as he thought about everything they had lost—and everything that they could still lose.

*At least we're together*, he thought. *And we're still brothers. They can't take that away from us.*

But he wasn't certain. So even though he let Kerren cry without saying anything or warning him not to, he held his own tears as if they were a secret.

They followed the brisk lead set by the black-armored Swords, watching the glint of light off the links of chain that they wore. No one spoke, but the feeling of dread grew as five more slaves were picked up from the tents that housed them.

As they continued to walk, a scream cut the air.

Darin froze.

A sharp nudge at his back reminded him of the imperative of not being noticed, and he began to walk by rote, one shaking foot following another.

He smelled it before he could see what was ahead. It was acrid and sharp, even wafted as it was by damp, earth-sodden breeze. His brow furrowed as he tried to identify what had caused it.

Then he froze, and even the sharp nudge at his back could not make him move forward again.

Kerren looked at him in confusion and tried to pull him along.

"Fire," Darin whispered. "They're burning people."

"Not people," a voice said from directly behind him. "Slaves."

Darin spun around. He saw the shadowed face of a Sword, black helm trailing down the wide, large nose like an iron finger. No comfort there, not in the wide, even grin that broke the line of the square jaw, not in the crinkles around the corners of dark eyes.

He stood transfixed a moment longer, and then Kerren swung him around, still maintaining a strong grip on his hand. "Come on," he whispered. "It's okay. They're lining us up."

He dragged Darin forward, and Darin didn't resist this time. The Sword at his back was a known death.

They joined the line that moved slowly forward. Darin studied the dirt-stained robes of the woman in front of him; caught a hint of a human smell that robbed the burning of some of its acridity. He inhaled sharply, trying not to breathe through his nose. Maybe he imagined things. Maybe he was wrong. Maybe—

Another scream cut the air. It lingered in the breeze before working its way firmly to the base of Darin's spine. He shivered, silent, as he felt other bodies huddle behind him.

"It's stopped," Kerren whispered.

Darin gave his friend a warning glance.

"No. It stopped. Look—if they were burning someone, don't you think it would go on longer?"

The thud of boots silenced them both. Darin looked down at his own white toes and flicked them gently against the flattened grass. He felt ashamed. He knew why Kerren was speaking— to try to comfort him.

He couldn't stop shaking.

"If they wanted to kill us, we'd be dead," Kerren whispered, before the footsteps had fully died away. The grip on Darin's hand tightened briefly and then relaxed. "It's okay."

Another scream.

Darin closed his eyes. He would never dream of being a hero again, never. He was the one who was line trained, or should have been if he had paid attention; he was the one who had some touch of the Bright Heart within him. Kerren was his best friend, but he didn't have any of the blood in him at all—and it was Kerren who was trying to comfort him. The worst thing of all was that he needed it. The trembling wouldn't stop.

Little by little the line was whittled away in blackness. Each person uttered a scream and then was gone; each person brought him closer to whatever fate awaited. He kept his eyes fixed on the brown robes in front of him, watching as they creased with movement, trying to discern whose hand had made them. And then these robes moved, and nothing stood between him and what lay ahead.

He saw it clearly then. A fire, stoked and roaring, was encompassed by a stone pit. A man—no, two—stood beside it, dressed as guards dress, but cleaner.

The woman moved forward. She looked back once, no wildness in her eyes, and no hope, and Darin met that gaze only because he couldn't look away in time.

He watched as one man pulled an iron from the fire; watched as another rolled the right sleeve of the woman's robe up and muttered something. The woman tensed, the man moved forward with the iron. Darin could see its end glowing red in the darkness, as if the Dark Heart's power hallowed it.

It touched white flesh, and Darin was struck by the scream and smell simultaneously. He stepped back, kicked the foot of the person who waited behind, and stopped.

The iron was pulled away; the woman's arm was wrapped roughly in gauze bandages, and she walked into the waiting Swords in a daze, stumbling with the shock.

They looked up then, these two, and he met their eyes.

"Boy," one man said curtly.

Kerren stepped forward. "I'll go first," he said. His voice was not even, but at least he could speak. He squeezed Darin's hand again and smiled tremulously, releasing it for the first time that evening.

Very quickly, as if afraid to change his mind, he covered the ground with his coltish, large stride. He held out his arm to the man with the bandages; it trembled, but not overmuch.

The man took it, looked appraisingly down at the slave, and then nodded, almost as if in approval.

It was done very quickly. Nor did Kerren scream, but a grunt of pain escaped between his clenched teeth. Even as the bandages were being tied around his lower right arm, he turned back to look at Darin.

*You see?* he seemed to say.

Then it was Darin's turn. There was no one to stand between him and the brand. He wanted to be able to do as Kerren had done, but he didn't have the strength. He walked, but his step was flat and slow. When the man reached out for his arm, he tried to pull back. It was useless, of course, and only got him a cuff in the side of the face.

The nightdress' sleeve came away, and his skin lay white and exposed in the darkness. He felt the breeze against it as he looked wildly up at the man with the poker. His eyes snapped shut before he could see the truth of the pain that followed.

And then it was over. The smell of the burning flesh in his nostrils was his own; Swords had to come to drag him, swaying, back to where the group had begun to gather.

The bandages on his arm helped. They hid the scar that would be forming even now. He heard somebody call it the mark of House Damion; heard somebody say that they, as slaves, belonged to that house; and heard the dire warnings given about a failure to obey its lord. All of these things were distant.

Kerren's hand was not. It slid into his left one and held it as firmly as Kerren could manage. Darin held on and only later did he realize that Kerren had offered the right hand; the injured one.

# chapter
# three

*Two people died of infection during the march through the prov-*
ince. They burned with a fever that Darin had seen once or twice
before, but was unable to do anything to stem. The high priest
was not amused by this, although he did not seem to be too
surprised, and it went the worse on the survivors. Many times
in the next two weeks, Darin wished it had been he who had
died. But if the Lernari blood that flowed so weakly in his veins
had not prevailed against the Darkness, it prevailed against this;
he remained whole and healthy.

It was cool at night, but the air was most often damp with the
hint of lingering rain. Tents had been provided for the slaves,
tents and meager blankets. But ten people crammed into a space
meant for four was anything but merciful. Food was also provided, and many were actually forced to eat, although they had
no appetite for it. House Damion had lost two of its levy to
infection; they had no intention of losing any to starvation.

The chains that had bound their ankles were removed on all
but the men, and even these were lengthened. It was a good
thing, as the high priest wished to return to the capital in haste,
and pushed them all as hard as he dared.

The days were hard. The slaves were chained by the wrists
and forced to march single file; Darin became used to the back
of the slave in front of him. Kerren became used to Darin's back.
They didn't speak to each other at all; they had no wish to draw
the attentions of those who drove them.

But if the days were hard, the nights were worse. The Swords
would come to the tent where Darin lay trying to sleep. The
flaps would open and they would walk in, booted feet not gentle
against the press of bodies, to choose among the slaves there.
Most often they took the younger women; occasionally the

29

younger men. In the beginning, those chosen would weep or plead. It did nothing beyond eliciting the occasional smile or blow.

Like pale shadows in the grip of the Swords they would go; and hours later they would return, bleeding at the mouth if they had caused too much struggle. They would fall back among their fellows, trembling at some fate that Darin didn't immediately understand. An older slave would tell him not to touch, and he would crawl back to his place.

The sobbing kept Darin awake far into the night. He tried, once or twice, to speak to the chosen, but they didn't seem to hear him.

Worse, though, were the ones who came back silent, and said no word, made no sound but the harshness of shallow breath in the dark of the tent.

One young man, Charis, died.

Not immediately. But he dwindled over the days; the guards would beat him, but they couldn't make him eat or speak; he was lost inside himself, and remained so.

They left his body at the side of the road; Darin saw it in his sleep through the weeks that followed. Vacant, brown eyes, looking up at the sky in a face that was slack-jawed and skeletal.

But that lingering death bought them peace for a week. No Swords came in the night. No one else died.

At the end of three weeks, they came to the city of Verdann. From the distance, Darin could see the spill of farms that had grown beyond the large, gray walls. Here and there, a large mansion proclaimed the presence of nobility. He wondered if those who worked the land were free. He wondered how a land so shadowed by the Dark Heart could be so green.

He was given no chance to find out; the high priest wished to make the inner wall by sundown. They passed the working farmers by without stopping for food or rest.

The city was large, larger, perhaps, than Dagothrin, and much more crowded. Litters, palanquins, and wagons lined one side of the street as they negotiated their way toward the city center. Because of the crowds, they could not walk quickly, and the urgings of the Swords were lost to the chatter and shouts of Verdann citizenry. For this at least Darin was grateful.

They stopped at the entrance of the market. Darin couldn't see exactly what was happening, but he could see the stalls that bordered the streets stretching out ahead on either side. He waited, putting his weight first on one foot and then on the other, glad of a chance to rest.

The sun blazed in the west; it would sink soon, retreating into shadow. He watched it, squinting at the light. In the background, yells and shouts of people hawking their wares reached his ears. Closing his eyes, he could almost imagine that this was an outing to market. He could see his mother's pursed lips and his father's sardonic grin as the maker of candles sidled along his rickety counter. He could hear the bickering that signaled the beginning of an eventual exchange of money; hear his father snort in amusement at the claim that the candles were made from only the finest animal fats; and hear his mother mutter under her breath.

*Honestly, Clav, you encourage that man.*

*Yes. He's got a good way with words, that one.*

And his mother would glance sideways at his father and roll her eyes in mock disgust. *Darin—come here; we'll lose you in the crowd otherwise.*

*We'll lose you.*

A tug at his wrists made him open his eyes. Chains.

*Mother.* Her face wavered before him, her fine, thin jaw clenched in anger, as it had been the last time he'd seen her.

*Father.* His face joined his mother's. His jaw, also gently pointed, was not caught in the same expression, and Darin thought he imagined just a hint of resigned amusement there. The eyes, brown and half-open, looked from his wife to his son before he gave a shrug of gray-covered shoulders.

*Mari, remember what you were like at his age.*

*I do. And that's why I want to avoid this all.*

*Mother. Father. I'm sorry. Where are you?*

The line began to move forward, and Darin was pulled along. He couldn't see where his feet were going. Everything was too blurred.

For the first time in four weeks, he cried.

A large, grand building loomed beyond the center of the market. Large, cut stone bricks covered the walls, leaving room for tall, thin windows with real glass. Even in the city proper, Darin had rarely seen glass. And there were certainly no structures as grand as this overshadowing the smaller stalls. He heard the muted gasp from behind him, and knew from it that Kerren thought the same.

They continued to stare at it as it grew nearer and impossibly larger.

"Here."

He glanced quickly to the side and saw that the Swords were directing them toward the wide, large staircase. Passersby moved to its gilded rails to gawk at them as they passed. One finely dressed man reached out to touch someone, and the Swords stepped briskly in his way.

"Not yet," he was told. "But a quarter of them will be sold by House Damion on the morrow."

"Damion?" the man asked. "Victory then?"

The Sword's smile was all the reply necessary.

"Well then, perhaps I shall see the lot. They'll make a fine memento of the occasion." He sighed, lips turning down in the slightest of frowns. "I assume the price—"

"Will be commensurate, yes."

"I see." The man nodded briefly, and the Swords dragged the slaves into the auction house.

From the entrance they were led past a wide, open space, which had a low, marble platform in its center. They went into one of several narrow corridors. The stone caught the sound of their flagging footsteps and echoed them dully.

They came at last to a wide set of wooden double doors.

"In here," the Sword at the lead said, although by this time it was hardly necessary. The doors swung smoothly open; it was obvious that they were well oiled and often used.

"Parget!"

"Coming, coming." A tall, thin man appeared at the door. "Ah!" His harassed expression faded into a delighted smile. "You've brought them, then." He gave a low bow. "I assure you, captain, that House Damion has made a wise choice in its representative. I've only just heard of our victory in the north, and I assure you that I've already several interested clients who would—"

"Save it for the block, Parget."

"Of course, sir. Of course." He stepped out of the doorway and clapped his hands loudly. Four men came rushing out. "Take these away, Lanos. Prepare to have them cleaned and groomed."

"Sir." One man bowed and turned to the Sword. A glint of metal caught the scant light as keys were exchanged.

"Clothing, sir?"

"Ah. Well, as usual, I will see that they are properly attired.

My thanks to Lord Vellen of Damion, the high priest who presides over the Greater Cabal.''

The Sword nodded brusquely. ''These last ten are for the personal use of House Damion. They are not to be sold, but Lord Vellen wishes them to be appropriately cleaned and attired before he makes his journey to the capital.''

Parget's smile faltered momentarily. ''Ten? But surely, captain, he cannot—ah, well.'' He sighed. ''Ten it is, then. And yes, we will see that they are attired as befits a house of that stature.''

''Do so.''

Darin was dragged out of his clothing. The attendant, and there was only one, snorted in disgust and dropped the rags of his night robe into the nearby fire. He grabbed Darin's right arm, inspected it, and nodded tersely.

''You can wash yourself, boy?''

Darin nodded. He felt uncomfortable being naked in front of so many people, and he sank into the small, warm bath immediately. His hands shook as he scrubbed ferociously at his pale skin in an attempt to rid himself of weeks of sweat and dirt.

When he finished, he was thrown a towel, and the water, blackened with filth, was removed with another disgusted snort. Dripping from head to toe, he moved to stand in silence by the red flicker of fire.

His muscles ached, and his eyelashes brushed his cheeks as he fought the urge to sleep away the long day's march. No permission had been granted yet to do so.

Kerren came to stand by him; his face was a rosy red, and water dripped freely from his hair. He wrapped the towel tightly over his shoulders and smiled nervously at Darin. Darin smiled back, but it was hard. They leaned against each other, feeling the closeness of the fire along their cheeks and feet.

If they had been at home—*home*—Helna or Darin's mother would have come in with steaming milk. A rug would take the chill of stone from beneath their feet; a chair the ache of standing from their legs.

But nothing would remove the brand that scarred their arms.

The slave house handled its merchandise carefully. After all of the ten had been bathed and cleaned, they were led to another room, one with pallets and blankets. Not one among them resented being ordered to sleep; they lay down on the rough mats, curled blankets over their naked bodies, and knew no more.

* * *

"Mommy, that one. I want that one!"

"Be good, Cyllia, and we shall see."

"I want that one!"

"Why don't we look at them all, daughter? You must learn to make no decision in haste."

This was the worst thing of all. Stories had come down from the few refugees that had made it to Dagothrin's shelter or to Culverne, but none had prepared Darin for this. He watched from behind a rope as the thirty slaves that had journeyed this far with him were inspected.

He had once seen horses bought, and it was little different than this, save that horses were not so scantily dressed or so finely chained.

The noble lady, bearing a crest upon the left shoulder of her robe that Darin guessed proclaimed her house, took her daughter's hand. The child pouted, a very pretty, very spoiled pout, and allowed herself to be led away from Ansen, a boy nearer to Darin's age than the child.

She was, perhaps, four seasons, maybe five, but certainly not older. He had imagined that any who would own slaves would be old, ugly, fat—and dressed in expensive jewelry, velvet, and silk.

Neither of these two lived up to the image.

The child was pretty; her skin was fine porcelain, her hair gold ringlets. She had a winsome smile, and a sparkle about the blue of her eyes that fit her rounded face exactly.

Her mother's face was longer, but still had much of youth about it, and was in many ways more lovely. She wore a single strand of gold about her long, perfect neck, and her gown, a deep blue, was both simple and modestly cut. She touched the smooth cheek of her daughter and smiled affectionately.

Yet she looked at the thirty as if they were expensive animals to be bought, like a kitten, for the amusement of a child.

He shivered, wishing they didn't look so normal.

"I still want that one. Mommy, please, please can't we get that one?" She smiled up at her mother, yanking at a slender finger. "He's the prettiest, Mommy. Please?"

"Hush, Cyllia."

But worse than this twisting of the everyday and the normal was the fact that Darin quietly prayed that the child would get her wish.

* * *

In the end, all thirty were sold.

Darin watched as each was led to the block—the large, marble platform, with its engraved lines and gilt edges. He watched as the spectators—and there were many—began alternately to raise their hands or shout out numbers as each slave was brought forward and his or her virtues were extolled loudly.

Sometimes he cringed as a slave was led away. Sometimes he breathed a quiet sigh of relief. The nine who stood with him, Kerren included, did likewise, although not always at the same time.

And not one among them did not wish that they were on the other side of the ropes, or on the block itself; they knew that it was the high priest of the Dark Heart that had claimed their service, and they had little doubt about how easy that service would be.

They remained in Verdann for one week. The high priest had matters to attend to that would not wait, and besides, it gave the Swords a full seven days to begin the training of the newly acquired.

Nor was the training as hard as the transport had been; now that the numbers were set, Vellen had no wish to lose more—not yet, and not without his specific command. The odd bruise or two might grace the face or sides of any individual, but there were no severe beatings.

There was no reason given for any.

Darin did as he was ordered almost before the command had left the lips of the Swords. He did not shy away from them—this was "bad bearing"—but he did not meet their eyes on the rare occasion that there was an opportunity. He saw more of his feet in these weeks than he had in the rest of his life.

The tunic and breeches that he wore were not that much different from those that he'd worn in Culverne—but they were blue and black, the colors of House Damion. He was given two sets, but no nightclothing, and these he carried with him on the long march.

The Swords also dispensed with the chains and allowed the slaves to walk two abreast between the large wagons that rolled out of the forbidding city gates. None of them tried to run.

Only at night, behind the padlocked doors of dormitories in the various inns that they sheltered at, did Darin ever relax. He would speak to Kerren in quiet whispers as they shared their hopes and fears. Sometimes he would daydream, but the laugh-

ing face of the thieving prince eluded him in the greater shadow
of the Empire. He would stop, half afraid that the Swords could
read his mind and find there a reason to take him.

He did not speak of escape.

But sometimes he prayed for it, using the old language of the
lines, with its delicate resonances and gentle pauses; he tried to
touch the Bright Heart both in the waking world and in dream.
Only darkness ever answered him.

The sun had browned his skin, and already the scar on his
arm was beginning its long fade into whiteness. He was stronger,
in some ways, than he had been at the beginning of the journey;
the muscles in both legs and arms had hardened in response to
the tasks demanded of them by the Swords and their master.

Master? Yes, Vellen of Damion was that, and more. If the
shadow of the Empire had a face, it was the high priest's—and
if it had once seemed strange to Darin that his master's face was
pale and wintry, as the First's had been, it did not seem strange
now. The winter sky of the cold northern province was warm
compared to those eyes, and the blackest of cloudy nights no
less dark. He felt the high priest's gaze at the back of his neck
even when the man himself was nowhere in sight, and he tried
as hard as he could to please him; it motivated his waking hours.

And it seemed, perhaps, that his efforts might be rewarded,
for as they approached the capital, the high priest became almost
jovial. Darin could almost understand why.

From some miles away, spires reached up toward the sky,
catching the glint of afternoon light and spinning it back like a
magical loom into a picture of grandeur and power.

Dagothrin had never seen such majesty.

"It is Malakar," a low voice said, and Darin started guiltily,
although he'd been allotted no tasks or duties this day. He
straightened the anxiety out of his face and turned in the man's
direction. His feet missed a step as he saw who it was.

The high priest was dressed in his formal attire. Darin had
seen it only once, but that once he would never forget. Robes
of soft, fine red, trimmed in a black that seemed to glitter, made
of an armor more invulnerable than solid steel. A simple gold
circlet, deeper in color than his hair, cut the line of his brow,
supporting a single, large ruby.

Darin felt a kick at his ankle, and suddenly came to his senses.
With an audible gasp he fell to his knees. Out of the corner of
one eye, he saw that Kerren had already done so.

*Thanks, Kerren,* he thought, as a tremble started in his throat.

But the high priest was in a good mood today; he even smiled indulgently as Darin raised his shaking face from the ground to receive his orders.

"You may rise. All of you."

"How may I serve you, lord?" Darin asked. No one else spoke.

"You were staring at the city, were you not?"

Darin nodded.

There was a swirl of red and Vellen gestured. The lump in Darin's throat tightened, but he showed no hesitance as he followed the priest's directions and came to stand beside him.

"Look well at it, boy. It will be your home." His long, large fingers pointed at the spires that still shone in the daylight. Black silk touched the edge of Darin's jaw like the tail of a cat. "We call it Malakar. It is not grand?"

Darin nodded again.

"There are no walls to guard or hide it. It is the heart of the world; it needs none."

*The Heart of the world. The Dark Heart.*

Vellen's lips lifted at the corners as if all of Darin's thoughts were laid bare.

"There is no Twinned Heart, not any longer." His voice was a warm whisper. "And Malakar will stand as evidence of that. It was built," he said, his voice growing distant, "in mere decades. The power of God Himself created those spires and towers. The poverty of your mortal eyes cannot contain the full glory of their sight." His hands snaked out suddenly, to grip Darin's shoulders. "And that will be your home; you will have the privilege of serving it." He released Darin abruptly, as if only becoming aware that he addressed a mere slave. "As will all." His smile grew grim, and therefore more familiar. "In one way or another."

There was a gate house on the main road into the city. It was small, but not plain; its walls were stained almost black, its edges trimmed by copper with runes along it that Darin couldn't understand.

But the guards, although well dressed, were not Swords. They, too, bowed, as the slaves did, when the presence of the high priest was announced, their knees touching the cobbled stone precisely, their foreheads shadowing the ground. Nor did they move until Vellen had given them leave, and he exercised his power here as if it were a luxury too long denied, staring down at the chained shirts that covered bent backs for minutes before he allowed them to rise.

*Are they slaves?* Darin thought, as he began to follow the wagons once again. Then he shook himself. The looks the guards gave them, half of pity and half of contempt, answered the question for him.

They had no trouble traversing the streets, although the crowds here were, if possible, larger and more oppressive than those in Verdann. Merchants with their wagons, nobles in their palanquins and litters, or drawn carriages—all managed to find the space and time to move aside for the crest of House Damion. The nobility did not bow, but they nodded their acknowledgment; all others did as the guards at the gatehouse had done. And if they grudged the bowing and scraping, they were wise enough not to let it show.

Here, however, Vellen was more inclined to be gracious; he allowed the bows proffered to be perfunctory and merely waved the citizens on.

Word spread up the street as they moved, and Darin felt the chill of *victory* wrap about him like a shroud. Of all the people on the streets now, that word had meaning to perhaps forty, and thirty of those were as he: slaves. He tried to ignore it as its dark edge burned into his heart. Defeat.

An hour passed, judging by the sun, before they at last found a place where the roads were wide and near empty. Walking here was hard. Darin kept looking from side to side at the expanse of walkways that suddenly stretched away from the street to end in manses such as he had never seen. Many were as large as the royal palace had been, but they looked newer, cleaner, and somehow more lofty. No two were alike; some boasted small towers, built with chunks of rough, gray stone; some were almost square and forbidding in their simplicity. On one or two, there were gargoyles caught in frozen relief as they watched their master's lands.

And color; there was color here to catch and mesmerize the eye. Flowers lined the walks, flowers in late bloom, but still quite beautiful. The reds of roses mingled with pinks and pale whites; the blue of some flower he had never seen looked askance as they passed. Each house bore large twin flags; one of red and black, and the other changing as he walked. Later he would come to know these as the house crests—the banners of the nobility of Veriloth.

Twice they passed guard patrols; the red and the black of their surcoated armor marked them as Swords. They saluted the high priest as he passed, but no more, and the high priest in turn nodded.

And then, finally, they turned to the left and began to walk up perhaps the largest of the drives that Darin had yet seen. His heart flipped high and landed squarely in his throat, and his breath became short and shallow.

The scent of flowers hit his nostrils; the shadows of trees touched the back of his neck. He could see greenery everywhere his eyes dared to wander. But it was organized, controlled green, as if even the things that grew did not dare to displease the high priest by being out of place. From high above, he heard the trill of small birds as they leaped from branch to branch in their agitation at the passing humans.

He forgot all these things as he looked up for the first time. And up. And up.

House Damion was indeed a palace. The walkway ended in a large, vaulted arch. Beyond it, he could see the sunlight touching the courtyard's flagstones. And above it, he could see four towers that grew as he approached. The stonework here was smooth, but it was far from simple. Along the side of each tower, masters must have labored for decades to create the statues of human likenesses that lined them. They seemed to look down upon the slaves as they entered, their expression and features distantly familiar. Only one tower was smooth—perhaps reserved for the future.

Flags flew here as well; the black and red was distinctly larger than that of the house. As they passed beneath them, the high priest stopped. An elderly man walked out to greet him.

Darin watched carefully, sure that the rest of the slaves did the same.

"Father." The high priest's voice was colorless.

"Vellen." The elderly man, Lord Damion proper, held out a firm hand. "You return in victory."

"News has traveled."

The man chuckled warmly. "Forgive them if it has; they spread your word."

"And the honor of the house, father?"

The man's smile fell away from his face as if it were water thrown there by the caprice of poor weather. He withdrew his hand and stared at his son, his eyebrows drawing together in a line. They were of a height, although perhaps the elder man was

still the larger; his shoulders were broad and remarkably un-
stooped for his age. Nor did he have the piercing eyes of the
younger Damion; his were dark and impenetrable. The elder
lord spoke first, although he did not look away.

"The Dark Heart comes first." It was not a question.

"Were it not for the weakness of past Damions, we would
have always borne the crest of the Karnari. We did not until
now."

Lord Damion did not move. "Vellen, the high priest does
not rule the empire. You would do well to remember it." He
turned, then turned back in a carefully executed afterthought.
"Or did the First not crusade with you?"

Vellen's face darkened. "The ruling of mortals is not of concern to the Servants of God."

"Do not forget your history," his father replied. "The Empire of Veriloth was founded by a Servant; the First. He carved
it, he destroyed the First of the Enemy. Power rules here, and
he is still the greater power."

If possible, Vellen's face darkened further. Although the anger was not directed at the slaves, Darin cringed.

"We serve the same God, Father."

"Then know the God *we* serve."

The emphasis was not lost on the high priest. He stood silent
a moment, and then turned to his Swords.

"Have them take the church flag down. It is to be redesigned
and replaced. *Now!*"

The Swords moved.

Darin saw the bitter smile that hardened the lines of Lord
Damion's mouth. It gave him little comfort to know that there
was at least one person in the Empire who did not fear its high
priest. He shivered and waited for word to enter. He could still
see the fury in the lines of Lord Vellen's shoulders, and it made
him cringe again. The stories he had heard about the rages of
slavemasters echoed loudly in his ears. What little of life that
slavery bought him could be lost in this instant.

He had much to learn.

Lord Damion himself led the slaves into the manor. His commands, as his son's, were terse and pointed; he was used to
being obeyed. They followed behind him, passing beneath the
arch and into the courtyard, and from there through a grand set
of double doors that footmen opened wordlessly.

"This," the lord said crisply, "is House Damion. You will
serve it well." He made no threat.

The long hall stretched out before them, a grand, empty throat. Silent, they began to follow him into the heart of a new life.

# chapter
# four

*Darin stared at the small walls of the room he and Kerren shared* with two of the younger men, David and Stev. They had no windows; the only light to come to the room was provided by small lamps, and even these were rarely afforded to the slaves. Nor did they possess a fireplace, but here in the south, or so they were told, there was little need of one; snow was a myth to David and Stev.

Darin learned how to clean the ground halls and the brass and silver that Damion possessed in quantity. That was his first task. Korven, an elderly, stout woman, had taken the newcomers firmly in hand and tried, in her sonorous bass, to make clear what the rules of their new life were.

"First of all, although you've probably learned it, there are rules about names. Names are important in Veriloth—and as far as the free men are concerned, slaves don't have 'em. Understood?"

Silent nods all around.

"You've probably been allowed to make a few mistakes with only a beating as a lesson. You won't be allowed that now; you're in House Damion, and it demands only the best behavior from the slaves it claims. Understood as well?"

Nods again.

"Good." The woman looked at each of them almost grimly. "Among the slaves, you have to have names. Your given ones are as good as any. But Lady help you if you ever answer to one when the nobles call."

Darin turned to look at Kerren. *Lady?* he mouthed.

Kerren shrugged.

"We'll lose a few of you," Korven continued, her voice matter-of-fact, and more chilling because of it. "It always happens. But the number we lose depends entirely on how you adjust to your new life here." She glanced at Peggy. "You, dear, will have light duties for the time. You're well along?"

Peggy nodded miserably. She rarely spoke now.

"Good." Korven shrugged. "Pregnancy is one of the few occasions when a doctor's summoned for slaves."

From there she had proceeded to assign the slaves to "partners," people who knew the duties their lives depended on learning. Darin drew Stev.

Stev was surprising. He was tall, almost two feet taller than Darin. But he was also thin; his arms and legs looked like sticks with gnarled knobs at the joints. His hair was a thatch of barely kempt red, and his pale face was dotted with brown freckles. His coloring was not what surprised Darin, although in itself it was unusual.

It was his demeanor. He always had a grin to spare, and words of cheer and support came freely from his laughing mouth. He picked up a bucket and a damp rag, and motioned for Darin to follow. Bemused, Darin did as he asked, occasionally glancing over his shoulder to see if the masters were watching. They weren't, but Stev also had an uncanny sense for their presence.

"You'll learn it." He chuckled. "They've a chill about them when they come." He looked down at his young charge. "You've done this before?"

Darin looked down at his feet.

"Well, never mind it; you'll learn soon enough, and with me as a teacher, I'm sure you'll do yourself proud." He picked up the rag and walked down toward the doors. "Outer brass is most important; it's got to shine like the sun, or somebody pays. Don't forget it; what other people see of the house had better be all spit and polish." He began to whistle a light tune as he brought the rag to the door fixtures. "Hmmm. Can you reach this? No? Well, you might have to carry a stool with you, at least for the first few years; you're small, but they won't take it into account."

Darin watched in silence.

"Darin," Stev said, lowering the rag for a moment, "they didn't cut out your tongue, did they?"

"No."

"Then don't be so gloomy."

*Gloomy?* Darin wanted to shout. His face paled, then took on a rosy color that had nothing to do with the warmth of the rising sun. "Gloomy?" He rolled up his sleeve, exposing the pale mark of Damion to the light. "Bright Heart, how can you be so—"

Stev shoved the damp rag into Darin's trembling mouth. His green eyes were wide, and he wheeled around, his gaze searching the empty courtyard.

"Never say that," he whispered. "Never say that here. They'll kill you for it without a second thought—even if slaves are expensive. Understand?" He gripped Darin's shoulders and kneeled down until their eyes were on a level.

Darin spat out the rag, choking slightly on the soapy water that trickled down his suddenly tight throat. Tears welled up in the corners of his eyes.

Stev sighed, his lanky frame relaxing. He still held the shoulders of his young charge as he began to speak more softly. "Darin, this is the Empire of Veriloth. We'd heard rumors of your arrival and we knew what it meant." A rare shadow darkened his eyes. "But it's happened. You're still alive. This Heart that you evoked—it didn't help you. Don't call it here. Never think it here. You're too young to die for something as trivial as that." He began to whistle again as he released Darin and bent to retrieve the rag.

Darin tried to watch what he did, but the tears blurred everything.

"See how it gleams?" Stev asked.

Darin shook his head.

Stev sighed for the second time. "Darin, if you've got to pray to someone, pray to the Lady."

"T-the Lady?"

"Aye. The Lady of Mercy. Haven't you heard of her?"

"N-no."

"Well then." He wiped the door fixtures clean. "They don't like her either, but they won't kill you for speaking of her. Come on; we'll do the silver in the mistress' collection. No one's there, and we can speak more openly."

He picked up his bucket, and Darin followed him in, his legs almost too shaky to carry him.

"Not like that, Darin. You'll wreck your wrists and you won't get half the job done. Here. There's a rough edge along the bottom of the rag; you use it to clean the silver, and the smooth part to polish. Understand?"

Darin looked dubious. "You have to do this all in one day?" He had never seen so much silver in his life.

"Aye." Stev smiled. "But you'll get good at it; you'll get faster." Indeed, he'd already done three times the number of forks that Darin had managed. "You're lucky you're not in the kitchen. There's *real* work."

"Stev, who's this Lady?"

"Ah. I thought you'd forgotten." His smile told Darin that he thought no such thing, but his hands kept working. "We've a story here, among the slaves. The Lady of Mercy once walked the world; she was consort to the darkness, but she was like the dawn."

"Light?"

Stev looked pained. "If you must, but that's a word you should watch as well."

"I don't remember hearing about it."

"You didn't grow up a slave, Darin."

Darin was silent, and for the third time that day, Stev sighed. "Come on, none of that. Let me finish my tale.

"The Lady of Mercy, that's what we call her, was consort, but her pity tempered the evil Lord, and he loved her greatly. She was a great noble, but it was not the nobility she loved; it was people like us. Slaves."

He smiled to himself, only this time the smile was tinged by sadness. "She was a spirit, Darin, or so we believe. She came to us, but something happened. She was forced to leave. And it's been a darker world since, without mercy."

"Then why pray to her?"

"We pray for her return. We pray for her rest and her peace. One day, each of us'll be with her. Some sooner than others, but all of us who've suffered here have earned her touch and her mercy."

Darin shook his head. He'd never heard of any such thing—and anyone who died went Beyond. Even the children knew that.

As if reading his thoughts, Stev's smile saddened yet further. "Darin," he said, putting a fork aside, "maybe in the world you came from, you didn't need her, and she didn't come to you. But you'll learn, soon enough, that we do."

"Why," Darin grunted, as he tried to lift the edge of a mahogany table, "are you always so cheerful?"

Stev swept deftly underneath the shaky space that Darin had created. "Why not?"

Thud. Leg hit carpet and settled firmly down. "For one, we're slaves here. They can kill us whenever they want."

"True." The broom was put aside as Stev began to oil the desk top. Darin wrinkled his nose at the smell, but grabbed another cloth. "So?"

"So?" He rubbed the oil into the wood and grimaced slightly; someone had been drinking at the desk, and not very carefully either. "So what's there to be cheerful about?"

"We're alive." Stev gave the boy a sly, happy smile. "Mara's agreed to bed me when we've time. We're not on stone duty."

"But you don't have any choice about what duty you're on."

"No," the older slave replied. "So?"

Darin vented most of his frustration on the wood. "I don't understand you."

Stev sighed. Then he smiled. "I've never sighed so much in my life as I have since you've come.

"Darin, if I'm miserable, does it change anything? Does it give me freedom or the ability to make my own choices?"

"Well, no, but—"

"Right. And if I'm miserable, does it hurt them?"

"No."

"Does it hurt me?"

"Well . . ." Darin turned back to the desk.

"I'm not asking you to be happy, at least not yet. But we're alive, and there's still some good in that." Stev started to whistle.

Six weeks later, Darin began to join him. He was young.

"You're lucky," Kerren mumbled, his voice muffled neatly by the thin pillow that adorned his bunk.

"Hmmm?" Darin looked up at the darkness that was the bottom of Kerren's bed. "How's that?"

"Lucky," Kerren repeated.

David and Stev laughed from across the room.

"Kitchen duty," David got out, by way of explanation. "Kerren was assigned to me, and I was transferred to the kitchen." He gave a theatrical groan. "It's the price for being too competent. Stev'd never get transferred there. He's barely capable enough not to have himself killed."

Stev whacked his detractor soundly with a pillow.

"Stev's good at what he does," Darin insisted, jumping to his new friend's defense.

"See?" Stev said to David. "I've got support."

"Aye, and you need it." David chuckled. "But I'm teasing

him, Darin. He's a better slave than most. Stupider than most as well.''

"Has to be," Kerren muttered. "He's always smiling." He rolled onto his elbows. "I'd trade places with you any day."

Darin laughed. "No way."

"I'll second it."

Across the room, Stev laughed. Kerren picked up his pillow. They had half an hour before they'd need to sleep, and he and Darin used the time as any children might. Darin almost forgot where he was, and why; it had been a long time since he could play this way.

But in the morning, he remembered.

The slaves were summoned en masse, with the exception of the kitchen staff. Korven sent the word around, and Stev frowned upon receiving it. It was rare that he frowned, and Darin felt the hairs on the back of his neck stand on end.

"Come on," Stev said shortly. "We'd best be quick; summons or no, we'll still be expected to finish what we've started here." He set the rag and bucket neatly away in one corner and gripped Darin's shoulder firmly. "The masters'll be there; maybe all of them. Remember what Korven taught you and don't make any mistakes."

Frightened, Darin nodded. "Why are they calling us?"

Stev looked down at Darin and shook his head. "It's that time, Darin. In a week or two, they'll blood the stones."

"Blood the—you mean sacrifices?"

"Yes and no," Stev replied. "The brown stains on the flag-stones in the courtyard are blood. They spill it in the grooves of the house crest." His frown deepened. "They don't usually choose among the house slaves; we're trained enough to be of some value."

From somewhere in memory, Stev's words returned to Darin: *We could be on stone duty.* He thought he understood now. If they chose him, though, his blood wouldn't flow for them; it was frozen in his veins.

Together they walked to the main hall in unnatural silence. They joined a slowly growing group of slaves. Darin saw Kerren standing beside David. Kerren smiled uneasily.

"I thought the kitchen staff—"

"Shhh."

He silenced himself, but the knots in his stomach grew.

In silence they waited. Just as the tension seemed to become unbearable, the large doors of the sitting room opened. Darin knew them well; he'd cleaned them every other day for seven weeks.

Instantly, the slaves fell in one neat motion to rest upon their knees.

Lord Vellen, Lord Damion, and a young girl entered the hall. Vellen was dressed in the black and red of the Karnari and moved like a shadow. Lord Damion chose instead the blue, black, and silver of his house. Of the two, the elder looked more finely accoutred, but the young lord carried himself more strongly.

The girl, on the other hand, wore a pale green dress. She must be of House Damion, Darin reasoned, but not even the house crest was in evidence upon her clothing. One fine, silver strand cut the line of her throat and sparkled in the sunlight. Her hair, like Lord Vellen's, was pale and wintry; her eyes, like his, were icy blue. But her face was softer and sweeter, rounded where his was sharp, and her lips were turned up in a friendly smile.

Darin hadn't seen her before. In fact, since his arrival, he had not seen any of the masters. He stared down at his feet.

"House mistress."

Korven separated herself from the ranks of the slaves and dropped to her knees in front of Lord Damion.

"Lord Damion." Her forehead touched the ground an inch away from the black leather of his boots.

"You've taken the newer slaves well into hand. I'm pleased with their progress."

"Thank you, lord. How may we serve?"

"Lady Cynthia wishes to acquire a new maid. Are there any among these that might be suitable?"

Korven didn't raise her head. "Yes, lord."

"Ah, good. You may rise."

"Thank you, lord."

"Father?" The Lady Cynthia's voice was high and sweet. "Might I not choose my own?"

Lord Damion frowned. "The house mistress knows the abilities of the slaves she directs, Cynthia. Would it not be best to leave the decision to her?"

Cynthia frowned, but even the frown was delicate and pretty. "But Father, would you not trust my decision over that of a slave?"

Lord Damion's answering frown had none of the delicacy of his daughter's. "Cynthia."

"Please?" Without waiting for an answer, she began to approach the ranks of the gathered slaves. "Do rise," she said softly.

Darin began to move, and Stev, from behind, grabbed the back of his tunic. He stopped, noticing that a few of the others had also started to obey.

Silence reigned as Cynthia turned back to her father.

"Very well," the older man replied. "Rise." His curt word unfolded the slaves' legs, where her pretty ones had not.

Darin glanced furtively back at his mentor, who gave him a tight-lipped shake of the head. Darin turned and did not look back again.

Cynthia's skirts rustled against the floor as she approached. The slaves stared straight ahead, standing as tall and still as they were able. She walked casually, stopping occasionally to look more carefully at one person or another. Her footsteps, light and ladylike, could scarce be heard, although no one spoke.

At last she stopped in front of Darin. He didn't have to look up to meet her eyes; she was only an inch or two taller than he. And perhaps a season or two older; it was hard to tell.

"What of this one?"

Korven came quickly to stand at her side. "He's young, lady, and he's just started with the cleaning staff."

"Oh. Does he do his tasks well?"

"Yes, lady."

"That's encouraging to hear." She smiled, her cheeks dimpling as she met Darin's eyes.

"Has he any training in serving the nobility?" Lord Damion asked. Korven looked almost grateful.

"No, lord. By your orders, he was assigned to cleaning."

"Very well. Cynthia?"

She ignored her father. Darin wondered how she dared. From where he stood he could see the lines that were etching themselves into the lord's brow.

"What is your name, boy?"

"I—I don't have a name," Darin said.

She smiled. "But you must have a name. Weren't you born with one?"

"I'm a—a slave, lady." He felt his knees falter and dearly wished that the lord had not given the order to rise.

"Cynthia." Lord Damion's word was more of a curse than a name.

"Yes, father?"

"Enough."

But she still didn't stop. Darin began to tremble.

"Tell me your name," she said, lowering her voice. "If I'm to have a new maid, hadn't I better have something to call him?"

He swallowed, his throat suddenly dry.

"Tell me your name. Now."

"Lady, I—"

"That's an order. Do you know what happens to slaves who disobey orders?"

Darin wasn't sure if the tension in the hall was just his. He began to sweat as her lips turned down into a dangerous frown.

"Your name."

He wanted to turn back to Stev, but didn't dare—not when she was so close. He looked down and saw that his hands were trembling visibly.

"D-Darin."

He heard the collective intake of breath. It came from all around. In panic, he looked back to see that Stev's eyes were closed. He wheeled around again.

Cynthia's smile was the smile of a cat.

And Darin knew how a mouse felt. It didn't help to know that the look of anger upon Lord Damion's face was not directed at him.

"House mistress," Lord Damion said, the word grating through clenched teeth. "Take this slave to the slavemaster."

"At once, lord." She reached out to catch Darin by the shoulder; he felt her hands trembling, although they looked steady.

"And tell him to wait upon my instruction before meting out punishment."

"Yes, lord."

"Cynthia, I will speak with you *now*. Your request for a new slave is denied."

Darin didn't hear her reply. He went with Korven. Only once did he dare to glance back, searching the crowd until he caught sight of Kerren's pale face.


"I'm sorry."

Darin bit back a cry of pain as Stev tended to his back. The warm, wet cloth stung the open strips that the whip had torn out of his flesh.

"I should have thought to warn you."

Tears squeezed themselves out of Darin's eyes. He reached out and felt another hand take his.

"Darin?" It was Kerren.

Darin tried to nod, gulping as Stev continued to clean him.

"It's a game," Stev murmured, "a game that the younger nobles will play. It doesn't often get anywhere." He looked down at the mess of Darin's back and sighed. "I've seen worse punishments. But they were on broader backs."

Darin wanted to close his eyes, but every time he did, he saw the grim smile of the slavemaster and felt his own fear well up as he stood there, naked, and was bid to turn around. The first three strokes cut the air at his sides, making him jump. That was bad enough—the fear.

But the whip was worse. Not for anything could he imagine enduring that again.

"They didn't kill you," Stev continued.

Darin hated the slight edge of surprise and curiosity in the words.

"And the lord almost chastised his daughter in front of the slaves."

"Are you finished yet?" Kerren asked, letting his voice show the fear and annoyance that Darin's didn't have strength for.

"Not yet, Ker. Be patient."

Kerren nearly shouted back. "You're hurting him."

"It's all right," Darin whispered, still very much aware that Kerren gripped his hand. "He needs to do it." It helped, to be able to say what he only half believed. *Clean the wounds, or there'll be infection. If the lord didn't see fit to kill the slave, he'll be furious if he dies now.*

"That's right." Stev nodded. "I'm sorry. It's just that most of us were born to the life; most of us understand the games better."

Kerren's hand tightened fiercely, and for a moment Darin wished that David were awake. Maybe he was, though. No one could sleep through the noise Darin made.

"I wonder at it, though. Why didn't they kill you? Ah, well. Best not to question luck."

Lady Cynthia was furious. The fine, high lines of her cheeks were stained with a red that was ugly and unbecoming to her station.

"You do realize that the slaves are laughing behind my back, don't you?'' She threw her hands in the air; a bracelet jangled against the taut muscles of her wrist as if it were hitting steel.

Lord Damion continued to read the document that had been placed on his desk in the morning.

''Father, are you listening?''

''Yes, dear,'' he replied, flipping a page.

''What's so special about that slave anyway? He's obviously not worthy of the house—he named himself in front of us!'' She took a deep breath and her toe skirted the rug. She was old enough now that dignity mattered a little; she stopped herself from stomping her feet.

''Nothing is special about a slave.''

Her face froze for a moment.

Her father looked up.

Lord Vellen entered the room. He was garbed as high priest, a swirl of red and black around the winter of his skin, robes for everyday Church use. He bowed in the direction of his father, a low bow, but not too low.

''Ah, Vellen.'' Lord Damion nodded. The documents that had been studied so earnestly were set aside. ''Have we been arguing this long?''

''My duties today were shortened, Father.'' He turned and smiled brittlely at Cynthia. ''Sister.''

She clenched her hands and walked over to the beveled glass of the study's bay window. Sunlight caught and framed her small, slender figure. It set off the warmer hue of the dress that she wore; she looked like a peach flower in bloom.

Vellen smiled sardonically.

''Vellen.'' She smiled as well. In this they were indeed of the same blood; neither smile reached the eye of the wearer.

''Lord Damion and I have matters of import to discuss, Cynthia. I fear you would find them tedious. Why don't you get ready for the dinner party that you've planned for this eve?''

''Vellen.'' She curtsied, the gesture insulting as only a sibling could make it. ''You are not Lord Damion yet. You can't just walk in and interrupt my discussion with Father.''

''Little sister, I am not Lord Damion yet, but I *am* High Priest and leader of the Karnari. Go.''

To that she had no response. She turned stiffly, walked to the door, and then wheeled. ''Lord Damion,'' she said formally.

''Cynthia?''

''As the life of the slave is not mine to claim, might I claim his service for the evening?''

"The eve—ah, yes, the dinner gathering." He frowned. "Cynthia, the house mistress made it clear that he is not fit for formal duties. Should you desire it, I can change his allocation to allow for this in the future."

She frowned and began to speak.

"No." Lord Damion lifted a tired hand. "What you choose as a personal slave is your own business, but a gathering of nobles, young though they are, is house business. I will not have the house embarrassed by an untrained slave."

She struggled for a moment and then nodded stiffly.

"Oh, and Cynthia?"

"Yes, Father?"

"Should you damage or kill one of your slaves this eve, or allow another to be damaged or killed, you will not have a replacement. Is this clear?"

Her cheeks flushed red again. "That wasn't my fault! Garok got drunk! I'm sorry he killed her, but what's done is done!"

"Garok was your choice of guest. You must learn to live with the responsibility of your choices." He turned to face his son; the interview with the younger Damion was obviously over.

She clamped her lips shut and walked out.

Lord Damion sighed. "This age—it is a difficult one. Perhaps you were right; perhaps I should have assigned the girl to the priesthood."

Vellen, politic, said nothing.

"And perhaps I was right; too much of value to the house is already invested in the Church." It was as much a true compliment as Lord Damion ever paid to his son. "You came to see me?"

"Yes, lord."

"About?"

"The third phase. In one week, the stones are to be blooded, and the sacrifices made."

Lord Damion nodded. He glanced down at the papers on his desk. "Have you seen these?"

Vellen made a show of curiosity. He held out one steady hand, and the paper rustled against his still fingers. "The seal of the Empire."

"Indeed."

Vellen flipped the leaves of paper without pausing to read the calligraphy.

"Vellen, what is so precious about this single slave?"

"Nothing that I have been able to learn." He allowed his

anger to color his words. "Nothing that excuses the *use* of House Damion as a holding ground for chattel."

Lord Damion saw the cold fire behind his son's eyes and smiled carefully. "The First is still Emperor."

"Yes."

"There are rumors that have come by way of the Swords, High Priest. Rumors about the fields of the fallen Line Culverne."

"Such as?"

"There was no blooding, no sacrifice."

Vellen said nothing. He did not move at all.

Lord Damion knew that he had been heard, and after a moment he continued. "And we hold a slave that we dare not punish. A pity."

A smile twisted itself out of Vellen's lips. "A pity? Yes. But it gives Cynthia a lesson she badly needed to learn, does it not?"

Lord Damion nodded, but Vellen didn't notice. He was seething. That he had been ordered to hold the slave was indignity enough; that the First Servant had seen fit to send this missive to his father only added to the fire.

*No*, he thought as he smoothed the lines of his face, *we cannot kill this insult. But there are other ways*.

Abruptly he rose. "Lord Damion," he said, bowing stiffly.

"Vellen? Did you not come to speak with me about a matter of import?"

"No, lord. Only to inform you that the levy should arrive in the three-day and the altars should be prepared."

He met his father's gaze firmly.

Lord Damion inclined his head, granting the permission to leave that Vellen required in this house alone.

They rose above the petty buildings in the streets, twin spires cutting sharp shadows into the path the sun laid. Stone walls, inlaid with bronze, leaped up from the street. Beyond the walls, a hint of other buildings could be seen; the fifty-foot stained glass windows of the nobility's chapel looked down upon passersby with the eyes of God. This was the home of the Church, the center from which all worship was dictated. Here, on top of thick, cut stone walls, Swords mounted their patrol, their steps crisp and even as they looked down upon the streets of the city. At this angle, only the north wall could be seen.

This was the heart of the city; indeed, it was almost a city unto itself. The laws and privileges enclosed herein separated the nobles and the free men from those who served God. The gates, black and solid, were open to those who cared to enter, but they were also guarded by the elite of the Swords.

Usually when he entered the temple complex, Vellen's anger gave way. The concerns of the outer world were left beyond the large trinity of arches.

Today was different.

Acolytes in the hall noticed his passing and gave ground; they moved toward the walls of cut stone and did not resume their speech or movement until he was well past them. Nor did he give them a second thought.

Varil, one of the Karnari, began to approach him as he strode toward the massive cathedral that the Karnari blessed four times yearly. But even Varil gave way, although not so obviously as the acolytes. This was well and good; any display of weakness from the Karnari was not be tolerated, and Vellen was certain he had chosen well.

He gestured at the guards in silence, the movement almost a curse.

They bowed, and he waited in irritation while they struggled to open the massive black doors that led into the cathedral. Those doors were heavy; much work had gone into them and their ebony inlays. Rubies glittered in the daylight, small specks of the earth's cold blood that bore witness to the greatness of the Dark Heart. They had been fashioned into the likeness of a hand and thus, fist clenched, they also bore witness to the power of the Dark Heart.

"Close them. Do not allow any to enter behind me until my word is given."

The Swords saluted smartly, and before his left foot had crossed the threshold, he heard the creak of the doors as they closed to defend his back.

The altar lay silent before him. It gleamed, reflecting the sunlight that the stained glass tainted into dark, new colors. But beneath those glints, all was black, cold rock. Its edges curved in toward its center to meet a small, clean hole that had been carefully chiseled through it. It was not large, nor particularly grand, and one large man could take up most of its exposed surface easily.

What made it special was the way it lay suspended in midair, casting its shadow upon a small circle of still, open water. To

the eyes of the nonblooded, and admittedly there were few allowed entrance here, it looked like a miracle.

And even to the eyes of the Malanthi priesthood, it held some
of that. A delicate, red web of power surrounded it, an inch
from its surface, and held it immobile above the water. The
power of God, the God that Vellen worshiped.

His anger held as he approached the altar. He brought his
hands out, held them a minute over the altar, and then spat into
the well beneath it.

"Dark Heart," he whispered, his eyes closed. "It was once
said that the Servants had your ear. They served You in ways
that we could not, and in turn, You granted them the power to
rule."

Silence, as always, answered him.

"The First among these Servants claims to rule still. At the
eve of our victory, he denied You Your due. Surely he must be
made to see that even he cannot so simply thwart Your will."

"Do you question God?"

Vellen raised his head slowly. The hair on the back of his
neck stood suddenly at attention. With measured, even steps,
he turned to face the voice.

He had seldom seen a Servant of the Dark Heart in its unen-
cumbered glory, and even though they served the same God, he
still felt a chill down his spine. Standing perhaps seven feet in
height, cloaked in a darkness that was absolute, the Servant's
red eyes flashed as they observed him. But he was ruler here, if
not in the outer world of the Empire. He controlled every facial
muscle as he performed a stiff bow.

"No," he answered softly.

"That is good," the Servant replied. His voice was dark and
sibilant. "But I have come to answer your . . . request of God.
I am Sargoth, the Second of the Sundered."

The chill radiated outward, and with it an excitement began
to grow. Never before had the Dark Heart seen fit to answer the
prayers of a priest—even if that priest were head of the Karnari.
Surely this was proof of His favor.

"The rulership of mortals," Sargoth continued, "is not my
domain, nor does it hold my interest. But the concern of the
Dark Heart does. We are aware of the transgressions of the
First—and they will grow, from this moment." He stepped for-
ward, his feet making no sound in the preternatural silence of
Vellen's hope.

"For now, High Priest, you must continue in your path. Obey the emperor's commands. Cause him no concern or trouble."

Vellen nodded, waiting.

"But soon, in our terms, perhaps years in yours, you will feel a sign, and that sign is your permission to move against him, with the power of God by your side. Is this understood?"

"When?"

Sargoth hesitated a moment. When he answered, his annoyance was evident. "Soon." He turned away from Vellen, then, and gazed upon the cathedral.

"Much work was done here," he said, as if to himself. "I remember the doing of it." He walked to the altar and gazed slowly down, his eyes glinting off the water. "Has so much passed, so quickly? Ah, well." He turned again. "I have much to teach you, High Priest. A magic and a power that is not of God alone. The doing will be hard, and it may be that you are not strong enough to survive it." A hint of amusement was there.

Vellen could not contain the smile that took his lips. His hands, at his sides, were trembling.

"Perhaps one day with my help, Second of those who serve, you shall be First."

Sargoth looked at him then, and Vellen thought he could make out contours of blackness that moved shiftlessly through the shadows.

"We shall see," he said, at length. "Come. We must begin."

# chapter
# five

*Lord Vellen handed his cloak to the waiting slave, who rose* immediately and took it carefully from his outstretched hand. He received a small smile in return, and forced himself not to step back. Lord Vellen's rare displays of temper were not feared among the slaves. Not so with his even rarer displays of good humor.

"I shall speak shortly with Lord Damion."

"Yes, lord."

"In half an hour, send out the guards to retrieve a certain slave. A new one; I believe he has been allocated to the kitchen."

The slave paled, but his expression of obeisance did not waver. "Yes, lord."

"Send word to another of the new slaves." Vellen's smile broadened slightly. "The one who humiliated Lady Cynthia by daring to give himself a name in her presence, as if he had rank equal to hers."

If possible, the slave paled further. "Yes, lord."

"At once. If you do not know these slaves personally, I suggest that you find the house mistress."

"Lord."

Vellen's smile grew yet further as he made his way to his father's study. He withdrew, from the folds of his sash, a small pouch that jangled noisily.

Lord Damion was rare for a noble; he valued a certain austerity that he claimed could be found in the elegance of simplicity. The door to his personal rooms made this quite clear; it was of solid material, but no brass inlay or crest touched its surface. Indeed, it was the only door to the lords' and lady's chambers that was not doubled.

Lord Vellen knocked on it precisely and, after a moment, heard his father's permission to enter.

"Lord Damion."

"Vellen. What brings you so late?"

"A matter of little import to the house, Father. But I wish to purchase the use of one of your slaves."

Lord Damion frowned as Vellen deposited the pouch neatly on the center of the desk.

Stev looked up at Andrew's broad face. Although Andrew often worked at the side of the gardeners, his tanned face was pale, and his brown eyes too wide.

"Lord Vellen asked for Darin?"

Andrew nodded. "Sorry, Stev," he murmured. His face was still chalky beneath the darkness of his hair.

"So am I," Stev said brusquely. "But it can't be helped." He turned and walked over to where Darin sat polishing silver. "Darin," he said.

Something in the tone of his voice made Darin look up in silence. No laughter lit the eyes now; no whistle was in the voice.

"What is it?" Darin asked uneasily.

Stev closed his eyes. "Lord Vellen has asked that you be sent to him in his study."

"The high priest?"

Stev nodded.

Darin swallowed and set the cutlery aside. He unfolded himself very gingerly; the marks that the whip had cut were still not fully healed. "W-what do you think he wants?"

Stev shook his head. "Don't think on it, Darin. He'll tell you when you arrive."

Darin tried to nod. "What have I done wrong?"

"Lad, it may be nothing." The tone of the voice said clearly that even Stev didn't believe this. "But go, or you'll face the slavemaster for certain."

Darin shuddered. He couldn't help it. He turned his gaze to Andrew, but Andrew had found something absorbing to stare at in the stonework floor. He passed Andrew, walked out of the open door, and stopped.

*Lernan, God, please* . . . But there was no answer. There was never any answer.

In silence he walked down the long hall.

The doors of the study were open. On either side, two armed guards looked down on him as he made his approach. They wore

the blue and black tunics of House Damion. They weren't
Swords, but their expression made clear that they served the high
priest anyway. He swallowed and gagged as the walls of his dry
throat stuck together.

"Ah, good. Enter."

Lead shoes would have been easier to walk in than the simple
sandals he wore. He dragged himself across the threshold and
then stopped abruptly.

Kerren was there, flanked and held by four guards. He was
almost green, and he looked across at Darin with such an expression of terror on his face that Darin couldn't help but respond. He began to walk over to where Kerren stood.

"Stop."

He froze then, remembering where he was.

"So. You're the slave that dared to name himself, as if free."

Darin dropped to his knees and let the stone cool the sudden
heat of his face. "Yes, lord."

"Lord Damion, in his infinite wisdom, decided to be merciful." The high priest's voice was a purr. "And I, slave, have
decided to be likewise merciful, considering your ignorance."

"Yes, lord." Nothing in Vellen's words reassured Darin.

"This evening, the rites of the third quarter are to take place
in the House temple," Vellen continued, his voice almost con-
versational. "Normally, no slave is allowed entrance there—at
least, not in the gallery."

Kerren whimpered. He began to struggle with the guards that
pinned his arms; one of the four casually slapped him with an
open, mailed, hand.

Darin could not even speak.

"But you, little slave, are to be granted that privilege. Having
named yourself," he added, darkly, "in ignorance, I wish you
to understand what the holding of a name means in Veriloth.
You too will be allowed to preside over the Dark Heart's ceremonies."

He sat back in his chair, a smile on his lips.

"And for this eve, by donation of the Church, we will not
even stain the altars with the usual criminal levy." He raised
one elegant hand and Darin slowly turned to look at Kerren.

"We will instead choose an innocent from among your number." His voice changed. "Guards, take him to the house priest.
Have him prepared."

It was almost too much for Darin. The words took moments

to sink in; moments in which Kerren's whimper had escalated to hysterical pleas.

"*Darin!*" he screamed, as the doors to the hall swallowed him. "*Darin!*"

Darin rose then, knowing the naming meant nothing, understanding what the high priest intended for his friend, his brother. He lunged forward.

"Stop!" the high priest's word was cutting and clear.

He couldn't obey immediately, but the guards at the door were prepared for this. A blow to the chest took the wind from his lungs, and he collapsed in a heap, gasping.

His name filled the hall with Kerren's despair and terror.

He was not allowed to return to his quarters. The house guards at the door were given care of him, and one at least was always within hand's reach. He cried, but his tears were silent, and the guards did not appear to notice them. But they were not completely aloof either; they wore tension as Darin did, but were more effective at hiding it.

Lord Vellen sent his summons to the study that served as a prison, and the guards received it with a nod, grateful to be able to do something other than listen to a child weep. They grabbed him roughly by the arms and began to lead him down the hall. The halls were silent, almost cavernous. Darin thought there was some chance that he might see Stev, but even the slaves were no longer on duty; everything was still. Even the lamps along the walls seemed low and dark.

They came at last to the one wing of the building that Darin had not entered before. It was austere; only one large tapestry colored the west wall, but it was done in subdued tones. Doors grew larger as they approached, stretching from floor to ceiling. A crack of light appeared around them.

"Here," one of the guards said softly. He continued to hold Darin's arms as the other man went to the doors. They slid smoothly and silently open.

Darin froze.

From where he stood, he could see the edge of a brass balcony; carpets, deep and red, lined the floor from the door to the rails. There were four large, mahogany chairs—he could see the backs of them clearly. A fifth, less fine but no less sturdy, stood between the third and the second.

"Ah, good." Lord Vellen rose from the third chair and turned toward the open door. "I feared you might be late."

"No sir," the guards replied in unison.

Vellen nodded. "This chair," he said, gesturing to his left. "Bind him."

Darin wanted to struggle, but the blue of Vellen's eyes pinned him like daggers. Nerveless, he allowed himself to be pushed into the chair. It was large, the back inches higher than his head, the arms, inches wider than his arms. They tied his wrists and shoulders firmly.

"Welcome to the galleries, slave," Vellen murmured, as he resumed his seat.

Darin turned his head to the side with some difficulty.

Lord Damion's gaze was impassive. Cynthia's was full of icy fury.

He sank back, trying to look at his feet.

"Not there." Cold fingers dug into his chin, forcing it up. "Below."

Darin shuddered and looked down.

Three robed figures stood around an obsidian altar. Inlaid in red along its surface was the crest of House Damion. It shone orange, catching the flicker of multiple torches. The three, priests all, seemed to be looking up at the gallery.

Vellen nodded grimly, not taking his fingers from Darin's face.

"Begin," he said softly. The word was caught by the arches of the vaulted ceiling; it drifted slowly but surely to the priests below.

The figure closest to the gallery bowed. Then he straightened and gave an order in a tongue that Darin did not fully understand.

He forgot those foreign words when Kerren was brought into the chamber. Kerren's voice, much louder than Vellen's, was shaky and hysterical. He was wearing nothing; his flesh, pale and white, was reflected briefly on the surface of the altar before he was chained to it by the Swords that had conveyed him to the priests.

Kerren could twist his head enough to look up. The gallery was perhaps thirty feet above the ground, and Kerren's eyes were young and sure.

Darin met them helplessly. He strained against both the ropes and the hand that held him.

"Oh, no, little slave. You *will* watch this."

The priest who had bowed walked over to the altar, and one of the robed figures handed him an ebony box.

All of the line stories about the blood ceremonies came back to Darin in force. He *knew* the knife, and it seemed that it winked balefully up at him as the priest took it firmly in hand.

"No . . ." Darin whispered, his throat too tight for any louder sound.

Kerren's voice echoed it, filling out the shadowed edges with hopelessness and fear.

Darin tried to drag his face away again, and Vellen's fingers bit deeper, drawing blood. No escape there.

He shut his eyes. The darkness behind his lids made Kerren's pleas grow louder and more urgent.

"Slave," the high priest said. "You will watch this, or you will see it repeated, again and again, until you do. Every slave that you have ever spoken with will follow this one. *Do you understand?*"

Chanting filled the room as Darin forced his lids open. His mouth was dry; his hands clenched the wood of the chair until they looked more bone than flesh.

"Good." Vellen's voice was smooth. He withdrew his hand and made a steeple beneath the edge of his jaw.

"Poor child," he said. "You cannot know what this feels like for those with the blood. It's a little like music, but wilder."

The chanting stopped. The priest raised the knife and circled the altar so that those watching from the gallery could see clearly what he intended.

*No.*

*NO.*

"Watch this carefully, slave."

The knife came down, but slowly, delicately. The caress of naked blade left a sudden, crimson stain in its dance across Kerren's chest.

Darin didn't know whose scream was louder or longer—his or Kerren's.

"Do you see the grooves in the altar? They catch the blood of the offering."

The knife moved again, rising and falling in a hypnotic cadence. It stopped, and the scream it evoked faded.

"The blood runs down to the silver pail at the far edge."

Kerren's eyes were clenched shut as he strained against the chains that rattled coldly against the stone.

Five minutes later, that was no longer a problem.

"It's surprising," Vellen said, "just how long a body can survive. But you will see."

The knife rose, the knife fell, the knife swam along a body more blood than flesh. And Darin's screams grew louder as Kerren's grew weaker. There was nothing else he had to offer.

Three chains were removed from two ankles and a wrist. The fourth had seen no use after the first half hour. Slaves came into the hall, pale shadows whose hands very carefully lifted the corpse from the slick obsidian at the directions of the priests.

Darin's bonds were cut at the same moment. His face fell forward into his lap.

"Not so quickly," Lord Vellen said softly. The hand that gripped the back of Darin's neck was not so gentle. "You must now work off the debt my favor has granted you. Guards!"

The door opened once again. The same two guards stepped into the gallery. They took care not to look beyond their lord as they saluted.

"Take the slave below. Give him over to the priest's care. Tell Kaleb that the stone duty is to be transferred to the boy."

The guards nodded and stepped forward to take hold of Darin's sagging body. He leaned into the strength of their hands as they began to turn him around.

"And tell Kaleb that he progresses well. Another few quarters and perhaps I shall let him serve in the Church proper."

It was such a relief to be free of the galleries that Darin did not immediately question his destination. But even if he had, he would have had no choice in it; either guard alone would have been strong enough to force him to walk.

His throat was hoarse, his breath shallow and rapid. Flickering torchlight outlined the step of his sandaled feet; he could not look up to see beyond them.

Stairs. The plain, slightly worn stonework did not look familiar to him. It was odd to find uncarpeted stone in the house. He shook his head from side to side, but even this exertion left him dizzy.

After a minute, he closed his eyes and let the guards almost carry him. He stumbled once or twice, but their grip was sure enough to spare him the inconvenience of a fall.

The fall would have been welcome.

*Kerren.*

*No. No, that wasn't Kerren. They didn't do it. That wasn't—*

He threw back his head, and a parched, strangled noise came

out of his lips. One of the guards took a moment to slap him gently across the face.

*Kerren!*

*No. No, Kerren never looked like that. Kerren never screamed like that.*

*Kerren . . .*

*Not because of me. Not because of me. Not my fault.*

But the halls echoed with screams now; the calling of Darin's name. And that name—the use of that name . . .

*It should have been* me.

But the worst thing of all was the knowledge that there was something beyond the guilt and the loss. He might have screamed as Kerren screamed, as Kerren died—but the knife did not do its work upon his body, had not called forth the splash of his blood. And he was afraid now, afraid of the black altar, of the black blade, of the black robes.

He was afraid that it might have been him.

He sagged further, and this time he felt a sharp pain in his leg; the guard had kicked him. It was nothing.

He moved in a trance, eyes closed, darkness all around.

Then the doors opened. Darkness receded to a blur of red, and he looked beyond the doors. From here, he could see the dark, wet stains along the sleeves of the priest's robes and hands.

"This is for you." One of the guards pushed him forward. "Stone duty. The high priest was pleased by your ceremony tonight."

The younger man raised an eyebrow and then nodded more formally. His face was longer than Vellen's, framed by black hair and colored by brown eyes—but his expression held that remoteness that came with a certainty of power.

The minute the guards released him, Darin fell naturally to his knees. His forehead struck the ground more forcefully than normal, sending a shock of pain through him.

"I am not lord here."

Darin froze, then struggled to his feet. It was hard to keep them.

The priest knew that. "Ah. The watcher from the gallery." Again an eyebrow flickered in the expanse of forehead before coming to rest. "Come."

He turned and walked into the room.

Darin followed. It wasn't easy. Each time he took a step, his legs threatened to throw him.

The priest appeared not to notice. He walked over to the altar, and Darin froze again. It was still glistening in the torchlight.

"Come." The word was sharper, darker.

Darin followed, looking down at his feet.

But even that wasn't safe; the blood had splattered here and there in a patchwork pattern on the marbled floor. Each drop seemed to come to life and struggle toward his wobbling feet.

No safety here. None. He swallowed. He followed.

The priest came to a stop and waited. Darin nearly ran into his back, but corrected himself in time. His arms, held so stiffly at his sides, were shaking.

The priest pointed.

Darin followed the line of his arm from shoulder to finger and beyond.

"Take this."

He was pointing to a pail. Silver; Darin knew silver well by this time. Stev had taught him all about how to recognize it. The pail before him gleamed; it was newly polished, but not by his hands.

"Are you deaf, slave?"

The pail. And in it, inches below its delicately fashioned rim, blood.

This was the closest he had come to Kerren since Kerren had been dragged out of Lord Vellen's study.

"If you spill a drop of it, slave, you will replace it. Is this clear?"

*No. Not me.*

Darin swallowed and reached out to the side of the pail. His nerveless fingers gripped the handle and pulled it. The blood rippled as if it had a life of its own.

"Take it up to the courtyard."

Darin wasn't sure he knew the way, but the priest's expression brooked no question. He lifted the pail; it was heavy. Heavier, he thought, than Kerren would have been.

And he walked, unsure of how he managed it, the bucket before him more of an encumbrance than manacles would have been. He stopped once or twice, always looking over his shoulder, as the halls passed in a daze around him.

The slavemaster was there to greet him.

At any other time, Darin might have frozen in terror, but the slavemaster was less to be feared than the bucket and the commands of the priest. Only when he reached the center did he dare to put it down.

*Kerren.*

No. No slaves had names. None.

He let his knees curl around him, and he fell to the stone. The slavemaster laughed.

The laughter almost sounded pleasant; it drowned out the screams.

"You're not finished yet, boy." The shadows of a torch outlined the thickset, balding man as he stepped forward. The torch was in his left hand, and in his right, he carried something. From its glint, Darin thought it might be a sword. He lowered his head, exposing the back of his neck.

He knew of the Beyond. For a fleeting moment, he thought he might join Kerren there, where he could apologize in peace and light.

But what struck him was blunt and metallic. It hurt without cutting.

"Get up, or you'll regret it. You've still more work to do." Something pulled him up by the back of his neck, bruising the muscles there.

The slavemaster's ragged smile leered at him. "Take this."

This? Darin looked numbly at it. Silver. It was silver, too. But it wasn't the pail; it was smooth and clean. He focused his eyes in the dim light. A spoon? A ladle? It was that shape, but larger, much larger.

His eyes widened. He could not move his hands.

"Stone duty," the slavemaster said. "You've got it." He shoved the ladle into the boy's face, striking his cheek. This time Darin lifted his hands, but his knees remained stubbornly locked beneath him.

"See that?" The slavemaster lifted his torch and pointed, another man in power showing him something he was suddenly certain he didn't want to see.

But he looked.

Cut into the stone in a runnel was the outline of a large cat, crossed by spear and sword. A crown stood in the air above it, and beneath its claws, the carcass of a long-necked bird.

He knew this; it was the crest of Damion, robbed of its blue and black and silver. He looked uncertainly at the silver ladle that he held in his hands. The slavemaster laughed again.

And Darin understood.

Wildly he looked at the pail. At Kerren's blood, all that remained of Kerren's life. He dropped the ladle as if it had suddenly seared his flesh; it clattered to the ground and left silence.

The slavemaster's smile vanished. "Pick it up."

Darin shook his head. Something had snapped.

"Pick it up." The slavemaster drew closer, the torch, lower.

Darin shook his head again. He could not do this. That Kerren had fed the Dark Heart was wrong enough, but that his blood should be used this way—no.

He felt a calm enshroud him, and for the first time in months thought of Renar. Renar would never do this.

Legs that would not move before creaked to life beneath him as he rolled out of the slavemaster's grip. His heart pounded in his chest as he got to his feet and saw his shadow stretch out shakily before him.

*"Guards!"*

He ran.

His legs were short, but so were the legs of the slavemaster. He reached the outer doors, scrambled futilely with the catch, and then darted away, along the wall. He felt fingers clutch at the back of his tunic and pushed himself harder.

He had to make his way clear of the courtyard. He had to escape the blooding and the stones and the evidence of Kerren's death. He reached the door by which he'd come this far, flung it open, and lunged forward.

He hurtled into the arms of four guards, four guards who were not so ill-prepared as the slavemaster had been.

He shouted, wordless with rage and fear. His feet struck out against mailed shins, causing him more pain than it did the guards. A mailed fist struck the side of his head, shattering his determination. He fell, felt hands lift him, and heard the slavemaster directing them to hold him fast.

His struggles grew wild; a moth trapped in hands might flutter just so, with equal results. He realized this, and stopped. The pulse that beat time with his heart could be felt at the base of his throat.

The slavemaster moved toward him. His hand was already raised, as if to strike. Darin watched him, aware of the fingers digging into his arms and his back.

*Renar—Renar wouldn't struggle like this.*

He held that thought firmly, trying to distance himself from his tormentor. It worked. He had seen what the priests could do; could the slavemaster, armed with neither blade nor whip, do worse? He was not afraid. Something grew around his thoughts like a wall, insulating him from the grim smile on the slavemaster's face.

But he was not Renar.

The slavemaster's fist struck him squarely in the abdomen, piercing the fragile wall that he'd built. Were it not for the grip of the guards, he would have doubled over.

The blow barely registered before another was struck. Open-handed, this one fell across his right cheek. Open-handed again, across his left, in a smooth, easy rhythm that spoke of years of practice. A boot struck his left side. A moment, and then his right. The slavemaster was a methodical man; he appreciated symmetry.

When the guards finally let go, Darin toppled forward. He looked up, and something dark struck his forehead.

His throat was raw; his lips slick and wet when he opened them to plead near-silently.

In answer, he felt a hand grab his left arm and jerk him to his feet. He swayed, the world spinning around him, and then screamed once. It muffled the snap of bone.

"I haven't broken the right one," the slavemaster said, his words coming between pants of exertion, "because you need it." His grip tightened on the broken arm.

*No please no stop* . . .

The ground moved beneath Darin as he was dragged across the courtyard to face blood and death once again.

This time, when the slavemaster placed the silver ladle in his hand, he did his best to hold it. He tried to rise twice and failed. The third time, fingers wound themselves into his hair and yanked. He came up then, his knees skirting stone.

"Blood the stones."

The ladle shook violently as Darin tried to force it into the silver pail.

*Missed. Bright Heart—I missed!*

"Please . . . please . . . I'll do it. I'm trying to do it. Please . . ."

The slavemaster said nothing. He held Darin up by the hair and waited until Darin finally managed to draw the liquid out. It glistened in the darkness, as if there were more light in it than just the reflection of the pale, pale moon.

And it screamed in Darin's heart as it formed little rivulets that filled the grooves of House Damion's crest.

"More."

Weeping, Darin did as he was ordered.

Hours later, it was over. The sun rose, entering the courtyard to see a small, unmoving body curled awkwardly around the proud crest of House Damion.

Darin woke alone. His eyes were swollen, and it hurt to open them.

The pain had stopped.

A knock sounded, as if at a great distance away.

"Yes?" He tensed then, before realizing that it really was his voice that had uttered the single word. He turned his head very gingerly to one side and wondered if his insides had turned to liquid; it felt much like that.

Stev entered the room.

"Darin?" he said, his voice soft and quiet. "I've brought you food."

"Where am I?"

"Your new room," Stev answered, coming closer. He carried a lamp with him; the tiny fire on the end of the wick seemed to dance.

"Room," Darin repeated. He rose onto his elbow and then cried out in pain.

"Your arm!" Stev put something down and quickly walked over to the bed. He placed a cool hand on Darin's forehead and pushed him back onto the pillows. "Careful of that; it's been set by a doctor, but you aren't to use it for near six weeks."

"Where am I?"

"It's all right, Darin. You were moved. You have your own room."

"My own . . ."

"You don't have to share it with any other slaves."

"I'm not with you?"

"No, lad. Hush. It's a miracle that you're alive at all."

*A miracle.* Tears began to roll down Darin's cheeks.

"The slavemaster overstepped himself a week ago. You've had a real doctor in to see you and you're abed for at least three weeks by the lord's command. You're to eat as often as you can, and to drink more so."

Darin closed his eyes.

Stev stopped speaking. He looked at Darin's still face, then bent gently down. "Darin, Darin lad. It's all right. It's over." He sat down on the bed and with infinite care drew Darin's head and shoulders to rest against him. There he began to rock very slowly, backward and forward.

Darin continued to cry. But it was no child's crying, this. He was silent, although his lips trembled. The arms around him were thin but strong.

"Ah, Lady, Lady," Stev whispered into Darin's matted hair. "Lady, grant your mercy here." He held Darin until he felt the muscles of the boy's arms and shoulders relax. Still he did not let go, but stayed in the near-darkness.

All of Stev's memories of life were of slavery; it was what he knew. He had seen much, both in House Damion and beyond its walls. He was as all slaves were: hardened to the injustice of the life he led. He was almost comfortable with it—or so he had thought.

But there was something about this sleeping boy that kept him here, although the tasks outside wouldn't wait. It kept him rocking and whispering meaningless prayers and words of comfort around the growing lump in his throat.

And when the child spoke, he thought he knew why he had waited.

"Daddy, I have no name anymore, no name."

Stev tightened his arms as if to somehow protect the boy from the bewildered pain in his own voice.

"No name. Kerren's dead. I have . . . I have no family." He tried to sit up, but Stev still held him, and slowly he sank back to rest against the warmth of another human being. "Wait for me, Daddy? Tell Mommy to wait, too. Tell Kerren I'm sorry— tell him I have no name."

"Ahh." Stev lost all words as he felt his own eyes begin to prickle. New slaves—and there were precious few—were always the worst; they were delicate, fragile, and lost. He had seen their anger and their pain, but this was as raw as it had ever been.

He knew why he had stayed. It was to lose what little heart his life had left him.

Darin's prayers to his parents may have been heeded, but it didn't matter; the one foot he had placed on the Bridge of the Beyond was lifted over the three weeks that he spent in bed. He ate automatically, drank a little, and regained his strength. Stev came to see him, but Darin spoke very little. He had learned the first lesson that new slaves often learn: have no friends.

As he grew stronger, he was once again ordered to the house mistress, and she put him back on cleaning duties. But he did these without the whistle or laughter of Stev to shorten the day.

Nor did he have the companionship of fellow slaves in the

evening. He spoke to the four walls of his bare room, slept with them, and occasionally cried. Only a few slaves might have tried to reach him, but it was difficult to risk the wrath of the lord and lady for one they hardly knew. Without being obvious, they shunned him.

He did not see Lord Vellen again, except occasionally from a distance. The lord became more and more involved with the politics of the Church—much to the anger of Lord Damion.

No matter; Darin still felt the high priest's presence in all that he did.

Every quarter, for the next four years, Darin was on stone duty. He took the silver pail and ladle and blooded the grooved stone. No slavemaster stood over him as he worked at his task; no witness held the torch or saw the tears that mingled with blood and rock.

Each time the stones were blooded he heard Kerren's screams; they never grew distant with time.

And then, near his fifth year in House Damion, he was summoned by Lord Damion himself. He felt a stir of fear as he walked down the halls, but he had learned not to show it; it would do him no good.

He entered the lord's chambers, and there met an older man— one he did not recall seeing before.

"This is Gervin," Lord Damion said, lines across his brow. It was obvious that the lord did not favor the free man.

Darin looked more closely at the stranger.

He was tall. Darin thought him older than the lord, but it was hard to tell; his shoulders were broad, and he bore himself without any trace of age. His nose was turned down at a slight angle, as if it had once been broken. His eyes, a green-brown, looked impassively at the slave before him.

"This is he?" he said to the lord, although he didn't look away.

Lord Damion grunted a reply.

"Good." Gervin gestured with one large hand. "Come, boy. Your tenure at House Damion is at an end. House Darclan claims your service now; it has already been arranged. We've far to travel, and we must travel it in no long time."

Darin automatically stepped to the older man's side. He heard the command behind the gesture, and knew enough to obey promptly.

Gervin turned and bowed—perhaps less formally than he

should have; it was hard to tell. "My lord thanks you for your service."

These were, Darin thought, the wrong words to say. He didn't know why, but Lord Damion did not reply at all.

Gervin shrugged and turned back to his charge. "Horses are outside."

Darin nodded automatically.

"Can you ride? Be honest, boy."

"N-not well."

Gervin sighed; the roll of his eyes told Darin that he had already guessed this. "That will have to do. Come; the Lord Darclan waits and he is not a patient lord."

Darin nodded and followed Gervin out of the open doors, into the sunlit court.

He had no belongings, nothing to call his own. He might have said good-bye to Stev, but he did not wish to ask for such a privilege when he knew so little about the temperament of his new owner. He had learned to be a good slave over the years. In time he might be one of the best.

Thus did he leave House Damion, as much a slave as he had been when he arrived.

# interlude

*Lord Darclan walked around the grounds of the gardens, his* face pale and expressionless. He surveyed the expanse of leashed wildlife—the hedges and brambles that had been extensively manicured into growing sculptures, the roses that grew upon the oddest of trees. He had never been particularly fond of gardens, and time had not changed this.

But *she* loved them.

He frowned as he continued to walk, his feet leaving no mark in the grass to speak of his passing. He wanted perfection, but he knew he was not a judge of it; not here, this was not his domain. The master gardener was off in some distant corner; his ears could hear the distinct clip of metal against stem or branch.

*No. I will not interrupt the gardener further this day.*

He turned and walked back toward his castle.

The stonework, smooth and seamless from this distance, looked as if it had been carved from one great piece of rock, a mountain perhaps. It had four corners; four wings, but the towers were short.

She had never become used to the height of the spires of Rennath; here she would have no need to. His fingers curled into fists. He caught them, straightened them, and continued his walk. But he was troubled.

*To wake you, Lady, is difficult. More difficult than I had imagined.*

And not without risk.

Fists. Fists again. A momentary flash of anger colored his eyes. He loathed, as always, this lack of self-control. What matter a few more months, after so many years?

*Naught. It matters not.*

But it was strange, this feeling, this apprehension and antic-ipation. To walk with her, here, in the sunlight; to see her smile, to see her light—

*Ahhhh.*

His long work was over. The Empire was complete. But this making anew he could not be certain of. He despised that weak-ness. He realized that he had once again stopped, and he moved forward.

Someone waited at the gates to greet him. Gervin. Lord Dar-clan's eyes could clearly see the fatigue in the lines of his ser-vant's face. He strode forward.

"You have made the passage in good time," he said softly.

Gervin nodded.

"The slave was still alive?"

Gervin nodded again, but the nod was grim. "Alive, yes. He awaits your word, Lord, in the sitting room to your study. Shall I see to him?"

"No." This at least was distraction. "I shall see him."

Gervin nodded. He straightened out the crease in his leathers and took a deep breath.

"How do you find him?"

It was an odd question; Gervin's eyebrows, black frosted with age, rose fractionally. "Quiet," he said at last. "Well trained. He asks no questions and volunteers nothing."

Lord Darclan inclined his head and entered the castle.

The boy was waiting for him, as Gervin had said.

Almost before the door was open, he had assumed the pos-ture. His knees were upon the ground, and a few inches from them, his forehead.

"Rise," Lord Darclan said softly.

All that Gervin had noted was true. The boy immediately gained his feet and stood, head down, awaiting his command. It was hard to believe that this child was the last of Culverne. Perhaps death would have been a kinder option to offer in her name.

"Boy, look at me."

The child did even this without hesitation. Darclan's eyes caught the trembling along the boy's jaw; it was the only thing that truly showed his fear.

*Does he recognize me?*

He waited for a moment, but the reaction did not change.

*Ah. No.*

"This is House Darclan." Its lord moved past the boy into the waiting study. "Come."

The child followed. He waited as Lord Darclan took a seat behind a large, plain desk. "You may sit. In the chair."

Once again the years of House Damion were evident; the boy did not look from right to left; he merely sat, stiffly, in the offered chair.

"You are now of my house."

"Yes, lord."

"The rules here differ slightly from the rules that govern noble houses; this is my privilege as master here."

"Yes, lord."

"Did you ever perform formal duty for your previous house?"

"No, lord."

"Ah. I suppose you are young. What duties did you have there?"

Only with this question did the boy's reactions change, and even these were minimal. His small face paled and stiffened, no more.

*Interesting.*

"I was with the household staff," the boy said, his head beginning to fall. "I cleaned the brass and silver. I kept the portrait gallery clean and prepared it for visitors." He swallowed then, convulsively. Fear was in the air; fear and pain. He opened his mouth, shut it, looked up, and then began again. "I blooded the stones."

"Look at me, child." Lord Darclan's voice was cold but clear. "Now."

The child obeyed. Brown eyes met black ones without flinching—the boy did not have even the will for this.

*Clever, Vellen. Very clever.* Lord Darclan had only seen this flat stillness about human eyes on one occasion: death. He thought back. How long had he been in this task? How many years had passed? Five, less three months. That was not a long span, even by normal reckoning. He looked again at the slack, lifeless eyes. *Careless.*

The boy could not know that the lord's sudden anger was not directed at him. But he waited.

"Child, we do not blood the stones here."

The boy said nothing. His face was of delicately painted alabaster, cool and immovable.

"Do you understand this?"

A nod.

"Say it, then."

The eyes closed. The child's head, sun-stained near white, bent as if strings were slowly being played out. "House Darclan does not blood the stones."

*Perhaps I have judged in error.* The lord stood then, his expression grim. *This child may not be a suitable slave for my Lady.*

He rose, motioning for the slave to do the same.

*But Lady, your province was healing; it gave you some joy.* He relaxed slightly.

"Come, boy. Let us walk to the courtyard."

The child stiffened again, but he moved.

# chapter
# six

*Darin met the house mistress; her name was Evayn. She was* younger than he expected, and taller, too. She assigned him, after intense questioning, to the household cleaning staff. He met other slaves, but here, as in House Damion, was given his own room. It, too, was beneath the ground levels and allowed no sunlight to enter, but he had torchlight and lamplight should he desire it.

He found the house to be a different place than Damion had been. Most notable was the absence of any colors or crest. The lord himself, seen now only at a distance, and only for minutes at a time, wore unadorned black. He did not require the slaves to do the same.

The seamstress for the slaves was a robust woman, large and fat as few slaves ever got. She had been at the house for seven years—since its beginning, she assured him—and took care and pride in varying the colors of smock, tunic, and trousers to please her eye.

"Lord's command," she would say cheerfully.

Darin could not understand it.

He worked well, as he had done in House Damion for over four years. He answered when spoken to, but rarely tried to ask any questions to which he did not need answers.

And he became accustomed to the castle. It was large, larger by far than House Damion, and much more severe in its grandeur. The halls, gray stone, were as unadorned as the lord himself. Brass torch holders hung at a height that required a stool to reach, and Darin cleaned them weekly, wondering at the lack of mirrors, paintings, and wall hangings. It was obvious that House Darclan was not too poor to afford them.

Over the next month, all this changed. When the south wing

opened up and it was added to Darin's list of duties, he saw that it was frescoed.

He hated it. He worked beneath colored panoramas of the Dark Heart's victories, steadily progressing from the fall of the Lady of Elliath to the fall of . . . Culverne.

After his duties there started, he never again wondered at the naked stone. He much preferred it.

He counted the days and the way the sun fell across the top of the open courtyard. At night he would watch the face of the moon, slowly unveiling itself as it aged across the days.

Second quarter was coming.

Forty days into his stay, he sat in bed, his knees curled beneath his chin, his ears listening across time to the opening scream of the high priest's command performance. His arms ached from the tension, his eyes blurred in the darkness. He wanted a torch, but could not move to get one. The second quarter was nigh.

*Bright Heart*. He thought, bowing his forehead. He had not prayed to the gentle God for years. *Bright Heart, Bright Heart let it be true*.

No knock came to trouble him, no light moved in the corridors. He did not, could not sleep.

But there was no blood on the flagstones.

Scurrying from one end of the castle to the other on an errand for the cook, the lack caught his attention.

He stopped, as he had stopped many times before, to look anew at the carved stone beneath the open sky. It was clean and gray, the eagle cresting the air with a branch clutched tightly in its glittering claws. But there was no brown stain, no sign etched with the dying blood of some poor slave, some unknown criminal.

*Here we do not blood the stones*.

He stopped, swallowing convulsively. On impulse he walked, looking quickly from side to side, to the colorless stone. He had never approached it this closely, partly from fear of the guards, and partly because he did not wish to diminish the wonder of hope by finding any telltale trace of old blood.

Yet now, on this day, he had no choice but to do so. His shaking legs carried him quickly to his goal, and he knelt, again snapping his head from side to side, to look at the stone, and to touch it.

It was completely clean, swept, no doubt, by another of the slaves, one assigned to the courtyard. But that was all that any slave had to do to maintain it.

He touched it and felt the warmth of the sun lingering against his fingertips. No blood. No blood on the stones; no house name filled in by a living trail. No screams, Bright Heart, no more screams.

He shuddered.

*There's no blood. Bright Heart—Bright Heart, where have you been until now?* In wonder he bowed his head, and his hand, shaking and cold, touched his forehead once, twice, three times in half-remembered benediction. *Bright Heart. Thank you. Thank you.* Words came to his young lips; the opening of a prayer.

He had never prayed like this before, in thanksgiving. His mouth moved without his will, the urge was so strong.

Then, of a sudden, his lips clamped shut in a whitened face. He had almost forgotten the rule that governed his existence: No prayer here; never here. That part of his life was dead, and it was a miracle—however he had cursed it—that he was not dead with it.

*Dead?* He looked up at the stones as they blurred. *No blood . . .*

He got to his feet rapidly, gave the courtyard yet another cursory scan, and ran back into the castle on light feet. Not even the fear of the prayer he had made could stop his lips from forming a dazed, wild smile. He entered into the side hall that led to the kitchen and continued to run down it, stopping just short of the doors in order to make a more dignified entrance.

The chief cook looked up as he entered.

"About time you got back here, boy. What's the word?" He went back to mixing a blend of odd herbs, some of which Darin recognized, most of which he did not.

"The lord will dine alone for the evening."

The older man allowed a glimmer of curiosity to show—there was no one but the boy to see it, and no harm done. "I thought the lord was to have a guest?"

Darin bobbed his head.

Cullen sighed. This was a strange one—all silence and misery. He wasn't likely to get more information than that out of him. He raised his knife over a long, thin stem.

For the first time in three years, he missed, as the boy spoke again.

"He does, Cullen. Have a guest, I mean. But I don't think she's well."

Cullen gave a cautious nod, glad that Old Merritt had taught him not to use his fingers to prop up what he was cutting.

"Darin, boy," he asked gingerly, as he set the knife aside, "are you feeling well?"

The boy's face suddenly creased. Cullen had never seen him smile. "Yes. Yes, I'm fine." He threw one hand in the direction of the courtyard, the picture of a younger boy with an important secret to share.

Cullen leaned slightly forward. "Yes?"

"There's no blood on the stones—no blood in the crest of the house!"

Cullen nodded, no longer mystified.

*What did he do at House Damion, Evayn? Entertain?*

*I don't know, Cullen. He wouldn't answer—not with all of the truth.*

He sighed, feeling older. *Stone duty.* Then he shook himself. That was for the other houses, not this one. Lady alone knew why, but he didn't question his fortune.

Besides, if Darin was in the mood to be talkative, he wasn't going to waste it.

"Well then, where's the guest staying?"

"The guest?" Darin asked, confused. Then he nodded. "Oh, her."

"Her? Yes, her."

"I'm not sure."

"The hell you're not, boy! Come on; I've little enough to do in the kitchen now—I could use something to occupy my mind." But his action belied his words, as he picked up the cutting knife once again.

"Well, I didn't see it for myself so I can't be sure." Darin wondered that Cullen wasn't more happy about the stones, but only for a minute—Cullen had been here long enough to know the truth of the lord's words.

"Just out with it."

"Well, I heard from Evayn that she's staying in the lord's wing. Possibly in his own chamber."

Cullen frowned thoughtfully. "That'd be a bit unusual for him. Do you know her house?"

The boy shook his head.

"Too bad; it's good to know what vipers we'll be dealing with." He shrugged his shoulders, knowing that they'd have to accept happily whatever walked into the castle. Stretching, he said, "Well, then, why don't you—"

The door swung open, hit the wall, and swung back. There was the sound of muffled cursing, and the door opened again, but this time somewhat more slowly. A boy about Darin's age—maybe fourteen seasons, rather than thirteen—walked into the kitchen, obviously out of breath.

He gave Darin a mixed look of sympathy and fear.

"Master Gervin's sent me to find you."

The slavemaster? Darin paled slightly, and his whole body stiffened. He said nothing, waiting for the worst news his imagination could conjure up. His imagination was not disappointed.

"The lord—he's requested your presence. In his study."

The stones were forgotten.

*Lady of Mercy,* he thought, *someone saw me in the courtyard.* "Why?"

"Don't know, but you're ordered to report now." The youth had finished catching his breath.

"Don't go scaring the boy, Kelm. The Lord's not had anyone killed for months—and the last one might well have deserved it."

Darin heard the lack of conviction in the cook's voice clearly. Nevertheless he obeyed automatically.

*Someone saw the blessing in the courtyard.*

It isn't fair! He wanted to shout, but his fear was too strong. He cursed himself, hating the familiarity of it. That same fear was the reason that he was still alive; it had forced him, against all that he'd been taught, to labor on the blooded stones for four years.

And now that he had finally been granted a measure of peace and freedom from it . . .

His feet automatically traced the path to the lord's study. He knew when he approached it, for the halls became suddenly silent and empty; no slave without errand ever came here.

With trembling hands he opened the door to the sitting room. His shadow fell upon the worn leather great chairs that kept company with the still fireplace.

*Why?* He thought. *Why was I so stupid in the courtyard? Anyone could have seen me.* Only once before had he done anything as stupid as this in Veriloth.

The door swung loosely shut behind him as he gave it a small push. Why? Because for the first time in over four years, God had answered his prayer.

There was no blood on the flagstones.

He allowed himself the faintest thread of hope, remembering that. Taking a deep breath, he crossed the length of the room. He paused for a moment to lean his forehead against the cool dark wood of the door.

"Enter."

He jumped, his light step making more noise than the gentle press of his forehead had. Swallowing, he did as bidden, opening the door into the large study. It was as it had been the only other time he'd seen it; books, row upon row of them, lined shelves that almost reached the ceiling. It was a library in miniature, dwarfed by the library in Culverne's hall. In Culverne . . .

For a moment the desk and the lord behind it did not exist. Instead, the room opened up into plain oak tables, with equally plain chairs. Acolytes and initiates lined them in silence, and Este's severe whisper warned him to join them in the same. The roof, old stonework, opened up to let the light of the sky flood down, giving day color to the grays and the browns and the endless row of books.

"Come here, boy."

The silence was broken; the world returned.

Darin's eyes shifted slightly to take in the man behind the desk. Carriage, bearing, and the slightly cruel expression that he wore made him out to be of high nobility. No matter that Darclan was not a house name that Darin recognized from his days in the capital. He had seen enough to recognize a man comfortable with power and to know the cost of thwarting it.

He forced himself to walk across the room to stand in front of the desk.

"What is your name, child?"

In a perfectly flat voice, Darin replied, "I have no name, lord."

"Good." Lord Darclan leaned slightly forward in his chair. "I have taken the liberty of relieving you from your current duties."

"Yes, lord."

Lord Darclan watched the boy's pale face, slightly amused by it. Then the amusement vanished as he spoke again.

"I have in my care a young lady. She is not well, but is expected to recover soon."

Curiosity flickered in Darin's eyes, but only in the eyes. He waited to hear his sentence.

"You are to tend to her needs for the time."

Relief. Darin felt his knees quiver, it was so strong.

"Do you understand?"

"Y-yes, lord."

"Good. She is not conscious now; you are to watch her carefully. If anything changes in her condition, you are to let me know."

"Yes, lord."

"Good. Go to the slavemaster. He will tell you the rest."

"Yes, lord." Darin pivoted on his heel then, to hide the relief that washed over his face. He hadn't been seen; the blessing hadn't been noted. He was safe, for now, and he swore to himself that he wouldn't risk his life like that again.

"Oh, and boy—"

The relief drained from Darin's face as he stopped.

"Yes, lord?"

"Do not answer her questions."

"Y-yes, lord."

He walked to the door then, waiting for the end of the game, and not until he passed through it did he breathe again.

The slavemaster looked up as Darin entered the room. He frowned for a moment, the lines of his face shifting, and then nodded. He gestured toward a chair, and Darin took it, sitting stiffly with his back pressed again the ribbed wood.

Gervin looked tired. "Ah, yes. You're Darin?"

Darin nodded quietly. Of all free men, only a slavemaster could use a name when speaking of slaves. Most chose not to, to avoid the stigma of making themselves slave equals. Gervin, however, was not given to this insecurity.

"Good. The lord has assigned you to keep watch over his guest."

Darin nodded again, and Gervin raised an eyebrow.

"Spoken with him?"

"Yes," the boy answered briefly.

"Ah." The brow was raised further. Then the older man shook his head. "Well." He folded his hands on the tabletop and looked across at Darin, the hazel of his eyes piercing.

"The lady is of importance to the lord. She is likely to be the only noble upon his grounds for some time. She is still unconscious, and wakes rarely."

Darin nodded.

"You are to feed her when she will eat, and to bring her water to drink."

Darin nodded again.

"And you are to see that she is happy here." Gervin took a deep breath. "This is the most important task that you will have to perform in House Darclan. You must know, by now, that the lord is not as cruel as many other lords choose to be—but fail in this, and the punishment meted out will be most severe."

"Yes, sir." Darin wanted to know who the lady was, but knew better than to ask. Still, he wondered. This slavemaster, this Gervin, was not like the other slavemasters he had met. It almost seemed, as he spoke of punishment, that he regretted it.

"Go, then. The lady occupies the north wing—the lord's wing. There are tapestries and paintings in the galleries there; they have just been brought into place, and there will be other slaves in the wing to tend to them. If anything happens and you need assistance, do not hesitate to call upon the working slaves. Understood?"

"Yes, sir."

Sleep always did such odd things to a face, and Darin noted it particularly in the lady he watched. In this case, it softened the lines; the white pallor of her skin seemed relaxed, almost gentle. He could almost believe, seeing her sleep, that she would be kind—nearly human—in her treatment of the slaves; something about her mouth, for it was soft and full. Her hair was an unusual color; much too dark for the rest of her, and touched by red highlights.

Her breathing came regularly, as it had for the last few days. He looked out at the setting sun, caught off center by rich blue velvet in the bay window that faced north. Soon it would be time to feed her a little. And that was another strange thing: Although she never woke, she could still swallow soft food and water without choking.

As he watched, she frowned slightly. Even this could not dim the gentleness of her face. He almost didn't want her to wake. His hope had given her the illusion of kindness, and he didn't want to have to face the reality. But the lord had said she would wake in a three-day.

Sighing, he left the room and went in search of water.

"Lady?" The voice was soft and timid. After a few seconds it came again into the darkness. If anything, it was softer.

"Lady?"

She felt the weight of sleep against her eyes, but it lay unnatural and heavy. She opened her mouth to reply, but her tongue felt thick and swollen. It would not respond. She gave up trying and instead concentrated on the timbre of that voice. It halted, faltered, and trembled in a way that tugged at her.

'Lady, please wake."

That was it—the voice, urgent now, was a young one. An older child's voice; a thin veneer of words over fear. She forced her eyes open, ignoring the strong desire to drift back to sleep.

Everything was blurred; indistinct shades of gray only slowly coalesced into normal vision. She blinked, her lids sticking, and was eventually rewarded by sight of a boy. He was older than his voice indicated, but she knew the age well; soon the voice of youth would begin to crack in an uncomfortable compromise with adulthood.

He seemed a dim shade in the soft lights of the chamber, flitting nervously from foot to foot, anchored to her by wide, brown eyes in a still, pale face.

"Yes?" The sound of her own voice surprised her; it was more a croak than a word.

The boy's face relaxed. "The lord sent me. He said you would be awake." He walked slowly over to the bedside.

Slowly? Warily. *Why?*

He stopped at her left shoulder, a small silver goblet cupped in his thin hands.

"He said you should drink this. It will help your strength."

A small arm slid gently round the back of her neck. The cloth of the tunic was cool and welcome. Cool, too, was the silver that slid between her parted lips and trickled liquid slowly down her throat.

Now that she was awake, the boy no longer seemed frightened. No, no that wasn't true. There was fear there, but it was a quiet one.

Still, he handled her gently, showing the same attentiveness that a child might show an injured puppy. He moved slowly, taking great care to see that the cup was tilted only enough to let a little water out, but not so much that it would spill from the corners of her mouth.

When she had finished, the boy rearranged the covers and blew out the candles. She could see his small form silhouetted in the door frame as he left.

Only as the darkness closed in did she realize that she had

forgotten to ask the boy where she was. She tried to call him back, but the words would not rise out of the chaos of her thoughts. The net of dreams took her in silence.

"Did she speak?"

"No, lord." Darin stood warily in front of the large ironwood desk. He had come to know it well.

The Lord smiled mirthlessly. "But she drank?"

"Yes, lord."

"And did she seem to be in any pain?"

Darin hesitated, unsure of what to say. It was obvious that the answer—the right one—was important, for the lord's eyes never left his face.

"Well?" He said, his voice soft and low.

"I think—maybe a little, lord. I'm not—"

"Good enough." His gaze slid off the boy's face, and to the shelves that lined the wall behind him.

Darin waited. His legs were stiff and his arms ached, but he held himself still.

After a time, the lord interrupted his musings and turned again to face him. "Come here, child. Around the desk."

Darin began to move uncertainly, his slight shoulders curling down.

"Come. There is nothing to fear." He reached out slowly and cupped the small chin in his hand.

Darin was rigid.

"Tell me—do you fear her?"

Wariness shadowed Darin's face. The lord's hand tightened.

"Do not try to give me a reply that will please me. I ask the question for reasons of my own—and those you will never question. I have said you have nothing to fear, and I am used to being taken at my word." The jaw he held trembled in his hand.

Darin took a deep breath. "No, lord."

Lord Darclan's stare grew more intent.

Darin could not look away, although he wanted to. He had no idea why he had answered the way he had—but he knew, suddenly, that it was true. It frightened him.

"Why not? Because she is weak? She *will* be well soon. And she is high born."

Darin's face grew thoughtful as fear momentarily gave way to a dangerous introspection. After a few minutes, he said, "It isn't because she's weak. It's—she's—" He turned a winter shade of white, remembering too late who his audience was.

To his surprise, the lord withdrew his hand. As if to himself, he said, "I see that I have chosen well. Go."

Darin did not hesitate. With as much dignity as he could muster, he sprang across the room and out of the partially opened door.

When he had gone, the lord rose from his chair and walked with restless grace to his bookshelf. There he picked out an ancient, leather-bound volume. He opened it, running his fingers along its edge.

"You always did like children. Perhaps, now, you will have the chance to enjoy them."

He wondered, at length, what she would be like upon waking.

She woke at dawn. The curtains had been pulled to allow the first tentative overtures of daylight to brush across her face. She sat up in bed and stretched her arms upward, ignoring the ache of—*how long has it been*?—days of inactivity. She could barely remember the time that had passed; blurred images of drifting half-awake returned slowly, and with it a sense of isolation and darkness.

She sat up abruptly, wrapping her arms around her shoulders.

A small cough came from the doorway, and she swiveled her head at the sound.

"Hello." Her word was soft with warmth and relief. Loneliness retreated with the last thread of sleep.

A boy hesitated in the doorway, a large, unwieldy tray in his hands. At the sight of her smile, he seemed to freeze for a moment, suddenly unsure of where he was going.

"Your breakfast, lady," he said, trying for all the world to be the perfect picture of diligent, sober obedience. And it would have worked, were it not for the unusually heavy tray that set his arms trembling.

She laughed then, grateful that she could, and the last of the darkness fell away. Her smile spread across her face, across the room to touch the boy. It was a warm, new laugh, full of a life that demanded an answering warmth.

Darin bowed his head. He had thought, maybe, that she would laugh like that. And now he didn't know what to do.

Mistaking him, the lady said, "I wasn't laughing at you, child."

"Well, maybe I was at that. But only a little. Here. I'm sorry. Won't you come in and set that heavy thing down? They really should have sent someone else." She started to rise, almost too eagerly. This child, this boy, was familiar somehow, and she didn't want him to leave. Not yet.

At this, Darin did look up. He was torn between fear and disappointment. The fear was obvious: If the lady found his service unsatisfactory, it could well mean his death.

But the disappointment was more dangerous. He realized that somehow, watching over her sleep and waking, feeding her and giving her the water that kept her alive, had become important. It shouldn't have mattered who served the lady—in fact he knew well that it would certainly be safer to do almost anything else in the castle. But he *had* watched her; he'd nursed her to health, and he'd discovered perhaps the one noble in all of Veriloth who might just be human.

Maybe it was the stones, so clean and gray beneath the rising sun of the quarter, that had given rise to his ridiculous hope. He didn't know. He only knew that he didn't want to give it up.

With determined authority, he brought the tray to her bedside table, and with no small effort, lifted it and placed it down.

With a tentative, nervous smile, she said, "I'm really making a mess of things, aren't I? It must be the morning. I feel as if I haven't seen one in centuries, and it's making me a bit thoughtless. Please forgive me. Yours is the only face I remember. I don't even know what mine looks like." She lifted her hands and ran them along her cheeks.

Darin watched as her fingers continued to play along the contours of her face. He wondered what she was doing, until she looked up and grinned.

"No scars."

He heard the words as if from a distance, and almost leaned over to catch them.

*There'll be no scarring. Well, you've not managed to do yourself permanent harm, Darin, lad. But you'll manage it yet if you're as careful as you've always been.*

He could clearly see, for the first time in years, the wrinkled face of the Grandmother that the shadow had obscured. The Grandmother, with her age-honed tongue, and the eyes that saw everything so clearly. The dull ache that had companioned him for nearly five years became a sharp pain and a sharper fear.

*No. Grandmother . . .*

The lady's face grew quiet as she saw the inexplicable change in his. She caught his chin before he could lower it, the tip of her finger a gentle restraint. *Child, what is it? What's wrong?*

"I'm sorry," she said softly. "I shouldn't be teasing you.

Thank you for bringing breakfast to such an impossible patient.''

Darin didn't know what to say. *Is this a game? Are you playing at something I can't see?* He looked up, met the wide, serious green of her eyes, and looked away.

He was awkward. He reminded her so much of—of . . . she tried to capture the image and felt it flitting away. She looked at the boy's bowed head, knowing that he expected her to recognize all of this.

*Maybe,* she thought as she straightened her back, *he's only troubled because I don't. Maybe he's just worried about me.* Sighing, she forced a smile to her lips for his sake.

He didn't look up.

"Have you eaten yet?"

At this, Darin did look up. The question was unusual—it was something she should have known well enough.

"No, lady."

"Oh. Well, then, as I've no company, would you care to join me?"

Darin's face turned blank. This type of trick, apparent and obvious, had trapped him once or twice before. He was not about to step into it now; not even for her.

And she caught the change again.

*He's afraid of me.* She didn't know why, but she knew it was true. Her face darkened—she couldn't remember whether or not she deserved his fear.

"I've done it again. I'm sorry. I don't understand what it is you expect of me—I wasn't joking when I told you I don't even know what I look like. Tell me. Tell me what I should be doing.''

Darin looked at her as she held out her hands, palms up. They were shaking. If she meant it, he could tell her anything, anything at all, and she'd believe it. He bit his lip, avoiding the way her eyes suddenly closed.

"Please," she said, her voice even softer than normal.

She meant it. She really meant it. He didn't know what to do. Of all the things he expected, being *asked* for help by a noble was not one.

*No,* he thought, as he took a deep breath. *No, I can't chance this. I can't.* But he couldn't leave, either, until she dismissed him.

So he stood, pinned by the helpless expression that transformed her whole body. Stood silent, waiting for the order.

Fifteen minutes passed, and she still would not give it. He felt
odd; his face was hot. *What am I supposed to do? Bright Heart,
what?*

*She doesn't even know what she looks like. Doesn't know . . .*

"Lady, would you like me to bring you a mirror?"

She started, as if the sound of his voice surprised her, and he
wondered what she had been thinking. But she smiled, her nod
pronounced.

With great relief, he fled the room in search of polished silver.
He would have to go back, and soon—but he needed the time
to think.

*The child was afraid of me.*

The lady looked down at her hands; they were white; they
were shaking.

*Why?*

She stood, belted the soft robe she wore, and began to pace
across the plushness of golden carpet.

*Where am I?*

The window was a source of light. She walked over to it,
turning her face to the sky as if it held answers.

*Who am I?*

*Who is she?* Darin rubbed his tunic yet again over the surface
of the silver mirror. He held it up, squinted at his slightly distorted image, and began to polish it anew. Not that any more
dirt was likely to be taken from it, but it would explain his
absence.

*Why doesn't she remember anything?*

He looked up at the sound of footsteps, but it was only Jen,
off across the hall to continue his cleaning duties.

The sun was near half-up; soon it would be time for lunch.
He'd have to arrange to get it to her and to clear the old food
away.

The growl of his stomach reminded him that he'd not yet had
the chance to eat either. Sighing, he stood. He'd been sent for a
mirror, and he'd have to get this over with sometime.

The door opened.

The lady looked up. Her hands gripped the edge of a large
chair tightly for a moment before relaxing. She smiled, but the
smile itself was shadowed and false.

"You came back! I was beginning to think you'd forgotten me."

"No, lady." Darin bowed low and took the opportunity to control the sudden flutter of his stomach. "There aren't many silver mirrors, and I wanted to find you the best."

She held out a hand without waiting for him to finish, and he walked over to where she sat, placing the cold frame of the mirror into her icy hand.

She didn't look at it.

Instead, she looked up at him.

"You're afraid of me," she said. It wasn't a question.

Darin was surprised again. He wondered then if anything the lady said would not surprise him. The lord's face flickered between them, with the echo of a similar question.

"No, lady," he said, speaking half to her and half to the man who claimed his ownership. And saying it for a second time, he found that he did believe it, as much as any slave could.

It frightened him, which was good: fear had kept him alive in House Damion. He needed it to keep him alive here. He turned and walked over to the breakfast dishes.

To his dismay, none of the food had been touched. Eggs, sausages, ham, bread—all of these things were cold and undisturbed.

He was not afraid of the lady.

He was too smart not to be afraid of the lord.

"Aren't you hungry?" he asked, his voice quiet and small.

She shook her head. The mirror still wavered in her hand. "Are you?"

He closed his eyes and nodded.

"You are?"

"Yes."

"Well, then." She rose, setting the mirror down carefully. "If you don't mind cold food, do you think you could join me?"

She had offered, again. Darin looked at her pale face, noticing for the first time how gaunt she looked, and noticing, as well, the way she watched him.

"If—if you don't mind."

The tension seemed to ebb out of her, and she stumbled as if it had been the only thing that kept her standing.

Without thinking about it, Darin was already at her side, his arm under her arms, his feet firmly planted in the wool of the carpet.

"Lady," he said, as he helped her back to her bed, "you haven't been awake very long. You must be careful."

"I'll try," she said softly.

"Do you want me to get warmer food? This has gone cold."

She shook her head. "I don't see any reason to waste it just because I didn't eat it when it was first brought."

He nodded automatically as he tried to pull the covers back. She had to help a little; he was not big enough to hold her and pull them as well.

He dragged the heavy bedside table over.

"There's only one set of cutlery," she said quietly.

Darin nodded.

"Could you get more, do you think?"

He nodded again. *You only have to order it*.

"We could share these?"

He shook his head. "I'll get—I'll get more."

He found the comfort of the quiet halls again.

*She doesn't want me to be afraid of her. It scares her*.

This time he returned promptly. His chest was still heaving; he had to run to and from the kitchen without even pausing to answer any of the cook's questions.

She still had not touched her food.

As the door opened she smiled, but the smile was hesitant.

"I waited for you," she said.

"Thank you," he replied. It was all very strange. But he felt no fear as she moved to make room for him; felt no fear as she began to divide, rather unevenly, the meal that he had brought earlier; and still felt none as he began to eat it.

He wasn't sure why.

# chapter
# seven

*The next meal was easier.*

Darin experienced a moment of panic, no more, when she asked him to stay. Then he nodded, left the room, and returned with cutlery and a small plate.

The meal after that, dinner, was easier still.

The following morning, when he brought the breakfast tray, he took the liberty of bringing his dishes with it. She asked few questions, and those that she did ask he could answer, questions about the size of the castle, the number of people it housed, the size of the gardens, and even about the weather.

Two more days passed like this; two days in which her smile grew stronger and less shadowed. For some reason, it made him happy.

". . . and I knew I shouldn't keep them; they burrow, after all, and the cows and horses break their legs in the holes." She sighed, her lips turning down in a delicate, self-deprecating smile. "I wasn't old. How was I supposed to know they were male and female? I thought they were, well, best friends or something."

Darin winced.

The lady laughed. "Right. Hundreds of the little monsters. My father nearly killed me."

Darin laughed. The expression on her face was one that had often been on his, and the words she used were words that he had often used himself.

Then she stopped.

"My father . . ." Her smile faded and she looked down at the hands that were already forming fists. Then she shook her head in frustration. "I almost had it. Almost . . ." She sat there, her lips clenched, and then her expression changed again. It often did; it was mercurial, unfixed, and entirely unpredictable. "You laughed!" The exaggerated roll of her eyes left Darin no room for fear. Even when she rose and grabbed either shoulder he felt none. "You've never laughed before."

He thought about it. "No," he said quietly.

For some reason, this cheered her immensely, and she put away the darker thoughts.

"I'll have to keep telling you about the stupid things I did as a child, then. God knows they might as well be of some use to someone!" And she chuckled.

*But lady, how can you remember things you did as a child, if you can't remember who—who you did them with, or where?* He didn't ask. But he worried for her.

And he laughed, too.

"But what is your name?"

Darin froze. The hair on the back of his neck stood on end. Such a harmless question. Such a guileless one. He swallowed, paling.

"I—I can't tell you." This, this was a risk. Not *I don't have one*, but *I can't tell you*. He hoped she would understand.

Maybe she did. She looked hurt. But she didn't ask again.

Lord Darclan sat in the large chair behind his desk. When Darin walked into the room, he looked up.

"Good. I have been waiting for your report."

Darin assumed his stance before the desk in silence.

"How does the lady fare?"

"Well, lord." Darin wanted to look away, but averting his eyes in the presence of his lord would certainly be worthy of note.

"Does she eat?"

"Yes, lord."

"Does she speak?"

*Speak?* Darin thought about gophers. "Yes, lord."

"Of what does she speak?"

"Her childhood. Things that happened when she was younger."

Lord Darclan caught the frown that Darin made and returned it.

"I see . . ." He glanced outward, into the darkening sky. "So soon.

"Does she also ask questions?"

Darin looked distinctly uncomfortable. "Yes, lord."

"And these?"

"She wants to know who she is. Where she is, and why. Everything."

"And your response?"

Something in the lord's tone shot down Darin's spine. He stiffened, his lips almost trembling. "I did as you ordered, lord." His voice was low. "I told her you would tell her. I told her that I didn't know the answers to her questions."

"Ah." A pause. Then, "You have done well, boy. Go."

The child was forgotten before he left the room; he was of little consequence. Lord Darclan rose, his movement silent and elegant. With one hand he gestured, and the remaining light in the room was guttered. The shadow felt good, familiar.

*Your childhood, lady. How is it that you remember this?* He turned, gave the curtains a vicious tug, and heard a tearing that marked the end of the fabric. *It is too soon.*

The darkness made a low noise. The lord regained his composure. *How much more will you remember?*

This was not in the parameter of his spell. But she was who she was. On reflection, that explained much. He straightened himself out to his full height, and his form shivered balefully where there was none to see.

*Very well. It begins. In the morning we will speak.*

A loud rapping on the door pulled Darin abruptly out of sleep. Groggy, he lifted his head as the noise grew louder.

"Darin!"

Bang. Bang.

He rolled out of bed, grabbed his tunic in clumsy hands, and tripped over his stool on the way to the door.

"Darin wake up!"

"I'm coming, Kelm. Leave off the door or you'll break it and we'll both be for trouble!"

The slighted door was yanked open, and Kelm nearly pitched over as his hand struck air with a forceful woosh. Darin yelped, stepped out of the way, and offered the unfortunate Kelm a hand up.

"Thank the Lady you're awake, boy." Sweat rolled off Kelm's tired, round face. His lids blinked rapidly, a nervous habit that obscured dull brown eyes.

"What? What is it?"

"The lord's guest. She's not awake—but Helen heard her crying out. Lord's orders say that you're to tend her, and you alone, so she woke me and sent me down to you."

Darin nodded crisply, sleep forgotten. He started to walk down the hall, then turned back.

"Does—does the lord know?"

"No one's been to him."

Darin nodded; more assurance than this Kelm could not give.


Before he reached her room, he could hear her voice. It was as unlike the gentle, quiet voice he'd come to know as it could be. But raw and wild as it was, he recognized it. He skidded to a halt before her door and threw it open without even bothering to knock.

The dim light from the hall transformed the room from darkness to shadows. With shaking hands, Darin fumbled with a lamp and, the moment a flare burned on the wick, he shut the door behind him.

The lady lay in her bed. She twisted from side to side, the covers disarrayed around her legs. Her face was white and strained with effort, but her eyes remained closed. This was bad enough. But her screams, too strangled to form words, cut into Darin as he ran to the bed.

Her arms shot up suddenly, straight and tense, and Darin reached out to grip one hand. The oil in the lamp sloshed ominously as he tried to put it down.

"Lady! Lady!" He held her hand tightly, forgetting for the moment who and what she was. Then her hands went limp in his, and her eyes snapped open. He could see a trail of tears in the corners of her eyes.

Her eyes focused slowly; her breath grew less ragged. She reached out as he set the lamp down, capturing his hand almost before it was free. She was very, very cold.

"I—I must have had a nightmare." The words came with great difficulty. Her eyes were too wide open for Darin to meet easily.

"It's all right, lady." Now that she was awake and aware, he felt suddenly awkward. He tried to let go of her hands.

"Wait." The word sounded as if it were dragged from her throat. She started to say more and then paused. Darin saw pain in her face, like the pain he had kept inside himself for years. It was gone quickly, but her voice, as she continued to speak, still held it.

"It's dark. It's very dark in here." She licked her lips nervously. "Can you bring more light?"

He nodded and started to move away. Then he cleared his throat. Very gently, he said, "Lady, my hands."

"Your—oh. Sorry." She released him then, but reluctantly.

He lit the two other lamps in the room with shaking hands. He felt her eyes upon him as he worked. Occasionally, he looked up to notice that her eyes would wander to the crack between the closed curtains of her window, to the night. Then they would find him again, and fasten onto him more tightly, as if her sight were a solid thing, an anchor.

When at last he was finished, he turned again toward the lady, half expecting her to be asleep. What he saw instead was a woman whose hands gripped the edge of her newly adjusted sheets as if they were the only solid thing the room offered.

In a voice as gentle as he could make it, he said, "Is there anything else you need?"

She shook her head.

He nodded and turned to leave, only to stop again at the sound of her voice.

"Yes, lady?"

"Can you—do you think you could stay?"

He froze for an instant, his face a mask of ice. Twice before this, two others had made such a request, and twice before he'd had no choice but to—he cut the thought short, burying the memories. She saw this, could not help but see it. He saw her face pale; saw a flash of pain and loneliness quickly submerged as her expression came under control. With a wan, tight smile, she said, "I'm sorry. I'll be fine." She turned her head, and once again the dark of night caught her eye, almost freezing her in place. She drew the covers high around her chin and tried to settle back into bed. Her eyes were shadowed by more than the lamplight.

Darin was almost immediately sorry for his reaction. He knew that she wasn't really aware of the reasons for it—she was barely aware at all.

He wanted to stay, then, and be of comfort. Something in her face brought back the sharp, bitter image of his first night as one among the nameless, listening to the footsteps of the Swords and holding Kerren's hand as tightly as he dared.

*Why,* he thought, *do you always bring memories?* He turned abruptly to pull a chair closer to the bed.

Of course, he had been a slave that night. It had been different for him. Hadn't it?

"No, really. I'm fine. I don't have any right to ask you . . ." She shivered. "I'm adult now." But all around her, the darkness was growing. The child seemed to be the only source of warmth and light in the room.

Seeing the way her eyes widened, Darin sat down.

"I'll stay. Sleep. I'll keep the lamps burning."

He held out a hand and she took it, her grip tight and fierce, just as his grip on Kerren's hand had been. Just so.

He wondered what her life had been like, then, wondered if all of the free men and women really had a pleasant, easy time of things. But he stayed, and his presence brought her a measure of comfort.

He nodded off when sleep forced her to relax her grip on the blanket.

The high, fluting sound of laughter reverberated in the stark stillness of the hall; one low, rich voice blending in subtle harmony with a high soft one.

The lord could hear it as he made his way toward the chamber. It called out into the stillness, a beacon of such strength that he failed to notice the slaves as they scattered before the familiar sound of his footsteps, suddenly busy with their allotted tasks.

He paused before the closed door, drinking in the sound of her laughter. Then he gripped the door firmly and entered.

At once the room froze in a tableau before him. *She* sat in his bed, her auburn hair in a clumsy topknot, her deceptively delicate hands clutching the end of a feather pillow. Her green eyes, crinkled just so at the corners, were upon him. He glanced at the white translucence of her skin beneath the dark blue robe—he would have to see that she spent time in the sunlight; she had always loved the sun.

It was almost too much for him. To see her awake, to see her respond to life after so long—no other victory could come close to this.

Then he noticed the boy. His hair was a tousled mess, and his hands also clutched a pillow. This in itself would have been cause for severe discipline. Worse still, the child was standing—standing!—on the bed, the pillow over his head. His face was almost a death mask. Nerveless hands let the pillow fall to the bed. The soft thud it made was like thunder in the silence.

"Lord!" Darin croaked. His voice failed him, as did all else but fear. What had he been doing?

But the sound returned a semblance of motion to the room. Darin jumped off the bed and came to stand stiffly beside it. He couldn't control the trembling in his limbs or the pallor of his face. The lady gently put her own pillow down. With a quick glance at Darin, she turned to face the man.

"My lord." She inclined her head slightly.

"My lady." Her eyes. He bowed. "I apologize for my rude interruption. Please forgive me. I had heard you were faring well and felt that I should make myself available to answer any questions you might have."

"You're very kind." The sentiment did not quite reach her voice as she looked back at Darin.

Darin did not appear to notice.

Turning to the slave, Lord Darclan said, "You may go."

Darin went.

*It isn't only me he's afraid of.* The lady looked coolly at the man who stood, resplendent in black, before her. She was angry; it had taken the better part of three days of quiet coaxing to get even the hint of a smile from her young companion, and with a few words, this lord had driven that away. From the sounds of the boy's retreating footsteps, she wondered if she would have to start to form their tentative friendship all over again.

His pale, fear-taut face wavered before her.

"Do you wish me to leave?"

"What?"

"You seem discomfited, lady. If it is my presence that has accomplished this, I will leave you. I did not wish to . . . disturb your rest." His dark eyes flickered to the disarray of the bed and the lopsided heap of two feather pillows.

Her silence was response enough for a moment. He knew the tightness of jaw and the clamp of lips well enough to know what she felt.

*But beyond that, Lady?* He did not ask; now was not the time.

"I am glad to see you are well. The physicians were not so certain of your health."

"The child . . ." she said.

"Yes?"

"Why was he so afraid of you?"

The lord's eyebrows raised a fraction, as if in surprise. "Do you not know this?"

"No." Her answer came quickly, a short, terse word of frustration. She had always been this direct.

"Lady, how else should he react? He is, after all, a slave."

Silence again. But this silence was colored by the sudden widening of the green of her eyes; the opening of her lips. He saw her brows furrow as she struggled with the information he had given her.

*You cannot remember.* The thought was a command.

"And I?" she asked woodenly.

"You, lady, are a noble of Veriloth. You are no one's slave."

"Oh." She turned, her heels digging into carpet. Her fists clenched tight and then relaxed.

"I will do nothing to the child if he was following your wishes. He was purchased to serve you, and if you will, he is yours."

She cringed at the last word. Shivered.

"Perhaps," he offered, "we might speak of other things."

She said nothing.

"Let me introduce myself. I am Lord Stefan of House Darclan."

"Lord Stefan . . ." Her hair tilted back as she raised her head. "House Darclan?"

"Indeed, lady."

The curve of her shoulders dipped down, and she turned as if grudging him sight of her. "And I?"

He frowned and shook his head. "Ah. The physicians warned me that this might be the case. You do not remember?"

"No."

"You are Lady Sara Laren. House Laren is located in Penderfield." He took a step forward.

*Penderfield. Laren.* He saw her lips move slightly over the words. "This—this is not my house."

"No, Lady." He smiled. "And yes. It is properly my house, but I willingly give you the run of it."

His smile changed his features; Lady Sara looked up at the curve of his lips. Her brows drew together, and she raised one hand. It stopped a few inches from his face, and then fell into her uncomfortable silence.

She turned again.

"I'm sorry." Her voice spoke of frustration more than regret. "None of this means anything to me."

"It will come to, lady."

Silence again. He wondered if she had ever before been this silent, although his perfect memory told him instantly that she had. It was not her silence that he wanted. Nor the struggle that she seemed to be going through before she chose to speak anew.

"But you, Lord Darclan, you seem familiar. Have I seen you before?"

His chin tilted up, ever so slightly. He closed his eyes for a moment. "Yes, lady."

"Were we friends?"

This time it was his turn for silence.

Ever aware, she caught it and turned.

He reached out and caught her hands. She started, but his grip, though gentle, was immovable. Silence deepened between them.

Lady Sara found that she could not meet the lord's eyes. Instead, she looked at the way their hands twined together, and knew a sudden sense of *rightness* that she hadn't felt since waking.

"What happened?" she asked, unwilling to look away from his hands, from hers.

"You were out boating with a few of the slaves in attendance. A summer storm caught you unprepared, lady. You hit your head when your boat capsized, and one of the slaves, who knew how to swim, pulled you to land." His voice grew sharper. "You had taken in much water, there. We almost lost you. It was a very close thing."

He could not keep the pain from his voice.

It was the only right thing that he did that day.

Her hands shook even as they relaxed just a little beneath his.

"Lord Darclan, was I important to you?"

"Was? That puts it in the past tense, lady." On purpose, he made his voice lighter and more gallant. "You are more important to me than life itself." As he watched the rising sheen of red take her cheeks, he acknowledged with a sharp, familiar pain that these words were the only completely truthful words he had yet spoken.

And he wondered for just a second if beginning with lies—to her, when truth was what she valued so—was any beginning at all.

But his concern lasted only for a second.

She was free of her memories, but he could not and would not part with his. And he remembered the dark, broken fury of eyes that no longer looked green.

*So.*
*I came here from a thousand miles away—from the other end of the Empire. I came here to take residence in House Darclan because the climate suited me better. I came here because of Lord Darclan.*

She walked the stretch of her room until she reached the wall and pivoted neatly on the carpet for perhaps the hundredth time.

*I'm a noble of Veriloth. There's a Church of the One here. There's slavery, and I should be used to it.*

She frowned, and her toes dug savagely into woolen pile.

*No. That feels wrong.*

She thought of the look on the boy's face—the boy who was nameless, as slaves always were. Thought of the fear in his eyes that she disliked—hated—so much. Fear of her.

*And no wonder. I couldn't have had slaves. I could not have owned them.* If the carpet hadn't been so convenient a target, she would have kicked herself. *I should have asked him right there and then.*

But she hadn't, and she knew why. It was obvious that the lord was worried for her; obvious that her near-death had hurt him deeply. She ground her teeth together.

*He can't be right.*

But inside of her, curled in a tight knot, was the doubt of that conviction. She wasn't a coward; she faced it squarely. Maybe she had been a part of this, this slavery, this ownership.

*Maybe it's a good thing that I don't remember anything.*

The next morning when Sara woke, she found that clothing had been laid out for her. Deeming its presence to be a request, she quickly rose and began to change. A small sound caught her attention and she wheeled around quickly, clutching the dress to her bosom.

The nameless slave stood warily in the door.

Sara smiled, a tentative, welcoming gesture.

He nodded stiffly in reply.

"What?" she said, keeping her voice light. "No breakfast this morn?" Her voice fell on the last word. She felt the walls around him, and they were pushing her away. She wondered if he would ever eat with her again, or relax enough to engage in a combat of feathers.

"No, lady. The lord says you are well enough to dine in the morning room with the guests if you'd like."

"Oh." She turned her back toward him and nimbly stepped into the soft, green folds of velvet dress. The front of it was paneled with a different material that shone and caught the light, turning it a deep, forest green. She liked it. What she didn't like were the small, cloth-covered buttons that ran from neck to hip on the back of the dress.

She grimaced. Buttons like these, dainty little showpieces, she had never liked. She scrabbled at them, managed to catch one or two, and then stopped.

*No, I never did like these. Did I wear them? Is this how I dress?* While she stood, her left elbow nearly planted in her cheek, the boy moved forward. She felt the quick, light touch of his small fingers as he unfastened the buttons that she'd done up, and then refastened them correctly.

He worked in silence. Sara stood completely still, partly because she wished the dressing to be done with, and partly out of surprise. When he finished, she turned, half-expecting him to bolt at the sight of her. He didn't.

Oh, the look on his face. *I never owned slaves.*

She knelt, although she did not stand much taller than the boy. His legs moved woodenly as he took a step back.

"I can't just call you 'boy' or 'child.' "

Her breath stopped for a moment as she waited a reply. *Please,* she thought as she reached out a hand, *this is important to both of us.*

"You can call me whatever you like."

A hint of memory touched her then; it was odd, but she felt she'd heard these words before. Only the tone was different; it was serious and dark.

His face bore her study stoically, its lines unmoved and unchanged. Then he opened his mouth and his eyes shifted.

"Why are you doing this to me?" The words were a whisper. But his eyes, as they caught hers, were full of longing, terror, and a hint of leashed fury.

"Because you're afraid of me." She lowered her head, and her hair, loose and long, obscured her face. "I can't—it's hard for me, to know that you fear me. I want you to understand that you don't have to." The pulse at her neck began to jump. An odd tingle ran along her spine, traveling to fill her arms, legs, and face.

She knew he would answer. And she knew, somehow, that the answer would be hard.

It was worse than she could have expected.

"Don't you understand anything?" The young voice rose on the last word, and she looked up to see that all of his control had fled. "Or are you just playing with me? Are you trying to trap me?"

She closed her eyes.

"Well why don't you have me beaten instead—or killed?" His voice was desperate and uneven. "It's your right, lady, and it would be easier—easier than this."

She looked up, then, as his hands spread outward in a gesture that encompassed the room. She said nothing; he was not yet finished.

"Why are you doing this? Why?" His face was white. "Why don't you stop?"

Very slowly, she reached out and touched his cheek with an open palm. It was not the slap he expected, but he flinched as if she had struck with mailed fist.

The tingle that ran down her arms seemed to shoot out through her fingers.

"It would be easier," he said, his voice once again a whisper. "I wouldn't have to worry about you anymore. I wouldn't have to wonder if you really mean it all. It would just be over."

She nodded.

He closed his mouth and said nothing as her hands continued to hold the strange territory of his desert face.

Sara wondered then how this person could eat with her, have pillow fights with her, and listen to her tales of misspent childhood. The wounds, invisible to the eye, went deep.

This at least she knew: She had never lived his life. But just the same, she felt oddly akin to him, as if some other pain, some other hurt, found an answering echo in the words that he spoke.

"It's no game," she told him quietly. "No trap. You have been the only friend I have in these walls. Lord Darclan I might once have known, but I do not remember him. I remember you. When I was sick, you tended me. When I was afraid, you sat with me. When I was lonely, you ate with me." Her fingers stroked his cheeks in a rhythmic movement.

"Lord Darclan told me a little about this land, but it doesn't feel real to me. It doesn't feel *right*."

He watched her, dry-eyed. But he did not pull away.

"Maybe my house was different from this one. Maybe not. I can't tell you for sure. But I do know what's important to me now. I need a friend."

She saw his eyes flutter.

"If I call you 'boy,' if I call you 'child' or 'slave,' no matter for who's sake, then I'm accepting that that's what you are."

"I am a slave." His voice was quivering. "I have no name. I promised."

His voice told her what that promise had cost, or how that promise had been made. In spite of herself, she shivered.

"Maybe, right now, that's what you are to every other person in the castle. But don't ask me to treat you as he does. Don't ask that of me. Please." She felt her stomach knot; she didn't know why, but God, the words made crystal clear her feelings. It was so important that he not ask that, that she not be it.

"I have no name," he repeated dully. "Call me whatever you like. I'll still do what you tell me."

*It's too late. I'm too late.* She thought it for a moment, and the feeling of panic welled up, more strongly than before. Then: *No. No. No.*

"Then I will. I'll give you a name, that we two can use. I'm Sara. And you . . ." She closed her eyes. She felt suddenly weary.

"Darin." As she said it, she felt a little flare of warmth ring the two of them, too subtle to be identified.

*Darin.* The word left her lips. He heard it as if it were a shout. It reverberated through him.

*Darin.* He could hear it clearly, as it had been spoken by anyone he'd lived with for the first eight years of his life. The Grandmother, with her patient exasperation, and her not-so-patient discipline; his mother, with her stern silences and the shadowed laughter that held all he knew of the future—and his year-mates, in the halls that he would never walk again.

*Darin.*

The mask crumpled. Uncertainty filtered through the cracks.

"How did you know?" he whispered, his voice stark. He met her eyes fully, probing them. She met his search without turning away, and he saw the sheen of tears in her eyes. Had they always been there?

He looked at her cheeks and saw that tears trailed along them. *Is it all a game?* he wanted to shout.

No. This was real. this stranger, this noble of Veriloth—she was real. His arms shot out and wrapped themselves around her as tightly as they could. It was awkward, but he didn't notice the way she juggled her elbows out of the way.

"Darin."

He looked up; she was blurred by the tears—his, this time. Looking at her this closely, he thought that she was limned in a light that left her eyes and surrounded her.

"We'll take care of each other, you and I."

He nodded, but he couldn't speak. The tears were dissolving him. Someone was shaking; he couldn't be sure who it was.

But the tears became sobs, and the sobs became silence and a haunting peace.

# chapter
# eight

*They were very late for breakfast.*

Sara, lady of Veriloth, walked hand in hand with Darin, low-liest of slaves, as they made their way from the north wing. It only made sense, she had said, because she certainly didn't know where she was going.

"Are you sure you want to do this, Sara?"

*Sara.* She smiled warmly at him. "The lord's orders were most specific." Her smile faded. "Are you sure that you do?"

It had seemed a good idea in the comfort of her rooms, but the domineering gray of solid stone made it seem a smaller, colder one.

"He told you that you could do what you pleased?"

She nodded seriously.

"And that I could do whatever you wanted?"

She nodded again.

It was a bad idea. He knew it was a bad idea.

But he wanted to enter the dining room with her. He wanted—he wanted to know that he could walk beside her, and she would treat him like a real person without her own walls to hide them.

"Darin?"

His name. His name, used by someone free—someone who had a choice, as he had once had a choice. That decided him. Heart racing, he said, "Yes, Sara. Yes, if you're still sure."

"I'm certain."

Something about her voice made him glad that she was his friend.

She walked over to the set of small double doors.

*These ones?* She mouthed at him.

He nodded, and she gave a little grunt as she pushed them open.

The room that unfolded before them was laid out with the precision of a heart board. *Heart board?* she wondered with a start. A game . . . Narrow, peaked windows lined the walls even between rounded, decorative pillars. Light hit wooden floors, revealing the intricate inlays that curled around the legs of the long, narrow table. Much design had gone into this.

Lady Sara looked up to see Lord Darclan at the head of the table. He, too, sat precisely. Not rigidly, but not . . . she shook her head. Like hearts, his presence spoke of power. The black heart, personified, waiting for the move. And like the game, on left and right were two older men, standing in as Servant pieces.

She felt no recognition, but she didn't like them. One was dressed in a variant of the black that Lord Darclan still wore, the other in green and silver finery. Sara had always hated hearts. As a game, it seemed to trivialize and reduce war itself. Too many people suffered too much to have their pain made so small.

But she thought it fitting, somehow, that she stood directly opposite the black heart piece, playing, instead, the white heart. She looked at Darin, who stood very close to her side, and smiled.

*White heart and Servant; we are outnumbered. He has three to our two, and we have no black-blood, no white-bloods to throw between us.* Perhaps this was why she hated the game so much. *But this move is ours.*

She took a step forward and stopped as she realized that she had seen the game played, but had never played in it. Who had played it? Where?

The pressure that Darin exerted on her hand allowed her to put the question aside for the moment. But the thought lost her the right of first move.

Lord Darclan stood and bowed very formally. "Lady Laren. I trust I do not tax your strength with my request for your company?"

She sighed and squeezed Darin's hand to reassure both of them. "Not at all, Lord Darclan. I apologize for taking so long to wake. Please forgive us for being late."

He smiled, then, and nodded. The man to his left, the one in the dark robes, started slightly in surprise.

"Please, lady, be seated."

Darin hovered behind her. Sara walked up to the table and immediately noted that there were only four places set—and three taken. She hesitated, running her tongue across the edge of her teeth.

Once again she felt the pressure of Darin's hand.

She made her move.

"Lord Darclan." She gave a bow to equal his, low and proper. The man in the green and silver gave her a disdainful look, and she realized that she had bowed instead of curtsied. Bowing, however, had seemed to her the more natural action. She colored, gritted her teeth, and began to speak.

"Lord Darclan, it would please me greatly to be able to continue as I've started."

He raised an eyebrow and waited in silence.

Sara felt awkward. "I would ask that another place be set here for Darin." She lifted his hand, which shook only a little more than hers did. But he was afraid; she felt anger.

Lord Darclan's eyebrows rose fractionally higher as he glanced at the slave at her side, seeming to become aware of the link their hands formed.

Both men looked also, and then turned incredulous stares at Sara.

She met their gaze with a brittle smile. Lord Darclan was lord here, not these two, and she cared little enough if she embarrassed or demeaned herself in their eyes.

She waited for the move that would answer hers, her green eyes staring into his dark ones. Silence stretched out between them; it felt odd. And then, strangest of all, he smiled.

"Lady Sara," he said softly.

"Stefan."

His smile deepened. "We need not bother to set another seat. Calven is just finished, and his place will be cleared. The boy may sit there."

She cleared her throat softly and looked once more at Darin. He met her eyes, hesitated once, and then nodded almost fiercely.

The man in the dark robes, presumably Calven, rose. With a not quite silent sputter, he turned a venomous glare at Sara. She turned it with the edge of her smile.

Without thinking, he took a step forward, toward her.

Lord Darclan's hand caught his arm. Even from this distance, it did not look gentle. "Go," he said, in the exact tone that he had used to dismiss Darin from her quarters yesterday.

"For the sake of a *slave*?"

"For the sake," Lord Darclan said quietly, "of your life, Priest."

Calven's eyes widened, and his robes swirled as he attempted to pull away. Then he stopped, suddenly, as if struck. He turned to look again at Sara. His eyes widened and then narrowed in quick succession.

Bowing was difficult with Lord Darclan's hand still entrenched in his forearm, but he managed to do so, stiffly and formally. Then he left.

Lady Sara looked for a long while at her host.

In the game of heart, if a move was too easily made, or a victory too easily won, each side had to be careful before accepting the fruit of it. Traps were often set so, if one player was more experienced, and one too eager.

She sighed. Perhaps it was time to abandon the game; reality was dangerous enough. She pulled out Calven's chair and sat lightly in it, motioning for Darin to take the seat before hers.

His hands shook as he pulled out the chair, but he showed no other sign of what he felt until he was truly seated in it. And then he looked at Sara.

His smile, shaky, almost stunned, made the game worth everything.

Lord Darclan clapped his hands, and slaves appeared. At his word, they moved forward to clear Calven's place.

But they were not as efficient this morning as they were on every other. Each of them—and there were four—stopped to stare at Darin. Then they turned to glance, much less obviously, at their lord.

Darin said nothing, but he swallowed. Later, there would be questions to answer, a lot of them. Cullen alone could probably demand his time for an evening.

But some of his triumph evaporated as he realized that eating at this table meant that he, too, would be waited on by slaves. As if he weren't one of them. As if there were a difference. He didn't like it at all.

He glanced at Lady Sara and saw what he felt mirrored in the still lines of her face. Wordless, she apologized, and he accepted that there were things she could not ask—not yet.

The table before him was set with silver cutlery—the very silver that he had spent his first month cleaning. His appetite deserted him as the slaves filed out.

But it returned when they did, bearing a plenitude of trays with a variety of foods in large quantities. At the nods of those seated, they began to place these foods carefully and precisely upon the plates, forming patterns with them that eating would only destroy.

Sara tried to keep a cheerful disposition as the slaves hovered like shadows around her. She succeeded—but only briefly.

Her knife and fork clattered to the table, and she looked up to meet Lord Darclan's eyes. They had not left her since she had entered the room, but this did not make her uncomfortable. She felt that she had always been under his gaze, and the familiar sensation gave her an anchor.

Taking a deep breath, she said, "Lord Darclan, I must ask you a question."

He smiled. "Another like the last one?"

"No," she replied gravely. "I want to know if I ever owned slaves."

His smile faltered. His voice did not. "What do you mean, Sara?"

"Exactly what I said. Did I ever own slaves?"

"Owning slaves is common in our culture, lady." He picked up a fork.

"That isn't an answer."

The fork returned to the table. "No, lady. It is not. If you must know, yes, yes you did."

He watched as she shut her eyes. Watched the way her hand trembled on the tabletop. Watched the way her shoulders curled inward. Gifting of pain.

*No*. He reached out one hand to touch hers. Both were cold. "Lady," he said.

She nodded.

"You did own them, yes. You often said it was the only way you could protect them within the Empire." He felt her hand relax slightly, a reward for his effort at honesty. "You were always too gentle with them. I believe this was a point of contention between your father and yourself."

Her eyes narrowed at something his voice betrayed.

"And between us, lord?"

He smiled. "I will not lie about this, lady. It was indeed a point of some bitter difficulty between us. You often said I resembled your father in many ways." A distant look touched his features as he stared through her. "You never did admire efficiency."

"I don't believe efficiency is the art of forcing another human being to do everything for you."

"So you have often said." He turned his gaze upon Darin.

The boy didn't notice the scrutiny—he was watching Sara, listening to her words.

*Yes, Sara. It starts here, and not in the way I had planned.*

But in the afternoon, he was prepared to do his best to ameliorate the damage to his plans. He felt anger, but it was not directed. No plans that had involved her ever worked quite as he expected. He asked for her presence in the garden, knowing that she would be happy to join him in the outside air on a day such as this.

And in this, at least, he was correct.

"It *is* beautiful out here." She stretched her hands out toward the sun. Dark velvet absorbed its heat, warming her. "I never want to go back inside." Her face surrendered a deep, wide smile. It was the first truly open one that she had given, and it was not for him. But he would change that.

Everything smelled green all around, and instead of the gray stone and gray walls, she was surrounded by bursts of brilliant color in the form of flowers and shrubs. Her element, this life.

He walked, in silence, beside her. A faint smile hovered in his eyes as he watched her. She was different, as he guessed she might be. She had always professed to love the sun, had always been able to find beauty in any natural phenomenon that was not inherently destructive, but she had never given her expression with such glee. She had been too adult for it, too responsible.

*This, Lady, this is what you should have been like, with no experience to teach you to shield your light beneath age. Perhaps the return of your memory will only play you false and deprive you of joy in such a day.*

It was not all of the truth, and he knew it, but he declined to acknowledge it. Here, perhaps, he could enjoy her smiles, her laughter, and her life. And maybe here he could begin to invoke her light.

They walked alone through the immense garden that surrounded the castle. Not even the distant clipping and digging of the master gardener, which never seemed to end, intruded.

Here and there, she would stop suddenly, bending down or reaching out to touch a leaf or petal. Sometimes her face would disappear, caught between hair and color. It would emerge again, brightened.

"I like this garden," she said softly.

He relaxed, which surprised him, and decided that he would commend the master gardener by ceasing to question his activities altogether.

"It's—it's not quite like other gardens I've seen. At least I don't think so."

"No?"

She shook her head, a frown rippling across her lips. It vanished as she stopped yet again. "It's not as . . . organized. It's got more of a wild feel to it."

"I am glad that you like it."

She stopped. "Do you?"

"Pardon, lady?"

"Do you like it?"

He paused and looked around him. *Like it?* It was an odd question—a question that she would ask.

She chuckled. "Never mind, lord. It's answer enough." She began to walk along the paths again.

He followed, for the moment content.

Until he saw where she wandered. Until he noted that the hedges had sprung up, like walls, along the path.

*No,* he thought, and tried to lead her elsewhere.

She followed, but again her feet led her back to that path, the one that led, in decreasing green circles, to the center of the garden.

*Does she know even now?* He took her arm.

"Lady, where do you walk?"

She shrugged delicately. "I'm not sure. But anything in this garden has to be beautiful. Does it matter?"

*Matter?* he thought bitterly. He regretted his decision to bring her here. But short of forbidding her to walk here, he knew he had no choice.

*Even now,* he thought as they walked in an ever decreasing spiral, *even now it calls you. Ah, Lady, Sara.* It had never been his way to avoid the inevitable, but recognizing it was hard, and acquiescing harder.

"Lady," he said softly, "there is something I wish to show you. It was something you knew."

"What?" Her face brightened and tensed. There was something of hunger in it.

"It is—" He shook his head. He could not name it. "It is something you knew. Walk further into the garden's center; you will see for yourself."

They began to move together. But she no longer paused at each bush, each flower. She no longer bent to let their fragrance touch her the more closely. He felt her tension, her anticipation, in every step.

*This is the test of the blood-magic, Lady.*

The sun made odd shadows that cut and blended. Her fingers curled more tightly into his arm, cooling even in the sun's warmth.

He understood.

They walked on, and the circles grew tighter as the center drew closer. The path seemed enclosed and more twisted than it had; the flowers, for an instant, seemed an empty, perfumed façade.

Then they were gone.

She had said that this garden seemed more "wild," and the truth of it, absolute and undeniable, was here. They had reached the center.

Sara gasped, and her nerveless hands fell slowly to her side. She stood a moment in his shadow, then walked out of it to approach the crumbling, rounded wall of rock that might once have been a well.

It stood, a forgotten monument, beneath a twisting wreath of ugly vines. She stepped forward, avoiding the thorned mass of small plants that sprung up around the circumference of weathered stone.

He did not move to follow. A sharp breath cut his lips as her hands very delicately touched the old, pocked stone of the ancient well. As hers, his eyes fell on the wild vines, the uneven grass, and the brambles. He knew she found nothing of beauty here.

"What—what is this?"

"The oldest part of all my lands." His voice was muted, absorbed by the small island of wilderness. Not even birds flew here. "It has stood thus for centuries. I will not let even the master gardener tend it." Much to the master gardener's grief.

"But why not? It's so . . ." Her words trailed away; they hadn't the power to describe what she felt.

"I know. And it was not always so. It is a matter of interest to me to see how long it takes these vines to eat their way through solid stone. I have watched them for much of my life, making a little progress here, a little there. The rock still prevails."

"But if you value it, why don't you tend it? Why don't you preserve it?" Her voice was rising and tightening. He liked it not, but still did not move.

"Ah, lady." He bowed his head a moment. "It is not my art. Do you understand this?" He looked down at his weathered hands, clenched them into white fists, and let them slowly unfurl. "I have no power over it; it stands or it falls."

"But I don't understand! The gardeners could remove these!" She stepped forward, gripping a large, gnarled vine. Dark against her white, it trembled in her grip, creaking and straining to maintain its hold on the pockmarked stone. With obvious effort, she yanked the vine away. She did not look back at him; he knew he was forgotten in the sudden urgency of her labor. She mouthed something and reached to her side. Her hands fluttered there uselessly.

Lord Darclan watched her intently. He made no move to interfere. She stopped her scramble for something that didn't exist and turned once again to the vines. She yanked another free, threw it aside, and began on a new tendril. Sun glinted off the sweat of her brow as she worked herself into a frenzy. The well was large, and the stranglehold of the foliage was complete, so she chose to clear off one section completely.

Bitterly, Lord Darclan noted which area she fought to free. It faced his castle, and cleared, it might even be visible from the window of his study. Twice he caught himself when the urge to stop her caused him to start forward. He kept his hands at his sides, and his mouth in a clamped, grim line.

*What do you see, Lady? Does memory guide you in this, or instinct alone? How can it still compel your obedience?*

But he said nothing. This woman, not the child who had run free in his garden, was one he knew well.

She worked for two hours; the sun marked the passage of time. He spoke only once in that time, moved only once, touched her stark face only once. She shrugged him off, in a silence heavy with determination and motion. He was left standing, the tears in his hand catching the breeze.

At the close of two hours, her dress was scored with multiple tears and rips; her hands torn and blistered. She turned glazed green eyes to him and spoke in an old, dead language—line language; the heritage of the Light that had faded. *"Help me."*

He stepped quickly forward and caught her in his arms as she staggered forward, shaking his head.

*"Help me, please."*

He gazed at her with shuttered eyes, not certain to whom she thought she spoke. "I cannot, Sara." His voice was more rigid than his arms. "I cannot touch it."

He heard the low rumbling in the back of her throat, half

snarl, half whimper. "Come, lady. Come and rest. Tomorrow—"

*"Too late!"*

"Yes."

Her knees crumpled. He gathered her up; she felt weightless. He knew a moment of panic when her eyes suddenly widened; when the sun's rays seemed to pass through her as if she were translucent. He turned away from the burning orb, shielding her from its light, his grip tight and defiant. Then the moment passed, her eyelids closed, and sleep eased the pain from her features.

*Oh, Sarillorn,* he thought. *Will the time never come? Will you never be free?*

He shivered, knowing the mortal answer.

*No. No, I spared you that.*

But what had he truly spared her? Even in Rennath she had never come to this frenzied pass.

*You will know peace, Lady. And I shall share in it.* Tenderly, with infinite care, he brushed her tangled hair aside and kissed her forehead.

# chapter
# nine

*He carried Sara in from the garden. The castle was conspicuous* in its severe and sudden silence; if any saw him enter, they did not trouble him with even the sight of their frightened faces. He strode through the main hall, up the stairs, and down the corridor to his room—Sara's room. He stopped outside of the wood of her door, bowed his head briefly, and cursed beneath his breath.

The door swung open, and in the center of the room that was to be his much needed privacy sat the slave that Sara had named. For a moment the lord wanted to kill the boy for daring to be present to see his lady in such a state. And it would be easy—just a word, the briefest of gestures, and the boy would be gone. His eyes wore his intent openly as he glared, his anger too deep for words.

*Why don't you run?*

Darin asked himself the same question as he met his lord's dark gaze. He saw clearly what was in that gaze; had seen it before in the service of House Damion. Each time, someone had graced the altars and the stones. It had not been turned on him.

But he saw, as well, the bruised and bleeding form of Lady Sara as she lay unconscious in the arms of his lord. He couldn't breathe. He could only wonder if his decision to accompany her in the morning had brought her to this.

Kerren's screams echoed clearly in the air all around— Kerren's screams, and the price he had paid for the last time that Darin had named himself in the presence of nobles.

But Kerren was a slave. The lady was of the nobility—the lord had said so himself. Nobles didn't die because a slave was named.

118

Did they?

He remembered the last time he had defied the command of nobility. His arm ached, his cheeks flushed with anger, with shame. His hands were red with the blood of the stones. But he had not died. And he had never questioned again; the pain had been too great, too final.

At least, it had been when he was eight summers.

He knew the rule well. There can be no friendship among slaves. And he had followed it, followed it so dearly to avoid feeling again the loss and pain and guilt of Kerren's death. Lady Sara was truly the first person, since the death of Kerren, that he had allowed himself to care about, because his mistake could never cost her life. Or so he had thought.

Maybe the beating of the slavemaster had dimmed with the years. Maybe physical pain just couldn't be remembered that clearly. Or maybe the fear of losing this friendship was just too much.

Too much? If the lord intended to kill her, what could he do? He was as powerless without her friendship as he had been four years ago.

No, not as powerless. For he wasn't bound; his arms and legs were free; the chair and the gallery did not contain him. With a cry that carried across four years, he launched himself at his lord, his small fists balled and flailing.

Lord Darclan reacted more quickly than even the Swords of the high priest. His hand lashed out, a controlled, even movement that sent Darin sprawling dizzily into the wall.

His head struck, hard enough to stun him, but not enough to silence his cry. "What have you done to her?"

Lord Darclan met the pale face of young Darin with a bitter, chill smile. At the boy's words, with their mixture of rage, fear, and defiance, the edge of his anger vanished. *Am I not, after all, the cause of this, Sara? Would his loss, his disappearance, not put a deeper wedge between us?*

*This,* he thought, *this is what I saw in the slave. If his light is weak, it is still alive.*

He made no answer, but Darin could see the change that came over his eyes. It was confusing.

"The lady has suffered an accident."

Darin did not move, although the wall at his back was cold and hard. White lips opened twice, but words would not come.

"Darin." Lord Darclan nodded to the bed.

Darin felt shock cut through the haze of pain and anger that held him motionless.

*Darin.*

Lord Darclan spoke deliberately. "Darin."

This time Darin gained his feet. He did not know what to think. But hope came, hope that the accident was only that: an accident. He scrambled to the bed and turned the covers down.

Lord Darclan moved past him and with consummate care laid Sara down on the bed. His fingers traced the line of her jaw. He knew that the boy still watched, but he was weary.

What of it, then? Let the slave watch. The boy, after all, had no true idea of who, or what, his lord was. Leaning over, Lord Darclan brushed Sara's hair aside, and again his lips brushed her forehead. She was so still . . .

"Sara."

That one word told Darin all he needed to know.

"I will go and get water, lord."

Lord Darclan shook his head briefly, clearing his eyes. "Please," he said softly. "Do that."

"Will you stay with her? If she wakes, she might be afraid."

"I will stay," he murmured. "I will stay."

Darin walked to the door and then looked back. Lord Darclan was bent over Sara, his hands clutching her shoulders gently but firmly, as if to hold her. As if to keep her.

The two on the bed seemed bound by the same stillness, the same sorrow. Darin couldn't understand all of what he saw, but he felt an age about them, and a sense of Lord Darclan's bitter hopelessness, and love.

*Darin. He called me Darin.*

For the sake of Sara. Or because Darin loved her, too. The boy wasn't sure which, but either way, he knew that House Darclan was about to change. And he knew, from the name and the gestures, that Lord Darclan would allow it.

Hope bit him sharply as he went for water.

The fire burned merrily in the grate, to protect the room against the lingering chill of night. Soon it wouldn't matter, but this was as much of winter as the southern castle received.

Lady Sara, dressed in clean bed clothing, slept soundly between thick feather quilting and bed. Darin sat by her side, content to watch over her, as he had watched before.

But this time, the gentle rise and fall of her breath and the softness of her face meant more than a daydream. When she wakened, he knew who she would be.

Their two shadows, trapped by the flickering flame, moved rapidly in contrast to their stillness.

Lord Darclan watched the sculpture they formed, apart from it, but a part of it.

"Darin," he said softly. The boy shifted in his seat. "I believe the worst is over."

"I think so." The color had not returned to her face, but her breath was not so shallow as it had been.

Lord Darclan could see the question in the boy's eyes. Concern for Lady Sara had robbed him of fear for himself.

*Darin, she called you. And I.* He knew that he could forbid the boy to speak of the day's events, forbid him to ask of his lady what had transpired—if indeed she woke remembering any of it. He opened his mouth to do so, but the words did not come.

Meeting his eyes, Darin realized that he could ask what had happened, without fear of reprisal. He, too, opened his mouth, but found that the question would not address itself to the wary man—man now, not lord alone. His gaze fell back to Sara.

"Lord," he said, almost timidly, "I know that you'd never hurt her."

At the same moment, unbidden, the lord said, "Darin, I would never willingly allow harm to come to my lady."

The same faltering smile touched their lips, and who it surprised more, neither could say. It was gone from sight in an instant, but it remained, taking strength in the roots of memory.

Lord Darclan walked to the door, paused, and then bowed very formally to his young slave. Darin accepted the bow and returned it, knowing what it acknowledged, and what it could not say in words.

"I will tell the rest of my household to attend your words; she is your charge, and you are now responsible for seeing that no harm comes to her. Is that clear?" *I am trusting you with my existence, child. Sara, Sara.* If she could have seen how she still wrought changes, in spite of all his best plans, she would have smiled.

And that smile would have paid several times for the inconvenience these changes made.

"Yes, lord," Darin said softly, an echo of any other time he had said it.

Lord Darclan walked out of the room and into the corridor. As he walked its length, he realized that the youth trusted him.

For her sake, yes, but nonetheless . . . Darin was only the second person in history to so gift him. He walked to his study, musing over this.

Darkness swirled around her, catching and closing her eyes with long, red nails. She felt the touch of it across her exposed cheek, fingers so cold that they burned. She reached for a hand, or something that could support her against it. Fingers closed on ice that split the hand to the bone.

She was alone.

Shuddering, she forced her eyes open, then snapped them shut again, and cried out something—a name?—that the darkness swallowed. Teetering uncertainly, she spun around, trying to see beyond the blackness that held her. She wrapped her arms around her shoulders.

She was alone. In desperation, she cried out for the one person she could remember.

*Darin!*

Her cry had brought him once before, but now something else responded to it. A ghost of a man, tall and gaunt, made itself visible through the darkness.

*He is not here.* The words were as thin, as cold, as the man. He raised one long arm and held his hand out, palm up. *But I am.* Along his arm, like a fine tracery of lace, cut a deep red line through the blackness.

Then, from nowhere, a ring of light surrounded Sara. The man grimaced and stepped backward slowly. Without thought, she took an involuntary step forward, toward him. The light grew tight around her, offering slight warmth. It would not allow her to pass.

*Darin! Lord—Lord Darclan!*

*These are not for you, not now. Come, little one.* He smiled. *I will wait.*

Because the castle was usually silent and somber, the sound of raised voices, or in this case one raised voice and one quiet one, carried more clearly than it might have. The mood that had lingered with Lord Darclan upon quitting Sara and Darin was shattered; his steps lost the subtle spring that had carried him this far.

"—and in matters of the Church, you are not privileged to speak with Lord Darclan's voice, regardless of what he has told you."

A heated voice responded to the condescension in the smooth one. "May I remind you, Priest—"

"You will be respectful. Nobility does not treat servants of the Church in that tone; it is certainly not fitting for one who is mere steps above slavery!"

There was a choked silence, and the louder voice, more controlled, began to speak again. "May I respectfully suggest that, regardless of your stature, you are in the domain of the Lord Darclan, and here his word is law. I have been given dispensation to deal with unexpected visitors, regardless of rank or affiliation. You have no right to contest the lord's command in his own land!"

"Malthan does not recognize political dominion."

Lord Darclan stepped, unnoticed, into the confrontation. "Nor," he said softly, "it seems, does his Church." He turned to face Gervin, noting the angry red lines of his face. "You have done well, old friend."

Gervin wore his years well, but they showed in the steely flint of his eyes—eyes that had seen much, and little enough of it good.

*It has been nearly forty years,* Darclan thought, with a shade of approval. *You have been good to your word, and I to mine.*

He looked more carefully at his slavemaster, at his right hand in House Darclan. He dressed not according to his full station; his clothing was plain, common really, but fully functional. It housed two visible pockets and a plethora of concealed ones. If Lord Darclan had ordered an uninvited guest disposed of, the man, along with his grating demands, would have died with one foot halfway over the door.

Looking now at the slightly arrogant young priest, Darclan regretted that he had not. This one wore the formal regalia of the priesthood: dark black robes, lined with gray and gold. His posture, likewise, was that of a priest: the dichotomy of energetic indolence.

"If your missive is so urgent that you attempt to undermine my commands in my domain, perhaps we should retire to my study to more quickly discuss it." Without waiting for a response, Darclan turned and walked into the room.

The priest stood back for a few moments, a flash of annoyance skirting his face. Then he shook his head and followed. Darclan gestured briefly at a chair in front of his desk, and the priest took it.

"You may begin."

The priest raised an eyebrow. "May I introduce myself, as you did not leave your servant time to announce my presence."

"I am not concerned with the particulars of what you are called. You are one of too many priests of the Dark Heart. You may state your business, and I will listen. But do it quickly and leave."

The priest blushed, a deep crimson color.

*Fool.* Darclan had never suffered this lack of grace well. And the priests were always the worst. Mere curtness could be used to bait them endlessly.

The priest took control of himself slowly; Darclan noted this with sardonic amusement.

"Very well. You know that the ceremony of renewal is to take place in the third quarter."

"Well enough," Lord Darclan said, "to need no reminders."

The priest gave a measured nod. His ringed hands gripped the edge of the chair on which he was seated, but his face betrayed nothing.

"Lord . . . Darclan," the priest began, knowing his irony was not lost, "while you are setting up a house for reasons which do not concern us, we are worried about—"

"Much that does not concern you." Several times Darclan had considered crushing the priesthood. Each time it was harder to ignore the desire, and he had forgotten in the years of battle with the lines just how strong this urge could be. "I am aware of the ceremony. It is petty and the province of the half-blooded. I do not believe you have anything else to say." Leaning slightly forward, he added, "And I am not one who has patience with those who would waste my time."

"My Lord"—the voice was now free from irony—"if you wish it so, then your desire is, of course, our command. It is your Empire, and we have followed your wishes in regards to this house. I will not waste further words on unnecessary politeness." His voice became sharper. "We have noted a disturbance of late. It is faint, but not inconsiderable."

Darclan leaned back into his chair; his arms rested on the desk, his hands came up to form a precise steeple. "Go on."

"As you desire, Lord. It has come to the attention of the High Priest Vellen that you have a guest. A young woman."

The words seemed to have no effect. After allowing the silence to lengthen, the young priest began again.

"Her name is, oddly enough, Sara Laren. Lady Sara Laren.

There are those scholars among us who believe this is to be a derivative of an older title that one line, long dead, once used."

The priest noted that Darclan's eyes had become strangely black; he could not discern the pupils, or tell where the gaze fell. The fingers on the armrest began to dance nervously.

*You are young,* Darclan thought with disdain. *You have not been on the fields. You have not seen who truly rules this Empire.* He smiled, and waited.

"The high priest wishes to meet this woman."

"For what reason?" The blackness of the Lord's eyes seemed to spread; no longer did any white mar them at all.

"He finds it unusual that this disturbance coincides with the unheard of presence of a particular young woman in the Darclan castle. It has been rumored that you have indulged her to the point of allowing her to dictate the presence of a slave at your table. He cannot think of any reason why you would allow this, unless she had her own power."

"And?" Flesh color gave way to shadow and clothing gave way to darkness, a darkness that gave him height.

Now the priest faltered. A thin sheen of perspiration broke across his rather pale face.

*Now you understand, but it has been too long in coming. A pity.*

"Go on."

"The high priest believes that a meeting with this woman would confirm her identity as an enemy of God. If this is the case, she is, by his command, to be the sacrifice for the ceremony."

"I see." Stefanos stood then, and the room was filled with his power. His eyes, black now, gave way to a silver-gray— Sargoth's gift. The young priest began to quiver uncontrollably, his mouth flopping sullenly in wet silence.

"A pity indeed." But the First Servant's voice held none.

The tremors contorting the man continued, building in strength. The muscles around his neck and shoulders grew taut. His hands, shaking visibly, reached out toward Stefanos.

But Stefanos only watched, a distant expression of vague distaste invisible in the darkness. The priest slumped forward in the chair, motionless.

The shadow withdrew, the countenance of the Lord Darclan returned. He walked to the door, opened it, and spoke a few curt words before returning to his desk.

Gervin soon entered the room and, ignoring the priest, stood before his lord.

"Very good, Gervin, I wish you to take a letter. It is brief."

Gervin nodded, walked over to the desk, and picked up a stylus.

"To the First Karnar of Malthan."

"Vellen of Damion, sir?"

"I believe that is what he is called."

"And the text, sir?"

"He is to refrain from interference in my personal business if he wishes to maintain his Church."

Gervin scribbled something down without raising an eyebrow. "Anything more?"

"No."

"And the visitor?"

"Ah. You may send his body with the letter. One other thing: Send the Priest Calven to me if he is still within my walls."

Blackness without end. Sara clung to the periphery of the light, trying futilely to drape it around her body. She felt skeletal but could not see herself clearly enough to know if this was just fear.

And beyond her stood the man of red. He had not moved since she had first seen him. She was afraid of him, but found an odd comfort while she could see him; the darkness that clung to her skin and the inside of her mouth did not seem to trouble him at all.

*No, little one.* He smiled. *The darkness does not affect me. If you would have this protection, merely step forward and I shall grant it to you.*

She started forward, as she had any number of times, only to be caught once again by the light.

*Where am I?*

He gave no answer, no matter how often she asked. But his lips curled over preternaturally sharp teeth.

*Someone,* she thought, as she had thought time beyond number, *someone will come for me.* But every time she told herself this, she believed it less.

*What care have they for one such as you? All of your kind are long past.*

Why? Why should they come? Why should anyone dare this—this blackness, this web?

*They'll come.* But her memory gave her no such assurance.

She was alone; she felt that she had been alone for centuries. Looking up again, she met the eyes of the man, and they were red.

She waited. And the darkness grew closer, and the light rimming her grew dim. She grew tired; too tired even to hate the darkness that surrounded her.

*Come. Have an end to your fear.* And he smiled again. *They have left you to me. Come. I shall not leave.*

She started to refuse, but her mouth was too frozen. Looking at him, tracing the outline of his face as she had done often, she thought his words true. For he had stood thus, it seemed, forever. He had not left her side, and she felt he would not, not without her. She shivered. She was afraid of him, but the darkness leeched her strength as she waited.

And slowly, she uncurled, and wordlessly she nodded.

She began to step across the threshold of the light and it flared up, grabbing her ankles. Another trap. She fought to wrench her foot loose.

*Come.*

*I am coming.* She tried to struggle free of the light and he stepped back—only a step—and opened his arms.

*I'm coming.*

"Ahem."

Darin started, nearly dropping the goblet he'd just filled. He knew the voice well, but had managed to avoid its owner over the last few days. Oh, well, it couldn't have lasted much longer.

He turned to see that Cullen was leaning over the cutting counter, drumming his ample fingers.

"I've been hoping to see you, Darin lad."

"Hi, Cullen." Darin gave what he hoped was a genuine smile. He liked Cullen, but he knew that the cook would press him for answers about the activities of the last few days, and wouldn't believe him when he said he didn't have most of them.

"Heard rumors this way that you spent yesterday morning in the dining hall."

Darin nodded.

"*At* the dining table."

"Well, yes, but . . ." Darin's voice trailed off.

"Heard that the lady was calling you by name."

Darin looked down at his hands, feeling guilty. "Yes," he said at length. "She did. All morning."

"By the Lady!" Cullen whispered. "It's true."

"But I'm sure that she'd name us all," Darin said quickly. "I'm sure that she'd have us know hers."

Cullen looked at Darin and shook his balding head. "It's not a game?" he asked.

"No." The answer was quick, but there was no defensivness in it. "I haven't met anybody like her since I was in the city."

"The city?" Cullen raised an eyebrow. "Are you from out-Empire, boy?" At Darin's solemn nod, Cullen's expression changed. This fact explained much. "Ah." Too much. "We'd heard that Dagothrin had fallen. Even here, we heard that." He shook his head, and then stopped. "Is she from outside, too?"

"No." Darin shook his head. "She's from the Empire. She was in a boating accident here a few weeks ago. She hit her head and almost drowned, and it's done something to her so that she doesn't remember anything."

"Darin, boy, use your thick little brains." Cullen rapped the counter. "If she'd been here a few weeks ago, wouldn't someone have noticed?" The cook shook his head.

"But I know she isn't lying. She—the lord told her about the accident. She told me."

"The lord," Cullen said softly. "Maybe there is a game being played. Be careful, Darin."

Darin didn't tell the cook that Lord Darclan had also called him by name. Instead, he thought over what Cullen had said as he made his way out of the kitchen.

He didn't see the way that Cullen stared at his curled shoulders. Didn't hear the whisper of a prayer that formed on Cullen's lips.

*Lady.*

For the next two days, Lord Darclan began and ended his daily routine on the same note: He would knock on the door of Sara's chamber, and Darin, greeting him, would shake his head from side to side. He did not believe that he could endure a third such start to a day, and so began the morning in the breakfast hall.

He sat at the head of his table, engaged in a vague conversation with Lord Daldrem, which interested him solely because he did not desire silence. The elderly man in the green and silver did not seem to notice this and continued his monologue unchecked, until the door to the inner hall flew open and crashed into the stone wall.

Darin stood, gripping the edge of the door and trying to catch his breath. Behind Darin, two male slaves also stood, their expressions worried as they looked up to meet the eyes of their lord.

"You have done well," Lord Darclan said, his crisp voice carrying the length of the hall. "Both this boy and master Gervin are to be given access to me even if I have indicated that I do not wish to be disturbed. At his request, he is to be given immediate access to my presence, regardless of time or circumstance."

They relaxed slightly and nodded at his command.

"Now, Darin." He saw the way that the two slaves looked at each other and then fixed their gaze on Darin's back. "What is the reason for this disturbance?"

"It's Sara!" His chest rose and fell as he tried to fit words between breaths. "I was sitting by her this morning and she went all tense. She started to kick and hit out at nothing."

"Did she wake?"

"No." He gasped. "I thought she was having a nightmare. I tried to wake her. It seemed to help." He bit his lip before continuing. "Then she screamed. Just screamed and fell back."

"She's sleeping, then?" He rose and walked over to Darin. His hands reached out to steady the boy's shoulders, and perhaps to steady himself.

"I don't think so. She's—it's like she's been broken. She's all pale and she doesn't move anything. It doesn't even look like she's breathing. But she keeps saying something, over and over. I thought it was nonsense at first, because I don't understand it. But it's the same thing."

Lord Darclan took a deep breath and closed his eyes. "Do you think you can repeat it?" He waited, listening intently.

"It's something like 'mayvanna.' "

"Mayvanna?" Lord Darclan's eyes snapped open. *"Me venna."* He cut the air with sudden intake of breath. He turned and ran, leaping deftly through the open doors of the breakfast hall. Darin followed at his heel.

Sara lay in bed. She was white and still; limbs and forehead were cool to the touch. Even her lips were colorless in the alabaster cast of her face. Lord Darclan's hands clenched in tight, large fists as he stood looking down upon her. Darin moved quietly to stand at the other side of the bed. The motion caught his lord's eyes. They met Darin's briefly—cold, smoldering blackness, no hint of white to allay their chill. Darin shivered and looked away, doubting what he had seen.

They stood for fifteen minutes, watching, caught in the red light of the curtained room. Sara did not move at all.

*Something's wrong*, Darin thought. It was several minutes before he realized what it was: The curtains of the room that filtered the sunlight were blue.

*Blood-magic.* He paled, clasping his hands tightly together to stop himself from drawing the two Wards he knew. Lord Darclan had named him, but he could not trust him further.

Sara's lips opened a crack, and the whisper of words came rasping out. The tone of her voice matched her eerie pallor; free from life or expression, it hovered between the two who stood watch.

*"Me venna. Me venna."*

*"No!"* Darclan grabbed Sara's hands, crushing them in his own. "You are not going anywhere!"

"Do you understand what she's saying? Is it a name?"

"Not a name, no," he answered. His eyes began to change, from black to steel gray, edged and hard. "It is an old tongue, Darin. Some of your scholars may have remembered it." He smiled bitterly. "It is a dead tongue, now." Closing his eyes, he bent his head over Sara and began to murmur. It was a strange, rhythmic litany of words, matched in meter by the swaying of his black-robed body. His voice grew quieter. Time faltered, warping itself to the timbre of his words and the cadence of their rise and fall.

Darin watched. He wanted to offer his help, but the words wouldn't come. His lord's knees gave, but he continued his chant until the words creaked out of a parched throat. Only then did he raise his bowed head. He gave a low, furious snarl and dropped Sara's hands. They fell limp to the covers. He stood, gripped her shoulders, and started to shake her. She didn't respond. He touched her face, called her name. No answer. At last he pulled her into the circle of his arms and rocked her body gently.

"Lord?"

Darclan shook his head. "She is—still alive."

"What's wrong with her?"

"Do not ask." He tucked her head under his chin. "Go to master Gervin. Tell him to send me a knife."

Darin's hands were on the door before Darclan could continue; he froze to catch the last few words.

"Tell him that I need you. Do not forget this. You are to wait until he gives you leave to return. Bear what he gives you to me."

Darin stood warily inside of the small vestibule outside Gervin's living quarters. He knocked tentatively on the door and waited. A brief rustle sounded, followed by quick, light steps, and the door opened a crack. Gervin peered through it. He wore a blue woolen robe; the belt had been clumsily tied and was already slipping. Gervin looked decidedly less friendly when newly awake than on his regular duties, something that Darin would have sworn to be impossible.

"What's urgent enough to wake me at this time of night, boy?"

"Night? But it's late morn, master."

Gervin slid his curious eyes over Darin's upturned face. "Morn, is it?"

Darin gazed around the vestibule searching futilely for windows. He thought back briefly. How long had he been with Lady Sara and Lord Darclan? Not that long. Certainly not that long.

"It—it must be morning. It was when we entered the Lady's room."

"Oh, it's morning all right, Darin, but I don't suppose you're here to debate which end of the morning it is." He opened the door and stood aside, allowing Darin to enter.

Darin glanced around the sparse, stone walls of the third tower. There was a grate for the fire in the far right corner and a small, neatly closed desk. At one end was a bed with a few blankets and no pillow. That was all. Gervin grinned at the boy's swift appraisal of his worldly possessions.

"Well, boy? Did the lord send you?"

Drawn back to the task at hand, Darin nodded. "He's with the Lady Sara."

"And what does the lady request? Shall I have the linen maids redress her bed? The women draw a bath? The boys start another fire in her grate? Or, worse still, shall I screw up all my courage and rouse Cullen, as she has missed meals this three-day?"

"None of those, master," Darin replied, serious in the face of the older man's teasing. "Lord Darclan says that you are to send him a knife."

The wrinkles around the corner of Gervin's mouth froze in a grizzled mask. Even his eyes seemed momentarily dead. He

turned and walked rigidly over to the small desk, his right hand
fumbling for a key.

"Did he say anything else, child?" he asked in a light, cold
voice.

Darin nodded, although Gervin couldn't see it. "He said that
he needs me. I'm to wait here until you give me something to
take back to him."

"I see." Old hands removed a plain wooden box from the
top drawer. Old eyes gazed bitterly at the symbol burned carefully into the sheen of its lid. "Then wait. Do not touch anything."

"Where are you going?"

"To do as we all do." The box shook gently in Gervin's grip.
"Stay; here you are safe."

Darin watched, as the old man left the room. Something coiled
tightly in his chest, waiting to spring.

He remembered suddenly the home and freedom of his childhood and the strong voice of the matriarch of the line as she
delivered, again, the old warnings. He wanted to shut the memory out, as he'd done many times before, but it was stronger in
the isolation of Gervin's tower than it had been in many years.

The shutters to the single window in the third tower swung
awkwardly in the breeze. There were no curtains—Gervin dis-
dained them—and starlight, clinical and distant, glittered like
frost in the night sky—little vicious eyes, pockmarks of light.
Words, buried deep, were unearthed.

*They stalk at night. Darin, pay attention when I speak. The
Darkness draws nearer and what you learn may save your life.
All power needs life, mind. All the costs of power are measured
in the blood. Lernan will only accept what is given willingly, but
the Darkness trades in any life. And they come in the—*

Moonlight, streaked and oddly painful, touched his upturned
face, mingled with breeze and a soft, acrid smell. The sound of
hoarse voices filled the inner courtyard and dwindled into a
silence suddenly unbearable beneath the naked sky. Darin
slammed the shutters into their stone frame, grappling with the
cold wire latch. He walked over to the bed and sat down, clap-
ping hands over his ears to ward off the voice of the past and the
choice of the choiceless present. He thought he knew why this
particular memory came.

The box should have been ebony, the blade, toothed and
curved.

Lord Darclan was a priest. Malanthi, born with the blood of the Dark Heart. It chilled him.

He sat there until Gervin returned. Although there were lamps, Gervin carried a heavy torch held high in his left hand. Darin could see a large purple bruise around the old man's right eye. Washed in torchlight, clutching the small wooden box in scratched hands, Gervin seemed ghostly. He stopped in front of Darin, roughly shoving the box toward him.

"Here. Take it. Tell the lord it's done."

Two small hands stretched out to relieve Gervin of his burden, but they stopped before touching it.

He had to know. "Master Gervin, what's been done?"

"Don't you know, boy?" he said, his voice a hoarse rasp. "How old are you?"

"Thirteen by the calendar of Malthan."

"Young, then," he muttered, almost to himself. "Keep your youth a little longer. Take the box."

Darin shook his head.

"And brave as well. If you'd been older when you were taken, you'd know." Keen eyes met the dull glint of young ones. Gervin gave a small start of surprise. "I believe you do know after all."

Darin scrambled backward and stopped when his back hit the wall. He eyed the box with fright and sick fascination. "I can't. I can't take it."

"You can take it all right." Gervin dropped the box at Darin's knees. "You *will* take it."

"No!" This was the stones all over again. This was supposed to have stopped.

A weary, bitter voice answered. "Now is not the time for heroics. The blade has been blooded; nothing you can do will change that." Darin still made no move toward it. "Damn you! Take it! I will not have done this for nothing!" His hands were shaking with rage and a rawness Darin knew for pain.

"I can't. Not for her. She'd never accept it."

"Do you think she'll care?" A red film coated Gervin's eyes; the reflection of firelight obscured his pupils. "Nobody important died!"

"She wouldn't want anyone to die for her sake!"

"She's a noble, isn't she? Maybe full of pleasant, meaningless words, but still above the rest of us! Maybe she will be upset if you tell her—she'll have to acknowledge a slight twinge of conscience! What are you staring at?"

Anger and pain stretched Darin out between them. He had been at the castle nearly two months and had seen Gervin many times, but never like this.

Tears sprouted down Darin's cheeks, and with them a sense of desolation so keen it splintered his visions of the past.

"You're wrong," he said, forcing a choked whisper from between clenched teeth. He grabbed the box and held it as if it burned him. "She's nothing like that—you aren't a slave, you haven't see the worst that nobles can do! I have—and I know her for better!"

Gervin watched Darin with eyes so full they seemed oddly vacant of expression. "Have I not?" he whispered, the anger gone suddenly from his voice. He walked over to the wall and placed the torch in the metallic ring. "Go. Lord Darclan will be waiting for you."

Darin glared at Gervin's back, knowing that the older man would not turn to face him again. "Even the lord knows she's special. He loves her, too."

"He must want something from her to order this." His head dropped a little, and Darin thought he was staring at his up-turned hands.

"He *loves* her!"

"Darin, I have been with the lord for forty years. Lady help us if what you believe is true." Gervin waited until he heard the loud thump of Darin's feet. Only when he heard the distant click of the vestibule door did he turn.

Blindly, he made his way to the bed that he knew would hold no sleep for him, no peace.

Darin's memories were not the only ones that were made strong by this solitude. And Darin's were the kinder.

*It isn't the same*, Darin told himself, the tears still running down his cheeks. But the box shook in his hands.

*Isn't it? Didn't someone die?*

He shook his head and forced his feet to keep moving. It wasn't easy; revulsion warred with the urgency of Sara's life.

*No. It isn't. He ordered it to save Sara's life.* But he knew that if he had said the words aloud, he would have choked on them. This was no death gained in war, to save the lives of innocents. It was the death of an innocent, and even the reason for it was tainted.

He shivered; he did not think he had stopped shivering since he'd left Gervin in the tower.

*If I'd known, I could have offered my life. Then it would have been all right.* And if he had thought about it, he would have known. He should have known.

But he didn't want to die, and he faced that knowledge with shame. He wanted to live. He wanted Sara to live.

And if Lord Darclan was a priest, he was still different from any other priest Darin had known or heard of: Only for love of Lady Sara had he ordered this death.

Darin slid the chamber door open and sidestepped into the room. It was as he remembered it; nothing had changed. A warm red glow bathed the darkness. Looking carefully, he could see that the center of that light came from the bed on which Sara lay.

His numb fingers clutched the wooden box, the absolute symbol of the loss of his former life. For he carried the blooded blade to its owner as accomplice.

Lord Darclan looked up. Wordlessly, he held out his hands, and Darin delivered his burden into them.

"I will need your help, Darin," he said, as he gently lifted the lid.

Darin did not move.

"Stand by me. Do not move; if I cause you pain, it is for her sake, and it will be brief."

Lord Darclan set the lid aside and raised the box itself. He spoke slowly, with crisp, full enunciation, in a language that Darin did not understand. Then he lowered the box and drew from it a small dagger that glinted in the red light. It was not the knife that Darin had seen previously, being a simple five inches of unornamented steel that extended from a plain ivory handle.

Darclan took it in his left hand. With his right hand he grabbed Darin's wrist. Darin made no protest. He could only watch in fascination.

Twice Lord Darclan spoke, dragging the knife's cold edge along Darin's right hand. The third time he said nothing. With a quick, strong jerk, the blade bit into Darin's shaking palm, making the shallowest of cuts. The blood came; Darclan clenched the wounded hand into a fist and watched the pattern that emerged on the carpet beneath them as the liquid crept around closed fingers to drip downward.

Darclan looked up at Sara's deathly pale face. She was in the grip of one of the Servants; he knew the feel of it. He allowed himself to accept that fact now that he had a chance to change it. Even more, he accepted that it was his fault for allowing her near the protections set round the well; without her memories she had been no match for what lay in wait. Still, it had been two days, and the nightwalker had not been able to take material form—her raw strength had at least guaranteed that. It was not too late.

He began to call it out of Sara, knowing that it would come to the strength of two bloods, life blood and the boy's. Nothing seemed to change in the room, but Darclan staggered slightly at the influx of power.

The dagger dropped to the floor, forgotten. The pattern the blood made on the carpet began to grow; out of the chaos, Darclan drew meaning. He shook his head sharply, imperatively. The pattern shifted before his eyes. It writhed, a dark thin line attempting to evade his grasp. Again he snapped his head in defiance, and again the pattern altered itself, with different results. The metallic gray of his eyes gave way to an eerie red that cut the beads of blood. They struggled, misted, and recongealed—the process was slower this time, and harder to achieve. Nor were the results any more acceptable.

Darin watched as Darclan worked. His legs grew tired, and sharp pangs of hunger struck home the fact that he had not eaten that day. He did not move, somehow knowing that his lord's concentration must not, at any cost, be broken. The red glow in the chamber began to pulse obscenely, like a heart beat. He held his place. Darclan's voice began to rise, slowly building to a shout. In response, Darin reached out to take one of Sara's hands. It was cold. A sense of fatality crept into him, numbing him by slow degree.

Darclan continued his chant. He was losing, and with that loss came an end. He redoubled his effort, bolstering his final attempt to control this lesser Servant with the last reserves of his strength. He had never taken such a risk, but the cost of failure was unthinkable. Bitterly, he accepted the fact that were it not for Sara's teachings, Sara's rules, he would be in the absolute position of strength that the First of the Dark Heart had always enjoyed.

He struggled to contain his spell and felt it slip like water from his flagging concentration. His voice broke, then; his eyes, once burning, became dull eyes. Human eyes.

He pulled at Darin's hand, unfurling it; it was clean—unscarred. He lost his voice at the sight of it, stricken. His hands fumbled for the dagger, but it too had vanished. No sign of this offering remained.

He turned bitter, ancient eyes to the carpet; the pattern that scarred it was dark and final. He stood and backed off, watching, waiting. A red mist began to lift itself off the floor. Rising and moving before him, it slowly took form. There was little definition to the features at first, but it gathered the blood—Darin's blood, mingled with lifeblood—to it. Lord Darclan closed his eyes wearily, and when he opened them he faced the ghostly image of shadow. Behind the translucent darkness of it, Sara lay waiting. She already belonged to the Seventh; he had lost her. Weariness overwhelmed him; only the habit of long years of self-control kept him on his feet.

He heard the gasp that trembled out of Darin's lips. Heard it, but did not turn.

"Nightwalker!"

The walker bowed. "Well met, Stefanos." His voice was dust.

"Seventh." Lord Darclan bowed stiffly.

"You have held me some time. But not as long as you once might have. You have grown weak since last we met."

"I have." It was hard to say it.

The Seventh of the Sundered looked long at him before speaking again. "I know what you ask, First and Lordling. I do not know why you ask it, but I would grant it willingly—were it within my power."

"I have no strength left, Kerlan. Not even for defense."

"It is true," the Seventh replied. "You have weakened yourself greatly."

"Then do it. You would then be First among the greatest."

"Ahhh. More is true than I would have thought, First. But the sun approaches. Even if I could destroy you it would cost me the time I need for her. She is strong, Stefanos.

"I do not know what your interest in this mortal is. But perhaps I shall find out in my own way." It turned then and drifted lazily toward Sara.

Darclan staggered to the bed. "Wait!"

"Wait?"

"I cannot stop you, Kerlan. Let me say my farewells, for if you do not destroy me, I shall remember this, and I shall grow stronger once again."

The nightwalker paused, deliberating. While he stood so,

Darclan passed through him and knelt by the bed. He kissed Sara, gently at first, and then more urgently. Her dead lips remained motionless. He gathered her into his arms, burying his face against the side of her neck. He ran his hands through her hair and then along her face, searching desperately for some sign of life. This could not be his last memory of her—not this cold, bitter silence. Not this reddened darkness.

"I grow bored of this, Stefanos. I do not know what game you play, but this one time you have lost." Kerlan drew closer and reached out for Sara. Snarling, Darclan struck out, his hand passing through the wraithlike body.

"You, of all, should know better. We are already bound, this one and I; I have tasted her blood." The walker touched Sara's cheek, and she stiffened beneath his insubstantial fingers.

Even this much response she had not given Stefanos.

And then Darin leaped up on the bed, scrambling over his huddled lord. His hands struck out at the air frantically. The wraith's expression altered.

"What a brave little boy you are," he said, in his chill, dead voice, "to come between me and my chosen. Leave now, or on the morrow I will walk for you. Your blood I have also tasted this eve."

Darin's eyes gleamed. He became still and silent. Stefanos could feel his fear.

"Go, child," he said, more harshly than he intended. "There is nothing that can be done for Sara."

The Seventh Servant bent slowly down to Sara's forehead, disregarding the boy. He had great faith in the fear of humanity; fear had fed and served him well in the past. The lord's eyes urged Darin to leave, to spare himself the upcoming feast.

They had both mistaken the boy. His fear was not only of the nightwalker. Even as he trembled, his mind had taken flight, rummaging through the shards of his shattered past. His fingers began to move automatically.

*The Lesser Ward is for what, Darin?*
*For imps, Grandmother.*
*And these are?* Her stern old eyes did not leave his face; he shrugged impatiently, hearing the laughter of his year-mates in the courtyard as they played through his detention.
*They are the little evils.* He grimaced. *The ones that are only strong enough to perform petty acts of malice: souring the milk,*

*rotting the wood, sowing dissension among friends, causing
bodily discomforts—*
*Good enough, child. Show me the Lesser Ward.*

From years away, Stefanos watched the boy's hands jerk upward in a smooth, lilting motion, across his chest. The Servant's
grip on Sara's face became stronger, more solid. She began to
whimper.

*What is the use of the Greater Ward, Darin? Darin! Pay at-
tention—you'll be out in the yard sooner.*
He dutifully turned his full attention to the Grandmother's
stern face. *The Greater Ward is for protection against the workings of the priests, Grandmother.* He did not say the name of
the master they served; it was forbidden to the uninitiated. Even
those of the Circle used it rarely, if at all.
*And the workings are?* She was always so impatient. Even
now, her bent fingers were tapping irritably along the edge of
her chair.
*Blood-magics. The magics that injure, or burn the blood that
belongs to God.*
*That will do. Show me the Greater Ward.*

Small arms swept across a trembling chest. Fingers flew in
the air; the red glow around Sara ebbed away. The Servant
looked up, disturbed from his feasting. Stefanos' eyes widened
in surprise; he drew a painful breath, cutting himself along the
fragile edge of hope.

*And now I will show you the True Ward, Darin, if you can
tear yourself away from the window. I don't know why they insist
on giving me the one room that faces the courtyard. Teaching
you is difficult at best—you don't need the distraction.*
Not that he was distracted anymore. The True Ward was the
test of adulthood, and if he could one day master it, he would
no longer be treated as a child. He leaned forward in his chair,
year-mates and their games forgotten.
*Well, I seem to have your attention for once. Maybe I'll try
to teach you some of the other things you should have learned
in the past.* She laughed when his mouth fell open in dismay,
and he knew she was only teasing him. At least he hoped she
was—with her, you could never tell. On impulse, his fingers
traced the Lesser Ward in the air between them. She laughed.

*I wish I could live to see the day that you have to **teach the lines**, Darin! In fact, in case you are somehow overlooked **for that** duty, I shall make it a last request that you be forced to do so.*

*Very well,* she said, the crinkles around her eyes smoothing. *The True Ward is never used lightly—nor does it always work. I will show you the gestures, but I will not invoke it. The cost, both to myself and to Lernan, is high.*

As he watched her slow, deliberate fingers, he listened.

*It is our truest shield against the Darkness. It stands between ourselves and the power of the shadow. When we call it, we stand for a moment in God's Hand. If blood is strong, it can evoke the white-fire, the greatest weapon against those of Dark blood. Such is its power, that even the Servants must feel some small measure of it.*

Light, quick movements accompanied the sound of her voice. Darin followed them awkwardly, his duplication slow and clumsy. Unlike the Lesser and Greater Ward, these gestures involved the hands alone; the arms did not sweep upward or before the face, and even the fingerplay across the air was sparse.

That had been the only time he had ever seen it. Sweat beaded his pale brow; his hands faltered in the air. The walker's face stiffened; he began to pull his hands away from Sara's strained face.

*I will never be able to do it,* Darin thought. It was the very core of his fear. *I'm not worthy. I've been party to the Dark Heart's ceremonies. I carried the blooded blade.* But still he struggled with fragments of memory that stung him.

*And the cost, Grandmother?* His fingers continued to try to repeat her motions. *What of the cost?*

Her answer returned to him. His eyes leaped to life, searching the room with haste and fear. There was nothing that would do it; nothing he could use. His entire body was tense, trembling. Stefanos silently urged the child onward, not knowing what the boy, taken too young, could do—but hoping.

The last of the walker's fingers left Sara's face, but slowly, heavy with the fruits of conquest, sluggish in its motion. Darin's eyes met the eyeless creature's face, and he decided.

With a quick, sharp yank, he drew his right hand to his mouth. His whole face taut with anticipation and terror, he opened his jaw and clenched a fold of his skin between his teeth. He did not cry out in pain, but gave an animal grunt as he pulled, and a small chunk of flesh gave way.

"My blood!" he cried, spitting the bits of his hand at the nightwalker. "*Lernan!* I give you my life freely! Aid me now, though I am not worthy!" He could hear the beat of his heart as he fought to still the fear that stopped any further speech. Lernan would not listen to one who had not been faithful; both he and Sara would be lost. He forced himself to remember that she was not lost yet; his mind recited a silent litany of prayers that his voice would not find the strength to utter.

His crippled hand flew awkwardly to life; desperation drove the pain of it from his mind. His fingers moved through the thick tension of the air, cutting it down with precise, spare strokes. His eyes were in the past, on aged, confident hands. He mimicked them, his actions becoming more concrete, less unsure. The Servant froze then, his expression a mixture of anger and disbelief.

"What treachery is this?" His head swiveled to Lord Darclan's silent countenance. He clawed at the air; it seemed to constrict around him, forcing the mist of his body inward. "The lines are dead! Your God has no voice here!"

Darin's blood dripped downward, splashing across the white sheets. Stefanos could hear it as it fell. Darin looked at him, caught his eyes, and continued to trace the invisible sigil in the air. In a high, tense voice, he said, "Nightwalker, I know you now. I am servant to Lernan, God, and I stand in your way."

The walker shook his head, writhing in pain. His clawed hands tried to curl around movements—counterwards. But they were too full, too slow. "*Malthan!*" he cried, tearing at nothing. His fingers began to fray, returning to mist. He screamed, a shrill, breathless sound, and then he was gone.

He was gone. Darin bowed his head. His whole hand cradled his injured one, and he let the pain in. It was a good pain, as the Grandmother had promised, for he bore the wound in triumph. He wished that she could see him now; Lernan had claimed him, finally, for the adult that he thought he could never be in his life as a slave.

The lord caught him as he fell. The color had returned, ever so faintly, to Sara's face.

"I did it!"

"Yes, Darin. For tonight, for many, you have saved Sara." He stopped, looking at Darin's pale, glowing face. "I shall not call you *child*, not any longer. Initiate, your adult life begins here. The Circle has opened to embrace you."

"Lord . . ." Darin held him in weak arms.

"Rest easy. You have done what I could not do. You have saved the lady, and you are safe."

Darin smiled. A hint of that smile remained to greet the first rays of dawn as he surrendered to exhaustion and hunger. Darclan placed him gently on the bed beside the woman he had saved. It hurt him to hold the child; the sigil of the True Ward, weak though it had been, lingered in the room. Even though it had not been called upon him, he felt its effects. He knew that he made his most dangerous choice; it had been his goal for centuries to see that the lines were destroyed. But he would not do so—could not, and that surprised him.

"Sleep," he whispered, stroking Darin's brow. "It may be that she is not out of danger yet." Yes, that was it. He would not kill the child because Sara might need him. He tried to believe it as he walked back to his study to contemplate the odd turn the future had taken.

# chapter
# ten

*Darin slept until noon, when the smell of food broke forcibly* into the half world of dream. His hand throbbed as it lay bandaged on the coverlet. He started to sit up, and a firm hand reached out to push him gently back onto the bed.

"Rest. Your hand has been tended to; I do not believe it will become infected."

Darin's eyes focused on the aged face of master Gervin. He shrunk as far back as the bed would allow.

"You've had a busy night."

Darin said nothing. His lips and throat were dry, but even if they hadn't been, he wasn't sure he could think of anything to say.

"I've brought food; it's been cooling." He rose, turned around, and lifted a large tray. Setting it down, with more ease than Darin had ever managed, he lifted a silver goblet. "The lord said that you are to drink this before you eat. It will help restore your strength." He held it out, and after a moment Darin took it. "Drink a little at a time. It'll be harsh going down, but you'll have to stomach that."

Nodding, Darin tilted the cup, his watchful eyes not leaving Gervin's face. He bit back a small cry of pain as he flexed his injured hand. It dropped back to the bed where it was regarded with dismay.

"Come, drink up." Catching the direction of Darin's widened eyes, Gervin shook his head. "To be expected, don't you think?"

"But my work! I'm to tend to the lady—" Darin stopped, looked to his right, and blushed furiously as he realized he was inches away from Sara. He started to pull himself out of the covers, and Gervin caught his arm.

"*I'm* to tend the lady for the time, and to you as well. You'll have your duties back as soon as you're fit for them."

Darin tilted the cup back slowly, taking great care not to look to his right. As warned, he found the liquid foul to the taste and painful on the back of the throat; it was thick and warm as it lingered on his tongue. He put it away from him with disgust.

"All of it."

Sighing, he took it up again and returned it to his mouth. "I know this type of cure," he said between mouthfuls. "It's so awful that you don't mind the pain after you drink it, as long as you don't have to drink it again."

Gervin laughed, and Darin almost lost his grip on the cup. Gervin had always been old, hard, and severe, but the laugh was none of those things; it spoke of hidden things and it scattered like light round the room. Seeing the obvious shock on Darin's face did nothing to stem the flow of Gervin's amusement; rather his laughter increased in volume before dying out slowly.

"Well done, Darin, well done. I wouldn't have finished it at the behest of even the Lady of Mercy!"

Darin grimaced. Whatever the liquid was, it had done something; the pain he had been suffering receded. In its place came hunger. He reached out quickly for the food on the tray.

"Don't eat so quickly. You'll make yourself sick."

Darin slowed down and began to take the time to chew his food. As hunger receded, a strange calm took him, and he felt somehow at home in this large bed and this warm room, with the slavemaster of House Darclan as a manservant. He set aside the cutlery and turned to look at Sara.

"Has she—"

"No. But she is closer to natural sleep than she has been."

With a certainty that Darin could not identify the source of, he knew that she wouldn't wake; not yet. His eyes returned to the bandaged hand. He flexed it gingerly, wondering.

"Oh, the pain's real enough. Cleaned it myself." Meeting Darin's warily curious gaze, Gervin continued. "You did a good job on it. I'm to ask you no questions—and you're to answer none, even the ones I won't ask." Something was shining in the old man's eyes, something that replaced the darkness of the previous evening. "The walls have ears, as the saying goes."

On impulse, Darin stretched out a hand—the wounded one—and after a taut moment, Gervin took it gingerly in his own.

In the merest of whispers, he said, "But I can guess. I can guess." His eyes, oh, his eyes! They caught Darin in the fine mesh of the unsaid, the unsayable. "I'm not worthy to know, but I—I know what you must have done. Bear the wound proudly."

Images of the previous night flowed back to rest between them. From the hazy events, Darin drew only one clear memory: Gervin's pain; the bitter self-loathing that had walked with him as he left to do their lord's bidding. It was the same thing Darin had felt himself.

Gervin had killed an innocent person, drawing lifeblood.

But Darin had carried the blade, knowing this.

Lernan had forgiven him his part in the unspeakable act, and in turn, Darin found himself forgiving Gervin. It puzzled him, for he knew that he couldn't have done so in the past. Maybe this was adulthood—it was the only thing about him that had changed in the night that marked his transition.

Or maybe not. He felt a vague disappointment as he realized that no deep mysteries had opened themselves up to him; that, in fact, although the nightwalker had felt the presence of Lernan, he himself had felt only fear, followed by abiding relief as the nightwalker had unraveled.

Gervin released Darin's hand. "I'll come back with dinner. I believe Lord Darclan will be with you shortly."

Darin nodded as Gervin continued to watch him.

"Darin, I cannot ask you questions about the night. But—are you afraid of the lord?" The words were low, intense. Without pausing, Gervin added, "Do you know who he is?"

"He is someone who loves the lady," Darin replied firmly, his mind shunting away the answer that he didn't want to acknowledge for himself.

*If he loves her enough, maybe the Church of the Enemy will have one less priest.*

"And no, master Gervin. I'm not afraid of him." Truthfully, he was forced to add, "I'm not sure why."

Gervin nodded sharply and left.

When Lord Darclan entered the room, Sara and Darin both slept. He walked over to the bed and touched Sara's cheek. It felt warm. Her lips were parted, her breathing regular; if it had been a different day, he would have waited for her eyes to flutter open. She had been, in Rennath, a light sleeper.

Today, however, was the day after she had borne the touch of a Servant. She lived, but he knew that she had been severely weakened. Putting his hands on either side of her face, he stared down at her intently.

When he at last released her, he noticed that Darin was awake and watching.

"I hope you are well rested, Darin."

The boy nodded shyly and sat up, disentangling himself from his blanket. "How is the lady?"

Frowning, Darclan walked across the room, returning to the bedside with a large, heavy chair. "She is sleeping."

Darin was instantly alert. "Will she wake?"

"Not on her own." Darclan looked at Darin, measuring the boy's strength. "You did well last night; the nightwalker took great harm from your Ward. He does not have the power to return to her, and I do not think he would do so if he could." His hands formed a familiar steeple as he continued to speak, his chin resting roughly against his fingertips. "It was well done, but it was not done quickly enough. Do not feel guilty; I know well where the blame lies."

Darin's face darkened in spite of his lord's words. He stood unsteadily and walked around the bed until he was facing his lord. "She can't just sleep."

"Not and live, no." He gave voice to their mutual fear in a distant tone.

That distance gave Darin an odd comfort. He looked up at his lord, a slight tilt to his head.

Darclan answered the question in the boy's eyes, his voice grim. "There is nothing that I can do to help her."

Darin nodded, taking a deep breath. "But you think I can do something."

"If you are strong enough."

"I'm not as strong as you are, lord. But I'm alive, and while she needs me, that's good enough. It has to be."

Looking away from the intensity of Darin's youthful fire, Darclan smiled sadly. The sentiment was not well put; it had no grace, no elegance, no finesse. How strange, then, that it mirrored his own so exactly in its starkness.

He nodded, then. "You will want heavier clothing. I will send Gervin with it. When you are dressed, have him lead you to the north path of the garden. Tell him that we are not to be disturbed by anyone, for any reason." He rose. "I must take care of a few things before we meet. If you arrive before I do, wait."

"What am I to do?"

"We will discuss it later. Is everything clear?"

Darin nodded.

"Good. Until later, then." Darclan turned and strode into the hall. Darin could hear the curt demand that he placed with one of the slaves. He sat down on the bed and drew the blankets lightly around his shoulders, waiting.

Nor did he wait long; Gervin returned in less than ten minutes with a small bundle tucked under his arm.

He gave an odd, low bow. At another time, Darin thought, he might have meant insult, but not now.

"Do you need help in dressing?"

"What?" Darin said, as he reached for the bundle that Gervin handled so carefully.

"These might give you difficulty, young master."

With a sharp look Darin unfurled the bundle. When he held it up, it trailed the floor. But he could see that it was a thick, gray robe, with a few buttons and a small hood. It had full, plain arms and the body fell a good five inches past his ankles.

"I can't wear this. I couldn't walk halfway across the courtyard without tripping."

"Look at it a little more carefully. I think you will find it suitable." He paused. "Round the back, young master."

"Don't call me that. It isn't—" He stopped. On the back of the robe, inseparable from the rest of the weave, was a plain silver circle. It was large, the top of it flush with the neckline, the bottom with what would have been a larger man's waist. Unadorned, it caught the daylight and sent it rippling outward.

Darin couldn't speak. His fingers clutched the robe to his chest. He lifted the cloth and brushed it gently against his cheek. It was cool, with no warmth of friendly body behind it—but seeing it, so familiar, brought back the ache. It smelled musty, which was wrong. It should have smelled slightly sweaty, slightly woody.

Gervin watched Darin quietly. "It is one of many things in my keeping."

"But this is part of the Circle."

Lowering his voice, Gervin said, "A robe of the initiates of the Bright Heart." The words fell like stones.

*Bright Heart.* No one had spoken these words in all of Darin's time in the Empire. His fingers contracted around the material, unwilling to let it go.

"Lord Darclan commanded it." Gervin walked forward and firmly took the robe from Darin. "I don't know why."

Darin stood numbly and allowed Gervin to put the robe around him.

"It's long. Whoever wore it last was certainly more than two days adult."

Again Darin looked at Gervin. *Two days adult.* There were so very few people, outside of Culverne, who understood the Bright Heart's calendar. For the first time, he wondered what Gervin's other life had been; it was clear to him that the slave-master had not started life in Veriloth.

*I am,* he thought, looking at the older man, *two days an adult. I completed the True Ward. I would have had robes of my own to wear, and a Circle to join.*

He was the Circle now.

Gervin took a step back to look at Darin. The shoulders of the robe were inches too long; the sleeves fell over his fingertips; the hem gathered on the floor at his ankles. In spite of this, he wore the awkward clothing with dignity.

"It will do. Your hand?"

Darin tried to move it. It throbbed more painfully than earlier. "It's fine."

Gervin smiled at the fleeting grimace.

"We're supposed to go to the north gate of the garden. You're to tell everyone that we're not to be disturbed no matter what."

"I will inform the household of his commands. Wait here; I will return momentarily."

Darin found himself waiting again. He folded the sleeves of the robe up. He gathered handfuls of the simple gray cloth and took a few steps. It was going to be hard to walk in it—hard, and wonderful. Something played around the corners of his eyes, but he kept his face bare of emotion. He could hear the teasing of the Grandmother.

*Can you see me, Grandmother? Mother? Father? Are you standing at the Bridge of the Beyond even now?*

"Are we ready?"

Looking up, Darin saw Gervin standing in the doorway.

"I hope so."

Lord Darclan was waiting for them as they made their way to the north gate. Although he appeared to be at ease as he stood casually by the hedge wall, Darin pulled the robe further up his legs and ran to meet him. Darclan turned and surveyed the garments on the panting youth.

"No need to run, Darin. You will need what little energy you have.'' He looked across the walk and nodded at Gervin, who hesitated slightly and then nodded.

For a long moment, Lord Darclan looked down at Darin. His mouth turned oddly at the corners, as if both a smile and a frown struggled for control.

"The robes fit poorly. Forgive me; I have not had the time to have them altered." He smiled crookedly. "Nor, I admit, the inclination. You will make do as you are."

"Don't change them. I'll grow."

Lord Darclan looked slightly pained and began to walk down the path. "Follow me."

Without question, Darin did as he was bidden, taking two steps for each of his lord's. Darclan did not look back. His graven face was turned inward, into the garden, his thoughts on the center. Each step he took felt irrevocable, marked in passing by more than fading sunlight and blades of turned grass. The shuffle of cloth and footsteps behind him was a whisper of past times. His progress grew more stilted as he fought the urge to turn back, to accept the unacceptable, to have an end. The smell of foliage and flowers grew cloying; it clung to him like little claws and drew invisible blood. He wanted to wither them all, to turn the entire garden into a vast, barren landscape leaving only the wreckage of the well as a centerpiece. He shuddered and stopped.

"Lord?"

"It is nothing. We are—almost there." Drawing the folds of his cloak more tightly around his shoulders, he forged on. Closing his eyes, he allowed his feet to trace the familiar path the last few steps.

Darin saw it first: the magnificent ruin of stonework and carving, choked with vines and weeds. He opened his mouth, but found no words to describe the sudden sense of wrongness that twisted his stomach. This was old, but there was a majesty about it—a familiarity . . .

Lord Darclan opened his eyes. He saw, with bitter pride, that Sara had left her mark upon it; the vines that she had cleared had not crept back. She earned it; she had paid for it.

Darin looked at it. "The Gifting." His mouth was dry. His words dropped like a pebble into the thick stillness.

"You know it, then."

"I've heard the old tales." Darin stepped forward and gingerly placed his hand upon the stone that Sara had worked so hard to clear. It tingled gently against the tentative brush of his fingers. "This—this is where the Lady Sara came."

"Yes." The word was a curse. "I should not have brought her here. I should have known what would happen."

"What happened?"

"She tried to clear the vines from the well. The vines are part of a larger—protection." He spoke with difficulty, anger punctuating each syllable. "The Servant—in blood-wraith form—was the other part. She wounded herself on the thorns of the vines. Her blood woke the creature."

"Why did you let her—"

"Enough! It was done, and badly. She would have been able to protect herself in the—" He broke off, swallowed, and strove to speak more slowly, measuring his words. "I erred. That is all you need to know."

Darin turned to face the ruined stone again. His hands flew upward across his body, his fingers doing the dance of the Greater Ward. Darclan took a deliberate step back.

"Darin," he said softly, "I cannot stay here."

"But I don't know what to do!" He too drew back, turning his face to his lord.

"Nor do I. The well and its workings are—forbidden to me." He gestured in a wide circle. "I have done what I can to ensure that you are undisturbed. You must do the rest."

"But lord—"

"You are of the lines; you are initiate to the Circle. You are the only person alive who is both of these things. I know little of the well, save this: Its power is my Enemy's, and His alone—and it is this that will save Sara." He drew further back along the pathway. "I cannot stay. I will return to Sara and wait for you." He turned away, stopped, then turned back again.

"This is not without risk to either of us. But for you, Darin, the risk is now. If you fail you will die—not by my hand, but I will be unable to save you.

"If you succeed, your chance of death is also high. Can you not feel it, even now? The well has old magic, and it is strong enough to be felt." Pink sunlight glinted off the silver weave of the circle on Darin's breast.

"And if I do nothing, Lady Sara will die."

"Yes."

Darin bowed his head. "Then I don't have any choice."

"You have the same choice that I have had for a long time." Lord Darclan shook his head wearily.

"You know I'll do it," Darin said, his voice a gentle accusation. "But I want to know something, if you'll tell me."

"I owe you at least that much, although you become bold."

"I know why I'm making my choice, and I know why you've made yours—I think it's the same reason. But this—this is the greatest work of my—of your Enemy."

"Yes," the lord replied. He turned, to protect his face from Darin's eyes. "And yes. It is because I love her that I risk these things. But how, and why? These are very good questions, Darin." Bitter, bitter voice. "Do you think I have not asked them of myself? I have no answer to give you. But think of this: Is love the province of the pure alone? Does it not exist in various guises throughout humanity? Can you answer these questions of even yourself?"

Darin was silent for a few moments. When at last he spoke, his voice was full, deeper than its youthful tone should have allowed. "All the things I love about her are things the priests of the Enemy have tried to destroy forever."

"Yes." Lord Darclan bowed, a formal, final salute. "Fare well and succeed, my little enemy."

Darin watched him leave, knowing that he would not turn back again. He felt tears push at his eyes.

*What do I do?*

He tried to remember anything that would make his path clearer to him. The well—the Gifting—was legend to the line; one of the two wells of Lernan. What had the Grandmother called it? The eyes of Lernan? He looked down at the wrinkled sleeves of his initiate's robe. It lay there, dull gray cloth that offered no answers. He looked at the bandages around his injured hand; a small red blotch had appeared through the last fold and was spreading slowly.

*I've opened it again,* he thought dully. *It'll get infected. I wish it would stop bleeding.*

Bleeding. Blood. The blood of God. She had called the two wells the blood of Lernan. A triumphant smile darted across his mouth, then fell away.

*Great. So it's blood. Does that help? Sara, what am I supposed to do to help you? What?*

He made tight fists of his hands, gasped, and relaxed the injured one. *Stupid.* He sighed again. *Lady Sara, you tried to clear the well. At least I can finish it for you now that the nightwalker is gone.*

Opening his eyes, he looked at the vines and again began to

trace the Greater Ward in the air. Then, steeling himself for a struggle, he put both of his hands on a large vine and pulled. To his great surprise, it gave way easily, and he left it, unregarded, on the ground. He moved on, traced the sigil, and again removed another section. It, too, he left behind him as he continued to work.

The routine became fixed in his mind as he walked around the large edifice. Greater Ward. Bend. Grip. Pull. The sun made its tumble into nightfall as he worked, marking time by the distance it had fallen. At no time did he become incautious; his fingers chose areas bare of thorn to grip, and he tugged each vine with enough force to remove it, no more.

Sunset came, and with it, the waning of the light; crimson splashed along the horizon. Darin pulled the robe tight. It was cooler; he could feel night wind creeping through the weave of fabric to touch his skin.

*Forget it,* he thought, as he surveyed the well. It was almost completely cleared, and he could see that the vines and creepers had not damaged the stone as much as he had first thought. He stopped to rest, lying back against the object of his labor. The night was clear; a sliver of moon appeared, face in shadow.

He stood, took a deep breath, and began again. The last of the vines were more difficult to clear than the rest; whether that was due to his exhaustion or the coming of the dark, he could not be sure, but it seemed to him that they moved away from his fingers in the shadows.

Not that it mattered; there were so few he would soon have the well cleared regardless of the difficulty. He moved more slowly; several times his fingers brushed the sharp point of near-invisible thorns.

*Sara, your blood called the nightwalker,* he thought, as his thumb nestled between the teeth of the vine. *I wonder what my blood would call.* It was an idle thought; he had no temptation to find an answer for his question. Not now, when the last of them rested in his hands. Smiling, he pulled it away, and the well was free. With a mingled sigh of exhaustion and triumph, he stepped back to survey his work.

The well seemed larger, newer somehow. Darin marveled at the way the stonework caught and held the frugal light of the night sky. It pulsed there, glimmering faintly. He reached out to touch the stone with his left hand and drew back; his hand glowed warmly.

*Lernan, God.* He did not speak, did not want the sound of

his voice to shatter the fragility of his miracle. The well was shining, he felt, for him alone, the light of it gentle and green. He reached for the bandages that concealed his right hand, and trembling slightly, began to unwind them. They fell away in his left hand and fluttered to the ground.

"That's quite a mess, youngster," a voice said. Wheeling around, he made out another figure in the darkness. The person chuckled as Darin backed toward the well. "Running in that direction won't do you any good, but never mind, I've no intention of harming you." Another soft laugh issued out of the darkness as Darin's fingers gripped the stone.

"What are you doing here?" Darin said, trying to give his shaking voice some semblance of authority. "The garden's been forbidden to the household."

"Quite true, quite true. More's the pity." The well began to glow more brightly; Darin could see it illuminating the grass. He wasn't sure if this was a good sign.

"Much better," the figure said, stepping into the light. "Well, don't just stand there, boy. Come give me a hand."

An old woman, clothed in tattered gray, hobbled forward. She walked with a gnarled cane gripped in equally gnarled hands. Her hair was an unruly white mass.

"You aren't supposed to be here. It's the lord's orders, ma'am. You'd better leave before anyone sees you."

"Nonsense. If no one's supposed to be here, then no one'll see me. Unless, of course, you count yourself." She continued her awkward gait. "No manners in children these days." She stopped and rapped the ground with the end of her cane. "Up to me to teach you some, I dare say. Get your back off that wall and help an old woman into the light!" She held out one arm expectantly.

Darin stared at it, and then at her. He felt sharply disappointed at her intrusion into his sense of divine isolation.

"Well? Are you going to keep me waiting all night?"

He wanted to say yes, but instead walked over to her. "You know you aren't supposed to be here, don't you?" he said as he took her arm. He'd seen many a similar old woman before, and he had no illusions about the effects his words would have. But he didn't recall seeing this one around the household, and he wondered if she tended the grounds.

"Says who? Careful, boy, you're gripping the arm too tight!" It would not have surprised Darin if she'd rapped him sharply on the knuckles with her cane; that she refrained from doing so seemed a small miracle. "Well, then. Well. What have we here?"

"Don't touch that!" Darin shoved her hand away from the circle on his robes.

"What's this? The cloth suddenly become too good for us commoners?" She sniffed, a loud harsh sound. "Since when do they let children wear the robes?"

Her question took him by surprise, and he gazed at her more sharply. She recognized his initiate's gown, of this there was no question—but he knew for fact that she had not been server to Line Culverne.

"Something wrong with your tongue, boy?"

He cursed himself for not studying his history more closely. But at her age, there was a chance that she had been server to one of two lines before they fell.

"They don't let *children* wear the robes, ma'am."

"You're wearing them, if I'm not mistaken."

"I'm not a child." He searched her face for a moment, then asked, "But you know of the robes of the initiates?"

"Recognized them, didn't I?"

He nodded.

"And don't think you can humor me, either. I'm not to be humored by children, even if they are initiates." She moved suddenly, dropping her cane. Before Darin could react, her hands gripped his shoulders, pressing the seams of his robe into them. "Look at me, boy. Look at me, I say!"

Darin met her eyes. They were a filmy brown, bloodshot and tired. She kept his gaze for a few moments before breaking away.

"Don't stand there staring, child, it's plain rude. Get my cane."

Bewildered, and not a little annoyed, Darin did as she ordered.

"Be careful with that! It's older than I am!"

He didn't believe it. The cane, for all its twists and the raw, dry quality of the wood, felt firm and strong in his hands. He held it out to her, but she reached for his arm instead.

"You carry it. It's getting too heavy for me."

*It isn't heavy at all,* Darin thought, his grip around it growing firmer. He looked carefully at it as they approached the well; it was not more than three feet long, and although the top was knotted grain, the last two feet were smooth. He tapped the ground with it experimentally, letting it support most of his weight. It felt solid and strong.

"You'll be doing that soon enough, child. Don't play at it now."

He blinked and, after a small hesitation, offered her the cane. "Here, you take it. You need it."

She returned his look quietly. Her grip on his arm tightened until it was almost painful. Without another word he helped her shuffle the last few feet to the well.

"Look at it, boy," she said, her voice smoother than it had been since she first spoke. She loosed her hold on his arm, and two weathered hands gripped the wide stone.

"It isn't as grand as it once was—but it's beautiful just the same. See the scars, boy?" She tilted her head until light caught her pale chin. "They're beautiful—they rest on the surface of the rock; they don't go much deeper than that.

"They don't shine. They don't glitter. But the well bears them like medals, like the testament they are." Noting Darin's puzzled look, she gave a sad shake of the head. "Maybe children can't appreciate the profound beauty inherent in endurance."

She released the rock and pulled the remnants of her clothing around her bent shoulders. The strange strength that had animated her voice drifted away as Darin watched her. Her face seemed to sag into wrinkles and irritable age.

"Don't just stand there. I'm thirsty. Get me some water."

"But—"

"I don't want feeble excuses! I want water!"

Darin looked at her in amazement. "Look—I've come here to do important things, not draw water! And anyway, there isn't anything to draw water with here—do you see any bucket?"

She snorted rudely and put a hand somewhere into the dirty folds of her robe. It emerged with a small tin cup. "Don't come prepared, do you? Here, take it!"

"I can't draw water with this!" He'd had about enough of her; his forehead began to fold and darken in an expression his mother would have known well, and hated more.

She shoved the cup into his hands. "You can. The water's almost to the edge. Look at it!"

He couldn't see any water and opened his mouth to tell her so in no uncertain words, but any thought of anger vanished as he met her ancient eyes. He found her very grating, but there was no doubt that she'd endured much. What harm could it do to humor her, as long as he did it quickly? His fingers closed around the edge of the cup.

"If I can get water for you, I will." He did not voice his doubts about the potability of anything pulled from the well. "But I'm only going to try once, and then you have to leave me alone. Okay?"

"Don't humor me," she said, but she nodded, her lips pursed in an unpleasant frown.

Darin turned from her and leaned into the side of the well; the rock gave off enough light to see by. If not for her, he might have continued to appreciate it—it was so oddly warm.

"I can't see any water, ma'am." He pushed his weight firmly against the stone and found, to his relief, that it didn't give at all. He set the staff aside on the grass and took a deep breath. Taking care to rest his weight upon his left hand, he pulled himself slowly up and onto the edge.

No glint of light indicated that there was water within reach. He sighed and gingerly bent further over. Still nothing. He looked at the tin cup and shrugged, pulling back.

"I'm sorry, ma'am, but if there's water here it's too far down for me to reach."

"Is it?" Her voice, in those two words, was chill and expressionless.

With a startled cry, Darin whirled around, but not quickly enough to avoid the two hands that had reached out to shove him forward. In panic, Darin's hands scrambled for a hold on the edge of the well; a stark pain shot through his right one and he yanked it back. He clung there frantically for a few seconds, then felt the rock recede slowly from the grip of his fingers. He looked up to meet her eyes.

"Help me!" he shouted, in a voice that held no hope.

"If you insist." She reached out for his hand as he held his breath, and then, with a hard downward arc, brought her aged fist down on it. He cried out at the pain of the blow; it was strong and sure. She brought her fist up and hammered it down again. He felt stone grind against the bones of his fingers as his feet tried to find purchase along the smooth inner walls.

"Why are you doing this?"

He didn't hear the answer to his question, if indeed there was any, for his hands slipped at that moment, and he felt himself falling into blackness. His arms and legs flailed wildly as he fell, trying desperately to find something to cling to.

He had just enough time to regret the foolishness of trusting a strange old woman in the darkness before he hit the water and went under.

# chapter
# eleven

*The water broke his fall.*

Thick and cold, it shot up his nostrils and whirled around the folds of his robe, flooding in an instant between cloth and skin.

He didn't want to drown. It was hard, but he forced himself to a state of calmness and tried to angle his body in such a way that he could reach the stone wall with either his legs or arms. Luck was with him in this; his feet skittered against a smooth surface, and he pushed upward in an attempt to break water. The oversized robe he was wearing didn't help. It drank the water greedily, becoming more heavy and cumbersome. He struggled to the surface.

The liquid gave as his face touched the stale air; he gasped wildly, went under again, and came up choking.

*Lernan!* he thought, his mouth too full to say the word. He hovered in water, pressing his body firmly against the side of the well. The taste of the liquid was bitter against his tongue; he could feel it, slimy and thick, as it lingered.

In the faint light he could make out the top of the well; with weary certainty, he accepted the fact that it was impossible for him to climb back up. His cheek touched the cold, wet stone. Rivulets of warm liquid ran down his face, and he realized that he was crying.

*It's no good. Lady Sara, please forgive me.* He wished that Lord Darclan had stayed by the well; his lord was far too wise to be tricked into death by an old woman.

But the lord would not give up, either. Darin took a deep breath, and the smell of bad water overwhelmed him. He slipped slightly but managed to keep his head in the air. Why was the water so foul? This was one of Lernan's wells; the water, if he remembered the Grandmother's tempered instruction, was supposed to be purifying. Maybe she had been wrong. Maybe the work of the Dark Heart and his Servants had destroyed the ancient properties of the well.

"There are Servants everywhere, child." Looking up, Darin could see the silhouette of a form leaning over the well. A surge of anger wiped exhaustion away. His hands clenched more tightly, turning white against the stone.

"Defiance will not help you." A dry chuckle echoed down to his upturned face. "Perhaps you should try to remove the robe. It weighs you down even now."

That decided him; foolish or no, he'd be damned if he discarded it. He clenched his teeth as another cold laugh echoed down the walls.

"The lines called this the Gifting of Lernan; the water was a symbol of his blood. I should say it's a rather appropriate title for sewage." The shadow moved, bending slightly further, and spat into the water.

"For the blood of the Bright Heart, child. Consider it your epitaph." Starlight filtered down the well in a faint circle; by the light Darin could see that his tormentor had left. He was alone, surrounded by the sound of water as it responded to his slight movements.

He scraped his forehead along the stone in soundless fury. How dare she spit into the well? How dare she mock the lines?

*The lines are dead now.*

*They aren't dead while I'm still alive!*

*They will be dead soon. You will drown in the blood of Lernan.*

The creature had *spit* into the water.

*What difference does it make?*

But it did make a difference. Dead leaves, mildew, algae—these were the marks of age, of neglect; there was no malice in them and no inherent evil. The saliva of this creature was defilement.

*So get angry, then. There isn't anything else you can do.*

Bitterness rose like bile. He choked on it, felt impotent tears start down his cheeks again. Angrily he shook them away.

*You're going to die, Darin. And because you can't do anything, your Sara will die as well. Maybe you'll meet at the Bridge of the Beyond—if the beyond has a use for the weak and the hopeless in the after.*

"I'm not useless!" Water dulled the edge of his words.

*You couldn't stop the defiling of this holy place. You thought*

*you were an initiate; you thought the Circle had accepted you.
How could it truly accept one in league with a priest of Veriloth?*

A priest of the Dark Heart. Tears fell faster than he could
shake them; salt mingled with foul water beneath his trembling
chin.

*He ordered the Dark Ceremonies. He called for the lifeblood
of the unwilling.*

"He did it for Sara."

*It doesn't matter why.*

But it did matter to Darin. He held onto the image of Lord
Darclan; the way he had kissed the helpless Sara; the reason
that he had exhausted himself in the grim and hopeless struggle
with the nightwalker. He thought of Sara, her arms wrapped
around his memory; the way she had named him; her defiance
in the breakfast hall. He thought of her pale forehead under the
fingers of the nightwalker, and the grisly way the creature had
taken on substance and form.

*We love her.*

*You have failed her.*

*Yes.* His right hand hurt. It was open again. *Yes.* His eyes
widened and then closed. *But I will not fail God.*

*You already have.*

*No. Watch.* Gritting his teeth to stop them from chattering,
he pulled his hands away from the wall. His robe spun about
him like a serpent, pulling him to an underwater lair.

For a moment he flailed, his hands reaching for the wall, and
then he forced himself to be still.

*I am an initiate of the Circle.* He began to sink and kicked at
the water with slow strokes to buoy himself up. It took effort—
the weariness of the day's work and the shock of the fall had
already started to take their toll.

*I gave you my blood once, Bright Heart, and you answered.
You spared my lady that death.*

His head bobbed under the water, and he spread his arms out
and down, propelling himself above the water again. Numb fingers began to dance sluggishly beneath the dark surface. Reaching out, he closed his eyes and dug his nails into the open wound
of his right hand.

*Come again. Take the lifeblood I offer you freely. Cleanse this
place of the stain of our Enemy.*

He felt sharp cold against warm flesh and opened his hand
further. He slipped under the water a final time and knew that

he wouldn't be able to reach air. He was tired, but he forced his fingers to twist against the water in the pattern of the True Ward.

*Let blood call blood, Lernan, God.*

His lungs cried out for air; his head felt light, almost translucent. A rumbling tremor took his arms and legs; they began to shake uncontrollably. He felt them strike the walls of the well. It seemed to him that he was moving upward, toward blessed air.

Darin tried desperately not to give in to false hope; to gain an acceptance of death that might calm him and lend him dignity. He tried to tell himself that the swirling rush of water that started at his ankles and moved up to his torso was imagination, nothing more. It did no good; he was caught in a sudden lurch of adrenaline, and his arms began to flail wildly in an attempt to propel himself upward.

He opened his eyes automatically as a rush of night air touched his face. Opened them and looked around in confusion. He was no longer surrounded by cold, smooth rock; he could perceive the dark shadows of the hedges through starlight and feel the breeze that lingered across the wetness of his hair and face. His mouth fell open, and he stopped moving for an instant. The water had risen.

He realized his mistake as the water took him again, filling his mouth. He choked and kicked upward, stretching his arms out to touch the solid stone of the well's lip. He felt its rough texture against his fingers and managed to pull himself to one side as water swirled gently around him.

With slow, deliberate movements, he pulled himself up and onto the stone, and after a few seconds he rolled off and came to rest on the dry grass. He lay there trembling, the smell of dirt and grass all around.

"Well done, Initiate."

All Darin could do in response was to raise his head at the sound of the voice. Blades of grass that had not been crushed by his roll blocked his sight.

"You have gone through much. Rest awhile; your strength will return to you." A shadow passed over his prone body. He could hear the tinkle of water and the low, soft murmur of words that he couldn't quite catch.

A battered tin cup appeared before his face, held in pale hands. The hands were smooth, not bent or gnarled, but he shivered nonetheless.

For the voice did not just touch his ears; it went deeper than that, it dwelt longer. It had little in common with the coarse roughness of age, but he knew that the voice was still the same.

He had survived the well. How much more could he take before succumbing? With a trembling hand, he reached out and deliberately knocked the cup over. Clear liquid trickled away into the grass; the ground absorbed it quickly. He closed his eyes and took a deep breath; the cost of the simple gesture made plain to him the extent of his helplessness. He lay there, determined to play no more of these games.

A fragrant smell caught his attention and tugged at wisps of memory. He opened his eyes; they shone with his pain and curiosity. In front of him, where the water had spilled, a small white flower had blossomed. It stood alone in the midst of poorly tended grass, the ivory of four petals gleaming preternaturally.

"Orvas," he whispered, and he reached out to touch it. It was cool and smooth beneath the tentative search of his hand.

"Yes, Initiate. The eye of God." Pale hands reclaimed the cup from where it had fallen. "I will return to the Gifting and draw the blood I have waited for these centuries. Will you drink this time, or will you try to grow a field of these flowers?"

Footsteps receded, paused, and returned. The tin cup gleamed dully as it came to rest again inches from his face. He looked at it in silence and then turned his gaze to the flower that bloomed beside it.

Weary fingers curled around the crude tin handle.

"You have accomplished a great task, Initiate. Lernan cleansed his blood with your blood; they have mingled, and they are one. Drink and accept his Gifting."

"Gifting?" The cup moved unevenly toward his mouth, spilling tiny drops as it bumped across the uneven earth.

"The Gifting of the lifeblood of Lernan. What you have offered twice, He offers back to you. Drink and be whole."

The water smelled clean and fresh. He looked at it, lifted the cup, and hesitated.

"Initiate, I am indeed a Servant; Keranya of Lernan. Do you think that only the Dark Heart has them?"

"Why?" His voice was harsh; the cup trembled against his lips.

"To tell you more, to do other than what I did, would have made the task nigh impossible." The voice seemed suddenly hollow. "It was no easy thing."

With a ghost of a sigh, Darin tilted the cup forward. Clean, icy water tumbled into his mouth. It was sweet, almost too sweet to bear, although it tasted like nothing he had ever drunk before. It slid easily down his throat, and although it was chill, he felt a warmth rise in response to it. That warmth touched all of him, quickening his limbs and mind in one strong surge.

He rolled over and sat up, amazed that he could. The night air seemed sharper, and the starlight brighter. He looked at the well; it shone in the remnants of wilderness like a radiant beacon.

"Yes. It is whole; you have cleansed the wound and the blood will flow freely, as it once did."

He looked up then to meet her eyes; they were green, and framed by the lines of an ancient, gentle smile. No Servant should have worn her age so harshly; indeed none of the stories that he had been raised with lent credence to her words. The tatters of robes were gone, as were the stoop and gnarled joints. But the hair was still pale, near white, and the age that she carried somehow more evident. She stood, her regard unblinking.

*This,* he thought, *is a Servant of God?*

As if she could hear him, she smiled sadly.

He tried to remember that *she* had pushed him down the well, to an almost certain watery death. But perhaps the Gifting had healed more than exhaustion, for he felt no anger. She didn't seem to have the strength just to stand, never mind to carry out such an attack.

He looked around in the grass and found the tin cup. Without hesitation, he picked it up and walked to the well. He could see the surface of the water bubble gently as he approached. No hint of death was in it now; the stigmata of decay and age had vanished. He dipped the cup into the water with care and felt a tingle rush through his fingers.

Only when he had pulled the cup away did he realize that he had done so with his right hand. Where there had been pain, he now felt a steady warmth. He looked at the back of his hand; a small white circle, with slender, pale filaments, was all that remained of his two offerings.

He returned and took a seat facing the Servant. The cup he held out in steady hands.

"Not for me, Initiate."

Her voice—if voice it was—seemed even weaker.

"But it helped me."

"Yes." Again she smiled, and again the smile was tinged

with shadows of pain. "But it will not aid me; I made my choice and must abide it. Yes, in this, the Lady of Elliath was correct. I have waited long." She sat, suddenly, as if her legs could not bear her weight.

"Let me explain, Initiate, as the Grandmother or Grandfather of your vanquished line might once have done. This meeting with God, as you have done, is the gateway to all that is adult. But many times, to the dismay of the lines, such a True Ward fails.

"It fails, not because of lack of faith, but because of too much faith. Fear, mortal fear, is the link between our Lord and your life.

"I am sorry for the pain I have caused you this evening. I still feel its echoes, and I am weary. But to tell you who I was was to risk your confidence, and therefore your failure. You must understand that that risk was unacceptable. Forgive me."

Here she stopped, passing a hand before her eyes. Darin thought it looked oddly translucent; he could see that the dark of the night was fading into the early gray of morning.

"This Gifting of God is one of two wounds that he accepted for love of his followers. And these two were taken by those who serve the Darkness." Again she paused.

Darin nodded; it made clear the presence of a priest of the Enemy. He still didn't understand why the lord had brought Lady Sara here, but he understood why the lord could not remain if the Gifting was to be invoked.

"Each of your kind made a pilgrimage to one of these two. They blooded themselves at the well, for by doing so they believed that they became brethren with God, and servitors no longer.

"You have made the last such journey. And yours was hardest of all." She bowed her head in respect, and then raised it, looking eastward.

"The sun . . . ah, light." Her arms stretched outward in supplication. Then she smiled again, but much that was bitter was in it.

"The Lady of Elliath foresaw one last journey here, one last initiate after the Fall. And one of the Servants of the Bright Heart chose to tie herself to the mortal Earth to wait, in darkness."

"You," Darin said softly. He looked at the Gifting. Even in the early traces of morning it had a distinct light of its own.

"Yes. And it will shine so until the Malanthi come again." She rose then, her back bent into pink sky.

Darin rose, also, and, walking over to the well, retrieved the staff that he had set aside.

"No, Initiate. That, too, was part of my task, and it is finished. The staff is yours."

He looked at it carefully; it seemed to shine the same way that the well did, but more faintly.

"You will have need of it. In the time I have watched, in the battles that have passed by me, the seven lines have become two."

"Two?"

"The line of Bethany of Culverne exists in you. And the line of the Lady of Elliath, First of the Sundered." A shadow crossed her face as she spoke the name. She turned then and began to walk toward the hedges.

"Wait!"

Her back stopped moving, but she did not turn. "The Gifting of Lernan was our greatest work, and the work most difficult to accomplish in all of our history. We paid the price for it willingly. But it is hard. I am alone. I am weary."

Darin dropped slowly to the ground and bowed his head. He could feel the words she continued to speak, but they came to him as if from a great distance.

"I am mostly dead, Initiate, as I was in a beginning I no longer clearly remember, for I am of the Sundered of the true Light. Do not feel pity; while these two lines exist, there is hope for an end to my task. And it is a hope I had almost forsaken, for it has been long in coming.

"But she saw, and saw truly, the events that the night has brought.

"Ah, First among us, may your vision not fail. May the cost buy us our Lord's hope."

She lifted her arm; it trailed shadow along the bones of her upturned face. "But the day—even mortal light—is not for me. I am truly a shadow, a shade of the past."

"But the Servants . . ." *were of the Light*. He stopped the words from leaving his lips and bent his head.

"Take the staff; it was fashioned by Bethany, and it may do more than serve as a symbol of your office. You are the line now."

He looked up as she faded, her face turned toward the sun. He didn't understand what her work was, but he knew that if what she had told him was true, she was of those closest to the Light in the beginning. It seemed a bitter fate for her to live in the dark and night alone. Now he understood the age she wore, that was like no other Servant's. What other Servant of Lernan had chosen to live only in Darkness?

And then her words penetrated his mood.

He was all that was left of the Line Culverne—but the line of the Lady, the greatest line of all, had somehow survived the butchery of the Servants of Malthan.

He was no longer alone.

The war wasn't really over.

A sharp, sweet joy pierced him, and a heady defiance as well. He swung the staff gleefully overhead and let out a great, wordless yell. He was *not* alone, he had survived the night, and the world in front of him seemed, for the moment, conquerable. He was young, then; for a moment his hope outshone the scars that the Empire had inflicted to shape and control him.

# chapter
# twelve

*Lord Darclan sat beside Sara, streams of curtained light trou-*
bling his brow. He smiled, a tenuous mixture of the grim and
the gentle. The waning of the night had seemed endless, but
this slow creep of silent dawn was infinitely worse.

"Sara." He stroked her hair softly. "Did you feel it, too? It
will not be long. Darin accomplished—what he had to." But he
didn't know if Darin had survived the task. The well, cleansed,
was useless to him without the boy—less than useless.

He was tired; he had depleted much of his power, and it was
slow to return to him. But he would not walk in the Dark Heart's
hand to restore it; he would wait. His head fell slowly and came
to rest on Sara's shoulder. He closed his eyes.

And snapped them open again as the door gave a loud creak
behind him. He whirled around as Darin slid into the room.
Darin's robe was damp and hung round his small frame like a
tent; his eyes were ringed black. He leaned against a small staff,
which his left hand curled around. The lord grimaced at the
sight of it, but forbore comment.

For Darin's right hand was unbandaged, and looking at it,
Darclan could see the silver of scar tissue. In this hand-made-
whole was a small, battered tin cup, one that slaves might use.

"Lord." Darin held out the cup. "For Sara."

Lord Darclan started forward with outstretched hand. His
face twisted slightly in pain, and he drew back.

"Yes," he murmured, with satisfaction and a profound sense
of relief. "Yes." He ignored the pain—what did it matter? Had
he been any other man he would have been laughing or crying
for sheer joy. He was Lord Darclan; he allowed himself a wide,
deep smile.

"Lord?"

Darclan shook his head. "No, you will not call me that here." His eyes traced the outline of the staff. "I know that wood well; I know who made it, and I know what it means." He bowed. "Patriarch of Culverne."

"And you?" Darin's fingers whitened against the grain of the staff. "Do you also serve . . . God?"

Darclan's voice hardened at the tone of Darin's. "I will not discuss that with you. Not now." He turned to look at Sara.

Darin accepted his words and walked forward. No matter what the lord said, his years of slavery were hard to put aside, even for minutes, in the presence of such nobility. But his steps were firm and sure, different from any that he had taken in any house of Veriloth.

The lord moved aside and Darin knelt by the bed, cup in hand, as he had done in the dark of a night not long past. It was not night now, nor was the cup of the lord's offering. He had brought it, and it was his to give—his and God's.

With gentle firmness, he eased his arm between her neck and the pillow it rested against. He lifted her head, raised the cup to her lips, and tilted it carefully. After a few seconds she swallowed, and her eyes immediately began to flicker. She didn't open them, but she drank more greedily, and Darin could see the color returning to her pale features.

When the water was gone, he stood and placed the cup down quietly on the table beside her. It was not silver or other such finery, and normally no slave would dare to bring it for the use of nobility, but it had its place of honor. Nor did the lord gainsay its presence.

Both of the watchers could hear the rustle of cloth against cloth as Sara stirred. Darin felt tired, then, but at peace. He'd saved her.

They'd saved her.

His stomach growled, and his face responded by darkening several shades. He shot an embarrassed glance at Lord Darclan, but the lord did not notice him; he had eyes for Sara alone. His face mirrored all his hope, and his hands, although they stayed at his side, were trembling slightly.

*He does love her,* Darin thought, although already he had ceased to doubt it. Sara moaned softly, and Darclan looked at Darin.

"I'm hungry," the boy said, his voice quiet. "I'd like to get something to eat."

"Don't you wish to stay? Don't you wish to see her wake? I

could not have done what you risked your life to do." Frustration in this, that and respect. The lord's voice was low and uneven. This was Darin's victory, and no victory such as this could go unclaimed.

Or could it? He looked again at Sara.

"I think she'll be safe with you, lord." Darin also looked at Lady Sara. "But she's waking, and she might be confused. Shouldn't one of us be beside her?"

"Yes," Lord Darclan said; it was all he desired. But it had not been his hand that had drawn the blood of the Enemy, nor his blood that had been spilled to cleanse it. It was not his privilege.

And perhaps because his feelings were always so naked where Sara was concerned, the boy realized how he felt. He turned his back on them and made his way to the door, the staff dragging along the carpet.

Lord Darclan watched his back retreat and then took the two steps necessary to bring him to her side.

"Darin." Lord Darclan's voice came to him; it was under control again. Darin stopped and looked back without turning. "Thank you."

"Tell her that I'll see her later." And he walked out of the room.

Darin had not lied to Lord Darclan; he *was* hungry, and his stomach continued to make a spectacle of itself as he traversed the halls. His appearance earned a few odd stares from the slaves that he passed, but they said nothing. He knew this wouldn't last.

He headed toward the kitchen, then thought of Cullen, and thought the better of it.

But he was very hungry.

Feeling slightly less heroic, he turned and made his way to his room. He had missed breakfast, but lunch would be in the hall soon, and he could eat his fill there. He hoped that sleep would dull the pangs of hunger that made the hours till lunch seem interminably long.

He met fewer and fewer people as he walked; they would be on their rounds of duty at this hour, and the slave's wing would be practically empty. He felt grateful for it; the quiet and solitude reminded him of the halls of Culverne during morning prayers. He could imagine his lonely walk as the triumphant procession of one newly born into adulthood. The cold stone of House

Darclan gave way to the ancestral temple of the line. Large,
arched doors appeared in front of him, engraved with the sym-
bols of Culverne and the old runes that spoke their welcome.
He walked up to the doors, stopped, and performed a low bow,
knowing what he would see when he opened them: They would
be waiting for him in the pews. The Grandmother, the matriarch, would be sitting in front of the white, marble altar, her
fingers no doubt drumming impatiently against the stone as she
waited for him to enter. He could almost see her expression of
irritable, maternal pride.

He lifted the staff, brought it to his chest, and put a small
hand on the impressive doors.

And the illusion crumpled. Oiled oak panels gave way to the
rough-hewn wood of his small, rectangular door. He was not in
the home of the lines; his year-mates were lost, the Grandmother
dead.

But the line survived. And one day, past the Bridge of the
Beyond, he would have all the things that daydreams brought
him today.

With a sigh he opened the door, but in the next instant he
stepped back in surprise.

A fire burned in the grate. Food was arranged on a small
wooden table in the center of the room. A set of clean, comfortable clothing was laid out on his small, hard bed. And slavemaster Gervin sat on a three-legged stool, waiting, his mouth
crooked in a slight smile.

Darin opened his mouth, closed it, then opened it again. He
could find nothing at all to say, but his stomach wasn't nearly
so inarticulate.

"Well met, young master." Gervin stood and bowed, a
quirky, formal salute.

"Uh—master Gervin."

Gervin chuckled. "Would you like to eat first, or can you
spare the time to change out of your robes? They're damp—"
This was a generous appraisal. "—but the fire should dry them."

"What are you doing here?"

"I should think it rather obvious."

"Oh." Darin looked at the food; the smell of it was over-
powering. Cheese, meat—and fruit! He took a step toward it,
caught himself, and walked over to the bed.

He looked at the clothing laid out there with some suspicion.
The tunic—it was really more of a blouse—was made of a soft,
fine fabric, with a collar and smallish buttons. The pants were

of more durable material, but these, too, were soft and finely made.

"Are they not to your liking?"

*Not to my liking? What's going on?* He touched the wet sleeve of the robe he still wore.

In a more serious voice, Gervin said, "The robe is yours to keep. You are the only one who has any right to it. I've not come to offer you an exchange; the clothing was ordered by the lord."

Darin relaxed. Quickly, with his back turned to the slave-master who showed no sign of leaving, he removed his robe and slid into the dry set of clothing. He looked up once at Gervin, who chuckled.

"I've already eaten. The food is entirely yours. Here, take the stool—once you've dulled the edge of your hunger, you're going to be uncomfortable standing. I can sit on the bed."

Darin began to eat, and Gervin walked over to the bed. He did not sit immediately, but rather gathered up the initiate's robe. With infinite care he spread it out, his fingers lingering longest on the silver circle around the back. He turned to look at Darin and pursed his lips slightly.

"Chew before you swallow or you'll make yourself sick."

Darin blushed without returning Gervin's glance, but did as he was told.

*You're still so young,* Gervin thought, watching. *You seem too . . . fragile to bear the burden you've accepted.* He cut his musing short; youth in the Empire meant little, except possibly an early death. *It was not always so. Ah, I grow too old and weak for this.* He ran his fingers along the edge of his chin.

Sometime soon, he would meet Lady Death and answer for his life, and in return he would demand his own answers, his own justice. He dreaded that confrontation, and longed for it, for an end to the task he had chosen.

Darin ate everything. At any other time this would have amused Gervin; now it merely signaled an end to his waiting. As soon as the youth had pushed the last plate away, Gervin knelt in front of him, head bowed.

It was the last thing that Darin expected.

"Priest of Lernan," he whispered. It was the first time he had used God's name in over thirty years. He drew his hands together to still their shaking.

Darin stared at the slavemaster in confusion. Without thinking, his fingers flew to his staff. "Gervin, what are you doing?"

"Priest of Lernan," he repeated, bowing his head, "I, who am not worthy, come before you. Hear me."

"Gervin—I'm not—"

But it came to him, even as he began to deny it, that he was. The robes, the blooding, the joining at the well, all of these things made him undeniably what Gervin had called him. He looked at the top of Gervin's gray head and wondered what comfort he could possibly give to the man; he himself was an adult of only two days, and Gervin had seen much more of life than he.

He had dreamed away years of his childhood wishing for the day that he would be called upon as priest—he could never have imagined that it would be here, in a cold stone room, with the brand of slavery upon his forearm.

The staff in his hand began to tingle. He tried to recall the rituals of the initiates; some of the words drifted back to him, but they felt stilted, too formal for him to utter. He drew his shoulders back, lifted his head, and straightened the worry from his face in an attempt to look more dignified. It didn't help; it only made him feel ridiculous.

*Well, I might be a priest of Lernan, but I'm still just Darin of Culverne.* His scarred hand reached out to touch Gervin's forehead. The man looked up.

"Gervin, please don't kneel like that." Gervin did not move, and Darin continued. "I don't know where you're from, but I know that you recognize the robes. Things are different now." He waved an arm around the room. "They have to be. And I don't know all the formal stuff."

Gervin rose and sat stiffly on the bed.

"I'm Darin," Darin said. He had to look up to meet Gervin's distant eyes. "I might have been a proper priest before—" If he had paid attention to the Grandmother, he thought. "But now I'm just me."

Gervin shook his head. "No other person could do what you did. You freed the Gifting. You cleansed the Bright Heart's blood."

"How do you know about the Gifting?"

In a voice both soft and far away, he replied, "I know of it."

"Well, you're wrong about one thing. It didn't have to be me."

It was plain that Gervin did not believe him. Inexplicably, the staff grew warmer. Surprised, Darin looked down at it and saw a soft green glow around its edges. He looked up at Gervin quickly, but the older man apparently did not notice. His eyes were on Darin's face alone, the yearned-for old ways writ clearly there.

With a weary sigh, Darin decided to try. "I am the patriarch of the line of Bethany of Culverne." His voice was very quiet. "Do you come seeking the guidance of Lernan?"

"No, holiness."

Darin cringed. "Do you come seeking His aid?"

"No, holiness."

"What, then, do you seek for?"

"His comfort, holiness. His forgiveness." Gervin's voice had never been so quiet; nor had it been so raw.

Darin's memories grew hazy; he opened his mouth to try, again, to cast off Gervin's image of priesthood. To his great surprise, he found himself saying, "If you are a follower of Lernan, what need have you of His forgiveness?" He tried to close his mouth and cut off the words. He couldn't.

In a broken voice, Gervin said, "I am no longer a follower of Lernan."

"Then why do you seek His help?" Darin tried to stand, but his legs wouldn't respond. His mouth continued to move, but the words were not his own. The harsh edge of them frightened him.

It had that effect on Gervin as well. Darin saw the sudden flood of hopelessness in the older man and knew then that even his expression was not his own.

Gervin covered his face with his hands. "I seek His comfort because I have lived too long without it. I seek His forgiveness for the choices I have had to make."

"Continue." Darin heard himself speak that cold, cold word.

"I was not always the slavemaster. I did not always work for the lord."

"Do not call him that in my presence." Darin had not known his voice could be so chill. He had never wanted it to be.

Gervin nodded shakily. "As you command, holiness. At one time, in my youth, I served the lines."

"You are not of the lines." It was not a question.

"No. I was there when the Servants of the Enemy came; the line that I served fell before them. I was younger, then. I could do nothing. They knew I was not of the lines, and I became a slave."

Darin wanted to reach out. He knew this story well; he had lived it. But his hands continued to grip the staff in silence.

"I was brought early into the household of the—of the master. I did my best to keep to the ways of Lernan in my captivity." He took a deep breath.

*No! Do not make me say that!* Darin screamed it silently. He could see the glow of the staff from the corner of one eye; it had grown into a brilliant halo. His protest meant nothing. The words went on.

"The dark ceremonies are no part of His way." Each word was a sharp, verbal stiletto. Gervin shuddered and covered his face with his hands.

"Holiness—I worked for years trying to preserve the ways." He brought his voice under control and let his hands fall away from his face. It was a pale mask; it seemed ancient and fragile. "And then the lord—the master—took note of me. He came to me, offered me a choice." Hands began to shake. "He would give me control of the castle and the lands, if I would serve him completely.

"I refused at first, holiness. I told him I would rather die." Gervin began to rock gently backward and forward. "I was younger then.

"But he believed that. He left me, and in the days and months to follow, he made clear what a house could be if run by—other people. The Empire has many evils, and he made sure that I saw all.

"And he came to me again and told me that I could control the fate of his slaves. I could make their lives as easy as possible in the Empire. All that I had to do in return was to pledge my loyalty to him, to serve him without question.

"I don't know why he chose me." Gervin's voice grew bitter. "Perhaps he enjoys the death of spirit more than the death of flesh. Part of me died when I made my pledge."

Darin saw Gervin with new eyes. The old man's pain at the blooding of the knife, the hope at the robes of the Circle, the fatigue and silence that accompanied him everywhere.

*Could I have done it?* Darin thought. *Could I have been slave-master and killed at the call of a priest of the Enemy, in order to save other lives?* He didn't know.

But words that were still not his own started to come.

*No! Whatever you are, you have no right to make this decision for me!* He struggled to stop the flow of words, his fear for himself replaced by his fear for Gervin. His mouth began to close, but sweat beaded his brow at the effort.

A voice, dry as ash, spoke for the first time.

*Why do you stop me, Initiate?*

Darin started in surprise. His mouth fell open and started to move before he regained control of it.

*I can't judge him. If you want to do it, find someone else to control.*

He could feel the white heat of an anger that was not his own. *I am the caretaker of the Line Culverne; I am the guidance that keeps the way clear. You know nothing of the way if you think to stop me. You are young; your training was never completed.*

*I am Darin, last of the line you guide. Control or compulsion is not the way of Lernan.* His mouth snapped shut.

Wind crept through the ash of the voice. It was silent, as if considering something. When it came again, it was cooler. *Then let me guide you, as I have done in the past for the patriarchs and matriarchs of your line.*

*I will not let you judge this man. He didn't come to you.*

Something lashed out at his mind, and his body stiffened in pain.

*You wish to forgive one who has performed the dark cere-monies of the Enemy? You wish to accept one who has taken the lifeblood of the unwilling? I will not accept this sacrilege!*

Darin looked at Gervin's clenched hands. Those hands had held the blooded knife. They were shaking now, as they had done that night.

*Who are you to judge? Don't you understand what he's say-ing? Can't you see why he had to make the choice he did?* For Darin finally understood why the slaves of House Darclan were different, a little more open, a little more friendly. And he un-derstood, at last, that he might claim friendship from the slaves, without paying the high price that Lord Vellen had demanded.

*I am the voice of Bethany of Culverne, planted here in case such a perversion should arise from the dilution of the line's blood. I know the way—let this man be damned to Darkness by his own actions!*

*You are not Bethany of Culverne!* But doubt crept into Darin and his lips flew open.

"Holiness, does something trouble you?"

"Yesssss—" Darin clamped his mouth shut. He forced his gaze to fall downward to the hand that held the staff. He could feel the unnatural heat of the wood against the tight circle of his palm and fingers.

*You are a traitor to the Circle! Follow the way, or be cast out!*

Darin slowly raised his head to meet Gervin's eyes. He

flinched at what was in them, the pity in the action his own. Gritting his teeth, he began to pry his fingers free from the staff. Grimly, he spoke to the voice in his mind.

*If I'm to be cast out, then I will be. But somehow I don't think I will.*

*If you offer him your aid, you are not of the Bright Heart.*

*I carried the blooded knife.* His thoughts were sharp and edged. *I knew what he was doing. I didn't want to accept it, but I did. I played my part in the darkness. I, too, have sinned against Lernan. I was not condemned.*

Again the voice grew cooler, shedding the heat of its anger. *You have been cleansed by the blood of Lernan. Lernan accepted you.*

Two fingers came free.

*Yes. He accepted me. You wouldn't have.*

Another finger gave way.

*You are of the line—the last of it. You acted without the wisdom of experience. Your part in the ceremony can be overlooked.*

A fourth finger's grip loosened. Only Darin's thumb remained attached to the staff.

*No. I acted on what I knew. And Gervin, on what he knew. I've seen some of the evils he spoke of, and I know the pain he tried to spare people. If another had been slavemaster, many would still have died at the lord's command.* The thumb began to tremble.

*If you throw me away, Initiate, you will be throwing away the power of the founder. How will you battle Malthan and his Servants without me?*

*I don't know. I don't care.* But he did. He teetered on the brink of indecision as the voice continued.

*But you do. You know that the patriarch or matriarch of your line had, in legend, more power than the initiates. Where do you think that power came from? It was mine. I will give it to you if you will follow the way.* In a harder voice it said, *Dismiss this man. He is your enemy. If you forgive him, will you not find excuse to forgive any sin? Will you not excuse any number of murders? Think of the one who died at his hands. Did that life have any choice? Did that life go willingly? Who is left to avenge that death?*

His fingers began to curl around the staff again. *Stop it!*

*Then you condone the murder.*

*No! No, I don't!*

*Give me a voice, Initiate. I will deal with this.*

Darin looked at Gervin. The silence of Darin's battle with the voice had withered any hope that remained. He looked years older, his face shadowed by pain and guilt. His eyes glimmered with firelight as he rose and bowed stiffly.

"I understand, holiness. I shall not trouble you further."

*Do not be weak, Initiate. Our war does not allow for weakness.* The staff flared up; a column of white fire touched the ceiling. Darin felt a giddy rush of warmth take his body. He tingled with the aftermath of the blast. *You can call the fire if you like. Just give me a voice.*

Gervin stopped walking, his face pale, and Darin knew that he could finally see the staff's power.

"Is my death required?" He sounded as if he had already met it; his voice, hollow and flat, struck Darin as painfully as the staff had done earlier. Gervin stood, waiting, some faint hint of pride encircled by the shroud of his eyes.

*Well?* The tingling sensation stopped abruptly, and Darin bit his lip at the loss of it; the room seemed suddenly chill and empty. He shivered.

*My voice. Let me do what must be done.*

"Holiness?"

With a cry, Darin threw the staff away. It slammed into the wall and clattered onto the stone floor. He turned to the waiting Gervin and reached out to touch the man's shoulders.

"No," he said, his voice unsteady. "No, Gervin. You blooded the knife, but I carried it. We're caught in a web of choices that are all evil. Think: If our lord had chosen a typical slavemaster, how many more would have died? How many would have wished for death? I know it—I still have the scars.

"You had the strength to choose death—I didn't. And for you, it would have been easier. If you've come for forgiveness, I forgive you. If you've come for comfort, take what small comfort you can. And if you've come for the blessing of Lernan, I bless you in His name." Darin's hands were shaking as Gervin reached up to clasp them.

"Holiness—"

"I'm no more holy than you. If you can't forgive yourself for your crimes, how can you forgive me? I knew what you were doing, and you knew I did."

Gervin pulled Darin's hands away, clenched them tightly, and let them go. He tilted his chin up, looking at something beyond.

''You are holy to me.'' A trace of tears glinted in firelight. ''You are peace.''

Darin said nothing.

Gervin dropped to his knees and, grasping Darin's right hand, said only two words. ''Thank you.'' And in that, everything. He kissed Darin's adult scar, rose, and walked unsteadily out of the room.

When he had gone, and only then, Darin dropped onto the bed. The robe that Gervin had laid out so carefully was still damp, and he buried his face into its rough folds.

*Please,* he prayed silently. *Please let my choice be the right one. I'm not strong enough to have done anything else.* An unfamiliar ache cut deeply into him. He longed for the staff and the giddy warmth that a single flare of power had granted him. His hands trembled as he looked at where it lay, plain and cool, in the corner of the room he'd thrown it into. He had made his choice; he intended to be strong enough to abide by it.

*You will be, Initiate. The line still runs true.* The voice returned to him. Bewildered, he looked at his hands. They were still empty.

*Yes. By your choice, I am not at your side.* Something was different; the tone of the voice had changed. It was full and soft; instead of ashes, it stirred up memories of something more solid. Culverne. Home.

*I am sorry for trying you so harshly; these are harsh times and I must know that you will withstand the taint of them. It is easy to judge poorly; it is easy to cast blame. You chose to do neither. Take me up, Patriarch. Pick me up if you choose it. I will never again subject you to such cruelty.*

''This was a *test*?''

*Another one, yes. And this, like the other, you have passed.*

''This isn't just a trick, is it?'' The question was halfhearted; already he found himself rising from the bed.

*No, no more tricks. You have cast aside the mantle of power for that of compassion. I will serve you, as you serve Lernan. I may question you in the future; I may advise you or try to guide you with the experience of others of the Line Culverne—but I will never again force your choice.*

Darin's hand curled around the staff. It was cool. He looked at it for a moment before drawing it to his chest. He felt something akin to warmth deep within him.

*If it helps, Darin, know this: All of your predecessors have been tried in this way, and all have succeeded. The line holds true.*

# chapter
# thirteen

*The soft glow of night light brushed through the curtained study.*
Lord Darclan sat with his back to the window, fingers leafing
idly through an open book. He found the light uncomfortable,
but did not rise to close the curtains; let the light be, for this one
night. The covers of the book closed soundlessly, and he pushed
it to one side—it was the past. It was forgotten.

Sara was whole, she was now, she had smiled upon seeing
him. An echo of that smile played upon his shadowed lips. She
had smiled, new again, his spell crushing the memories that
might separate them.

He frowned. That same spell, that same suppression of her
experience and knowledge, had almost cost her life at the hands
of the guardian. He toyed with the idea of allowing her some of
her memory, but never seriously. As it was, was she not happier?
Was her life not now free of the pain that had previously plagued
her so? If she had some portion of her memory, would she not
soon after have all? Yes.

But the risk . . . Never mind it.

*I have won.*

But what of later? He could feel the power that stirred within
the walls of the castle; it slept because Darin slept, but it would
rise with dawn—a newly born thing, and a dangerous one.

*Even Sargoth did not know what became of the voice of Bethany of Culverne. And now, now I do. But how? How did it come
to be here?*

*I did not know the child could call the fire.* He pushed his
chair away from the desk and stood. The white-fire of the
Lernari burned in his castle; it was the strongest of their
magics. Darin's blood alone was not strong enough to contain
it—but Bethany's . . .

He had felt it; the ice of its touch through his spine still burned faintly. He picked up the book that lay on his desk and walked over to the shelves along the wall. It was dark, but he had no difficulty returning it to its place.

An image of Darin's face formed before him, stirring the barest hint of something he would not name. He smiled, this time a grim, bitter smile. There was strength in the child, and an odd sort of bravery that lay behind his mask of fear and weakness. He had the naïveté of youth about him, and the naïveté of trust; his death, when it came, would be a quick thing, if not a painless one.

*The fire. I did not know he could call the fire.*

He shrugged, a brief, economical gesture, a human habit. If he had known, it would have made no difference. What did it matter if the Line Culverne rose again for a few days more? What harm could it do, carried as it was upon the shoulders of a young boy?

His fingers curved tensely inward and then relaxed.

He would not kill the boy.

Yet that meant no clean break, no new beginning. The lines had always been the point of contention that could not be laid to rest.

He walked back to his desk, resumed his seat, and let his eyes absorb the darkness. Too much had happened in the days since Sara's awakening, and much of it unforeseen. He did not appreciate the unforeseen; it robbed him of the control he valued so highly.

*The fire.*

So close, he could feel it without searching. Without searching, the half blooded would not. But if they did . . . Ah, the old dangers.

*Vellen.*

His fingers curled inward again, but he was slower to relax them. Almost casually, his hands made a pass through the air. His eyes grew silver in the blackness, a small crackle of dangerous light. He repeated the gesture, more sharply and elegantly.

*Perhaps,* he thought, *it is time.*

But he hesitated, knowing well that the cost of the spell he contemplated would be unavoidably high. His hands stopped, falling to rest on the desk.

*Alariel. Lady. Where did you wander? What did you see beyond the veil that made such a taint of your end?*

Many times in the past century, he had toyed with the spell, learned from Sargoth's studies. But the face of the Lady of El- liath had always had this effect: It stopped him from moving further. Her resignation chilled him more than her fire might once have.

Until now.

Too much had happened. What hope of control had he, if he had no knowledge?

He called forth an image of Sara's face. For her sake, he was willing to pierce the veil that separated the present from the future; for her life he was willing to pay the cost that had doomed the Lady of Elliath.

*Let me see, now, what the future holds.*

His lips opened on soundless words, over and over again in an endless litany. By morning, the future was no clearer, but the path to sight had been opened to him, a journey for another night.


Darin waited quietly in the sitting room outside of Lord Dar- clan's study. He wore the fine clothing that the lord had ordered for him somewhat uncomfortably. He also carried the staff.

After a few minutes, Gervin emerged. He looked much better for the night's sleep; the dark circles under his eyes had been completely erased. Darin thought he could detect a restless en- ergy in the older man that had not been there before. His step was brisk and formal as he walked over to Darin and bowed.

"Lord Darclan will see you now."

Darin nodded and rose. He paused once outside the closed door, gripped his staff more firmly, and entered in. The study still evoked a tremor of fear.

Lord Darclan looked up when he entered, and set aside a small sheaf of papers. "I hope I have not kept you waiting long."

Darin looked at his feet, fully aware that he had overslept the dawn by a good three hours.

"No, lord," he replied. "I just arrived."

"Good. If it would please you to do so, you may sit." He gestured at the chair in front of the desk.

Darin took the seat quietly. He didn't know why Lord Darclan had summoned him, and habit kept him wary.

But Lord Darclan was not entirely certain as to the reason for the summons either. He fixed both boy and staff with the dark- ness of his eyes before shifting restlessly in his seat.

"Might I remind you, Darin, that I have asked you to refrain from called me lord?" He smiled then, a wintry, edged expression. "It is a force of habit you would be better without."

"What should I call you instead?"

The question confused Lord Darclan, and his smile became fixed and hard. "Enemy, perhaps. Or peer. It matters little." He knew the boy could use neither.

"I hope—I hope not to have to use the first."

"Or the second?" He shrugged. "And I had hoped as well." *Lady, Lady.* "Such is the whim of fate; hope is fragile and easily crushed." He looked at the boy seated so carefully in front of him. Yes, there was strength in that small form, strength in the eyes that returned his regard so openly. The child who had lived in the shadow of his fear was gone; the lord found himself regretting the absence with a bittersweet pleasure.

"But it isn't easily killed." Darin thought of Gervin.

"In men, perhaps, and in the young." Darclan's fingers rose to form their familiar steeple. Changing the subject, he said, "I have not had a proper chance to congratulate you on your victory, Darin. Let me correct that oversight; you have survived much in the past few nights, and you have my gratitude for all that you have accomplished." He meant each word, and each for a moment was unalloyed by darkness.

"Thank you, lord." Darin looked down at the staff of Culverne; to his dismay he could see the bright green halo that had grown to surround it.

Lord Darclan saw it as well; his body tensed slightly, although he betrayed none of this tension. He remained still, his eyes bitter upon Darin.

*Is this what I seek by my summons, Darin? Are victory and peace so alien to me?*

He could never have anticipated what happened next, for Darin, with a pained but determined expression, set the staff to one side of the chair, withdrawing his fingers slowly.

"My lord." He bowed his head softly.

"Why did you set it aside?"

Darin did not reply. Instead, he pulled his hands up and clutched them firmly together in front of his chest. He glanced once at the staff, but made no move toward it.

"Darin, why did you set it aside?"

"I don't want to be your enemy," he said quietly. "I don't think we have to be. We both love the same things, or some of the same, anyway."

The lord's eyes closed tightly.

"Darin, child." Darclan's voice was slow, careful. "Do you not know who I am?" His fingers were white as they pressed together beneath the line of his jaw.

"A priest." Darin whispered, looked down at his hands. "A priest of the—the Enemy."

They watched each other for a few minutes, wholly focused but unable to speak. Young eyes clashed with old. Darin broke away first.

With stark, beautiful simplicity, he spoke. His voice was a whisper, but it was steady. "I trust you, lord."

His words fell into silence, each one striking Darclan forcefully. He began to laugh, and the laughter, like Darin's words, was wholly strange. "You trust me." He laughed again, in dark, rich despair. "You trust *me*!"

The staff of Culverne flared white and hot. Darclan could see Darin's brow crease momentarily. The white-fire was coming. Darclan felt sure of it. The last of his laughter faded into a grim smile. He watched with mirthless satisfaction as Darin bent to retrieve the fallen symbol of his office.

And once again, the child did the unthinkable, the unforeseeable. He rose, staff in hand, and walked over to the door. It opened, and he left, only to return a few seconds later. Without the staff. He found his way to the chair he had occupied and sat, unarmed. He looked oddly the stronger for it.

Darclan stared at him.

"Child, you do not know what you are doing."

"Maybe not. But I know that *I'm* doing it." His voice was steady.

"Do you realize that you have deprived yourself of the only weapon in your possession that might possibly stop me?" His voice was harsh. He rose, suddenly, his movement overturning his chair. He began to walk slowly around the desk. "I could kill you. Now. You would stand no chance." He moved with feline grace, his eyes unblinking.

Darin's lips tightened.

"You should have listened to the voice of Bethany. Yes, I recognize the staff; it is older and wiser than you. It knows me for what I am; it knows that we are enemies." He was close enough to touch Darin now; his hands moved smoothly and came to rest under the boy's upturned chin. "It knows, better than you, all that I am capable of." His fingers tightened suddenly. Darin closed his eyes but made no attempt to wrest his neck from Darclan's painful grip.

"No, lord." His voice was faint but sure. "It can't know what I know."

Darclan's fingers bit into the pale skin of the boy; small beads of blood began to well up beneath his nails. He smiled, a cold, dark smile.

"And what do you know?"

Wearily, Darin answered as if he had had this discussion many times. "That you love Sara."

The smile died.

"If you can love her, you can love. If you can love, you can be touched by the Light of God, even if you are blooded by the Enemy."

"It may be that you have deceived yourself. Self-deception is the art that men learn first." But his fingers were suddenly numb. Unable to maintain his grip on the boy, he drew away and walked over to the window. Only the breadth of his back faced Darin.

Darin watched him. The marks that the lord had left stung, but he said nothing.

"Yes. Yes, I love her." The voice was suddenly ancient. Lord Darclan turned slowly, but did not look at Darin. "You trust me," he said to the wall, to the past, to things that Darin could never see. "I thought that might change. In truth, you are cruel, Priest of Lernan." Shaky hands found their way to the desk top. Lord Darclan braced himself against it. "Nor are you the first to be so foolish. You and one other, in all of time."

His head came up, and this time Darin did move, thrusting back into his chair.

The lord's eyes were red—a deep, dark, red, threaded through with blackness.

*I should have known better than to choose you, child. I should never have tried to find one so like her. And yet, you were different. Smaller, more frightened. More mortal.*

But as always, he pushed regret away—the deed was done; the consequences, complex and somehow painful, would be endured as they had been endured before.

"Darin." His voice was changing, deepening. The boy's trust hurt him somehow. It was the Bright Heart's legacy, the Bright Heart's taint. It was the same pain that Sara always caused.

And the same twisted pleasure.

He knew now why he had summoned the boy, the initiate, the priest. It was as close as he had come in hundreds of years to this feeling—for Sara, newly wakened, had not yet come to trust him so.

And he missed it.

But the boy's trust was given to a priest of Malthan. He bowed his head, then, and took the final step.

He summoned the darkness. It came, swirling around his human form and robbing it of its semblance of life. The room went chill. He shivered as he raised his head again, knowing that Darin's eyes could not pierce all of his shadow.

"Can you trust me, Darin?" he whispered.

Darin sat frozen. *Death*, he thought, as he had thought one night so long ago. *Death walks here.*

For the Lord's power was no longer veiled, and Darin's blood responded to its revealed strength. He knew the Lord now. He knew the Servant who had presided over the death of all Culverne. With a cry of fear, he bolted for the door.

The shadow made no move as he flung it open and scrambled for the staff that was his office.

*So.* Stefanos stood, withdrawing his hands from the desk. He felt relieved as the white-fire of Bethany flared like a clarion call. But he felt pain, too.

Darin turned, the staff forming a cross with his body.

"This," Stefanos said, "is all that I am. Do you remember me now, little Priest?"

The staff came up as the First of Malthan began to walk.

*Yes. Let us have an end.*

Tears began to fall from Darin's mortal eyes. Tears that the heritage of the Sundered could never allow to fall.

"You," Darin said. The staff was shaking.

"Yes."

*Yes. I am Stefanos, First of the Sundered. I carry the Darkness that is your line's death.* He raised his arm, his eyes flashing.

The staff faltered. Darin's eyes closed, and the tears grew stronger. And then he said one word, as if to himself.

"Sara."

Stefanos stopped. He knew that Darin spoke not to him, but to one long dead. He also knew that he would not kill the boy. His arm fell to his side, and the shadows slipped away. Cloaked beneath the façade of Lord Darclan, master of the house, he stepped back.

Darin watched in the numbness of shock. The staff, though not raised to strike, still surrounded him with a nimbus of green light so pale it was almost white. He was shaking, but stood unshakeable as he watched the transformation.

"So," Lord Darclan said softly. "You know." He wanted to order the boy to leave, but refrained, his eyes caught and held by the patterns of a light inimical to his nature. Arrested, he let the red flare of his eyes gutter, and wondered if the boy—if any Lernari—could see in the shadow what he saw in the light.

He smiled, bitter. For he understood, through this meeting, the error he had made. Sara's light, Sara's love—it was not separate from the blood that ran through her.

"You aren't human," Darin began.

"No."

"Not even half-blood."

"No."

"You killed my line."

"All but you."

There was silence again. Silence in which Darin's pain filtered out and danced in confusion around Stefanos' senses.

"And now?"

*Now?* Ah, the question. "I do not know." He stepped forward, reached out to touch Darin's shoulder. "I might ask the same of you."

Darin didn't move away. Instead, he shook his head. "The lady?"

"She is safe." Stefanos reached out with his other arm. Darin was caught in the circle he had formed, although neither knew why.

It was hard for Stefanos, hard to stand in the presence of something so fragile without breaking it. Centuries had done nothing to alleviate the dichotomies that Sara had formed. But turning away was hard as well. He understood the nature of fragility intimately; it was not the life that was before him, but something more complicated.

"Why?" Darin said, his voice closer and muffled. "Why don't you blood the stones?"

Lord Darclan smiled, although the boy could not see it. "Why?" he said softly. He shook his head. "Because she always hated the blooding."

"Why doesn't she remember?" Darin murmured, his voice already fading.

But this question Lord Darclan would not answer.

"Who is she?" The question was so quiet that none but a Servant would have caught it.

"Elliath," the lord whispered. "Elliath, as you are Culverne."

He felt Darin stiffen, heard the intake of the boy's breath.

*And perhaps it is time,* Stefanos thought, *that she remember this.* There was no resignation in the words.

Darin did not ask why Lord Darclan held him; Darclan did not ask why Darin allowed it. The silence gave them the tenuous peace that they needed for the moment.


"It's very frustrating."

"I realize that, lady. But you should not tax yourself so; the memories will return in time." He watched the stiffness of her shoulders give way for a moment as she stared out of the window. Daylight robbed him of the reflection of her face in the glass. He stood near her; the tremor in her voice drew him.

"It's just that I can almost remember—I can feel everything on the periphery just waiting for me to wake up."

Lord Darclan nodded, although Sara could not see him. He knew how she felt; knew it, but could not stop it. The cursed blood of the Enemy had revived her and weakened his bindings in the process.

And they should have held. They were strong; much blood and magic had formed their base. But all of his dealings with Sara were tainted by his weakness for her; why should this be different?

"And I don't understand what I'm doing here. None of this feels right to me, no matter what you've said, what Darin's said."

He shook his head; realized that he had not been listening. "Pardon?"

"I feel as if I should be somewhere else." She turned to face him then. Her face was pale and strained, her eyelashes matted with tears that she had not cared to share with him. "Something's happened; I know it—I feel it here. I'm needed."

Lord Darclan cursed silently. "Yes, lady. I need you."

"You don't have to humor me, lord. I'm in better shape than that." She bit her lip. "I just feel . . ."

"Trapped, Sara?" He reached out to touch her face, and felt the wetness of her colorless cheeks beneath his fingers. Tears he remembered—shaking his head, he smiled, willing her to smile in return.

She did, but it was an echo, repetition without substance.

"Lady, this mood is due to your exhaustion. If you rest now, on the morrow you will be better."

"I'm tired," she whispered, "of not knowing."

"This is natural. Rest. It will help."

He started to turn, but she grabbed both of his hands. "Why am I here? What was I doing?" There was a wild quality to the words; her hands trembled as they pressed into his.

He said nothing.

She was different with Darin, relaxed. He found that he did not resent this as he once might have; each man reaps what he sows.

If she had not held his hands so tightly, he would have withdrawn. But she did, and instead he found himself following a path familiar and painful—one that he had hoped could wait until she was somehow stronger. He drew her toward him, his pull firm but gentle. Her hands slid away from his and, after a moment, settled around his stiff back.

Beginning is always awkward. There was tension in both of them; undefined, unnamed. He stroked her hair and face precisely, rhythmically. They were caught in a halo of uncomfortable silence; it settled round them, a suffocating, invisible mist.

Sara raised her head; her chin was tilted at an angle both defiant and vulnerable. Light glimmered in her eyes—light and a distorted reflection of the man she gazed at. He saw himself then, visible and unknown.

He caught her chin between his fingers. It trembled as her lips parted.

"Say nothing, Sara." With just the slightest hesitation, he bent down. He stopped for long enough to realize that he stood upon a precipice. He could taste a trace of the breath that met his mouth before he made a choice that was no choice. His lips met hers, briefly and fiercely.

Pulling back was the most difficult thing he had done in years. He pushed her away more roughly than he had intended, and found, to his surprise, that the trembling he felt was not Sara's alone. He turned sharply, his eyes on the carpet.

"Don't go." Sara's words put up a wall in front of the closed door. "Please. I have to know . . ."

Without turning, he said, "I cannot stay, lady. Please forgive me for any liberties I have taken."

"No, please."

He shook his head. "You do not know what you ask, lady. Sleep. I will return in the morning."

He heard the rustle of clothing. Behind, her voice drew closer. "Please turn around." From the corner of his eye he could see the small hand that touched his shoulder, fluttering there. He shrugged it off brusquely and reached for the handle of the door.

Her hand stopped him; her fingers curled around his.

"Sara—"

He found himself turning. Something in her eyes caused him to flinch; they were both bright and dark, the light and the depth of them compelling.

"Why did you—do that?"

"Sara . . ." All explanation was lost, as absent as the will that had carried him to the door.

She stood perfectly still, his hand in hers, an inch away from his body. Her hair fell about her shoulders and around the line of her neck; a few strands obscured the question in her eyes.

"We've been here before, haven't we?" The words were soft, dim echoes. Her lips hardly moved at all. He could just catch the whisper of her voice. He pulled her hand away from his, and leaning forward, cupped her face in his palms. His thumbs hovered in the air before her moving lips.

"Yes."

She began to speak more quickly. "And you were here, at least once. You wore black, I don't remember what, just that it was black. And cool."

"Yes." He caught her eyes as they began to dart around the room—caught and held them.

She swallowed. "And I was with you here, and I was wearing . . ."

"Yes." His thumbs pressed firmly against her open lips, stilling her words. "And you were afraid." His grip on her face tightened perceptibly. The green glaze of her eyes burned.

"I—"

"Are you afraid of me now, Sara?"

"No—"

"No?" His lips brushed against hers. He smiled thinly.

"Yes, then!" She tried to wrench herself free; he stopped her with a slow, soft kiss. Her breath was quick and short and sweet.

"Shall I leave, Sara?"

"I don't know! I don't know who you are. I don't remember you at all except for this one—"

He kissed her again, like the first kiss, briefly and fiercely, drawing her to him.

"Do you want me to leave?" His voice was harsh.

"I—"

He knew that she was confused. He was an unknown benefactor; he was dark and somehow forbidding; he was alone with her, and she wanted him without knowing why or how she could feel so about someone she hardly knew. He could see all of these thoughts as they circled about the chaos of her mind.

And it no longer mattered. Yes, he wanted her answer, yes, he wanted her trust, and yes, he wanted her acknowledgment of the desire that lay between them. But more than that, more than any other thing, he wanted her.

She started to speak, but he no longer wanted words from her. He slid one arm around her waist, the other around her neck, and gave himself over to the feel of her mouth, the pulse of her throat, the delicate, insistent touch of her hands upon his back, caught between pulling and pushing.


There.

A flicker of light, hesitant and faint; no eyes but his could catch it. Hers, already closing, did not.

He watched, tense, in the silence. He watched it curl around the slight tilt of her lips as if it were a child's hands, watched it move gently outward, seeking. Light. Her light.

It touched him, an echo of the past, a whisper of tomorrow. For this, four centuries had passed. He felt its oddness, its warmth, and knew again that memory alone was not the truth, but a reflection of it.

Only when it was gone did he move, encircling her shoulders gently in his arms.

And then, in darkness, peace.

Perhaps he had been wrong; perhaps her memories were not needed at all. Not when presence alone could begin to evoke the light that lay dormant.

He rested his chin against the top of her head and let his mind wander as he held her. Even now it was hard to believe that they were together. She had fallen asleep so quickly; any questions that she might have asked would have to wait until morning.

Or longer. He shifted.

The past was the past. Let it lie dead; let it remain buried. Yet even that . . .

He knew that this night was not a new thing—it was a shadow, a trace of all that had been before. His eyes grew hard and gray; the reflection of Sara dimmed into clouds as he concentrated. *Let something new be born*, he thought, *something strong enough to defy our history*. He caught the strands of her dreams and memories as they rolled together, binding them fast.

He smiled as he worked; the smell and the feel of her lingered in the air around him. His eyes slowly darkened; blackness returned to them, and his lids fell shut as a deep satisfaction began to build. His fingers traced the edges of Sara's eyes, her nose, her mouth. She smiled into his hand, and one word shattered his peace as she drifted deeper into the realm of sleep.

"Darkling . . ."

And he accepted, then, what he had been unwilling to accept during their long separation: There was nothing he could do to change her mind or alter her memory—the mark of the past was a scar beyond his healing. It was only a matter of time—time was always his enemy—until she broke his binding; the seed of all that had happened grew in her, eluding his control.

He held her tightly.

There was so little time, and he wanted all of it.

Afterward, in the silence of his study, he recommenced the weaving of a different spell, the one that would give him the sight he wanted. Gesturing and murmuring, he threw off the shackles of the *now* that he inhabited and began to push himself forward. He could see the veil of years just ahead of him, a shifting gray wall. It rolled back like mist as he advanced.

*Just a little longer.* Images coalesced from the shadows, flitting by too quickly to be identified. He paused to catch one, and saw Sara's dirt-stained face as she reached out to touch—

The veil fell forward again before he could completely grasp the image. He cursed softly.

Time. Time. Time. Could he take it, he would have his answers, but the spell would hold him while the mortal years passed. This, this he could not afford.

The dawn had come.

# chapter
# fourteen

*Sara woke to a knock at her door. She was alone; the bed showed no trace of Lord Darclan's passing.* She frowned and then shook her head; she wasn't really surprised.

The knock came again, and she turned to face the door as it opened. She smiled and relaxed as Darin's head peered around the door.

"It is breakfast already?"

"Uh—not exactly."

" 'Not exactly'?"

"It's midday, lady. The lord said you were to sleep."

"Oh." She looked mildly sheepish.

Darin walked over to the window and drew the curtains back. She hadn't recalled closing them, but shrugged and stood as sunlight poured into the room.

The warmth and light of the day caught her by surprise. Sleep and hunger forgotten, she rose and walked over to the large window. "It's beautiful outside." Her tone was wistful and far away.

"It is, isn't it?" Darin smiled as she came to stand beside him. More carefully, he said, "Lord Darclan gave orders for lunch to be packed, if you want to eat out."

"Packed?" she said, confused. "Do you mean a picnic lunch?"

He nodded.

"Yes!"

"I'll wait outside—unless you need help dressing."

She shook her head and almost danced over to the closet. "I won't wear anything too elaborate. With my luck I'll just tear it or stain it." Her feet kept jumping. "I'll be out in just a moment."

As Sara stepped into the closet, Darin stepped out of the room. The hall was empty, and aside from the occasional shout that carried up the main stairs, quite quiet. He leaned against the wall, folding his arms around the staff of Culverne.

Sara looked better for the night's sleep. He wished, as he jerked his nodding head up, that he could say the same. Too many questions, unasked and unanswered, had plagued him during the previous evening, and try as he might to put them aside, he had gotten little sleep.

If Sara was of Elliath, why didn't she remember anything?

Because the lord did not wish her to. He knew it and sighed.

*If he loves the lady, Darin—and I will grant you the possibility—he is the first of all the Servants of the Enemy to be so blessed. What strange circumstance would allow this? And if those circumstances have existed, what strange emotion have they birthed? He is not mortal; he is of the Dark Heart's blood. Do not expect his actions to coincide with your understanding of love.*

*But should I tell her?*

*I cannot decide that for you, but it seems to me that you have little reason to hide what you know.*

*Except that Lord Darclan trusts me,* Darin thought. He kept that secret. He had not been forbidden to speak of the events of the past few nights, and he knew, without question, that Sara remembered none of them. But the lord's eyes—he could not bring himself to call him Servant—his voice, his posture when speaking or thinking of Sara—there was a trust implicit in them, a request, a hope. Hope for what?

*I'm not strong enough,* Darin thought with a sigh. *I think it will hurt him.*

*Hurt him? Darin, do you not know what evil he has caused in his time here?*

Darin closed his eyes; he felt colder than the stone his back rested against. *I think he wants her to love him back.*

*Love him without knowing him?*

*Not—not—I don't know.* He remembered the touch of the lord's shadow, the darkness that heralded the end of the lines; it had felt like the end of life, even though Darin knew he was safe. *Maybe he's changed; maybe he'll change when she returns what he feels.*

The staff was oddly silent for a few moments, and then the breath of a mental sigh crept forward; a musky, ancient breath. *Child, what hope of change is worth the present Empire?*

Darin did not answer, knowing that no answer was expected. *But I think you are wrong. The lady loves him yet.*

*What do you mean?*

Bethany did not answer, and the quality of her silence told Darin that she would not. When he pressed, she said, *We all have hope, and that hope exacts its steep price.*

She would say nothing else.

Frustrated, Darin gave a disguised snort and settled back against the wall. Some sound crept into the silence of the hall, a faint, muffled gasping. Listening more closely, he traced it back to its source.

It came from Sara's room.

He was halfway into the room before he thought of asking her permission to enter. He stopped moving and looked around. She was nowhere in sight. The sound was louder now; Darin identified it easily. Someone was weeping.

"Sara!"

He looked around in one quick, frantic circle, and the open door of the closet caught his attention. In the shadowed gloom of the long, narrow room he found her. She sat on her knees, back toward the door, head bent into hands that were covered with some sort of cloth.

He walked over to where she sat. She held an elaborate robe in her hands; the folds of its pale brown cloth draped themselves over her arms. Her face was buried into the fabric. It shook as she did.

He didn't know what to do. She was crying, curled tightly into herself in the darkness. But would she want him to notice? Would she want him to help? What could he do?

After a moment longer she stopped, the sound of her tears dying off into stillness.

*She knows I'm here.*

But she turned and looked through him, her eyes distant and unfocused. Whatever she saw beyond his back was imagination.

*Or memory,* Bethany's voice said, sadness tinging its clarity.

Her back trembled, then stiffened as she looked down at her hands. She spoke in a voice that was at once too young, too old, and too empty.

"There's too much blood." Her voice was stilted and unnatural. Nerveless hands began to fold the robe. "I never touched you. You could never have done this if I had ever touched you." She stopped folding and stared down at the robe for a long time.

Darin could see it; it was embroidered with a pattern that the shadows obscured. A wool, he thought, a finely spun fabric by the way it hung. As far as he could see it was unmarred by anything save Sara's tears. But she saw something there.

"I will never again believe that you can love." Her words were cold. She threw the robe weakly, and it lay, half folded, on the dark floor of the closet. She stood, wavering slightly, her eyes half-closed. The shadows seemed to reach up for her.

Her fall snapped Darin back to life; he ran the few feet to her in time to catch her in his arms. He braced himself, but her weight was more than he expected; he stumbled.

Her eyes fluttered open.

"Darin? What are you doing here?" Groggily she pulled away from his support and looked around in confusion.

"I heard you—" He stopped. "I thought you might need help."

She brushed her hands across her eyes and looked around the walls of the closet again. Darin looked as well. Row upon row of dusty, dark clothing—and none of it Sara's, judging by the lengths.

"I was looking for something. I think I thought it was important." She groped for the edge of that memory and then shook her head angrily. "I guess I must have gotten dizzy. But I—I don't understand where my clothing's gone. Do you know?"

Darin shook his head. "I'm sorry. I didn't think of it."

She smiled, barely. "If it's my room and my closet and I don't know, there isn't any reason you should have." Taking a deep breath, she withdrew from the shadow. The sun on her face was warm, but she felt chilled.

"I'll just lie down for a minute, while you bring clothes." The bed creaked beneath her as she curled up; her body was lost beneath covers.

Darin didn't leave at once. He watched her for a minute and then darted quickly back to the closet. His eyes lit upon the robe, and he scooped it up quickly.

Seeing it had upset her greatly; he wasn't going to take that chance again. He had to get it out of there, without her noticing. He crouched down and peered around the closet door. For just a moment, with the shadows protecting him, he felt like Renar.

He had not played at Renar for years. He froze, remembering. And then he smiled, but the smile didn't suit his face at all. He thought of Sara, straightened, and made a dash for the door.

"Darin?"

"Yes?"

"Don't tell him . . . that I was dizzy."

"I won't." The door was impossibly far away.

"Darin?"

He stopped, his back half-turned toward her.

"What are you carrying?"

"I—uh, it's just, uh, something that the lord, um, wanted cleaned."

"Oh."

A monosyllable had never sounded so welcome. He began to scuttle forward again.

Then he cringed as Sara spoke, an edge of curiosity in her voice. "What is it?"

"Just work clothing."

"Oh." Then, "Is it all right if I see what it is?"

Lying was not a thing that the Grandmother had ever approved of. He had done his best to learn the art, but without any help, he failed miserably.

He walked slowly over to her bed, still shunting the robe to one side. "It's just a robe, Sara."

She held out her arms; they were pale.

The robe passed from his hands as if it were a viper.

"Oh Darin!" Her eyes widened. "Do you know what this is?"

"No," he answered; best use truth when he could.

"I—I remember this!" Mouth wide, she drew it to her face and took a deep breath. "I remember it!" She gave a little laugh, so unlike the chill of her previous words that Darin's mouth half opened.

*If the lord could see you now,* Darin thought, as her eyes crinkled, *if he could see how happy you are with just a scrap of memory, he'd give them all back to you.* Then he thought of her shadowed form, bent and crying in the darkness.

She wrinkled her nose. "It does need cleaning. It smells like centuries of dust." Yet all the while she patted and smoothed at folds and wrinkles.

"I made this." Fingers brushed against the fabric, holding to embroidery as if it were an anchor. "I remember making it— this pattern was the hardest thing I've ever done!"

He didn't believe it.

"It took forever." She smiled. "Well, maybe not forever. But it felt like it. I blistered my hands. I remember." She looked down at her right palm; it was annoyingly smooth. "I remember the loom that held it. All old wood, but well oiled. It smelled like—like work does. And Eva. I remember her—sitting just to the right of me on the stool.'' She laughed softly. ''She wouldn't have high-backed chairs. Said it wasn't good for the back. I never thought so, but she knew her craft better than I.'' A tinge of red heightened her cheeks. ''I wasn't the best of students.

''But I made it for him—for Lord Darclan.''

Darin didn't doubt it.

''Do you think I could keep it? I mean, I could take it to be cleaned later—no, wait, I have a better idea. I'll take it with me when—'' She stopped and looked out the window. Hugged the robe more tightly, as if the lord were in it. ''I'll surprise him. Do you think you could get some clothing for me? Nothing fancy.''

Darin nodded slowly.

''Hurry, hurry!'' She was practically jumping in a little dance on the bed; the sheets rippled with every move.

Darin backed slowly out of the room. When he reached the hall he broke into a run. He wanted to do Sara's bidding and return as quickly as possible in case she should remember—and need him.

Lord Darclan stood in the main hall. At his feet a large, brown basket rested in the shadows of the arches. His arms were folded precisely across his chest, and his eyes never left the stairs. He was not given to pacing, always preferring economy of movement. But he was given to being impatient, and this time more so than usual.

Where were they? A flurry of slaves coming from their allotted tasks fell silent at the sight of their lord. They averted their eyes quickly and moved on.

He ignored them.

*Sara, what have you come up with now? I was certain that you would be happy to have leave to go out.* Still, she had never been punctual.

He heard the patter of footsteps—light, quick ones. Darin burst around the corner and rushed down the stairs, three at a time. The lord frowned slightly; noticeably absent was Sara's slightly heavier tread.

''Lord Darclan.''

''Where is Lady Sara?''

''She's waiting upstairs.'' He gulped. ''She wants to ask you something.''

The lord raised an eyebrow. ''And she couldn't ask it here, I suppose?'' But he was already moving before Darin could reply. He sensed the uneasiness in the boy's face, and Sara's requests were hardly the child's fault. "Very well."

They walked back up to the stairs and turned down the hall that led to Sara's room. Darin paused in front of the door, but before he could knock, it swung open. Sara's hearing was second only to the lord's—and at that, not by much.

"Come in," she said brightly.

He stopped to look down at her and she blushed; it was the first time that she had seen him since the previous evening. A gentle smile played back on his lips as she looked away.

He walked into the room, followed closely by Darin.

"See what we found?"

Lord Darclan looked toward the bed and stopped. A pale brown robe had been laid out on it with some care; no wrinkle in the fabric was evident. Against that pale brown backing, an embroidered emblem caught the day, a large, silver eagle, with a branch of some plant in its talons. On that branch grew a flower in full bloom, one that had not in any way been injured by its passage with the great bird. Darclan stood staring at it, remembering.

She spoke. "Lord Darclan?"

"Stefan," he corrected.

"Uh, Stefan. You remember this." As his silence lengthened, her smile faltered. "Don't you?"

He turned then, his eyes opaque, the lines of his mouth tautly drawn.

"Yes, Sara." There was more than recognition in his voice. "I remember it well." He bent down and touched it gently, his fingers moving over it as Sara's had done earlier. She turned to smile at Darin with relief. Neither of them saw the way that Darclan's hands curled into fists around the robe; neither saw the single tremor that took him and vanished.

"I made it for you."

"Yes. You thought I needed—something different from the robes I normally wear." The eagle was there. But instead of a carcass, there was the branch—the blooming flower—that was her gift.

She looked at his dark, heavy clothing. "Well," she said hesitantly, "it is warm outside. Don't you think it would be more comfortable?"

"Sara."

"You—you could wear it now."

He knew that nothing but an outright refusal to wear the robe would stop her from requesting it. He could not dim the hope in her eyes by doing so.

"If you like, Sara, I will wear it. Wait outside for a moment."

He picked up the robe as the door clicked sharply.

*It has been long since I have worn this for you, Sara. And long since you have asked me to do so. I should have destroyed it.*

But he held it gently.

*I wanted something new,* he thought, beginning to slide out of his clothing. *I wanted no taint of the past to come between us.* He smiled, a humorless, grim smile. *There is nothing new for us. Let me embrace the memories I have kept from you.*

And he did, sliding into the fabric of past times with elegant grace, remembering the happy pride that Sara had shown when she presented this fruit of the months of her "secret" labor. She had never known that he knew what she worked at. He shrugged, remembering the strange feeling the robe had given him when he had first donned it. Remembering that she had loved him, then.

And memory became more than the past; it grew round him as he belted the robe. He felt, at that moment, all the love that Sara had ever given him. It came on like the tide does in the fading light of day, fully, and finally, for any trapped by it. He was Stefanos, not Lord Darclan; he was the First of the Sundered; he was, as she had always called him, her Darkling. And she was his.

The day fulfilled its promise. It was preternaturally bright, clouds flirting with sunshine in the blue of the sky. Stefanos walked arm in arm with his lady, and Darin, lugging the large basket, followed in silence.

*Almost,* Stefanos mused, *as if he knows what I know.*

He shoved the thought aside; what was coming would come— he could not prevent it. But he could linger here, with Sara and the child. He would make the day a timeless one. He would trap it in the crystal shards of his eternal memory.

"Is something wrong?"

He smiled down at Sara's upturned face. To see it move, even now, was a small miracle.

"No, Sara."

Her grip on his arm faltered as she frowned slightly. "Stefan. If I ask you about my past—"

He touched her cheek gently, and she stopped speaking.

"Sara, must we speak of that today?"

In a very stark voice, she said, "Stefan, you can't know what it's like for me to have no past. There's some reason you won't tell me, isn't there? Something I did? Something I left undone?" She frowned, her grip tightening. "I know that Eva was a slave, but she wasn't afraid of me at all. Have I done something to scare the slaves here?"

"Lady, are you so certain that I know the answers to these questions?"

"I'm not a child, Stefan. I haven't been one for years. You do know."

"Your pardon, lady." His fingers traced her jaw lightly. "It is not as a child that I envision you. My manners are at fault."

She pushed his hand away. "This isn't a game to me. I know something's wrong, and I have the right to know what it is. I don't care if it's terrible—it's still me; I still have to face it."

For a moment his eyes clouded. He wanted to bind that thought, bind and erase it. The desire vanished as he again accepted its futility. His eyes remained dark as he responded.

"Sara, lady, please ask no more questions. In a week, if your memory has not returned, I will restore what I can of it. But now, now I want your untroubled company."

She met his black eyes with the green of hers, seeing in the shadows there more than he would say. He was open now, vulnerable. Her anger vanished and she swallowed, wondering if her *need* to know could be stifled for that span of days. With a sigh, she wrapped her arm more firmly around his, her fingers lingering over the pale wool.

A smile curbed her sense of desperation—she had remembered this robe, and the making of it. In a seven-day it was possible that more would become clear.

"I'll try."

"Thank you, lady." He kissed her forehead gently, and then they began to walk once more.

It appeared that they were wandering aimlessly, but that was not Stefanos' way, and soon they emerged into a green clearing several feet away from the edge of a small lake. Here, too, the day danced on the water's surface, winking and rippling as it moved. Sara did not give voice to her pleasure at the sight of it, but her smile was enough. The sun dimpled her mouth and brought the whiteness of her skin to light.

"I believe this to be a suitable location," Stefanos said, nodding to Darin. Darin replied by setting down his basket and removing a large blanket from it.

"May I help?" Sara asked.

Darin shook his head. "You're supposed to be resting."

"I am," she said, grabbing one of the blanket's corners. The cloth was heavy, soft wool, intended to keep the sting of dry grass from tender skin. At this time of year, with the grass new and young, that was not much of a concern.

"Lady Sara." The lord's voice drifted back as she and Darin spread the blanket out against the ground. "You make a most difficult patient."

She laughed. "Doctors always do."

Then she stopped, met the black of his eyes, and smiled more broadly. He nodded in silence.

"A doctor," she whispered to Darin, her voice jumping almost as much as her fingers against the blanket.

The meal passed in almost companionable silence. Stefanos ate little. Darin ate more, but he was very self-conscious. The use of manners had been taught to him, but he'd never fully understood all of their nuances. Only Sara was completely relaxed, her fingers darting to various dishes and fruits. The basket was half-empty before she had eaten her fill.

"That," she said, "was wonderful." She reclined, tilting her face to catch the wide swathe of sunlight. "We should do this every day."

"I imagine it would be more difficult in the winter."

"Winter?" She laughed. "Winter's a lifetime away! How can you think about storm and wind when it's so warm and bright?"

She turned in time to catch an arched brow.

"I have told you before, Sara, that I think about many things."

She sat up suddenly and reached out for him. "And now you are going to *stop* thinking for a minute and enjoy yourself!"

Darin watched with shock as he realized what Sara had started to do. She was tickling the lord. To little effect; the lord stiffened slightly, but looked down with a grimace, both surprised and amused.

"Darin!" Sara shouted, as the lord caught one of her hands. "Help me!"

Darin shifted uncertainly.

"Well don't just sit there! Do you want to be in his morose company for the rest of the afternoon? Help me!"

"But—"

"Darin!"

The lord turned to face Darin. In a soft, even voice, he said, "Darin, the water's edge is a mere four yards away. Before you listen to the lady's plea, consider that fact carefully."

Darin looked at Sara and his lord. He thought they had both gone insane. Lord Darclan was a Servant of the Dark Heart, Sara the last of the Line Elliath; they were in the middle of the Empire of Veriloth, with misery and death hedging them in. They were mad.

But he looked down at the unaccustomed finery of his clothing, then across at the rippling sheen of water. If they were mad, he knew the madness. He remembered it keenly.

"Darin," Sara continued, her voice dropping, "he won't be able to throw you in the lake if we work together."

"Won't I?" The lord's arms closed round Sara as he lifted her, in one motion, from the ground. "Sara, all the love in the world would not stop me from meting out just punishment. I am a man of my word."

She gave a little squeal as he began to walk toward the water.

"Darin!" She doubled her efforts to break free; her feet and hands rained soft blows about the lord's torso.

Dazed, Darin stood and followed them to the lake's edge. When he was five seasons, he might have done this. He might have walked, as the Servant did, to the edge of the water. Might have walked in, as the lord did, until that water lapped gently against the soles of his boots.

"The water here is quite interesting, Sara. I am standing on a small shelf. One step further, and we will both be wet."

Sara stopped struggling and twined her arms around his neck.

"If I go in," she said sweetly, "you come with me."

Her arms tightened. "But if I go in, lady, I shall be concerned with swimming, and not so much with the thinking you disparage in so bold a fashion."

Yes, Darin thought as he listened, they were both insane. Adults didn't behave like this. He thought about it, trying to remember more clearly those who were newly adult. He grimaced suddenly.

Peggy and Robert had been like this before they were married. And after, if he thought about it. They always wanted to be alone, and they always behaved almost as if they were.

For a long while he watched them.

Then he closed his eyes and began to move forward. Remembering, still remembering.

* * *

Stefanos saw the widening of Sara's eyes as she suddenly threw her arms out. His head came around in time to see a small burst of motion heading toward them.

Darin's smile was one his year-mates would have recognized—and run from. His hands hit their target with the full force of his weight. The lord let out a wordless exclamation and stumbled forward.

"Look out!" Sara wrapped her arms around his head. It was the last sound that either of them made before they hit the water. Sara choked between little gasps of laughter; the water was not deep enough to cover her completely. She wiped her eyes to clear them, and shoved her hair back. Dark, damp curls clung to her face and neck.

Stefanos was not nearly so inarticulate. He was on his knees almost before the water touched him. The damp robe he wore wrapped itself inconveniently around his body, slowing him.

"You dare?"

Darin stood on the grass, doubled over with laughter.

Stefanos rose and began to walk toward him. He heard the giggle and splash at his back as Sara caught his ankle and gave it a sweeping tug. There was another splash, another laugh, and another splutter as Stefanos resurfaced, rivulets of water running down his face and body.

"Sara," he said through gritted teeth as she drifted away, "I am not, in general, a man who plays games."

"Pity," she replied, as an arching spray leaped toward him. "I guess that means this won't bother you."

"And when I do," he said, advancing a few steps as the water ran down his face, "I do not lose."

She darted away as his hands closed on a current.

"Hey!"

They both turned to look at Darin, although they kept an eye on each other.

"If you two are just going to play in the lake, I'm going back to the castle to do *serious* work."

The lord looked at Sara and Darin. Both faces wore similar expressions—playful, slightly malicious grins devoid of the fear or hatred that he found in all others. He could almost feel an answering laughter strain to leave his lips; he hovered on the brink of it, awash in a peculiar warmth. The laugh would not come, but he stood there, savoring its nearness.

Sara toppled him over.

He lunged for her, but the water slowed him again; it was an unfamiliar medium for him. She glided away easily, her smile a reflection that the water wiped clean.

On the shore, Darin watched them and sighed wistfully. They were mad, yes, and he wanted to stay awhile and share that madness. But he remembered Peggy and Robert. He packed up the basket, but left the blanket lying on the grass. If they didn't get out of the water sometime soon, they'd need it.

Although he walked alone to the castle, he felt the warmth of their company as it lingered with him. And as he walked, other memories returned to him, and he let them come for the first time in years. At his side, he could hear the remarkably agile step of the Grandmother; in the distance, the sound of his year-mates' heated discussions. Just ahead, the hall of Culverne loomed high, imposed upon the turrets and towers of the castle.

*Days like today, Darin—are you listening?*

Yes, Grandmother.

*Days like today, you treasure. Sun's up and out, the borders are secure. You've the time just to enjoy life.*

Yes. Yes, Grandmother.

*I'll tell you something, boy—and don't grimace like that— even your father's still a boy to me. At my age, everyone is.*

He sighed.

*You take this day and make a memory out of it. Then, some-day, in a battle or God knows what, dig it out of yourself as if it were a diamond; cut it to catch today's light, and look at it. Remember moments like these have happened, and still happen. It might keep you sane.*

She disappeared, and he walked on alone, remembering who he had been, who he was, and who he hoped, someday, to be.

*I'll try, Grandmother, not to be afraid of your memory any-more.*

Sara swept her hair back and wrung it dry for the fourth time. A few drops fell from the ends and onto the stone floor of the main hall. On impulse, Stefanos bent over and brushed his lips against her forehead. She leaned into them, her smile soft and hidden.

Two slaves, on their way to the dining hall, stopped for a moment. Sara looked up, met the eyes of the older man, and blushed. The lord looked up, and they suddenly found their legs. He was almost sorry for their fear, then; he did not mind if the world shared his sight of Sara, or his love of her.

"Do you know something?" Sara said.

He smiled.

"These halls are so dim. And gray. They're gray and colorless." She wandered away from him, trailing her hand against the smooth stone. "There were tapestries where we stayed before, weren't there?"

He nodded.

She sighed. "And slaves."

He nodded again, watching her face. Her lips were turned down in a thoughtful frown. "They're afraid of us, aren't they?" She reached out to touch the emblem on his chest.

"Not 'us,' lady," he answered gently, knowing it hurt her, this fear—hurt her, as it warmed him. She relaxed, and then frowned again.

"Maybe it's because you always play 'lord of the manor' with them, all grim and forbidding."

"I *am* lord of the manor." He smiled, because he knew well why he was feared, and knew that somewhere, in his keeping, she remembered as well. But not here. Not now.

The frown grew, and she looked up hesitantly. "But maybe you could help them to stop being afraid."

"Sara . . ."

"If you stopped hiding in your study the way you always do, they'd see more of you, you'd see more of them, and maybe you'd understand each other better."

He touched her cheek gently, and smiled. It kept the pain at bay. *Sara, Sarillorn.* Leaning down, he kissed her forehead again. *I would be more for you, if I could. But that is not my nature. Would that you knew what you asked.*

She trembled.

"Lady," he said softly, "I think it best that you change for dinner. I shall do the same, if you will excuse me for a few moments."

She nodded, turned, and then turned again.

"Stefan," she said, her voice very quiet, "is their fear important to you?"

"It is—my custom, Sara." He waited a moment. "I am sorry."

She smiled. It surprised him, for it was very gentle. "Fear isn't the best way."

He knew what she would say, knew it so well he was surprised at how deeply it could still cut.

"Love is."

* * *

"I won." She whispered it softly as the vegetables were laid out on her plate. She turned a gentle smile and murmured a word of thanks to the slave who stood at her right. He started slightly, and then nodded in return, wondering.

Darin ducked his head to hide his smile.

"He can't swim at all. I almost had to pull him out of the lake."

"Probably because the robe weighed him down," Darin said charitably. "The lake wouldn't hurt him regardless."

She chuckled and lowered her voice further. "He doesn't know anything about water. Serves him right for threatening to throw me in."

"Sara," Darin whispered, remembering the slaves that surrounded the table, "maybe we should talk about this later."

"I think it best that both of you never speak about it again."

They looked up to meet their lord's gracious smile.

"Oh, hells," Sara said softly, picking up her fork. In a more normal voice, she added, "I forgot your hearing was that good. It's cheating."

"Cheating? Lady, you wound me. But come, let us speak of something different. Is the dinner to your liking?"

"Oh yes." She smiled. "But not nearly so much as lunch."

"I see." He turned politely and nodded his head at Darin. "And to yours?"

Darin did nod, but Sara's smile was infectious. "But I should agree with the lady to be polite." He laughed and nudged her. "Besides, neither of you won. *I* did. I was the only one who came back dry."

*Ah, now it comes.*

The veil was thinner tonight. For three days he had worked to unravel its edges. It was frustrating to know that this passage, cleared once before by the Lady of Elliath, was no easy road. And she had five years of time, a luxury he could not afford.

Time.

Images shot by him quickly. Even his sight could not translate them immediately. But they were sharper now, clearer for his effort. He moved heavily, the veil of *now* still bound tightly around him. He concentrated on finding one image, one face.

*There.*

And indeed she was. Her clothing was torn and dirt-stained,

her face wreathed by tangled hair. Her eyes glowed almost green as she reached out to touch—

The image broke free of him, flowing past. Cursing, he pursued it.

But with no time to harden it, the path he tried to follow was shifting and formless. As if aware of his pursuit, Sara moved past and was gone. Easily.

He started to concentrate again, and then broke off. House Darclan loomed before him. It was dark, but firelight flickered through some of the windows. He approached it closely enough to see that the gates were open. Someone drifted through them.

Recognition flared to life as he counted. Four.

*When?* He thought, furious. *When is this?*

Something red and ugly caught his sight, pulling it away.

He gazed at it a long time in silence.

Then, with a bitter sense of fatality, he turned back to the castle, determined to find a time frame for it and its unwelcome visitors. Time . . .

*No.* The future was lost to him; the study resumed its steady presence of darkness. For some moments he sat in a shroud of tense silence. Then he rose. Quickly, his feet making no sound on stone, he left his refuge, seeking.

The halls opened before him, cavernous and empty. He walked through them. He paused at the foot of the grand stairs to look up.

Although stone walls and wooden doors barred his vision, he knew with certainty that Sara was sleeping. His foot hit the first stair and then stopped.

Not yet.

Turning, he walked out of the front doors. A slave bowed to the ground as he passed. He nodded—pure habit—and continued.

The gardens and grounds passed him by; the lake glimmered palely in moonlight, surrendering no reflection. He moved too quickly for it to be captured. The hills opened out before him, and he followed their gentle slope, up and then down.

*No.*

But it was already there, a great wall of power, three times Sara's height, maybe four. It glimmered with no natural light, too red and too dark. Threads of black, like mortar, ran throughout it. He followed it to the horizon on either side. Red-fire might burn less painfully than this when laid against her skin.

*Who dares?* he thought, his arms outstretched as he approached the barrier. His hands touched it and passed through it to swim in a miasma of red.

No mortal hand had created this, nor any servant's power. Not alone.

*My Lord.* It was bitter, this. He looked long at it, and hard, and knew that the time had already come.

Sara could never pass it. Its touch would be her death.

In silence, he followed the circumference of the wall. But he knew already that he would find it seamless and whole; Sara was not meant to leave these grounds that he had built for her new life. Not with him.

*Lady.* He turned then. *There is so little time.*

After all that he had done, time was still his enemy. He returned to the castle. She was sleeping. He would not wake her, but he wanted her presence now.

# chapter
# fifteen

*Sara sat in her bed. She had thrown the curtains open to catch* the moon in her window frame, and its touch lingered on her back and the whiteness of her neck like a warning. She felt her hands as they shook and twisted them into the covers. Cold touched her skin, the chill of fear no summer night could prevent.

It was dark.

She shivered as she cast her gaze around the room. Too dark.

And she knew, now, why the darkness had always frightened her; it was her enemy, this crippled twin of light.

Bedclothing, like a shroud in its white simplicity, lay tangled around her body as if she were already dead, as if she awaited attendants and their ceremonies.

*What am I doing here?*

With a gesture, she called a little light into being and sent it traveling outward. It touched the walls lightly and then passed through the closed window.

She waited, taking a deep breath.

But it returned, melting into the palm of her hands, with no answers.

She unfurled her fingers and looked at the shadowed palm. As if it were yesterday, she could hear the Lady's words and see the Lady's face, bent over hers, as it mirrored her guilt and her concern.

This place was not Elliath, not even a nightmare image of the holdings that had been her home. Games and words came to her, but didn't reach her lips or her heart; she knew where she was. Somehow, she had come to be a citizen of the Dark Heart's Empire.

There was a gentle knock; someone had chosen to forsake polished brass and strike quietly at wood instead.

"Come in."

The door slid open, and a shadow crossed the threshold. That shadow held her memories, held her life somehow.

It stopped to meet her eyes.

"You are awake."

"Yes." Although he stood in the cover of darkness, she could sense tension in him akin to her own. *Fear.*

She stood and walked over to him as the words fell away, covering his lips with her fingers. He stiffened and then pressed the line of his mouth into them, bowing his head.

"Lady," he whispered, "I am so sorry."

*Pain.*

Without thinking, she sent herself outward and felt him stiffen in shock. He pulled back.

*Pain.* A pain that she had not touched.

"No, Sarillorn." He caught her hands. "This touch is not for me."

*Sarillorn.* The word sent a jolt through her. *Yes.*

He caught her chin and held it tightly as he looked into her eyes. His own, he closed. It was to be a night of losses. "You remember," he said softly.

She nodded. "Some. I know who I was. But I don't know where—"

"Not now."

He let go of himself abruptly, circling her with his arms. He wished again that the gentleness that was her nature might somehow become his, for his arms about her were tight and hard, and his lips on her mouth fierce.

Sara stirred slightly as Stefanos eased himself out of the bed. He moved silently, if somewhat more clumsily than usual, as he lifted her head from the pillow of his chest and lowered her down.

Perhaps she felt the absence of his body, or perhaps the rustle of the sheets disturbed her, although he doubted it—she had never been a light sleeper. Whatever it was that had caught her attention held it fast: She was almost instantly awake as his feet touched the floor.

"Stefan?"

"Shhh, Sara. Sleep."

She sat up and brushed the tangled strands of her hair from

her eyes. It was an automatic motion; hair or no, she could see no more than his silhouette against the window.

"Where are you going?"

"I am restless, lady. I am going—elsewhere."

She reached out and caught his arm with her hand; it was cool and dry against his skin. "Don't go."

"I must leave, Sara. But I will return in the morning." She could not see his expression in the darkness.

"Why? What must you do that can't wait until morning?"

He stiffened, raising his head as she wrapped her arms around his torso.

"Stefan?" Her voice was muffled, the words warm against him. "Please, please stay. I'd like just to wake up once and have you beside me. I don't want to be alone."

He heard the quaver in her voice and shook his head slowly. Her memory here was truer than she knew; he had never stayed with her through the night. He wondered if she thought only of the last few days.

"I would dearly love to do so, lady, but I have matters that I must attend to."

He had forgotten just how perceptive she could be after making love; had forgotten how much of himself he opened up in the act, and after. She knew instantly that he was lying, although his voice was smooth and diffident. Her arms circled him more tightly.

"You don't want to leave. I don't want you to either. Why can't you stay?"

*Because, Sara, in sleep you are fragile and defenseless. Because it is not day, but night, and night is the domain of the Servants. Because I cannot rest at night with you so close and so open—you call me to feed, lady; you call me unknowing. And if I stay, I do not think I can resist the call.* He said nothing, his hands cupping her chin almost protectively. He could feel the lifeblood in the flesh between his hands; the faintest of pulses, the most dangerous of distant musics. Yes, he wanted to stay, but he had stayed too long already, flirting with the extremes of his nature until the desire to stay in the warmth of her light was only slightly stronger than the desire to consume her.

*And if I did?* he thought bitterly. If he took her now, as he had always resisted doing in the past, what difference would it make? A few days, at best, for her, and no less a pleasant death than the one she would have to face. His hands tightened slightly.

Why should he leave her for another Servant? He was First, oldest and most powerful of all Servants—why should another be able to take what he had denied himself for so long? He looked at her face, clear and stark in the darkness, as he pondered. He could see the trace of pain in her eyes, and it, too, was dangerous.

Why should he not just have an end?

He smiled as he bent to kiss her forehead. *Why not, indeed.*

"I cannot stay, Sara."

His voice was full and final.

She let her arms fall away and lay back, staring sightlessly at the ceiling.

He wanted to tell her then; he wanted to free her from the bindings that held her, to slip the noose of his magic from around her memory. His own memories held him in check, but barely. He had six days. He would not lose any of them.


"Darin!"

Darin's shoulders sagged. He was wearing his old clothing now, and looked for all the world like any other slave. But he wasn't treated quite like one anymore. The other slaves, when he saw them, whispered among themselves; he could feel both fear and anger in the stares that they threw at his back.

*This is going to be bad,* he thought, as he turned to face Cullen.

But it wasn't just bad; Evayn was with the chief cook, not a foot from his side. He hoped, briefly, that she was just there to charge him with dereliction of duty. But it wasn't as house mistress that she chose to question him.

Her sleeves were long, as were Cullen's, but he knew they both bore the brands.

"Yes?" Darin said weakly.

"I've been wanting to talk to you for three days now, and you've been dodging me."

"Dodging?" Darin tried to draw himself up. "I've been following the—"

" 'Lord's orders.' We know." Cullen frowned. "Have you angered him, then?"

Darin's confusion was enough of an answer.

"But you're back on duties." This was Evayn. Her voice was low, with a thread of anger running through the curiosity in it.

He nodded.

"Good. You might start by telling us what's going on."

Darin shook his head.

Cullen was not to be deterred. He moved closer and caught Darin's arm a little too firmly. "Darin, lad," he said in a low voice, "we know that something's happening here. I've served this house for years and I've never seen a slave at the table. The dinner table, at that."

"Oh, he's been in the morning hall as well."

"Missed it," Cullen muttered. "But that's not the strangest." He shook his head. "Look, Darin, we're not so small that we'd grudge you anything you'd earned." The grip tightened, belying the words. "But if you won't tell us that, can't you at least tell us why the lord was wearing the crest of the lady?"

Darin's look of confusion was genuine. "The lady?"

"The Lady of Mercy."

"He's from outland, Ev," Cullen whispered.

*Lady of Mercy?* Darin thought. *Crest?*

"When was this?"

"Yesterday. The three of you went off together, and you came back alone."

*Yesterday? But he was wearing—* Darin's eyes grew wide, and Cullen looked almost smug as he rolled his eyes at Evayn. Evayn frowned.

"You honestly don't know much of our customs, even after five years." She shook her head, and to Darin's relief, Cullen relaxed his grip.

"Darin," he said, his voice a whisper, "who is the lady?"

"Who," Darin answered, "was the Lady of Mercy?" His voice became quieter, if that was possible. "Who did she love?"

Silence.

"That isn't possible." Evayn's tone was guarded—guarded and worried.

"Her name is Sara," Darin said. He leaned gently against the wall. "She has no memories . . ."

Darin's jaw hadn't moved for fifteen minutes, and Sara was quick to note this.

She tilted her head to one side as she watched his expression of astonishment, but didn't stop talking.

At length, she said, "What do you think?"

"You remember." It was all he could think of to say.

She nodded. "Not everything, no. But I remember more of

who I am—and who I was." She folded her arms around her knees. She knew who Darin reminded her so well of; she should have known it in an instant, they were so alike.

*Belfas.* She missed him, and wondered how by the Hearts he was surviving without her.

"But you—you know who you are."

"Yes." Her reply, simple and elegant, told Darin that she wouldn't stop there. "I do."

"What are you going to do?"

"I don't know." She stood then, and turned to face the window. The day was already paling, and clouds had turned blue sky to ash. "I don't know where in the Empire I am—but I know that I am in the Empire."

"Yes." He hesitated, and then began to fidget with the staff of Culverne. Bethany was silent; she always was at difficult moments. "But what do you want to do?"

"I want to know what I'm doing here. I want to know why I came." She sighed, and then turned again, her eyes narrowed. "Darin, are you of the lines?"

He looked down at his feet and caught the staff out of the corner of his eyes. He nodded, swallowing. "I'm of Line Culverne."

"Culverne." She frowned. "It's north, is it not?"

"North." His lips were numb. Casting about for something, he said, "Are you going to try to escape?"

"Escape?" She turned the word over in her mouth. "Escape. I don't know. I don't think I'm a captive here." She took a sudden step forward and grabbed his arm—his right arm. Before he could pull away, she rolled up the sleeve, exposing for an instant the pale lattice of dead flesh that House Damion had left him.

The sleeve fell loose again as she released his arm. Her face was as white as the scar had become.

"Darin, why are you here?" She was trembling. "Why am I? What's happened?"

"I don't know." He could say this truthfully. It was a relief.

She heard that, and sighed. "How long, Darin? How long since Culverne fell?"

He was surprised at how the question cut him. He drew a breath; it caught in his throat and dragged across it with invisible claws.

Bethany warmed briefly in his hand, but he ignored her, looking instead at the long-healed scar on his right arm. Remembering Kerren.

She stopped asking questions then, the way the Grandmother had often stopped, and rose. He felt her arm around his shoulder as if it were steel; as if he could let everything go and still be safe.

But the words wouldn't come. Tears did, tears and then silence.

They were late for lunch.

Darin held the staff as if it were a crutch, and Sara kept a hand on his shoulder. It felt right, somehow, that they should walk this way, the last two of the lines of the Bright Heart.

"We're late again," Sara said, because it was something to say.

He nodded, looking around the empty hall.

"Come on." Her fingers squeezed his shoulder and then relaxed. "We'd best run—Stefan doesn't like to be kept."

He didn't ask how she knew it; if she remembered this much, it wouldn't be long until she had the answer for herself. But the running brought his mind into the present, into the long, stone halls of House Darclan; into the Empire that they had to live within.

He fell behind, surprised at just how swift Sara could be. She reached the foot of the steps, gripped the banister, and swung around to the bottom of the stairs.

"Sara, look out!"

She heard him in just enough time to throw herself out of the way; she hit the ground with a hard thump and rolled. A small little gasp, mingled with high gurgling laughter, filled the hall. Sara looked up to meet the astonished—and pleased—eyes of a very young girl.

The girl's mother was a few feet away, her face suddenly white as she rushed over to her child. The child, surprised by her mother's harsh grip, exchanged the quickness of wonder for a loud wail; tears began to trickle down cheeks that had already turned red.

"I'm sorry," Sara said as she gained her feet.

"Please, lady, the child didn't mean to get in your way." The woman clutched the shrieking girl tightly to her breast. "It won't happen again, I swear it. She doesn't know what she's doing yet, lady. I'll make sure she doesn't do this again."

Sara took a step forward, and the woman took two steps back, fear and protectiveness wrapped around her child more thickly than her arms.

"Hello." Sara slowly extended her hand, as if approaching a wild creature. The woman's eyes darkened, but she remembered, this time, to hold her ground. "I'm sorry I almost ran into your daughter."

The woman met her eyes rigidly.

Very slowly, with infinite care, Sara reached out to touch the small girl's hand. The child was too old to reflexively grip the finger that she found in her palm, but her curiosity was piqued enough to stop her tears.

"She's beautiful." Sara avoided the mother's gaze and wrinkled her nose at the girl, who stared at her with the hint of a shy smile. She pulled back and shoved her face into her mother's shoulder, and then peered sideways at this new person.

"Thank you, lady." The woman's voice was as rigid as her posture.

They stood that way for a moment before the child picked up Sara's finger and bit down on it.

Her mother gasped.

"Ouch!" Sara made an exaggerated face—she was good at that—and then chuckled slightly. "Well, little one, I don't think your bite is all that it could be." She gave a little tug. "Can I have my finger back, or are you going to gum me to death?"

The child gurgled, and a few indistinct words came tumbling out.

"Baby talk," Sara said, stroking the soft skin of the child's cheek. Without looking up, she spoke to the mother. "I don't suppose you understand what she tried to say? It always seems to me that each child has its own language before it learns ours."

"Yes, lady."

Sara flinched, and then she did look up. Her green eyes flared, brightening and deepening at the same moment. She reached out to catch the woman's arm, and a trickle of light flared, a binding around and between the two of them.

The woman closed her eyes for a moment, and her breathing became more relaxed.

"I'm sorry," Sara said. "Truly, you have no need to fear me. I don't have children, but I've always liked to see them."

"Yes, lady."

Light continued to pulse; power continued to flow between them. "Please, don't break your child for my sake."

Brown eyes seemed to flash. And then the mother smiled, the first genuine smile that Sara had seen on any face but Darin's or Stefan's.

"I understand," the woman said softly. She looked at her daughter. The child was already trying to reach for the long swathe of Sara's hair.

Sara chuckled, but the sound was weaker. She withdrew her hand, and after a moment the slave bowed and left, young daughter still trying futilely to catch the wisps of Sara's hair before they floated past.

It was Darin's turn to be a support.

He caught Sara's elbow as she steadied herself against the wall. Her face was white once more.

She shook her head at the expression on Darin's face. "I'm all right." She took a deep breath, but the shadow wouldn't leave her eyes. "It's just hard—she was so frightened of me—of what I might do to her child."

Darin knew. But he also knew that explanations wouldn't help; Sara probably understood the reasons for the fear.

"Lunch," she said, and held out her arm. He took it and began to lead her toward the dining hall. But he watched her face, unable to understand all the things that passed across it.

They reached the door in silence, and then Sara stopped. Her hands were shaking as she grabbed Darin's shoulders.

"It's no good," she said softly. "I can't continue like this. Darin, please, you have to tell me what you know. I know it's hard for you—but I can't keep meeting people who fear me as much as that woman did."

Darin didn't know what to say.

"Why am I here, Darin? Why am I not on the front?" Her fingers tightened. "Is there no front anymore?" Her face paled further, her fingers now a vise. "Did I betray the lines somehow? Did I fail them?"

Darin shook his head. "No—"

"Do you even know?"

"No, Sara. He does not. But I do."

Lord Darclan stood between the open doors of the hall. He stepped forward and gently brushed the corners of Sara's eyes. She looked up at him and then tried to pull away; she was too tired to ease the pain that flared between them, but not too weak to feel it. She was never too weak for that.

And he, he was strong enough. Her pain answered his, an echo of the same. He looked at her white, white face, at the shadows in her eyes that spoke of a pain he had grown to hate.

"Lady," he said softly. He drew her into his arms, and after a moment she relaxed enough to allow it.

"I'm sorry." Her voice was muffled against his robes.

"Do not be. It was my desire that we wait, my desire that we not speak of the things you need to know."

He caught her chin and held it, seeing the years that had passed between them. *Time*. His fingers tightened as if he desired nothing more than to hold this.

"Lady Sara, you never betrayed the lines."

She sagged against him with relief.

"Thank you," she said, her voice very small.

She could not know that he was lying.

But he knew it, knew it well. She was tired; even he could see this. He had forgotten how strongly fear affected her; without all of her memories she probably had no defense against it. And he was weary. All of his plans had collapsed and lay around them in ruins. He had wanted to give her life eternal; five days were all that remained.

"Lady," he said, his lips against her hair. "Come. The day is cloudy, but it is still warm without. Let us go to the grounds."

*It is time.* He closed his eyes, drew her closer. Five days, and for those five, he suddenly desired what he had put behind him— the past.

He met Darin's eyes over Sara's head.

*Go.* His lips moved soundlessly over the order.

Darin left.

She was tense; the promise he had extracted still hung between them, a wall now, not a solace. But she rode well, or at least as well as four years of experience had gained her. He remembered the teaching of this with a bitter smile. It was lost, but it remained. His own mare was a calm, tired beast, one of the few in the stables that would carry him.

"Where do we ride to?" she asked, her hands almost slack on the reins.

"There is a simple trail just beyond the castle grounds. I believe that should do well enough for today. I shall lead."

She nodded, and he set his horse in motion.

They rode for some time with only the crunch of hooves and the slap of low branches providing any noise at all. If there were leaves there, forest flowers, soft mosses—if there were birds or squirrels, rabbits or other small woodland creatures—Sara didn't notice them. She saw the path, thin and scraggly as it lay across the undergrowth; she saw the shadows branches cast in front of rounded hooves; she saw her lord.

At last they rode out of the forested trail and into a small clearing. It was bisected by a clear, small stream with a visible rocky bottom; on either side of it were large, moss-covered rocks and a few fallen tree trunks.

Stefanos dismounted at the edge of the trees and quickly secured his horse. Sara mimed his actions slowly; it had been long since she'd ridden, and the trail had been difficult.

But he had chosen it because the blood-wall would not be visible. She steadied her horse as he brushed by, and he caught the meaningless murmur of comfort that she provided.

It was a comfort that could not touch him.

Angry, he nimbly made his way past, over the large rocks that the water swirled around.

She watched him go, the tension growing as the silence did. It seemed to her that he only touched the rocks with his shadow; his step was that quick and that sure. He crossed the stream without pausing to look at it, and after a few concise half steps and jumps he stopped, his back toward her. She moved forward more slowly, aware of the size of the rocks, and the large gaps between them. A fall here would certainly not be fatal, but it would be painful and hard to land on the rocks. She chose her steps with care and caution, planting one foot firmly against the moss before venturing another step forward.

She stopped for a minute when she reached the stream, her gaze caught by a continual distortion of rock as water rushed glibly over it. She could see the bobbing green of leaves and branches that had been trapped by the narrow current and imagined, briefly, that they pursued some futile struggle against its pull. On impulse, she bent down and, leaning precariously forward, swept one bedraggled leaf up into a cupped palm. It lay, wet and glistening, against the droplets of water on her skin, its veins branching delicately outward within the green of its flesh. With careful, slow movements, she set it down on the rock beside her.

"Be careful of the metaphors you force out of nature, Sara."

She looked up quickly at the sound of his voice. His back was still turned toward her, his shadow a cloak on the rock. He was dark.

"Very well, you have saved a single leaf from the ravages of the stream it has fallen into; but does it have a better fate now? We will stop here awhile, we will speak or not as our whim dictates, and we will leave it behind for the sun to scorch or a random breeze to begin again the journey you have interrupted."

There was pain in the words, distant and undefined, but there was anger as well. She picked up the leaf defiantly and slipped it into her pocket. He laughed.

The laughter was dark, wild.

"Do I make you nervous, Sara?"

"No." It was a lie; she had never been good at lying. But she didn't understand the way the tension honed itself into a fine, sharp blade that pressed, invisible, against her throat.

He turned then, his eyes flashing brilliantly in the shadowed glade.

Instinctively, Sara took a step backward, lifting and dragging her arms across her face. The motion was over before it had begun, but he recognized it easily. The Greater Ward. Smiling, he stepped forward, but she stood her ground, just as she had always done.

"Little Sara"—his voice was a whisper—"do you remember the first time we met? Do you remember what you offered me, and what I accepted?" He held out a hand; it was shaking. "Come."

She moved then, as if in a trance. Her feet touched the flat surfaces of rocks jutting above the water that rushed past. He caught her arm as she came the last few steps and pulled her up. His fingers caught her chin.

Very slowly he raised her head until he met her eyes. There was shock, pain.

"You don't remember."

"And you do."

He nodded. "Clearly. I forget little." He wanted to tell her then, tell her all of his grand plans for the life that he wished to lead—the life that he wished to share with her alone. Words whirled past him like ash in the breeze. He could not speak.

"Have you finished playing with me? Is the game over? You know. I don't. You've proved some point that I can't understand." She pulled her chin away from his hand and took a step back.

"The game *is* over, Sara. If you feel that you have lost it, you are not alone. This was new for both of us, but I am not accustomed to dealing with new things.'' He gestured, the movement brief and final. For a moment a spasm crossed and caught his face, and then his features began to alter subtly, his form becoming gaunter, nearly insubstantial in the daylight, his face sharpening and hardening into gray angles. His eyes grew wider, rounded, the white of them engulfed by a spread of black and red that swallowed Sara's reflection.

He watched as her face mirrored his transformation; as realization took in what memory would not yet supply. One word broke through the trembling of her lips.

''Nightwalker.''

And with one word, spoken in a dead language, he replied. ''Sarillorn.''

His eyes flashed again, gleaming briefly like light on a blade raised to strike. Sara cried out and, taking a step backward, huddled down, her hands gently stroking the cold rock beneath her fingertips.

''Anders, Anders, can you hear me?''

Stefanos watched impassively as tears began to roll freely down her cheeks. He gestured; she stiffened. A step, and his arms were there to catch her and lay her gently against the moss. He unraveled the binding of memory with delicate care. The power flowing out of him was a peculiar pain, an echo of loss.

He watched, again, the fall of her little outpost; watched her fight and her flight; carried her back in the darkness of his arms, in the blanket of his power.

He stiffened as she made her offer, shivered as he received it, and flinched as the sunlight touched his back. And he watched as she struggled to ease the pain of the Karnar—watched as she succeeded, fully and finally.

*And it was then, lady, that I wondered.* His hands touched the paleness of her skin as she lay insensate against the rock. She didn't respond, but he didn't expect it; she had been forced to relive the memories he had returned to her—as had he. She would sleep a few hours, and he would watch over her, as he had watched through the passing of that earlier day.

*I wondered what you were—how your strength could support your weakness, how the light could be so strange and so haunting.* Yes, the desire to understand the oddity that was the Lernari had taken root that night, and that morning.

Stefanos laughed, silently and bitterly.

*And I still do not understand it, lady.*

*Rest awhile; there is more to come.*

He stood, eyeing the baleful sun. *It never ceases to amaze me.* He tilted his head upward defiantly. *The memory of physical pain passes so quickly. It has been long since your touch has had any power over me.*

Physical pain could break a man; it was short and sweet in its immediate reward. Yet he had seen men come through the fire of intense agony whole. Their skin might be scarred, perhaps a limb lost or crippled, but what had been shattered so easily could yet be reclaimed.

He thought of physical pain as black and red, explosive, immediate, and powerful. *Powerful?*

Bending down, he touched her forehead. It was warm; he could feel the intricate network of veins beneath the paleness of her exposed skin.

*Powerful.*

*And yet . . .*

Why was intangible suffering so impossible to elude? A mother could lose her child, and the memory would never cease to shadow her existence; a husband might lose a wife, and although he could carry on as before, an emptiness remained that caused echoes throughout a lifetime.

And Stefanos knew, as he stroked her brow, that he would lose her. The spells woven in the dark of his study had at last borne fruit, had showed him what he least wanted to know in a way that made it impossible to refute. She would be lost. The mark of her passing would define loss for him; already he could feel the scar of it, indelible, upon his mind. Yet he was no victim of ceremony, no fodder for the contemptible priests. No pain would rack his body, no torture break his consciousness.

*Physical pain* is *powerful.*

But he caused her no pain as his fingers continued to touch the contours of her face; the sun caused him no pain as it touched him—he knew a strange numbness before the two of them, the chosen banes of an earlier life.

He felt the gray of the day close round him like a web.

Sara stirred, and he was thankful for it, for although it meant the exacerbation of memory, it was still something he could share with her.

His eyes flashed silver anew, the gray of the day above and the shadow within. He spiraled down through the chaos of memory, catching strands of it that were mutual between them.

He walked with her again on the long road away from the Lernari border; walked the path to the heart of his Empire under the chill of her mistrust; walked in strength while she followed in weakness. But she walked free.

He rose again, walking in a tight circle around her body.

Memory. Although he knew all that had passed before, something existed in it that burned anew each time he stirred its embers. Sara was still unaware of the forest, the glade, the touch of his hand on her brow; her eyelids flickered every so often, her mouth creased in smile or frown, but she was not with him.

She was in Rennath, dying the slow death that mortals called age. He felt his fear of it still, felt it strongly. And accepted it; time at least had done this.

But he remembered much beyond that. And these memories, these were beautiful. They lived still in the way his hands now caressed her face, pressed gently against her closed, still lips.

*When did you first talk of love, Sara? When did you ask it of me?*

*Why did I grant to you what no Servant in all of time has ever felt?*

He relived, alone, his own doubts, his own anger, his own resentment—and his own desire. He faced again the oddest truth that he had had to come to terms with: That the happiness of the Sarillorn was something he valued, something he wished to increase where he could.

And thus had it started. He had given her one life, and the one life became many. Where she walked, mercy walked.

He had done all that he could for her sake, but the one thing he would not give up was his power, his Empire. Her inability to accept it troubled him greatly, but never so much that he would—could—stop. No. He would build his Empire across the whole of the Twin Hearts' body—and everything in it would be at his disposal. Let her then change what she liked; let her ask for what mercy she wished—he would grant it. But it would be his to give or to deny her. His. As she was his.

For four years.

She had become Lady Sara. Her birth-name and her line name were cast aside with a regret he could only now feel.

His fingers curled into fists. They shook.

Time.

*Sara, Sarillorn. I pulled you from Lernari gardens, from the sway of the Lady herself. I killed my descendants for your sake; I left my heritage behind to enable you to forget yours a little. I was building an Empire I intended to let you live in, in peace. I loved you, Sarillorn. You were mine.*

The sun was almost beneath the horizon.

*Did you not understand that? Could you not see what you had become to me? You were mine. Not some subject of time or mortality. Did I not say that I would never release you?*

Something welled up in him as he held her, as the last of her bound memories began to return. It was strong, stronger even than his desire to keep her at his side had been; stronger than his great and ancient hatred.

With a low, vicious snarl his eyes flashed red. He pulled his hands away from her face, whirling in a low crouch to face— pain.

Not physical pain; that would have been welcome.

He remembered; and although he had decided that she should know all, he could not bring himself to share this last thing with her. Could not pay again the price of her anger, her hatred, her loss. He cursed his weakness, cursed his fear, cursed his desire. All of these, these were the flowers of seeds that the Sarillorn had planted; these were the harvest of four years that he might have easily missed in the blink of an eye.

The emotion in him would not subside. This was the Sarillorn's last teaching to him. He faced it, wary, but at last aware of the truth: Physical pain was nothing to this. Nothing.

And because he had not been willing to accept her loss through time, he had deprived himself of even the span of her short life.

Twilight would come soon; twilight, half-dark, a time of safety for him and for her. She slept under the bands of his enchantment, her back warming rock grown cool at the passage of several hours.

But he had those hours. Very gently, he lowered himself down to the rock. He pulled her limp form into his arms, and she responded by snuggling into his chest, a faint hint of a smile around her lips. She did not wake; he would not allow that. This time was his; it might be the last that he could hold her so.

He had learned to love her, learned to see her moods and emotions clearly enough to be able to please her.

He pulled her closer, breathing in her scent. It seemed bitter indeed that the last lesson of the Sarillorn, his Sara, should be this one.

She had taught him the meaning of sorrow.

# chapter
# sixteen

*But in the morning, she woke alone.*

As she had always done in Rennath.

She jumped up, her head spinning from side to side, and then relaxed. They day stretched out before her, but she had much work to do. She leaned back for a moment, her hair spilling in a dark splash over the pillows.

She could not remember all of the previous day; it was hazy and somehow shadowed. But she knew that she remembered nearly everything. She balled her hands into fists.

*There's so much to do. And I've been lying here, doing none of it.*

Well, that would stop here. She slid her legs over the side of the bed, thinking about the castle. Creases etched themselves into her forehead as she realized that she knew very little of its geography.

But there was no infirmary here. That much she knew. Frustrated, she rose and began to hunt about for clothing.

Gervin rose as the door to his chambers creaked open. Only one person in the castle ever entered without knocking, and even he only in times of urgency.

"Lord," he said, bowing.

Lord Darclan cast a long shadow that no light could explain as the door moved toward the wall. But he stayed a moment in the door frame, his dark gaze sweeping the sparse room.

"You have been here many years," he said, almost to himself.

"Yes, lord."

"Gervin." The lord stepped into the room and let the door swing shut behind him. "I must speak with you."

Gervin did not rise from his bow until the door had clicked, trapping him with the lord he had vowed to serve.

He looked up then, weary.

*What new task?* he thought, although he let none of it show.

But perhaps had he, this one day, his lord would not have noticed.

"Gervin, the lady will come to you, if I am not mistaken, and she will request any variety of changes. I believe she may also call upon Darin; I do not know. It is not important." He stepped forward. Gervin did not move.

"Grant her what she desires."

"Pardon, lord?"

"Do what you can to give her the things she will ask for. An infirmary, I believe. Perhaps some type of religious service. Again, I do not know. You came from the lines, and if it is not too long past, you will remember."

He looked at Gervin keenly and then bowed his head.

"Have you ever wished vengeance, my faithful slave?" He put his hands behind his back; even now he did not wish one beneath him to see the way they were shaking.

"Yes, lord."

It was Gervin's way to speak only the truth. It had been Lord Darclan's command, and Gervin had followed it to the letter. As he had done all else.

"You have it, then."

Gervin raised an eyebrow.

"The lady will not be here long, and perhaps I too shall join her in departing. But I wish her to be happy here. Serve her, as you have served me. You will find her the kinder master." He turned, and then stopped, remembering. "Gervin, do this, and I will call no more upon you for the blooding of the knife."

"L-lord.' He could hear the rustle of cloth that was Gervin's formal bow.

He opened the door, and then stopped again; he could not have said why. But there was one more thing that he wished Gervin to know.

"She is the last," he whispered, "Of the Line Elliath."

He did not wait to hear Gervin's response. Now that the words were spoken, he was suddenly free to leave. And he did, to seek the silence and the comfort of the study that he had governed the Empire from for so many human years.

* * *

'But I don't understand what you're doing.''

"The last two beds at right angles to the east wall," Sara said, pointing. She had one arm full of what looked like bandages. "Where is the table beneath all this mess?"

"Sara?"

She nodded as she found the table, and then frowned. "Help me move this.''

Darin sighed and grabbed an end of it. Sara plunked the bandages down and grabbed the other end.

It was very heavy. "What is this made of?" Sara muttered. But it didn't matter; before she or Darin could try to lift it again, two of the slaves appeared on either side. Their larger hands gripped the table, and they lifted it with an ease that made Sara sigh.

"Lady?" one asked. Darin had not seen him often, and thought perhaps he was one of the house guards. While he puzzled over this, Sara pointed at the wall.

"There.''

The door swung open and a man entered, followed in procession by three men who carried a set of drawers between them. Given their expressions, neither Darin nor Sara felt obliged to offer their help.

"Other side of the door," Sara called quickly. She looked around the room as it began to take shape, counted the beds, and frowned slightly.

"Linens?" she murmured.

Darin nodded. He too stopped to count and then took off lightly through the door before some other piece of furniture blocked his way.

*The lady is different today.* Bethany's voice was calm but edged with curiosity.

Darin nodded his agreement.

*I wonder what passed between them.*

*Them?*

*The First and the lady.*

Darin wondered as well, but that didn't stop him from moving. He hurried off in search of the house mistress.

And he found her, sitting behind a smallish desk, a smile tugging at the corners of her lips. She almost never smiled.

"Uh—Evayn?" Darin asked, as he hesitated in the doorway.

"Come in, come in," she said briskly. The tone of her voice relaxed him, and he stepped across the threshold. "What can I do for you?''

"I need sheets for ten beds," he answered quickly.

"Ten?" She frowned.

"Ten. Singles, like we use."

She nodded and stood, walked over to the door, halted, and then turned to face Darin. The smile was still around the corners of her mouth. "They're for the infirmary?"

"Infirmary?"

Evayn sighed. "About time I knew something that you don't yet. The lady's setting up an infirmary for the house. For the slaves."

"Oh."

"Oh," she repeated, rolling her eyes. "Don't you know what this means, Darin? No, I don't suppose you do. But ten sets of sheets can easily be spared." She walked out of the door, a hint of song on her breath.

It sounded familiar to Darin, but only after a few moments did he recognize it—it was something that Stev used to hum.


"My lord, a messenger has come from the Vale. He carries a letter from the Church."

The lord looked up to meet Gervin's still face. With a curt shake of the head, he said, "I will see him."

The bow showed none of the older man's relief; the Vale was part of the territories of the house, and so under his care.

Gervin opened the door and murmured a few soft words of introduction. A young man entered the room. He stood, his back almost against the door, and waited nervously for permission to do something. The lord considered telling the man that it was permissible to breathe in his presence. *Ah, Sarillorn. Your effect is felt even here.*

"Please be seated."

The young man bowed to the ground.

*Not of the Church, then.* Taking in both the style and manner of the man's dress—common and rough—the lord decided that the man was probably a villager of the Vale; the message had been sent by relay. It appeared that Vellen was taking more caution with the lives of his priests—and utilizing, in their stead, the people of House Darclan's domain. The Lord Darclan was not amused.

"It appears that you have a message of some import."

The man nodded, and managed a shaky, "Yes, lord."

Darclan held out his hand, and an envelope was placed in it. It bore Vellen's seal, blood red wax with the stamp of a severed circle.

"It's from—from a high priest of the Greater Cabal, lord."
The man's face was almost in his lap.

"Thank you for that information."

Darclan looked at the seal with distaste and amusement—
Vellen's choice of emblem was too arrogant for any other reaction. Did he mistakenly assume that the destruction of the lines
had been the crowning work of *his* insignificant life? Something
would have to be done to correct that assumption.

Still, Vellen was almost a worthy opponent, crafty, cunning
and skilled in the ways of men. For that reason, his grip on the
letter was tight. He began to open it and realized that the messenger was still there.

"You may go."

The man almost tripped over his feet in his haste to reach the
door. He swung it open and did trip over Gervin, who waited a
few feet to the side of it. Again Gervin's eyes met the lord's, and
Darclan affirmed his previous decision with a sharp shake of the
head. Gervin closed the door of the study and helped the man
to his feet.

"You're a very lucky young man," he said. "Your lord is
one of the few who would not hold you responsible for any
information you have brought."

The man nodded shakily.

Behind the doors of the study, the lord opened the letter. He
read it once, but before he could reach the end of it, his eyes
were already becoming silver. The paper began to curl, and was
slowly consumed by blackness.

Sara looked up as Darin entered the room, his face almost
obscured by the pile of blankets he held. She nodded, but her
attention was clearly on one of the slaves who sat before her.

It was an older woman, Emilee, assistant to the seamstress.
Her joints ached, she said, and Sara nodded, her face the very
picture of seriousness.

Darin began to make the beds.

*I've never heard Emilee so polite. I didn't know she knew how
to be.* But he said nothing; he understood the cautious fear of
the older woman.

Only when she muttered, "Hearts damn the thing, then," did
he know that she, too, had decided to trust this rather unusual
noble. He wondered if Sara's grip on her arm had anything to
do with it. But Sara asked no names, indeed asked no information beyond that of the ailment she was attempting to treat.

Her voice was even and quiet, and her movements were slow and sure.

After Emilee, there was a quiet lull and Sara helped him make the rest of the beds. She looked tired already, but there was little time left before dinner, and Darin was certain that the lord would confine her to bed for the eve.

She sat down, and Darin took a seat on a vacant bed beside her.

"I can't believe how much work there is to do here. I've only seen five people and I'm already exhausted. Still, I think it's going rather well; in a few days, I don't imagine they'll still wonder if it's some sort of trap. And then, maybe, I'll have something like a name from them." She sighed. "But it *is* hard. I guess Marcus must've done more than I'd realized."

"Marcus?"

"He was the physician in Rennath." At Darin's quizzical look, she added, "The capital."

*Capital of what?* He looked down at Bethany, but she said nothing at all. From the tone of the silence, Darin knew that she knew what Sara was talking about. Sometimes Bethany could be infuriating.

*You must ask for yourself,* Bethany said softly. *But go cautiously, Initiate. I do not believe that your two worlds are as similar as either of you would like.*

*Do you do this on purpose?* Darin thought, frustrated. But at least she had a suggestion this time. He opened his mouth to speak, and the door burst open.

Sara's head turned immediately as she gained her feet. And then she paled, for she recognized the woman who stood, ghost-pale, in the doorway.

It was the young slave with the child, and the child was cradled in her arms.

"Lady," the woman said, her voice a shaky whisper, "master Gervin said you'd help if you could."

Sara was already at the door. She held out her arms.

"What happened?" she asked, more to give the woman something to do than because she needed the information.

"She was climbing on the banisters, in the wing." The woman took a deep breath. "She fell, I think. I didn't hear her; that's why I checked." Her words came faster. "But she isn't moving at all—she's breathing, but it sounds strange."

A little flare of green, invisible to the slave's eyes, wrapped itself gently around the young girl before passing through her.

Sara closed her eyes and bowed her head. The child was in no pain; even were she awake she would feel none. Not now, and not ever.

She forced herself to look up, and the knowledge that she'd gained was written clearly in the taut lines of her face.

"No," the woman breathed. She shook her head, her mouth open.

Pain. And a pain like this was too deep for Sara to touch. She was already tired, but as often happened, she had the energy to feel what the woman was feeling.

She looked down at the child again.

*She's trusting me.* Sara's hands tightened slightly. *And I can't do it. Not alone.*

It came back to this. Always to this. Had she been Kerlinda's equal—had she been a true adult—she could save the child's life. She could touch God, and He would respond, granting her some measure of His power.

But not even with the power of Sarillorn could she now complete this task. It was beyond her mortal ken.

This day, the first of her infirmary, she had already failed.

*No,* she thought.

"Darin."

He was already at her side.

"Bring me a dagger. A small one. Make sure it's clean."

He nodded, knowing what she wanted it for. He paused at the door to touch the young woman's shoulder gently.

"It's all right, Helen. Trust her."

And he was gone.

*Trust me?* If she could have, Sara would have laughed. But she did nothing but wait for the sound of Darin's return.

When he came, he held the dagger carefully in the palms of his hands. Once before, in the house, he had carried a dagger to a noble. It seemed fitting, then, that he should also be the one to carry this new, clean blade.

He handed it to her, his wide eyes upon her face.

And she hated the look in them more than she could say. For the moment, he was just another person to fail.

She handed the baby carefully to Helen.

"I cannot promise anything," she said, her lips burning on the lie. "But I will do what I can."

Helen nodded, wide-eyed and silent.

Sara looked down at the truth of the metal that pressed against her palm. She lifted it carefully, looking only at the unscarred white of her hands.

*Lernan,* she prayed, *please, God, listen just this once.*

Blade bit into flesh, as it had done time beyond number before this. Blood welled into cupped palm as her hand began its silent dance.

She willed it to happen. Her lips were pressed firmly into a thin, white line. She gestured. She prayed. She pleaded. All this in a silence that knew no end.

God would not answer.

She looked at the blood in her hands. The blood on the floor. Without looking up, she whispered, "I'm sorry."

Helen's breathing seemed to stop, and Sara braced herself for what followed. The pain of even this lost hope hit her like a sword, but she stood in its path, paying its price.

It was Darin who eventually sent Helen on her way; Sara did not have the strength left to do even that. But she felt the curiosity and, yes, the pity in his eyes as he left her alone with the failure.

And when he left, the tears came. And the anger. And the fear.


"Darin, where is the lady?"

Darin looked up slowly from the food that he'd not touched. "Maybe she'll be down soon." His voice said it wasn't likely.

The lord's frown, subtle and slight, was still unpleasant to behold.

"What passed today?"

Darin's frown held no menace, but it was no less unpleasant to Lord Darclan.

"She tried to ward," he answered quietly. "One of the children fell."

Lord Darclan raised an eyebrow. "And this is enough to keep her from dining?"

"She failed." Darin's cheeks burned with shame for her.

Silence, then, always silence.

"I see," the lord said at last. He rose, and motioned for Darin to remain.


He found her in her rooms, sitting in the largest chair with her legs curled forlornly beneath her. Her head was propped up on one elbow, and a blood-stained hand sat loosely in her lap. It was dark; only one of the lamps had been lit, and its flame burned low. He would have to see that it was replaced, but not now.

He looked closely at her. Her eyes were closed. She seemed almost translucent, as if the dying light could pass through her without leaving even a trace of shadow.

"Sara," he said softly, as he walked toward her.

She looked up, her green eyes ringed by the shadow of circles. Wearily, she nodded to acknowledge his presence. Her eyes fell again.

"Lady?"

She didn't answer, not with words. But for the few seconds that they stayed open, her eyes lingered upon the blood that had failed her.

He put his arms around her gently and lifted her.

"This is no place for sleep," he said. He tried to smile. She would have liked that expression, but it failed him.

Her breath punctuated his thoughts as he held her.

*I have lost, Sara. I have lost all. I was foolish. Why am I always so foolish where you are concerned?*

He looked at the hand that lay open.

She was Lernan's; she was always Lernan's—no matter what the cost and strength of the binding he placed upon her had been, he could not change that fact.

And now, now he wasn't certain that he really wanted to. For her sake, at this moment, perhaps. But still . . .

*What have you done to me, Sara? How did you accomplish this? Why have the years not erased your mark? All else mortal passes.*

*Ah. It is dark, and too soon.*

He laid her down upon the bed, pulling the covers over her still form.

"I must leave, Sara. I shall return in the morning."

But her hand, wounded, fluttered at his robes. She was exhausted, and this was as much of a request as she could make.

He caught her hand and held it, cradling her tightly.

*A moment,* he thought, stroking her hair. *A moment for you, lady.*

And he held her for as long as his nature allowed it in the face of the darkening sky. In the day it would have been easy, the feel of her breath against his cheek an unalloyed pleasure. But it was night now, and she lay so helpless. His arms did not tire under her weight, and he moved only when she stirred slightly.

"Sara, I must go."

Her eyes never opened, although her arms tightened briefly around him. If she had asked, with words, he could have answered.

But he stayed; when he could stand it no longer, he still remained. And the brown stains on her hand seemed to redden before his eyes, to become a damp, limpid thing that struggled to leave her body. It strained, as if the flesh contained it, and he watched, mesmerized, as it tried to come to him.

To him.

With a silent cry, he threw her aside and bolted out of the room, his steps loud and lingering as they splintered the silence of the castle. The halls stretched out before him, comforting and infuriating in their emptiness.

It was cold, and the cold was steady and patient, for its waiting was almost over.

The details of the hall were lost to him; they melted into the background of a purely physical and unimportant world. Only the feel of the desk beneath his fingertips told him that he had made it to his study. He wheeled around, his nocturnal sight revealing the indistinct outline of a door slightly ajar in the dark room.

"Gervin!" His voice was a half snarl.

A form radiating heat appeared between the door and the wall. The features were indistinct, blurred by the taint of the living. Almost as an afterthought, the hardwood of the desk beneath his fingers buckled. The form took a quick step backward, stopped, and surged forward again. Stefanos could feel the small splinters of wood drive their way into his flesh—but the pain of it was distant, almost hollow.

"Go—get—Darin. Tell him—ward—study—door—from—outside."

"Lord?"

*'Now!'* His lips curled around the wood with a resistance that was more real than the wood that continued to burrow into him. More real, more painful. The walls of his mind, so precise and so logical, could barely contain the urge that drove him.

*I am First!* His fingers curled more tightly into the desk.

"Heart's blood." Two small, hushed syllables and the heat was gone. Gone before Stefanos' sudden leap forward could prevent it from escaping. The door, dead and cold, slammed shut, and he staggered backward into the center of the room. Little spears struck him from behind, and he whirled, his fingers becoming curved like claws. Moonlight streamed into the study. It hurt him. He knew that it had been long since the light had hurt him. With a blind lurch, he jumped out of the path of the uncurtained window and rolled into the darkness.

His hunger jerked him up and shoved him forward. It had been long since the light had hurt, but longer still since he had truly felt warm—since the blood of the living had filled him, permeated him, with its necessary heat.

Darin rolled over and sat up sharply. There was a loud pounding on his door, and an indistinct shouting filtered into the room. Shaking the sleep out of his eyes, he grabbed the wool blanket from his bed, and tying it loosely around his shoulders, got up and opened the door a crack.

In the dim light of the hall, he could see Gervin's frantic face.

"Gervin?"

"Darin, you must come, and quickly!" The older man was breathing heavily, his shoulders rising and falling with the effort of running from one end of the castle to the other.

Darin nodded swiftly and turned to retrieve his clothing. Gervin's shaking hand caught his shoulder before he could leave the door.

"You've no time to change! Come with me now, or many lives will be lost!"

"It'll only take a few—"

"Darin." Gervin lowered his voice, making up for the lack of volume with a terrifying intensity of tone. "The lord will walk if you cannot prevent it."

"Walk? Gervin, what are you talking—Bright Heart!" Any idea of clothing vanished as the weight of Gervin's words hit home. A whisper of memory chilled him. *Nightwalker. Lifeblood.* Brushing Gervin's hands aside, Darin ran into the room, picked up Bethany, and returned. With one hand he gripped the ends of the blanket around his shoulders. His face was white with fear and loathing.

"It isn't what you think," Gervin said over his shoulder; already he had started to run up the halls. "The lord sent me to you himself—told me to tell you to ward the study from the outside."

Darin didn't feel the cold stone of the floor against his bare feet. That sensation was lost as a sudden warmth flared to life in his right hand; the staff of Culverne was glowing more brightly than it had ever done.

He thought he was never going to reach the study; the halls suddenly seemed treacherously long. He had no time to worry about what he would have to face—all of his effort was funneled into reaching Lord Darclan. His breath grew ragged as he turned the bend of the hall that led to the study.

Darin stopped in the hall as an arm suddenly shot through the closed door of the outer room to the Lord's study. It moved so quickly that it had vanished before Darin fully understood what it had done; but he could see that a large, jagged hole remained in the wood. He felt the blanket slip from his shoulders as he brought his left hand down to the staff. The door shivered again, as if alive; the hole grew larger. Darin began to walk toward it, only now noticing that Gervin was not at his side. The crash of breaking wood obscured the sound his feet made as they lightly touched the floor. He raised the staff as if to bar the passage of whatever came through.

*Too late,* he thought numbly.

Because he was prepared, he stood his ground as the shadow crawled out. It was dark with a blackness that Darin had seen only twice in his life.

*Nightwalker.*

*Lord Darclan.*

But this was not the lord that Darin knew. Bethany flared brightly, and a shaft of light struck out. The creature snarled and backed away. Red flared indistinctly, and Darin realized that the eyes of the walker were upon him.

*What's happened?*

Light flared again, in a bright ring around Darin's feet.

*He has not fed in a while. Be wary.* Everything in Bethany's words told Darin that her voice still felt the darkness keenly.

He didn't need the warning; his hands gripped the staff as if it were an extension of his body. It burned steadily.

*The barrier will hold, but I do not know for how long. I have never seen a Servant in this state.*

The shadow moved forward slowly.

Again the staff flared brightly, but this time the nightwalker stopped outside of its reach, cringing into a slight retreat.

"Lord Darclan."

The creature became absolutely still. Darin took his right hand from the staff and raised it, palm up, hesitantly.

*Darin, you cannot reach him thus.*

*How, then?*

"Do you know me?"

Silence.

"Do you know Lady Sara?"

Something flickered in the wild eyes that met his; a brief, almost human pain. It looked out of place in the redness of the Dark Heart, but it was gone so quickly that Darin wondered if he'd imagined it.

And then the shadow spoke.

Darin could not recognize the voice; it was sibilant and low, as if the vocal chords had not been made for human speech.

"Initiate." Long, that word, as if spoken by a dying man. "Stay." Tendrils of shadow moved in a short circle. "Light. Here."

Darin responded with Bethany's power, and the light that had surrounded him moved outward until it lay around the Lord like a wall.

He heard the answering cry of pain and hesitated.

*"Light!"*

Closing his eyes, Darin nodded.

Gervin walked around the bend in the hall, his chest rising and falling visibly. He stopped to lean against the wall, just beneath the ring of a large torch. The flickering shadows underlined the fatigue and relief in his face.

"In time," he murmured.

Darin nodded, but he kept both hands on the staff.

"Gervin."

The eyes of the slavemaster penetrated the shadow. He shivered and started to turn away. "Tell him." The voice, strangled and gutteral, was still the command of his master.

"Lord," Gervin whispered. He bowed, although the bow was out of place in this strange tableau.

"Darin, the lord is a nightwalker; you know of it. You know he is different from the others, perhaps better than I. But the one thing I do know is this: He hasn't fed in all the time I've served him.

"I've watched for signs of it; if he were trying to be subtle there would be disappearances. If he weren't, there would be husks of bodies. I haven't seen either.

"Do you understand? He hasn't fed for over forty years."

*Longer.* It was Bethany's voice. *Much longer. Ah, Lady . . .*

*"Light,"* the lord said, and cringed anew. His face was only shadow now, but that shadow twisted and writhed around two red points. Hunger drove him; pain kept him at bay—but between

these two forces there was room for shame. Stefanos, First of the Sundered, had never asked for help in his long history.

"How long?" Darin whispered, hoping that the Lord would understand. "How long?"

"Dawn . . ." One tendril reached out and stopped a hair's breadth from the barrier that Culverne had called. "For Sara . . ."

Darin closed his eyes. He felt the uncertainly in Bethany without having to ask.

"Darin, can you hold him?"

"I don't know," Darin whispered.

Gervin had no reply, but Darin felt him draw closer. There was no comfort in words, and no encouragement, but Gervin was prepared to offer what he could. Sometimes, silences were best.

He held the staff high until his arms ached with its slight weight. It inched toward the ground, drawn there by gravity and exhaustion, but the circle it had drawn shone no less brilliantly.

Time seemed to slow; the torches in the hall began to flicker— a signal of the end of their life. Darkness fell, but the light of Culverne burned on, casting its white and green along Darin's bowed head.

It was cold here.

It grew colder still when the circle began to dim.

Darin's heart froze for an instant as the shadows around the Lord began to take more solid form.

*Not yet!*

*No,* Bethany's voice said. It was weaker now, as the light was weaker. *But I can hold this no longer. Call the Bright Heart, Darin. Ward.*

*But I don't know what to do!*

*I do. Call His power; I will direct it.*

Darin looked down at the staff in his hands. Panic rose; he was completely naked, no robes, no knife. And he could not put the staff aside; the Lord would walk then, and all of this would mean nothing.

But Gervin was prepared, somehow. A hand touched his shoulder in the darkness.

"A knife," the old man said softly.

Darin's hand found Gervin's and clasped it tightly.

"Do it," he said softly. "I can't let go of the staff."

He felt a sharp pain; his right hand again. And the cut was deeper than he might have made it, but Gervin was not sighted: the light of Culverne didn't guide him. Darin shook his head as blood filled his cupped hand. Then he looked at the shadow until the darkness was the only thing he could see.

Chill air filled his lungs. He called God; God answered.

And the light that ringed the Lord grew brighter. The shadows retreated.

*Thank you, Initiate,* Bethany said. *No one of us can stand alone.*

*Is this what it was like?* Darin thought. He imagined, for a moment, that the priests of the line stood in a ring around him, each offering their blood and its power in turn, each taking up the burden when it became too heavy for another to bear.

Or maybe it was the presence of God that took the stone corridors of House Darclan and replaced them with trees and starlight and family. It didn't matter; he was pleased to stand among them as an equal. They spoke no words, but their nods and smiles, their encouragements, were enough.

They stood for some time, and then, one by one, they approached him. They bowed, each in turn, and he saw the light that limned them. It was the same, measure for measure, as the one that ringed him.

And then they were gone; the clearing was gone; the halls stood around him.

He looked up, shaking his head, to meet the eyes of the lord. Human eyes; darker than any he had seen before, but cast in a human face. Only a trace of shadow remained, and even that was fading.

"Initiate."

Darin nodded. He was weary suddenly, but at peace; the night had passed. He waited for the lord to speak, but no words came. As Gervin before him, the lord offered his silence.

But this silence was forged in a different fire. The First of the Sundered held it about him as a shield. He watched as the light that had hindered him faded, leaving unmarked stone in its wake. He met the boy's eyes briefly, and then nodded again. Later, if there was time for it, he would have his words.

The outer door was a ruin; he remembered splintering it with the force of near-unleashed darkness. It had been foolish; it had cost much. He opened the door and walked beyond it, into the light of his study.

It was brighter, but the light no longer cut him.

*Sarillorn.* He touched the glass pane, spreading his palm against it. *A few days later and it would not have mattered.*

But she was still alive, and still his. And no death, no feeding, would mar that yet.

He was a Servant who had accepted the blood of a priestess, freely given.

*The hunger has never been so strong. I should not have stayed.*

He shifted restlessly. Was he not First among the Sundered? Yes, and in his nature was all that the Dark had been on the first Awakening. Nature called its own.

Dim sensations, centuries older than the world on which he walked, returned, and with them the hatred for the harsh, rigid spears of the Light. He could feel the stirring of scars wrought before wounds were invented. *I am of the Dark.*

*Yes, Stefanos, but the Dark itself changed with the coming of the Light, and the Light with the touch of the Dark.*

Her voice. Always her voice and her face, her light.

He did not know how long he stayed by the window, nor did it concern him; if he was left with nothing else, he would always have time. Time. His fist slammed into the wall.

# chapter
# seventeen

*Morning*.

She was alone, again. Always alone.

The sun was low on the horizon, but already its upward creep was noticeable. She rose in silence, seeing Helen's face, unable to see anything but Helen's face. Even the little child whose death was assured was not as clearly graven.

Her hands shook slightly as she rose. Clothing was laid out; somebody had come and gone, having seen to this task without waking her. She took advantage of it, sliding into the dress provided without even resenting its complicated finery.

There was a knock on the door.

*Darin*. She put a smile on and found to her surprise that it was only half-forced. It would be nice to have company.

"Come in."

It was not Darin who entered. Stefan walked through the door. He caught her faltering smile as it faded and winced.

"Darin is asleep," he said quietly. "I thought I might escort you to the hall in his stead. Shall I have him awakened, lady?"

"No."

"Sara." He took a step forward, then another, to bring him closer. Then he stopped, inches away from her, his dark eyes seeing nothing else. "Lady." He touched her shoulders as gently as he could and bowed his head. "I am sorry."

She mistook his meaning—how could she do otherwise?—and said, "It wasn't your fault. It was mine."

He only smiled, but no smile should have contained what his did.

"It is late, lady."

"Late? I don't think it's noon yet."

"Late," he repeated, as his eyes drifted windowward. "I

243

have guests, or I will have soon. Come, let us spend what we have of the day.''

He looked up a moment, and two slaves came in bearing two large trays. "Midday, Sara. Would it trouble you if I remained?''

"But the infirmary—''

"It will wait. Gervin tends those he can, and he will make his report to you. Please, lady.''

Something in his voice touched her, and she laid a hand against his cheek. Her smile echoed the sadness in his without ever touching its depths.

"We never have much time for each other, do we?'' she asked softly. "You in your night, I in my day.''

He closed his eyes, and on impulse she stretched to her toes to kiss his lids. They were cool; they trembled ever so slightly.

This was the last day. Night came soon, and it would be endless. He held her. He held her very tightly.


They walked together down the long hall. Day had come and gone, its passage too quick and too clean. Sara leaned against him, her arm entwined with his, a hint of smile across her lips.

*Now,* he thought. *It comes now.*

Gervin turned around a corner. His step was quick and firm, but it was obvious that the message he bore was an urgent one.

"Lord.''

Lord Darclan nodded gravely. "The high priest has come.''

Gervin's eyes widened fractionally and then he nodded.

"Where?''

"In the outer hall.'' Gervin smiled; it was not pleasant. "Waiting your command.''

"Very well. I will go to him now.''

He turned, kissed Sara's forehead, and then pushed her gently in Gervin's direction. "Lady, go to Darin.''

Their eyes locked for a few moments before Sara looked away. She nodded, tense, and he released her.

"Gervin, go with the lady. Make sure she arrives safely and without interruption.''

"Yes, lord.''

*Do not fail.* But the lord felt no need to say the words aloud. He turned and began to walk almost casually down the stairs while Sara and Gervin watched his retreating back.

\* \* \*

The halls were completely empty. A grim smile touched Stefanos' face as his ears picked up what his eyes could not; the muted, half-hysterical murmuring of slaves locked in their quarters, awaiting the pleasure of the Church. His thoughts were clean and sharp, focused on one thing alone: the high priest of the Greater Cabal, leader of the Karnari.

*Ah Vellen, Vellen. I should have killed you years ago. You showed promise, even then.* But there was no real anger to his thoughts, and not as much pain as there might have been.

*It has been long since any have provided a challenge to me.* His smile was the one that Sara had always found so distressing. It faded into a lean, straight line.

*Too long, perhaps.*

He rounded the last corner and entered the outer hall.

The Swords were there; four, well armed and armored, clean as if newly brought to the encounter. And at their head, Vellen.

A thought struck him, and he looked more closely at the Swords. Malanthi, and not as weak of blood as most he had seen in this generation.

But the Swords were beneath his concern. The high priest, surprisingly, was not. Lord Vellen. He wore the common regalia of the Church, but it had been altered to suit better his station. Across the front of the robe—and doubtless the back as well— was a large, severed circle. It was a metallic red, but hints of gold surrounded it, catching the torchlight in the hall.

Vellen stood tall, almost as tall as the Lord himself, but where Stefanos chose dark hair with eyes that were black, the high priest was fair-haired, and his eyes were the blue of sapphires, clear and cold.

The high priest stepped forward and bowed.

"Lord Darclan." The gesture was completely correct and deferential. The black of his robe swept the floor as he held the bow for just the right length of time. "It has been long since I've had the grace of your presence, First Servant."

"Indeed." Lord Darclan returned the bow, in every way as meticulous about its performance as Vellen had been.

"I apologize for the need to impose upon you with such short notice. I've taken care to keep my party small to avoid causing you inconvenience."

"Thoughtful, as always." He gestured briefly. "Is this the whole of your entourage, then?"

The briefest of smiles touched Vellen's face. It was like ice, and gone in an instant, but it left no room for hope.

"No, Lord. I am afraid that the rest of my traveling companions have not yet arrived. I expect them shortly, and apologize for their delay. They should be here momentarily."

Again the ice flickered across Vellen's lips, lingering like a chill in the air. "They stopped to provision in the Vale, Lord. They did not wish to . . . deplete the resources of your house proper."

"High Priest," Stefanos said softly, "I have always suspected you of being the superior of any who have held your title." He meant every word. "If you will permit it, I will wait with you while your rooms are seen to. I would like to see my suspicions confirmed."

There was a small trace of surprise. "I would be honored by your company, Lord."

Both stood in the silence of the hall, watching each other, their faces masked by a respect that was only half lie. They waited, their tension hidden but palpable.

Stefanos heard the sound first; the bars of the gate were being lifted. All present heard the gates as they began to open, but no one looked toward the main doors until they swung wide.

Only when people began to enter did the Swords turn. The high priest, however, did not look away from Lord Darclan's gaze—for this he had come, and this he would not deny himself.

They entered one by one, until they stood, four abreast, in the hall. The Swords of the Church bowed as one before allowing the four to pass.

Each of the four was of a height with Lord Darclan. Their feet, where they touched the stone, made no sound. They walked in shadow, *were* shadow. Where skin could be seen at all, it was deathly and chill in its pallor.

They moved without speaking until they stood two on either side of the high priest. Lord Vellen lifted his arms slightly to either side.

"Lord Darclan, my entourage is now complete." He let his arms fall casually.

The Servant furthest to his left bowed slightly. Shadow wavered, swallowing torchlight.

"It has been long by even the reckoning of the Sundered, Stefanos."

Stefanos inclined his head slightly, no trace of what he felt on his face. "Longer indeed than I thought, Kirlan, if the Sundered now serve the Church."

Kirlan's head snapped up; his eyes flared red for an instant.

"Come, Stefanos," another said, stepping forward. "There is no need for insult." His voice was more sibilant than Kirlan's had been. Vellen's head turned sharply to the right, but his expression remained smooth.

Stefanos allowed himself the luxury of a smile; it was the same as Vellen's had been, and gone as quickly. "Sargoth. I did not know you ventured still into the mortal realm."

"I venture when called."

"And what has called the Second of the Sundered on such a journey?"

The third Servant stepped forward. "You already know, Stefanos." Her voice, like Kirlan's, sounded hollow but smooth. It had none of the rasping quality of the Second's.

Stefanos met her eyes for a moment and then gave a terse nod. "Perceptive, Vashel."

"Always; yet not so much as the First. I believe that you know why we are called." Her bow was low; her words were a gesture of respect for power that was not yet her own.

The fourth and last of the Servants stepped forward.

"But perhaps it needs to be expanded upon." A grim malice contorted his face. "We were summoned by the Dark Heart, Lordling. Malthan bade us come in the company of this—" he did not bother to grant Vellen his title. "You shelter something he seeks, Stefanos. And we mean to bring it to our God. Stand in our way and perhaps you will no longer be First among us; you are weaker now than you have been."

"That may be true, Algrak." Stefanos inclined his head slightly, and the Servant smiled triumphantly.

Too soon. In a blur that Vellen could barely see, Darclan crossed the ten feet that separated him from Algrak. His hands closed round the Servant's throat, and his eyes flared, first silver, then a bright crimson that engulfed all present. With contemptuous ease, he hauled Algrak off his feet.

"There is always a fool in any order, Algrak, even that of the Sundered." His voice was low and furious. "You insult those of us who are not by behaving like a mortal fool; but anger me further in *my* domains, and I will see you destroyed."

No one made move to interfere. Vellen gave Algrak one disdainful glance before turning to speak with his Swords.

"Stefanos, you are ever First among us," Sargoth interjected. "Algrak has spent too long in mortal lands, but even he must remember this now."

"Perhaps, but perhaps not." With casual ease, Stefanos murmured a few words while Algrak clawed, almost effectively, at his hands. The First Servant's eyes flashed silver again, and with an almost gentle push, he caved in Algrak's throat. Algrak's eyes widened in agony at the red claws in his flesh.

Stefanos looked down the hall, and the doors swung suddenly open, slamming into the stonework.

"High Priest, please have your men move to the side."

"At your command, lord." He nodded slightly, and the Swords moved toward either wall.

Stefanos looked down at Algrak. "Remember this if you are capable of it, Algrak. I have never suffered fools gladly. Repair the damage to your chosen form as you are able—but do not dare to replenish the power you spend from any who dwell within my halls." He lifted Algrak over his head and threw him out of the opened doors. He made another gesture, and the doors slammed shut.

His expression was still smooth, but none there could mistake the red-fire that swirled in the lines of his face—they were all of the Dark Heart's blood.

What surprised Vellen was that the Servant survived at all.

As if that surprise were spoken, Stefanos turned to stare at him.

"I believe your rooms will be ready if you care to retire."

"That would be greatly appreciated, lord." Vellen smiled. "But as high priest, there are duties that I must attend to."

"I understand." Stefanos played smile for smile while the Servants watched with vague disinterest. "But surely your journey was somewhat tiring. These duties can wait until the morn."

Sargoth's gaze swung to Stefanos and remained there as if riveted.

"Morning, Lord?" Vellen asked.

"Indeed. I have already arranged for breakfast. I believe if you join me on the terrace, we will have more time to consider our respective situations."

"Perhaps you are correct. The journey here has been tiring. I believe, if you will have someone guide us to our rooms, we will be thankful for the opportunity to relax." He smiled, but he was seething. *Algrak is a fool.*

But Algrak had served the purpose of the First well; the demonstration was not lost upon the high priest. He bowed.

Stefanos nodded.

Neither relaxed; the time for that luxury would come soon enough.

"I will lead you to your rooms personally to assure myself that nothing is lacking."

"We are honored."

Stefanos led them to the east wing. It was seldom used, but had been designed to impress visiting dignitaries of any importance; it was easily the most magnificent portion of the castle.

Tapestries, depicting scenes of battle, lined the walls with their dark, rich colors and their legacy of death. Frescoes on the arched ceilings portrayed the fall of each of the Dark Heart's true Enemies, many of whom the high priest could not identify.

At the end of the hall, Stefanos paused in front of a set of large double doors. He opened them and stood to one side.

"I hope you will find these suitable, High Priest. I was expecting your personal company to be larger; there are subsidiary rooms which will house the Swords."

Vellen motioned to his men, and they entered, disappearing from view.

"I look forward to our meeting on the morrow, Lord."

"And I." He, too, bowed, and then walked away.

Lord Vellen watched him leave. He had developed a grim understanding of how such a Servant had built the Empire of Veriloth and ruled it for so many centuries. He did not understand why the First harbored the last of their ancient enemies—nor indeed how that event had come to pass. Nor was it clear to him how the well of the Enemy had been released. Not that it mattered now—he had met the Servant face to face and knew that whatever the reasons, there was still no weakness in him.

Not that Vellen's success was in doubt, but he could appreciate now why the Dark Heart had called four of the Sundered to aid him; they would be necessary—it would be close.

*Still,* he thought, *a pity.*

*But with your fall, I will have accomplished the work of a lifetime; the fall of Culverne will pale by comparison.*

The night held a faint breeze that fanned Stefanos' hair gently.

*Damn him.*

He stared bitterly through a haze that human eyes could not see. The barrier.

"You still wander the night then."

"And you, Sargoth," he replied without turning.

Sargoth drifted over to Stefanos' side. "Yes. though this is the first time in centuries that I have wandered for a reason other than hunger."

"That hunger has been satisfied for the time?"

He felt, rather than saw, Sargoth nod. He did not look back; the sight of the barrier, translucent and red, still held him fast.

"It is powerful, is it not?" How like Sargoth, to avoid answering a question by asking another.

"Indeed."

There was a glint of teeth. "No, Stefanos. It is not mine. Had I the power, I doubt I would waste it so. The Sundered of the Enemy have long since passed, and they alone were worthy of such a display."

"You never cared much for our descendants."

"*Your* descendants."

"And the Lernari?"

"Precocious mortals, deserving of some notice in the past, but then only the Line Elliath—the Lady's children."

"I see."

They were silent, the darkness robed around them.

"Do you remember the first time we stood upon the body of the world? There were more of us then; we were stronger."

"Are we weaker now, Sargoth?"

"Not all of us."

Again, silence. Any other would have suffered for those words.

"Word reaches far." Stefanos began to walk again, crushing the grass beneath his feet. Sargoth followed behind.

"Do you even remember what it is like, Stefanos?"

All Servants had perfect recall, should they choose to exercise it; Sargoth knew this well, but Stefanos chose not to rise to the comment. "I remember."

"Ah." The hiss of something, perhaps a sigh. "And yet you refrain. It is curious; I would have thought the only interest that humans could have would be in the dying—but in dying, they achieve some spark of glory. Nothing feels pain quite so clearly."

"Sargoth—"

"You were First among the Sundered, First of the Servants, the strongest of our number. Tell me, have you become sundered anew?" He paused to place one cold hand upon Stefanos' shoulder. Slowly, the First turned to face him.

Sargoth wore a veil of darkness around his form, one too thick for even Stefanos to penetrate without expending power. "I am curious."

"As I have been about you in the past, before the mortals caught my interest."

"If that was ever true, it was long before the Twin Hearts rose to shape our existence. May I?"

"I am hardly likely to waste the power necessary to stop you. I can ill afford it."

Sargoth nodded, and a ring of red rose from the darkness, encircling them both. It flared once around Stefanos, a fiery aurora, and then faded into gray.

"You are changed, but I do not know how," Sargoth said.

"Yes."

"It is strange. I would like to meet the one that you shelter."

"No."

"Perhaps not yet, Stefanos. But the time will come, and shortly, by our standards. He waits."

"I know it."

"Have you spoken with Him?"

"No."

Sargoth turned to face the barrier. "It is costly, even for Him. The blood flowed freely on the altars of the priesthood for this; Algrak supervised it." One dark limb passed thoughtfully through the perimeter. "Not even for the Lady of Elliath was such power used. And yet He uses it now. Do you not wonder why?"

"No."

A low, broken hiss touched the air like a cloud. Sargoth was laughing.

"Changed indeed, Stefanos, if I believe your word. But I will tell you this—I am curious. I say again that I will meet your Sarillorn."

Dryly, Darclan replied. "I do not think that meeting will give you much pleasure, Sargoth. I believe that was always your complaint about the Lernari; they died before you could consume them fully."

"True. Yet if I recall correctly, Stefanos, it was yours as well. I did not work as hard as the rest of you to try to claim the reward of their death. And that is curious as well, for you wished to destroy one fully, but now that the means and time for this is at your disposal, you do nothing."

Stefanos saw Sara then, briefly, as a glow in the heart of the night. Saw her smile touch his face and linger like kisses against his eyelids.

"Your curiosity was always your undoing, Sargoth."

"Yes. But I at least have the courage to accept what will

unmake me." He laughed again. "And you, you will not even ask Him why."

"I leave that to those who care for the answer."

"A pity. For I have asked Him often since I returned, and He will tell me nothing. I believe, if you asked, you would have the answer that I desire."

"Then I will definitely not ask; I am aware of the difficulties that arise between Servants when one has what another desires."

"And yet, if both have something that the other desires, there can be some sort of negotiation."

"I was not aware that you have in your possession something that would serve me." Stefanos chose his words with care.

"I do not have it yet, but I believe I shall. If that is the case, First among us, I shall make my offer then."

Stefanos looked at Sargoth carefully. *You were always different, Second of the Sundered.* "Ah, Sargoth. Even when you come at Malthan's bidding, you play your games."

"But I still come at His bidding. You alone among us have ever refused—and even then, only once." The hidden face turned away. "It appears that you have found a way to master the sunlight. If we meet again after this, perhaps you can teach me the same." He began to drift backward.

"Answer one last question, Stefanos; the answer will not be of relevance to you, but I am—"

"Curious. Ask."

"Has He not spoken of this affair to you?"

"No."

"I see."

# chapter
## eighteen

*Darin answered the door.*

He caught Gervin's bow and looked in astonishment at Sara. Although she had become the best of his friends, he had never seen her in the slaves' wing—and was certain that the lord would have forbidden it.

On the other hand, Gervin did nothing without the lord's express command, and he stood at her side.

They were both tense, both silent.

After a moment, Darin realized that they meant to stand outside in the hall until he got out of the doorway, and he took a few steps back.

Sara entered first and came to a stop in the room's center. Gervin followed and then closed the door gently behind them. "Your pardon, Darin," Gervin said, his voice very quiet. "But we are to wait here for the hour."

"Here? Why?"

"I'm sorry." Gervin bowed his head. "But Lord Vellen of Damion has come." He knew what the name meant to the boy, and was uncomfortable in even mentioning it.

Nor was he mistaken. Darin paled visibly. He reached for the staff of Culverne and drew it very tightly to his chest.

"I haven't done anything wrong, have I?"

Gervin shook his head at the sudden fear in Darin's voice. "It is not for you that he has come, I fear."

Darin relaxed then; Gervin was not known for his ability to lie. But the words left a question hanging in the air. Darin felt guilty at the rush of relief he felt.

"Who?"

"Me, I think." It was Lady Sara who answered. Her arms

253

were wrapped tightly around her shoulders. "Lord Vellen, of Damion." She looked quietly at her feet. "The high priest."

Gervin nodded.

"When?" she asked, as if to someone not present. "When did Derlac cease to lead the Karnari?"

"Derlac, lady?"

She looked at Gervin. "Derlac was High Priest."

Gervin looked askance at Darin. Darin shook his head in reply.

"How long? How long has this Vellen claimed rulership of the Church?"

"Twelve summers." It was Darin who answered.

*Twelve years.* Sara's mouth made no sound as it moved over the words. *Twelve.* She unfurled her arms and looked at the veins of her white hands. *How?*

"Gervin." Her voice was soft. "I have been with the lord for four years. We lived in Rennath. We traveled the Empire three times." She took a deep breath, steadying herself. "Derlac was High Priest then. Stefanos did not love him, but of the priest-hood, Derlac made himself least offensive."

Gervin said nothing.

"The last time the Church tried to interfere with my lord, he devastated its upper ranks. The Karnari had to be rebuilt from the less trained and less powerful." She met his eyes squarely, her own dark. "Why would they choose to interfere here? Why are we here?"

"Lady." He bowed. "I have served the lord for near forty years. I have never seen you." His words struck her deeply, but not so deeply as hers had cut him. "Lady, do you know what the lord is?"

"What he is?" The words seemed so far away. "We are rited. He is my bond-mate." But her eyes looked through him as she said it. She shivered. "He is old, Gervin, old. He knows much, has much power. He is—" She shook her head and smiled, but the smile was pale. "Yes."

*Yes.*

*Lady. Lady of—*

Elliath. Light.

Gervin had seen much of the Empire. Now, his memories turned to a small, cramped holding cell for criminals and run-aways and the newly acquired slaves.

The smell was harsh; sweat, urine, and blood mingled to-gether so strongly that no one scent was distinct. An old man shared the small cell with him, but Gervin knew that it would not be for long; the aged chest cavity sank inward as if nothing prevented it; blood ran down his gaunt rib cage. A runner.

What had he said?

*Even the darkest of lords was not proof against the Lady; and he loved her as she loved us. Life cannot be forever without mercy; she who is gone will return, and we who slave await her coming.*

He was busy tearing strips of his own tunic off, in a vain attempt to bind the man's wounds.

*It does little good to you now. Or me. We're trapped here, under the hand of the Dark Heart.*

He had been young then, younger in every possible way. His anger was fresh, clean, consuming.

And the dying man—what was his name?—had found the strength, through his pain, to smile crookedly. *The Lady of Mercy comes for me now; I will certainly go with her. I will go with her knowing that there is hope yet for those I must leave behind. Hope is precious. It is her legacy.*

*Hope is foolish*, Gervin had said dully. He could hear the words struggle to leave his throat even now. *They've won.* His gaze was full of pity and horror, but he knew that he would not die, not yet. It was not death that he wanted, even though his life was already lost.

Young, then. Young indeed.

*Ah, child*, the man had said, although Gervin was no child at the time, *from Beyond, in the Lady of Mercy's care, I will pray that you, too, will find hope. She will come. She will return. It was promised to us.* And he had died.

*I cried for you*, Gervin thought. Then, with wonder, *and I am crying still.* It was true; he could feel the warm water slide down his cheeks almost peacefully. *Old man.*

*I found absolution at the hands of Culverne. I found healing.*

He looked up to see Sara's bowed head.

*Wherever you are, stop praying. I see her now. I know. I know who she is. And Bright Heart, I don't know how, or why, but the slave's tale was true.*

He brought his hand up to his cheek. His voice, when it came, was soft—but the strength in it, the strength! Just for the moment, Vellen was forgotten and the Church was a pale and passing mist, dissipated by sunlight's touch.

"Lady of Mercy."

Hearing his voice, Sara's head jerked up, as if pulled by invisible strings. "Gervin?" she said. He was crying, but his tears were not those of pain; they were rarer than that, and held, for the moment, a hypnotic beauty.

Darin, too, turned to look at Gervin. He saw what Sara saw, and more. He saw Stev, and all those other slaves who had held to their faith in the Lady.

"Gervin?" Sara said again.

"It is hope, lady." He shook his head, wiped the tears away, and walked to the door. "I would tell you a little of what you do not know, but I must go now. The patriarch will keep you company." He nodded to Darin and walked out.

Darin stood alone with Sara. Alone with the prayers, half-jaunty, half-earnest, of almost any slave he had ever known.

The light of Gervin's peace touched Sara's face; it was the first such that she had felt in House Darclan, and she was grateful for it.

"Darin." Her voice was quiet. "Tell me now, how you came to be in the Empire."

Gervin's face was still shining as he strode down the halls, unmindful of who he might meet there. He was full of purpose now, in a way that he had not been in living memory. The memories he had once interred were stirring, their ashes blowing across his mind in the wake of a clean, crisp breeze.

He walked along the stone floor, his footsteps light and resonant. He'd followed this same path many times, for many reasons, but none so dear to him as this one. The distance seemed to compress as he went, and before he knew it, he faced the sitting room door. Just beyond that, his lord's study lay waiting. He had no doubt he would find him there.

Nor was he wrong. He knocked once on the door, heard the terse, familiar command to enter, and walked directly in. He stopped for a moment in the door frame, as light assailed his vision. A fire burned in the grate. An oil lamp shone on the desk. On the wall, torches flickered merrily, tossing their shadows haphazardly across a small sphere of the room.

And surrounded by the light sat Stefanos, Lord Darclan, First of the Sundered, and the lord of Gervin's adult life.

Lord Darclan smiled grimly at Gervin's unconcealed surprise.

"It looks different in the light, does it not?"

"Lord." Gervin bowed.

"Do you have news to report?"

"No."

"Then why have you left the lady?" He waited for a reply, his eyes dark and glittering.

"It is of the lady I wish to speak."

"Speak then. No, wait. Before you ask, know this: the grounds are barriered against her passing; if she leaves now, she will be consumed in red-fire."

Almost as if to himself, Gervin said, "She will not leave now."

Lord Darclan raised an eyebrow, but the gesture held no menace. He laid his hands out, palms down, on the desk and looked at them in the play of the light.

"Gervin," he said, his voice calm and clear. "There are four Servants here." Just that.

Gervin's eyes seemed to darken. "Servants? Of the Enemy?"

Stefanos smiled grimly. "Of Malthan, yes. Do not forget to whom you speak." But again, his tone held only a shadow of danger.

Gervin stood silent for a few moments, and Darclan watched as the lines of his face grew once again more pronounced.

"Lord," he said at last. He pushed his shoulders back. *Perhaps,* he thought, *I am old indeed, to need such faith in hope.* But it was not dead, not yet. "I know her now."

"Know her?"

"She is the one that they call the Lady of Mercy; they have prayed for her return, and it has been granted."

"Prayed to her? Gervin, you served under the lines—you at least should know better than to put faith in superstition and children's tales. How can Lady Sara be this revered godling, when she is, as you know well, of the lines herself?"

Gerven mulled over his words for a few minutes. "She is Initiate, yes. But this does not mean that she cannot be more than that. Whether she knows it or not—and I believe she does not—her return here, at a time when darkness has seemed absolute and unshakeable, heralds a change."

"Really?" Darclan's fingers began to drum the surface of the desk unevenly. "And why do you think this?"

Gervin looked up, and for the first time in his years of service, met the eyes of the First Sundered without fear of pain. "Because, lord, you love her. And the Lady was the consort of the Dark Lord."

*At a time when darkness seems absolute, the Lady of Mercy will return to guide her people into the Light.* Stefanos wanted to laugh. *I know the words well, Gervin. I wrote them. Lady of Mercy. Lady.*

A bitter mirth twisted his face. What a human irony, this. What an ugly, strangled thing. Almost against his will, he said, "And how has that love served her?" He would not deny it. "If it brought her here, it brought her to death at the hands of His Servants. By her will, by her request, for her happiness, I have forsaken much of my heritage as nightwalker—and much of my power. The others have not. Against any one of them, I would prevail; perhaps against two. But the Second has come to mortal lands, and with the aid of the others, I will be unable to aid the Lady. And they know well the powers she wields—they will not be vulnerable to her fire or her light."

"Lord—by morning the Servants must retreat. There is only the high priest, and I believe she can master him with Darin's aid."

"She can master him well enough without the aid of the boy, but Malthan's wall will hold true; it is anchored today by the Malanthi. If she crosses it, she *will* perish."

Gervin leaned forward, an almost triumphant expression on his face. "But she can call upon the power of the gifting of Lernan to bring that barrier down."

"Do you think I have not thought on this?" Darclan's face was bleak and hollow. "If she calls upon the power of Lernan to undo Malthan's work, the effect will be the same; it is too much for one mortal to hold, and she will be consumed. The barrier is God's work.

"And if, by some chance, she should succeed, the power that she calls to destroy the barrier would also destroy me. During the night, I have some chance of survival—but in the day my strongest of wards would avail nothing." His hands curled into smooth fists. "Listen well, Gervin. You will never hear this again—and if you speak of it to the Lady, you will die after witnessing the deaths of all those in your care."

Gervin nodded, strangely unafraid.

"If the Lady could call upon the blood of the Bright Heart to destroy the barrier without herself being consumed, and the cost of it were my life alone, I would grant it to her now. But should she succeed, she will fail, for if I fall, she will fall at the same instant."

Gervin was silent for a few minutes more, pondering the grim visage of his lord. Darkness gathered round him, dulling his eyes, for he knew that the lord did not lie.

"Perhaps it is better that she perish thus. The alternative is—"

"I know."

Sara was very, very tired. Darin, who ushered people into her presence, was worse. Darin, on the other hand, didn't have to smile when he really felt like crawling into—or under—a bed.

She sighed as he led away a rather foolhardy young boy. At least today there had been no emergencies. And if there were no brilliant successes, there had been no tragic failures.

Yet.

*I am tired.* She heard a knock at the door and straightened her shoulders. If she wanted to feel miserable, best do it on her own time. Darin went to answer it and froze.

He met Lord Vellen's gaze squarely, barely noticing that here the lord wore robes of the Church, not the house.

Lord Vellen looked down at him, and for a moment, he too froze.

"Out of my way," he said softly at last.

To his great regret, Darin moved automatically, casting his eyes to the ground. But he didn't bow. Didn't scrape the floor with his forehead.

And maybe that would have been wiser.

Lord Vellen passed him without another backward glance. His Swords stayed stationed in the hall, to warn off any who came to this unusual infirmary. He walked over to Lady Sara, black robes swirling around a complexion as fair as hers, but colder.

"Lady Sara Laren, I believe. I hoped to have the opportunity to make your acquaintance. One of the slaves told me, most reluctantly, that I would find you here."

Sara felt slightly sick, but held on to her frozen smile. "I'm afraid that I won't have much time to speak with you. I've a busy day ahead of me."

"Indeed." He looked casually around the room, his eyes taking in—and dismissing—the medical supplies that lay to one side of the small bed. "I do not believe, however, that we will be disturbed for the next few minutes at least." He turned and nodded to one of the Swords. The door creaked shut.

Sara remembered the only time that the priests had entered her infirmary. She tensed.

"Please, lady, be seated. It would be rather inconsiderate of me to make you stand for the duration of our interview."

"Oh. Does this mean that the priests of the Church now only indulge in acts that are extremely inconsiderate?"

He smiled, and Sara was surprised to see that it was genuine. The lines of his face moved around his mouth, giving them a younger, almost carefree look. The dark color of his clothing heightened the flawless fairness of his skin and hair.

"Please allow me to introduce myself. I am Vellen of House Damion, and High Priest of the Church of Malthan."

"As you already know who I am, I shall spare you a like introduction."

"Nonsense, lady. I would be pleased to hear your name and title."

*I'm sure you would.* She ignored his request. "Is there anything I can do for you?"

He was silent a few moments. "Perhaps, lady, you might tell me what I've done to offend you."

"Offend me?"

"Indeed; you seem to be displeased at something, and I can only assume it is my presence."

This surprised her. Whoever this Vellen was, he was unlike Derlac, the high priest she'd been forced to deal with too often.

"I'm not used to having the infirmary sealed off by armed guards." She turned warily to face him again, arms crossed, head to one side.

He saw in her expression fear, confusion, and irritation. All amused him. Clearly her stay with the First of the Sundered had not broken her. The fact that she was whole pleased him immensely.

"Forgive me, lady." He bowed. "I shall have the Swords removed at once."

Standing in front of a perfectly attired, perfectly civil priest made her feel suddenly awkward and gawky. She had never imagined that any Malanthi could carry such an air of beauty about him. It made her very uncomfortable. Motionless, Kandor might once have looked as Vellen did.

"Look, Lord Vellen," she said, drawing her arms tighter around her body. "I'm rather busy, rather tired, and rather disinclined to play at word games. If you want something, state it plainly. If you don't, you can leave with your Swords."

"It appears that I have caught you at an inconvenient time." He turned to the door. "But I assure you, Lady Sara, that I only wished to meet you. For the moment you have nothing more to fear from me."

She nodded, not trusting the words. She did not relax at all. He turned back, his smile faltering only fractionally.

"Your bravery is commendable. I believe I shall see you at this evening's meal."

He opened the door, and Lord Darclan walked into the room. They watched each other without a trace of surprise.

"Lord Darclan."

"High Priest."

They fenced with their smiles; Sara saw the identical glint of teeth on each face, and noted that the warmth had left Vellen's. Stefanos looked up to meet Sara's eyes.

"Stefanos."

"Lady."

She smiled, very conscious of Vellen's gaze.

"Darin?"

This caused the only discomfort that Lord Vellen had yet shown. His brows rose, and the look he shot his former slave held all of the anger he had not yet shown.

"Lord," Darin said quietly.

"You are both well?"

They nodded, and Stefanos stepped quietly toward Sara.

"I will leave now, Lady," Lord Vellen said, plainly aware that he was about to be forgotten. "I will have the pleasure of your company later this eve." He bowed a last time and left the room.

When the door had closed, Sara walked into the waiting circle of Stefanos' arms. She leaned into his chest.

"He's dangerous," she told him quietly.

He held her tightly, too tightly. She looked up.

"Stefanos, what is it?"

"Nothing, lady."

"Not nothing. Something troubles you. Please, look at me."

He did, with pain and an odd sort of hunger.

"Lady, will you close the infirmary for the day?"

Quietly she looked at Darin and nodded. She walked around the room, putting things away. When she finished, she followed him out of the infirmary, and with shaking hands locked it.

Darin asked his leave, and Stefanos gave it without paying too much attention. He turned to Sara, caught her hands, and kissed her forehead.

Together, by mutual silent consent, they walked toward Sara's chambers. There, in the curtained light, they held each other against the coming of the night.

* * *

Vellen stared down at the corpse in front of him. With a slight grimace of irritation, he rolled down his sleeves. Taking care to avoid blood, he wiped the blade of his knife clean and placed it, almost reverently, into the box that the Sword to his left held.

*Risky,* he thought, *but I may need the power.*

Still, he felt annoyance. He was not inclined to rush through a ceremony, or to end a life too quickly. The need for a semblance of secrecy annoyed him further, not that it would matter in the end. With the coming of dawn, he would blood the altars several times, free from the constraints that held him now.

"Redak, take the body out through the slaves' quarters. Make sure you are seen by no one but the slaves. On your way back, tell them this: The Lady Sara is not to leave the premises again; if she is seen, she is to be stopped. At midnight, those unwilling to serve the Church in this fashion will serve it in another."

Redak gave a low bow and set to his task. It was a fairly easy job, for since disposing of the body might have posed a problem, Vellen had chosen a young child, one easily carried by a single Sword.

*Risk.*

He turned to look out of the window. *What game do you play, Servant?*

He had wanted to see the blood of the Enemy, wanted more to defile it and destroy its potency. That desire was not to be granted to him. On the three occasions that he had tried to leave the castle and enter the grounds, he had been firmly, fearfully, and forcibly halted. Without the four Servants as escort, he could do nothing short of cutting down those who opposed him, which would accomplish little.

But the evening approached, and with it the power he needed. If the First Servant wished to guard the blood of the Enemy against him, it mattered little—no one else would reach it. They were two against nine, and they would be overpowered.

But it vexed him, and not a little. He was patient when necessity decreed it, but he had no love of waiting.

*I will be home soon. And when I arrive, my rule will be undisputed.*

Good enough. He noted the sun's position and began to lay out clothing for the evening meal. The only thing he would regret was lack of time to satisfy his curiosity about Lady Sara. What did she hold that could bind the First Servant so strongly?

What about her, among all others, had elevated her to such a level?

Stefanos held Sara, feeling again the warmth of her, seeing without sight the luminosity of her life. Already the sun was cooling into its daily death and the chamber was sinking into darkness. He knew that he would never again hold her or know the peace that she could bring him.

*What did you say about the light, Sarillorn? That you would hold it within you, hold it against me like a shield?*

He tried to smile, but there was too much grim bitterness to allow for it. She had always kept her word. And now, now there was no like thing he could call up within himself to use as a shield against the loss. He felt like the husk of a living thing and pulled her closer to share the warmth of her life.

Without speaking, Sara returned his embrace. She knew what he was feeling, and the intensity of it banished her desire to know why.

"No, Darin, you can still see the staff."

Darin reached down and pulled at the hem of his tunic. It was slightly oversized, but both he and Gervin agreed that this would probably not be noticed or remarked on—the occupants of the dining hall would hopefully have their attentions focused elsewhere.

"Better?"

"Slightly." Gervin rubbed wearily at his eyes. Between the two of them they had gotten maybe four hours of sleep, and sleep was badly needed. No time for it, though. No time at all. "Now practice walking again."

Nodding, Darin crossed the length of the room.

"Still limping, Darin. Try again."

It was perhaps the fiftieth time he had done so, but he made no complaint—the cost of a mistake was too near and too high.

"Did you find out if the Swords will be dining?"

Gervin smiled grimly. "Yes. They won't be dining formally." He did not expand upon this, but Darin shivered at the darkness of the smile.

"The Servants?"

"Places will be set for them. Don't think they'll be eating much—not yet. That's better. Can you get it out of the strap?"

They both knew the answer, but Darin pulled the staff out from under the side of his tunic anyway.

"Good. Put it back."

Easily said, and after hours of practice, almost easily done. *Are you sure they won't be able to see you?*

The voice of Bethany replied firmly, but wearily. *As I've said many times, Darin, I will not put out the power. Without it, there is little reason for them to suspect your existence. But if I am visible at all, they will know me, as your lord did.*

*Right.* Self-consciously, he checked the length of the tunic, pulling it again into position.

*The Sarillorn is strong. They are expecting her; they will be warded against her power. They won't be warded against all of mine. Perhaps we may surprise them.*

*I hope so.* He continued to walk, more out of nervousness than any desire for perfection.

Gervin checked his dagger sheaths almost casually.

"The Swords will be my problem, Darin. I believe I can accomplish something against them."

Darin stopped walking and checked the staff again. He sighed. "When shall I report to the kitchen?"

"You've another hour. Keep walking."

"I'll want some time to practice balancing dishes."

Gervin shrugged. "How difficult can that be? You've served before."

"Not in the dining hall. They said I was too small."

"True. But I've told you all you'll need to know here."

"I know. But if I start serving from the wrong side, or in the wrong order—"

"You won't, Darin. Have some faith in yourself." Gervin sat down, stood up, and sat down again. He shrugged, trying to relax muscles that were riveted with tension. "I've taken the liberty of providing a dinner here for the both of us."

"I'm not very hungry," Darin said quietly.

"Neither am I," Gervin confessed. "But we'll need the energy, so we're both going to eat." He tried to smile, and for the most part succeeded. "Besides, if your stomach starts growling while you're serving dinner to our exalted guests, you're liable to come under some scrutiny."

Darin nodded seriously and sat down. He grimaced and set the staff of Culverne aside.

"Gervin, if we do make it as far as—"

"Don't think of it. Think as far as the dinner. If we're still around after that, we'll have time." He frowned.

They sat together in tense silence until someone knocked at

the door. In a flurry of motion, Darin grabbed the staff and jammed in into the strap beneath the tunic. Gervin rose and answered the door.

"Master Gervin, we've brought your dinner."

"Come in, quickly."

Two men walked into the room, carrying large trays with an ease that Darin envied. One was an older man, his dark hair streaked with steel gray, his eyes sunk into his face and ringed with dark circles. The man beside him was younger, but his face no less gaunt. Many people had had sleepless nights.

"Set them down on the bed."

They did as he commanded and turned to face him.

"The doors?"

"It's been arranged."

"Good. The gate?"

"Also arranged."

"The children?"

One of the speakers, Reynis, paled. Wordless, he shook his head.

"Why not?"

"The Swords of the Church are keeping an eye on our quarters at all times. If we evacuate the children to the Vale, it will rouse their suspicions."

Gervin nodded grimly. "Very well. Begin the evacuation of the children when the Swords are in the dining hall. I believe they'll be sufficiently distracted at that point."

Michael nodded.

"Anything else to report?"

A shadow flickered dimly across Reynis' face, a hint of grim doubt. Then he swallowed and made his choice. He said nothing.

"Good. Go back to your families."

They left the room as quietly as they had entered.

"Dinner, Darin." Gervin waved a hand toward the trays. "Best eat up now. You'll be wanted in the kitchen soon enough."

Darin did as he was bidden; he found it easier to follow directions now than to try to decide what to do on his own. His hands shook—there was nothing he could do to stop that—but he managed to lift food from the tray to his mouth. Everything had the texture of sand; it clung tastelessly to the inside of his throat until washed down with tepid water.

"Darin." Gervin's voice was soft. "It's time. Go to the kitchen now."

Numbly he put down the fork. He stood and straightened his tunic awkwardly.

"Darin." This time Gervin's voice was sharper. "I know how you feel, but this isn't the time for it. Be stronger. She'll need you."

Darin nodded, and Gervin sighed.

"You aren't a child now. You don't have that luxury. You're a priest of Lernan, an Initiate of the Circle—and head of your line. Honor that."

Again Darin nodded, trying to draw strength out of titles that now felt hollow. He thought of Sara, of the lord, of the slaves in the castle.

"I understand, Gervin." His voice was soft but steady. "It isn't the fear—it's the hope. We've got a chance—a small one—and I'm afraid that I'll fail."

"You won't. Take the time to feel this way now, if you must, but leave it behind when you enter the hall." Gervin stepped forward and hugged him; it was the first time that he had ever done so. "Go. I will see you there."

Taking a deep breath, Darin opened the door and walked out into the deserted hallway.

# chapter
# nineteen

*"Come, Lady. Our guests await."*

Sara stood, looking at the closed door. She swiveled her head around to take in the contents of the darkened room before she turned to look at him, her eyes obscured by shadow.

"Stefanos."

"Sara?"

"You think that Vellen is going to win whatever game he's playing." It was not a question.

In reply, he gently kissed her forehead.

"Dinner, lady," he said, and this time she offered him her arm. She asked no further questions, for which he was thankful.

Together they walked down the conspicuously silent halls, aware of each other, and aware of the fate that awaited, although they walked toward it with outward civility and acceptance.

The doors to the hall were open, although no people were in evidence. There was a hush over everything; Sara's footsteps sounded unnaturally loud and hollow. In silence, Stefanos walked her to her usual chair and pulled it out, allowing her to sit. She did not thank him; words seemed foreign and suddenly out of place.

He nodded, as if to say, *you understand*, then took the seat beside her. He watched as Sara looked at the place setting, a faraway cast to her eyes. Even the normal and the usual now seemed a prop for the unknown. They waited.

Nor was it long, but for Sara, unused to the tension of such a confrontation, the arrival of the high priest came almost as a relief. He entered through the doors in full regalia, the simple, embroidered robes exchanged for darker, richer ones, red entirely except where bordered by shadow, belted by darkness. These were the robes of the Karnari—the Greater Cabal's priesthood; she knew it although she had rarely seen them worn in Rennath. She could see, quite easily, the gold line that bordered them. Broken.

Across his brow, still fair and smooth, he wore a simple band that held a ruby in its triangular peak. He bowed slightly as he entered, his eye falling on the chair beside Lord Darclan. Wordless, Stefanos gave an almost imperceptible nod, and the high priest approached his seat.

Behind him, more noisily, followed the Swords. They stopped, two on either side of the open door, as their master claimed his chair.

"Lady Sara," Vellen bowed. "I am pleased to be graced again by your presence."

With a smile that held all the warmth of mere politeness, Sara responded. "Thank you. I'm honored."

She thought she caught the flicker of a smile from Stefanos, but when she looked to the side his face was set and expressionless.

"It is well to know that, lady," Vellen said, his voice no less pleasant. "For I believe we will be availed of the opportunity to travel together."

"Travel together? I believe you're mistaken."

He smiled then, and again Sara was caught out by it; his teeth, cold and white, brought a startling warmth to the rest of his face.

"Let us leave that matter until after we have dined. Perhaps you will find reason to believe otherwise. Ah." He looked up, his smile choreographed and deliberate. "I believe the rest of my party has arrived."

Sara turned to face the door.

*Dear God.* Everything became clear then—Stefanos' weary acceptance, his certainty, his pain.

Her expression became fixed and gray. Stefanos casually covered one of her hands with his as Sargoth entered the room, bringing the fall of night with him. He glided across the floor silently, pausing to look at the occupants of the hall. The red of his eyes touched Sara once, deeply, before he came to the seat beside hers.

"May I?"

She shuddered at the rasp of breath that was his voice. She started to bring her hands up, and found one of them in Stefanos' grip.

"Please be seated, Sargoth."

"Stefanos." He gestured once, briefly, and then sat. "The others are coming."

"We are here, Sargoth."

Sara looked up again, and the three Servants, lesser in stature than the two seated, entered the hall. She paled further, but this time refrained from gesturing.

Stefanos was the only Servant who had ever showed her a face she could remember. These, however, were night creatures, fell and dark, so much like the one who had presided over her mother's death. Her eyes swung around the room, searching. There were no noncombatants in it, and she relaxed.

"We wish privacy, Redak. Please close the doors."

The Sword nodded at Lord Vellen's words, and the large doors swung slowly shut.

"The castle is magnificent, Lord Darclan." Vellen gave a measured frown. "A pity that we've not had a chance to see the grounds; I'm sure they would prove of interest."

"I am afraid that the grounds are in some disarray. You would not find them comfortable or suitable to wander through."

Vellen's smile became edged. "Ah, but I have varied tastes and interests. I hope to be able to see at least the garden."

Stefanos replied vaguely, and Vellen allowed the matter to drop. Sara looked curiously at the two of them as they spoke.

The door to the kitchen swung open.

"I believe dinner is ready," Stefanos announced.

Sara turned to look and saw Gervin, dressed far differently from his usual spare, coarse clothing, enter the hall at the head of a group of young men. Her heart sank. It was obvious those selected to serve the meal knew who they would be serving; a tension was evident in the way they walked and the way the trays were gripped at the edge by white hands. She stopped herself from raising an eye at the sight of Darin at the end of the train.

Neither of the two appeared to recognize her, and she returned the favor. Perhaps, if they came as slaves, they would not be caught up in whatever came to pass.

*Four.*

Sargoth was a name that she recognized. Second of the Sundered—he who wanders. But he had not interfered with the wars in hundreds of years, long before the formation of the lines.

She stole a surreptitious glance around the table, and stopped when she met Sargoth's eyes. They were nightwalker eyes, small bursts of red and black embedded in shadow. She could feel his gaze pinning her down and barely resisted the urge to rise out of her chair. The hair on her neck stood on edge. These were her enemies, and she had come without sword, armor, or shield, without unit or commander, to stand before them.

*Stefanos, did you know?* But she would not ask, not here, where it would be conceived as fear or weakness.

"You are very quiet for a mortal, lady," Sargoth said.

Her chin rose slightly. Everyone seated could see the green aurora that flared from her eyes. But she smiled. "And you're very curious."

The breeze of an almost silent chuckle touched her ears. Servant's laughter; a Servant's humor.

"A fault of mine."

"And one he takes pride in," Stefanos said. "You must ask him, when time permits, where he has been for the last few centuries. The answer would almost certainly be illuminating."

"You might consider asking yourself, Stefanos."

"Perhaps." One of the young men appeared briefly at his lord's shoulder holding a bottle of wine. With a deft, practiced flourish, he poured a small amount into the empty glass that stood before him. Stefanos lifted the glass and let the fluid slide down his throat. He nodded, his glass was filled, and the man moved on.

"Would you care to join us?"

Sargoth eyed the wine for a moment before dismissing it. "Not this time, Stefanos. It seems unpleasant."

"As you wish."

Sara lifted her own glass, brought it to her lips, and put it down, in an almost continuous motion. The wine swirled in the glass, catching the light in its red depths. She felt it tingle as it traveled down her throat, but could not really taste it at all.

Vellen drank and smiled. A very good wine, and one appropriate for the evening. He toyed with the idea of making a toast, but rejected it. He was not used to celebrating a victory before it became a reality, no matter how sure a thing it was.

"Lady Sara," he said, his fingers running along the stem of his glass, "you are something of a mystery to those of us gathered here. Perhaps you would care to tell us a little of your life."

She pursed her lips slightly in response, her mind not on her own life but on the deaths others had suffered at the hands of the Dark Heart's minions.

Her silence annoyed Vellen, but the irritation was fleeting; the lines were never known for their ability to appreciate a Malanthi victory—or in fact to acknowledge one—with anything but their death. At least in this she proved true to heritage. He still hoped to be able to discern the quality that bound her to the Servant, but he had time, and much of it, before they reached the capital. If patience was required, he could afford it. He did not repeat his question.

"A pity, lady." Sargoth's whispered voice now. "For I too am curious. I would like very much to know how you came to meet Stefanos."

Sara moved slightly to the side as a clear soup was placed in front of her. Her hands taut, she picked up the larger spoon, sighed, and turned to Sargoth.

"In a Malanthi border raid."

The soup, like the wine, was tasteless. But it was warm; she drank it hoping to stem the rising chill.

"A border raid?" Sargoth pointedly ignored the bowl that was hurriedly brought to him. "I see. But how did you survive it?"

Very quietly, and very distinctly, she said, "Luck."

"Ah. And when was this?"

"Sargoth, I do not believe the lady is used to being interrogated."

"She will become so."

Hair bristled at the back of Sara's neck. Power flowed around her skin until it prickled. In a cool, clearly enunciated voice, she said, "I rather doubt that." She pushed the soup, half-finished, away. She started to open her mouth and then snapped it shut. Anger would serve her poorly here; of this she was certain.

The meal passed in a slow haze of tasteless food, brought and taken away hardly touched. Sara nodded once or twice, at what she could not have honestly said, but for the most part concentrated on maintaining a smooth façade. When her hands started to shake—whether from fear or anger she couldn't decide—she would set her fork and knife aside for a moment until it had passed.

And then it was over. The last dish was removed. She sat perfectly still, tension threading its way round her spine. She linked her hands in her lap, kept her chin low, and waited.

Vellen was speaking.

". . . and I must thank you, Lord, for the excellent meal you've provided, and for your hospitality. This will hopefully be the last time you are imposed upon in this fashion."

He raised his head and nodded slightly. The four Swords moved forward, away from the doors. "However, it is now urgent that we return to the capital; we must leave this evening. I trust that our horses are readied?"

"One of the Swords nodded wordlessly.

"Very good. Lady Sara, if you would be so good as to prepare yourself for a journey." He nodded in her direction, and the Swords moved as one man to stand at the back of her chair.

"I was not aware that I was to travel anywhere."

"An oversight on Lord Darclan's part." Vellen's voice became much quieter, stripped of the vague good humor that he'd shown throughout the meal. "Not one, however, that I can afford to make allowances for."

Very slowly, Sara turned to face Stefanos. His expression was etched in ice, or so it seemed. His eyes met hers only once, and that very briefly, before he nodded.

She saw silver in them, a quick mercurial flash, and pushed her chair away from the table, scraping it along the stone. Very quietly, she stood, and the guards looked neutrally at Vellen.

Vellen smiled. Catching the First Servant's nod, he allowed himself that. *This may not be as difficult as we thought.* He nodded at each of the Servants, and they too rose.

The Swords closed in on Sara. Her hands trembled as she balled them into fists at her side.

"Come. It is time." With that, Vellen also stood, laying his napkin aside. "The doors, please."

Two of the Swords walked quickly over to the large doors, and with little effort opened them to reveal the darkened halls. Sargoth, moving more quickly than his companions, stood behind them. The two Swords who remained with Sara started to push her forward.

And one of them fell. With no warning, his knees buckled. He gave an abrupt gurgle, and collapsed against the stone, face first. From the back of his neck, black and matted, the handle of a dagger protruded. Blood from the wound obscured the back of his throat.

Sara gasped and started away from the second Sword, whose hand now gripped a readied sword. They were good, these. The blade rose, wavered, and then clattered to the ground, as the second Sword joined the first upon the floor, blade in side of throat. This time, however, Sara had seen the direction the dagger had come from. She brought her hands up in a complicated weave of motion and whirled around.

Some ten feet from the kitchen door, Gervin stood, legs apart and feet firmly planted. Both of his hands were empty.

Vellen spun at the exact moment that Sara did, and saw the same man. He recognized him only now and cursed himself for a careless fool. In wordless fury, he raised an arm, homing in on Gervin.

And in the hollow behind the furthest hanging on the west wall, Darin saw what no one but Gervin could: That the high priest's eyes glowed an icy, familiar silver. He had no time to digest the import of the observation—and no time truly to fear it. With fingers curved tight around the pale wood of the staff, he swung outward in complete silence, a move he'd practiced several times. The staff was already level and pointed; it needed no further guidance or coaxing. A brilliant bolt cut the distance between him and the nearest Servant in two. It crackled white, with a hint of the palest green, as it sped, unerring, to its target.

The Servant screamed, her hands flailing in the air fractions of a second too late.

*Got her!*

Gervin threw himself to the side and rolled to his feet as the high priest's eyes lost their silver glow, dimming to a brief blue before changing once again. He looked at Darin, staff in hand, and his eyes widened.

"Are you watching, Vellen?" Darin shouted, the staff already leveled. "Do you have a good view?"

Vellen brought his hands up in a precision dance, but he was not a Servant; he hadn't their speed. The light of Culverne smashed into his chest and sent him staggering back.

And even though the hall bristled with sudden movements, Darin was silent, the staff across his chest. He watched as Vellen's legs jerked slightly. Watched with grim satisfaction, hoping he was in pain, hoping it would last. He fired again; white cut the room. Was there a scream, or was it only an echo?

The two remaining Swords rushed forward as Stefanos leaped out of his chair, throwing it to one side. Algrak and Kirlan, both outlined in red haze, drew back, circling the First of their number. Almost all of the power in the hall was centered around the long, wooden table; Stefanos was already causing his wary hunters to circle.

He looked once to see Sargoth standing quietly between the open doors. He smiled as the Second nodded, wordless.

"Stefanos, you cannot hope to win this," Algrak proclaimed.

Stefanos merely smiled, cruelly. "Least of the Sundered," he said, "I am arrayed against only two, less than two if you are to be counted among them. Prepare yourself."

And with that, a silver arc cut the air between them. Algrak spoke no more, but the red around him tightened and solidified.

Along the east wall, Vellen lay slumped in an awkward heap. From the north and the south, different figures ran a race to reach him. Gervin cursed bitterly as he realized that Darin's blast had pushed Vellen just a little too far out of range. He stopped short as the two Swords that had not been dealt with came in, weapons raised.

*This is it,* he thought, his grip on his own blade tightening. *This is where it counts.* Adrenaline surged and time blurred as the two men came to the protection of their lord. He forgot, as he raised his arm to meet the first strike, that they were younger, stronger, and better equipped than he; he was good, had always been good, and he'd never felt it so keenly. Although he was silent as blade bit into blade, his mind reverberated with a long-dead wail, wolfish in its absolute intensity.

Nor did the Swords speak as they tried to gain the advantage of their number. Already two of them lay dead at the hands of this adversary, and the stance that he took with bare blade spoke of knowledge and skill.

They circled, offering strike and parry, as they watched for an opening.

Darin, hands on staff, began to run down the length of the hall.

"Sara! Beware the Servant in the door!"

The warning was wasted; Sara's wards were as full as she could make them.

*Lernan!* Furiously she dug her nails into the flesh of her palms, trying to tear them open. Her fingers would not respond, and instead she bit down on her lip, hard. Her mouth filled with the taste of warm salt. *Lernan, Bright Heart, please!*

And as always, as always there was no answer.

For an instant she was twelve again. She turned, unarmed, fists raised and shaking, to meet her enemy. To face the death that she had avoided only through the deaths of all the others in the caravan from Hillrock.

"Sara!"

Darin's voice pierced the thorned wall of memory, and she

was once again the crippled Sarillorn of Elliath. And Darin, sometimes charge and sometimes friend, was still alive. Still alive, untortured, unwounded, and counting on her.

She could see, glowing brilliantly, Sargoth's counterwarding, and wondered why he alone stood implacable while all others in the hall prepared for mortal combat. Whatever the reasons, he made no move toward her. Perhaps he smiled as she turned away, perhaps not. His countenance was veiled under the darkness of shadow.

Darin!

Darin stopped short as a tongue of red-fire shot out at him. Instinctively he clutched the staff to his chest as the red whirled all round him, trying to find purchase. It sparked angrily against the green of the staff of Culverne; Darin could almost feel its unnatural heat.

*Bethany!*

*It's red-fire, Darin. Hold.*

He pushed his fear back and drew a shaking breath before calling again the white-fire of his line. The fires joined and flared, crackling in a pink haze. Slowly, the white grew weaker, and Darin grayer, as the red began to push inward.

*Bethany—the flames—*

No voice answered him; all of the staff's power was involved in keeping the red at bay—in protecting the last of her line. He tried to lend her his aid, but knew, without knowing how, that it did no good. The red crept closer, and then closer still, until he could feel the fan of it along his face. Now, instead of head, he felt the fingers of a deathly chill trace his cheekbones. He wanted to pull back, but there was nowhere to retreat to—the red was all around, like a hazy cocoon.

*Bethany . . .*

Another light flared in the room; another light battered against the red that surrounded him. It was white, pure, blazing—and unexpected. Darin's sight dimmed as it caught his eye unaware, but he kept panic far enough at bay to continue to stand still, arms and hands wrapped about the symbol of his line.

Caught between the white-fire of Culverne and the white-fire of Elliath, the red-fire was forced both backward and forward, slowly—too slowly—crumbling into itself.

Somewhere in the hall, as if from a great distance, the sound of screaming began. It was low and unnatural, and Darin couldn't place it—but Sara could. She smiled as she ran along the west wall, the first genuine smile that had touched her lips all evening. It was a dark, grim expression; if Darin could have seen it, he would not have recognized her.

Her lord was in his element, in his glory.

She kept her wards up and reached Darin's side. Her hand touched his arms and he spun into a crouch, the staff held lengthwise in two shaking fists.

"It's Sara, Darin. I'm here."

He relaxed, but only slightly. His eyes focused poorly; the light was still upon them.

"Sara, are you all right?"

She nodded. "Yes."

"You have to get out of here."

"I'd guessed."

"Where's Gervin?"

She turned around quickly, her eyes scanning the room. Swift impressions of steel, of magic, and of motion danced before her eyes. She could see Stefanos at the vertex of a static triangle, his arms raised and pointed; could see one of the Servants writhing in midair—still screaming—while the other poured out streamers of fire that fell just a little short of their target. The scene captured her eyes for a fraction of a second before she looked elsewhere. At Gervin. Her eyes grew wide as she started forward and stopped in a sudden, jerky movement.

*This is it,* he thought again. He was sweating and bleeding—it was hard to tell which was which—but so was the last of the Swords. Gervin was the better swordsman, but he'd taken the more severe injury; he was not good enough to stand alone and unarmored against two of Vellen's elite guard without paying some steep price for the action. The Sword feinted low and brought his weapon up at almost a right angle. Gervin parried and swung almost wildly to the right, feinting as well. He felt the satisfaction of knowing that his strike was not a miss before the Sword attacked again, this time calling on the reserves of his energy for a series of lightning-quick lunges. Not the usual method of attack for such a heavy weapon.

*Hells.* Steel bit deeply into his left arm, glancing off bone only because of the angle of attack. He staggered back a few steps, and the Sword pressed his advantage. Both men were breathing heavily. Gervin felt a black wave dance before his eyes and lunged into an attack to drive it back. *Blood loss,* he thought dimly. He danced out of the way of another strike, allowing it to graze his calf instead of removing his lower leg.

*Is this the best you can do?*

The Sword attacked again, and Gervin cried out as steel slid neatly between his ribs. He tottered once and then fell backward to lie face up under a stone sky.

With a grim nod of mingled satisfaction and relief, the Sword walked over to his adversary's body. He gave it a vicious kick, and Gervin slid across the slick, red floor. Then, wiping his brow, he turned to look across the hall.

Gervin rolled up, grabbed the weapon that had "fallen" so strategically, and brought it down in an angle that ended with the weary Sword's neck.

Just that simple.

*Just . . . that . . .* He sighed, sunk slowly down to his knees, his eyes searching the hall for sight of the lady. Already everything was dimming. *Damn blood anyway.* He dragged one hand across his face, trying to clear his eyes.

*Lady? Lady—it's cold—*

And then he saw her, shrouded in white. Her eyes, green and glowing, like new grass or new leaves, grew closer and closer.

*Have I finished my task now, Lady? May I rest?*

He could almost feel the touch of her lips across his eyelids as her gentle fingers closed them. He smiled, and the sword clattered to the stone, never again to be raised by his hands.


"Can you see Gervin?"

"I think—I think he's engaging the Swords." Sara turned firmly around toward the kitchen door.

Darin didn't look down the hall; he didn't need to. Sara's voice told him all he needed to know. A spasm of anger and pain flickered briefly across his face.

But Gervin had paid the price for one reason only. He began to run toward the end of the hall and heard Sara rustling behind him.

*Darin, stop now!*

His feet skidded along the stone as Bethany's mental shout covered him. He lost his footing and slid a few feet before coming to an awkward halt. Sara reached down and pulled him up.

"What? What is it?" he said.

"Can't you see it?"

"See what?"

"Look straight ahead."

He did as she bade, while she cast a furtive glance backward. He heard her curse softly under her breath.

"I don't see—" and then he did, for a few seconds. Inches away from where he stood, a slight red haze touched the air. "What is it?" He started to put a hand out, and the staff of Culverne flared brilliantly in his hand.

*Don't touch it, Darin. it's a ward barrier.*

*It isn't solid.*

*No. And you could probably cross it; it would hurt, but it would not kill you. The Sarillorn cannot.*

*What?*

*She used some power to aid us against the red-fire. Her wards will not get her through the barrier unharmed; her blood is too strong not to be touched.*

"Darin, stay behind me."

He turned and nearly buried his face in her shoulder. Taking a cautious step to the side, he saw the cause for her curses: One of the Servants was approaching them. His movements were slow, almost casual, and his expression could not be seen for shadow.

But Sara knew him. "Sargoth," she said, raising her hands. "I wondered when you would enter this fray."

The Second of the Sundered did not reply. Instead he drew closer, until he stood less than an arm's length away. Sara faced him unflinching. He raised one hand, reached out, and touched her chin. Sparks flared angrily at the connection, and Darin gasped aloud. Neither Sara nor Sargoth deigned to notice.

"You are of older blood. I am certain of it." He pulled his hand away. "Ah, Stefanos. The question—I had forgotten it."

None of Sara's confusion showed; Telvar would have been proud of her. She faced Sargoth, knowing that he was her death and knowing that he knew it, without faltering once.

"Shall we wait for this to finish, lady? It will not be long now; nor is the outcome in much doubt."

*What game are you playing, Servant?* She looked quietly around the hall. Six bodies lay upon the stone floor: four Swords, the high priest, and Gervin. None of them stirred.

The three Servants, however, were still in motion. One now lay against the floor, quivering. The other was upon his knees. Only Stefanos stood, as he had done so many times before, in the face of battle. His arms fell slowly to the side, keeping time with the collapse of Kirlan. From her distance, Sara could see the strain across his features. Human features—she could not understand why he would expend his power in so trivial a way, but was glad of it.

He gave his opponents one last careful glance before turning to look down the end of the hall.

Sargoth met his eyes and bowed.

"First among us," he said, the sibilance of his voice carrying.

"Second." Stefanos returned the bow, his eyes going to Sara. He started forward.

"A moment." Sargoth held up one hand, and Stefanos stopped. "I wish you to recall a conversation we had in the closing hours of night."

"I recall it."

"Very well. At that time, I had nothing with which to bargain." He waved one arm to the side, taking in both Sara and Darin. "I believe that situation has now changed."

"Perhaps it has." He began to walk forward again. "I am willing to entertain the notion of negotiations."

"How unusual. I see your battle has taken its toll."

"Your offer, Sargoth."

"As you can see, neither Sarillorn nor Priest—and that was clever, Stefanos—can yet leave this hall. Algrak and Kirlan will stir soon. If I am not mistaken, so will the high priest. Should I choose to join my strength to theirs, all of your effort and planning will come to naught."

"Agreed." He drew closer.

"Good. I do not understand what transpires here, and it vexes me. This Lernari, unlike the other half bloods on either side, is quite strong; all here can feel it. Yet I believe I can come to understand this on my own."

"What exactly do you wish to know?" It was superfluous, but he asked anyway.

"Malthan has always allowed those of us who choose to serve him to do as they pleased in the mortal domain."

*Sarillorn.* Ignoring Sargoth, Stefanos stretched out one hand, and after the slightest of hesitations, Sara took it and allowed herself to be drawn into his embrace. It was cool, as always, but she could feel tremors of exhaustion run through him.

Without releasing her, Stefanos turned to look at Sargoth. "And?"

"Even if this woman should be as I suspect, it should in no way explain the unprecedented interference that the Dark Heart 'requested' of us in this matter. Yet He chose to send us here, against you.''

''Yes.''

''Why, Stefanos? With very little aid, He could have seen you destroyed if your actions annoyed Him. He did not ask for your destruction. Only the destruction of . . . the Sarillorn.''

Darin spun around at the words, his face a mixture of confusion and dread. No one noticed, and he did not dare to voice his question.

''I have told you, Second of the Sundered, that I do not know why.''

Sargoth's dry chuckle did not seem out of place. ''Indeed you have. And I have told you that I believe He would answer you should you ask the question.''

''Your curiosity, old friend.''

''Will be my downfall yet, I know. But as it has entertained me these many centuries, I will count on it yet.''

''And your bargain?''

''The child and the woman will be free to leave the hall, if they can find an escape from what waits without. I will not interfere with their progress at this time should you choose to satisfy my curiosity.''

''At this time?''

Sargoth nodded. ''I can promise little else.''

''And if He chooses not to answer?''

''Only ask, then. That will be sufficient.''

Stefanos' arm tightened around Sara briefly. She turned her face to his and met his eyes a fraction of a second before his lips brushed hers. She saw all that was in them. Nothing could be put into the few words she had time for, so she too said nothing, but clung to him.

Then he lifted his head and took a step away from her.

''Use the time well, Sara.''

''Stefanos . . .''

Shaking his head, he turned completely away from her to face the waiting Sargoth.

''I will do as you ask. But the Lernari are to leave now.''

''That is not the way that the Sundered deal among themselves.''

''That is the only way I will do so now.'' His voice was lean and dark; he was still First.

''Very well.''

Sara turned to the kitchen door and saw the barrier fade. It had been strong, but even though Sargoth had spent much power to maintain it, she knew he was stronger than Stefanos for the moment. She hesitated.

Without turning, Stefanos said, "Sara, you will leave with Darin. Now."

"But—"

"But?" She caught the faint glimmer of bitter humor in his voice. "No buts, Sara. Not this eve."

Still she faltered, and Darin moved forward to take her arm.

"Sara, I know you don't want to leave him, but you heard the Servant—it isn't his death that's called for. It's yours. I don't know what Lord Darclan has agreed to, but it's only to buy us time. We've got to go."

The price for life was always this: another's sacrifice. But this way she could buy Darin's life with it as well as her own. She had no right to take that from him.

She nodded firmly and moved toward the door. Darin swung it open, and she stepped through. She turned and saw Stefanos' gaze, unfathomable, upon her. She stopped, her lips moving without sound.

And in return his lips wavered, equally soundless.

The door swung loosely shut behind her. She was gone, and Darin with her. In her wake, the hall seemed suddenly dark and strange.

"Stefanos."

"I will not speak of her further." He raised his head grimly. "But I will honor our bargain."

"I thought you might. You have grown strange these centuries. Perhaps I should have stayed to watch the change."

"Enough, Sargoth." He lowered his head again, eyes flashing a dim, hollow red. "Do not play your games with me."

"Ask Him, then. Occupy my curiosity another way."

Stefanos didn't hear his words; the harsh sibilance had already become distant, as had the sound of odd movements in the hall, the rustle of cloth or gentle groaning. A different sense overwhelmed that of the ordinary, a type of hearing that Stefanos had not called upon for centuries. He concentrated, brow furrowed at the unexpected difficulty. He called the image of his goal into his mind and slowly saw, without truly seeing, the vast expanse of endless darkness, constantly in motion, constantly unbalanced. It grew closer as he approached it.

An inner sight took his vision to a place where light had no meaning or texture. It was odd, strangely different—he had not expected time so to warp his perception of the place of meeting.

*A mortal life*, he thought, flexing his hands before he realized that they were not truly there. *How odd that so short a life can change so long a habit.*

He felt no fear as he waited. Nor did he feel love or hate, anger or pain. There was no place for these things here, for here there was no life.

And then the darkness coiled and rumbled in front of him. It opened—he knew this with a sense that lay too far beneath the surface to be identified—and sent out a tendril.

Without hesitation, Stefanos, First of the Sundered, walked into the grasp of his eternal parent—into the part of him so long denied it had grown alien and unsettling. He waited there for his Lord's voice.

*Stefanos.*

*My Lord.*

*You have not rested thus for a time.* Around him darkness undulated.

*No, Lord.*

*You have not spoken to me, nor called yourself to the place of meeting.*

*No.*

*Yet you come now.*

*Yes.*

*Speak, then. Yours has always been the strongest voice among those who serve. I would hear it.*

Stefanos refrained from speaking as a small spark of anger flashed within him. Again the darkness rippled, touching him and moving through him like a current.

*Come, Servant. You are not so proud that you have not come; not so proud that you have not called. Is it aid that you require? Power? Do the Servants of my Enemy still plague the mortal planes?*

There was no place, in the palm of the Dark Heart, for emotion. Even knowing it, Stefanos could not stem the anger that flared.

*Ah, Stefanos. What is this you bring to me? You have been long sundered, Servant, to yet feel something here.*

*I bring you nothing, Lord. Nor do I require anything of you.*

*No?* The darkness shuddered, heaving almost aimlessly.

*No.*

*A pity. But tell me, Servant, if this is true, why have you come?*

Here, with the chill of darkness creeping around him in such a familiar way, he wondered. Was he not the First of the Sundered? Was he not the most powerful of his Lord's Servants? Was he not worthy of more than this—this game in which he was somehow a pawn? Was he not—

Sara's lover.

Sara. Sarillorn. Daughter of the line of the Lady, First of the Sundered of the Light, First of the Enemy.

But the Lady was gone now, through his gamble, his artifice, his strength. Her line was the first to fall to the march of human history, the tide of human time. What power she had possessed was now eclipsed and forgotten, surrendered to darkness and lost.

Yet in darkness, he remembered her.

In darkness he remembered her descendant.

In Malthan's hand he called upon the last of Elliath's Sarillorn, and her image came to him, wreathed with the strange translucence of her light. Her lips moved silently around the play of her human words, her human smile; her eyes shone green in the white of her perfectly flawed face.

*Why have you come?*

Sara.

*Stefanos, Servant, you have indeed brought me something. A gift. The last of my Enemy's line.*

Something stretched within Stefanos; it wrapped itself around him with a tension close to breaking. He would not name it. He waited for his Lord to speak.

*I have little concern for her; she is mortal.*

*Why, then, do you interfere?*

*Have I not said that you have the strongest voice of all those Sundered who serve me?*

*Of what import is that?*

*I have watched you, Servant. You stand between the mortal plane and the place of meeting; through you I have touched on much of the fruit of my goals. You gave me many deaths, sent to me the lifeblood of the tainted who are mortal. Your sendings were stronger than those of your brethren; in return I made sure that you continued to stand First among them.*

*But now, First Sundered, you have given me something sweeter and stronger than the lifeblood of the tainted. The death of the last of Elliath will not satisfy me; of this I am certain. But through you—through you, First Sundered, her death will be lasting. Even now it has already started, and she has not yet touched my altar.*

*She has taught you something; you have learned it well.*

Paralysis suddenly held fear for Stefanos. Recalling the quiet moments of a few days past, he pulled back, lurching away from the hand of God. The darkness heaved and shuddered as he sloughed it off; it receded into a distance that was never far enough away.

Light returned as he hit his body; a light that seemed brilliant and warm for all that it was dim. The walls of the hall wavered around him as he fell to his knees, to touch the welcome of the stone floor.

*Sara.* His hand crept slowly forward as he pushed himself up. *Sara.*

But it was not his Sarillorn that he faced upon his return from the place of meeting. He had not expected to, so the sting of disappointment was a bitter surprise. Ringed around him he could see the wavering forms of Algrak, Kirlan, and Sargoth. They were dark, almost a beaded mist. The fourth Servant who had fallen to the strike of Bethany was gone; she would not return to haunt him this evening.

He came to his feet as quickly as he could. He started forward, to find the way blocked. From each of the three Servants, bands of red-laced black sprouted forward, passing through one another in a tight, fine mesh. He wheeled around, but did not attempt to move further; the net was closing and he was at its center.

*This,* he thought bitterly, *from the hand of God. I will serve no more.*

From a distance, the smallest whisper brushed his inner ear. *You will serve me best of all.*

Stefanos was weary; he felt, for a moment, the centuries of existence that he had passed through as if they were a solid wall. *Mortal games. Is this what age feels like?*

The net closed in on him, its radius shrinking toward his body. He stopped moving completely and watched it come. It seemed to eat through the inches of stone beneath his feet, absorbing the solidity and transforming it. The power of God was truly here.

But it stopped. It was close enough to touch on all sides, but its embrace grew no tighter.

*No, Lord! Let us finish this!*

One strand of the web bulged in toward Stefanos, straining to reach him. With a snap it fell back into place, but the fine strain of red throughout it had been broken.

Beyond the wall, Stefanos could hear the growl of frustration that tore through Algrak's throat, much as Stefanos' hands had done earlier. He smiled.

"Come, Algrak, this is futile." Kirlan's voice wavered, but was stronger than Stefanos' would have been had he chosen to speak. "Do not argue with the will of our Lord. The woman has escaped the hall, and perhaps the grounds themselves—and the Lord wishes her to be taken."

Again a snarl, but this time accompanied by words. "To give her to that?"

"Spare your contempt." Kirlan responded. "Vashel is banished from the plane for a time, but the same strike did not destroy the mortal Priest."

"Then we will find the one responsible. But the First—"

"It is not in our hands. But if you wish it so, make your challenge. I am sure He will be most understanding."

Silence, then the sound of the door creaking open.

"Sargoth?"

"A moment, Kirlan. Just a moment. First Sundered?"

"Second."

"Did you honor our bargain?"

"I asked the question you wished asked."

There was stillness, followed by a subtle movement of air that might have been the raising of an arm or the shake of a head.

"And did he answer it?"

For a moment, Stefanos pondered the question, considering the usefulness of a lie. Let Sargoth's curiosity burn in him; let him be kept suspended in the state of ignorance that most annoyed him. He could not ask for Sara's life. *Ah Sargoth.* "He did."

"Then tell me. Tell me what he said. Let me know why he pursues this mortal with the power of four."

"Perhaps. But it may be that I am Servant still, and will honor our agreement in the manner of His Servants."

Silence, then sibilant breath across the air.

"You will tell me, Stefanos."

"Yes." He reoriented himself in his standing prison to face the direction the Second of the Sundered spoke from. He drew breath, although he did not need it—a habit so old it felt natural.

''He wants the Sarillorn because I will suffer for it.''

And because Sargoth could not see his face, he allowed himself the grace of a pain too precious to have physical origin.

# chapter
# twenty

*"This way."*

Darin's voice was barely loud enough to be heard over the sound of shallow breathing and hurried footsteps.

"Where are we going?" Sara glanced backward, at the darkness over her shoulder. They weren't being followed—not yet.

"The gardens," he replied, praying silently that all had gone as Lord Darclan and Gervin had planned.

*Gervin . . .* He pushed the thought away almost easily; years of living in the Empire had taught him that much control. Time enough for mourning later, one way or the other.

"Here, Sara. It's here somewhere."

"What?"

"Exit."

Sara shook her head; he heard her hair in the darkness. She had never left the castle by this door. Neither had he, but it was where Gervin had said it would be. He hoped it was open.

His hands shook as he found the latch in the shadows. A click, barely audible over the sound of their breathing, and the door slid open to the night sky.

"We have to run," he whispered between his teeth.

She nodded, swinging the door shut behind them. "Wait a minute." Leaning over, she pulled up the hem of her skirt, and with a quick decisive tug, tore it up the middle.

"Ready."

"Right." He took her nerveless hand in his and ran across the courtyard to the gate of the maze. Together they entered the first passage of the neatly clipped, twisting hedges.

"Darin, where are we going?"

"To the center," he replied. He knew that she didn't remember her first encounter with the Gifting, but hoped that seeing it again would give her some hint of what to do. He had none.

"Left," he whispered.

She nodded, looking nervously over her shoulder. The courtyard, or what she could see of it, was still clear.

"Left then." With that she pulled Darin's hand and the rest of him followed.

They ran, the soft grass providing slight relief from the noise their feet made.

"Left again."

She made no reply, following his directions almost before he made them. She quickly lost count of the number of turns they took, or the direction they chose to run in, but noted that Darin's directions became more sure and more confident as they ran. She paused to look over her shoulder a few times, but if pursuit was coming, she couldn't detect it.

Then, at the last turn, Darin stopped short. She shuddered, hoping they hadn't run into a dead end.

"Darin?"

"Sara, we've made it." Saying that, he turned to look at her, the outline of his face barely visible. "I don't know what happens next." He felt inexplicably more afraid now that the last few yards lay open before them; a part of his mind had been sure they wouldn't make it this far.

"Do we go on?" she asked him, raising her hands to cup his sweating cheeks.

"We can't go back."

She knew he was afraid; it was impossible not to feel it. Gently, although she knew their time was short, she drew him into a solid, warm hug.

"No," she said softly. "We can never go back."

And he knew she was not thinking of the here and now. His small arms shot out and wrapped themselves around her waist. Then he pulled away, almost embarrassed.

"Come, Darin. Whatever waits for us here, we'll face together."

He nodded, wordless, and turned the final corner. Sara followed closely behind.

They came together into the clearing and found the well. Darin smiled on sighting it; it still glowed faintly, a deep, bright green that lessened the night. He saw that the stone, pale and clean, seemed somehow newer, as if the well itself were a living thing and had healed time's injury. He started forward and stopped when Sara's hand fell away from his.

"Bright Heart, no."

"Sara?"

In the dim glow of the well, he could see the stillness of her face, and the whiteness of it. For a moment, she appeared to be carved from the same stone as the well itself.

"Sara?"

"Lernan." Her lips were the only thing that moved.

Darin tried to take her hand and found it cold and stiff.

She pulled away, moving but still lifeless, and brought those cold hands up to her face.

"Lernan," she whispered again. As if the word were a release, she began to move forward, walking like one caught in dream. Darin moved out of her way as she stepped toward the well. Her hands were shaking where they gripped the edge of glowing stone.

*Lernan.* Leaning across the stone, she reached out to suspend one hand above the water's surface. Where she stood, the light seemed to gather, and the water seemed to ripple just beneath her, as if trying to reach out. Her mouth moved again, completely soundless, as Darin stepped closer. He stopped before he could touch her, knowing that to do so at this moment would be wrong.

As if invisible string had been cut, her hand plunged downward to break the clear surface. It shattered, the sound of a splash mingled with a wordless cry. Her knees buckled as she pushed herself away from the support of the stone; the grass took her as she sank to the ground and covered her face with her hands. In the light, one of them was shining.

And that light hurt her. She looked at it, shaking her head from side to side.

Darin started forward and felt a hand at his shoulder. He spun around.

"No, child."

In front of him, an old woman was standing. His fear fell away as he recognized her tattered clothing and her perpetually bent back. Her voice, though, still aged and cracked, held a strength that he did not remember.

And her eyes—her eyes were a green so deep they caught him and held him fast.

"I have been waiting for you child, for you and your companion. Wait by the Gifting. There are Servants of the Enemy abroad this night, and in greater numbers than—'' She shook her aged head. ''Wait. Your companion needs my aid.''

Then she was gone, floating across the grass to where Sara lay. She bent down, curved hands running across the back of Sara's head, stroking her hair as if they had all the time in the world.

''Little one,'' she said softly. ''There is no time for this yet. You have come to me, and I have waited long to meet you.''

Sara's face came out of her hands. Darin couldn't see her clearly, but felt that at that moment the eyes of the Servant and the eyes of his lady were the same—aged, wise, and somehow beyond him.

''Elliath,'' Sara murmured, her voice flat.

''Gone, little one, as you must know now. As is the Lady.'' One crooked finger reached out to catch Sara's chin before it folded again into the grass. ''She saw it, child. She knew it would come and knew that she could not avoid it. But there was peace in it, in the end.''

''How long has it been?''

''Since the fall of Elliath, three hundred years.''

In a lower voice, Sara said, ''And the other lines?'' For she understood, bitterly and finally, Darin's presence in the castle.

''Culverne was the last to fall. The land still remembers their influence.''

''How long?''

''Five years ago.''

Sara's eyes swept shut as she huddled against the grass. If she felt any sorrow at the loss, it was buried deeply beneath her rage.

*The Gifting of Lernan—here.* She could not look up; the sight of it was a bitter accusation. *Three hundred years.* Belfas, Carla, Deirdre—all of these dead, buried, forgotten. She didn't even know how they died, or when; nor could she ask.

Instead, she remembered Rennath, in all its dark glory; remembered the years she had spent traveling through Veriloth, tending to those she could aid and turning her back on those she could not. She remembered the Church and the Dark Heart, its attempts to destroy her, and the way she had stood, alive and defiant, to fly in the face of their God. And she remembered her laughter, her faltering determination, her . . . love.

She stood quickly, then, shaking.

Her love for the—no. What had he said?

*I shall build an empire across this world, Sarillorn.*

Her love.

She cried out again, a wordless denial, and wrapped her arms tightly around her body to stave off the sudden chill in the air. Centuries had passed her by, somehow, to bring her neatly to this pass. She felt a sharp and bitter ache, and the undeniable terror of waking from a nightmare only to acknowledge its truth.

"Sarillorn."

She looked up, clutching her arms all the tighter around her body. In a dull voice, she said, "How?"

The Servant shook her head. "I do not know. But against all hope, you have come to me, to return once again my faith in the Lady's vision. Lernan's Hope."

*Hope?* She wanted to shout. "What must I do?"

"Leave here, and soon. The Servants of the Enemy are stronger, both in number and in power, than I."

Darin stepped forward. "The Enemy has raised a barrier around the castle. Lord Darclan believed it would destroy us both to cross it."

"It would."

"Then how are we to leave?"

Raising one hand, the Servant turned to face the well. "Take power from the Gifting of God. Call it into yourselves to bring the barrier down." It was clear to her that Darin did not understand what she said, so it was not to Darin that she spoke.

"Lady," Sara whispered, "I do not think, if the barrier was built by the Enemy, that we will be able to contain the power necessary."

"It will be hard, but what other choice do you have? To wait here as steward, until your return, I had to choose between the night and the day; and my power was of the Light. I am as you see me, Sarillorn; I could not wander, I have felt each minute of these several hundred years. I am . . . old. I have not waited in vain."

"For *my* return?"

"Yes. The Lady spoke of it to those of us who would listen. Remember that she named you Lernan's Hope."

"And what did she hope I would do?" Sara's voice shook with emotion that could not be expressed with either words or tears; it was too strong and too new for that. "I have failed you all; the Servants of the Enemy and his Church—all of these reign because I should have—"

"I cannot say yet what she hoped for, Sarillorn. But if it eases your burden, know that she saw you here, and now, and that she

asked the Servants to select one among their number who would
be able to wait the years until your return, tied to the mortal
world.

"I was chosen. I have waited, and it has been hard, as was
promised. No one should have to live so long with the weight
of mortality upon them." She spoke with the faintest hint of
pity in her ageless eyes. Her voice grew softer and more somber
as she continued.

"But my choice and my labor are not the hardest. I cannot
tell you what to do, should you escape the trap of the Enemy,
but I know you will not fail us. Child, the seed of the future is
yours; how you sow it, and in what soil, must be your choice.
For you are human, but of the Light, and in you the end to the
ancient wars is possible."

"And what must I choose?"

"You know the power of the Gifting. Use it. And if you
survive this, search for the Woodhall. Do not forget this. The
Woodhall."

"The—but—"

"No. Now there is no time."

Nodding, Sara came to stand beside Darin. Her face, still
white and fixed, was barren of expression.

"Sara, what are you going to do?"

Without answering, she reached into her dress and pulled out
a small dagger. It trembled, cold against her hand, before she
gripped it tightly.

Darin watched as she drew a thin red line across her palm.
Even her blood moved slowly, welling into perfect, tiny beads
along the length of the cut. She gazed out over the water, her
hands following her eyes.

She stood there, caught in the light, a small, dark shadow
reaching for something beyond Darin's vision. Then, with an
almost curt shake, the hand became a fist, and the fist sank
down. The breath of a silent prayer touched her lips as her skin
broke the water.

She faltered once and then raised her head. Her green eyes
shone brilliantly. They had never looked so cold.

The fist beneath the curtain of glowing water unfurled slowly.

*Lernan, God.* It was a bitter invocation. *Will you answer
now?*

*Granddaughter.*

Water rippled up, a living pillar of God's clear blood.

Only now. Now. Sara stood on the edge of a precipice, beyond which lay the heart of Lernan. If only she dared look, she might see it revealed, might understand fully His hope and His desire. She could not look at it. Nor could she look away.

Standing suspended, she felt the power of the solitary Circle come to her in silver strands. Her skin began to tingle.

As Darin watched, she began to glow with the same faint green that the well did. The light surrounding her grew stronger until she became a part of it. She did not look quite human.

"Initiate." The Servant stood forward, no longer bent or bowed, but still aged. Darin swung around to see Sara clearly, to know what she most resembled.

"Call upon Bethany's power. Ring the well with it."

The staff, forgotten till now, found its way to Darin's hand.

"Do it *now*. The Enemy is almost upon us—can you not feel them?"

Bethany's light sprang up like a beacon that eclipsed the light of the Gifting. it curved into a circle that surrounded Darin, Sara, and the well. No sound of danger disturbed him as he continued to hold the circle, but he felt no relief.

"Steady," the Servant said.

Darin nodded, glancing around at the area that Bethany lit. Just beyond it, the dark seemed unnaturally dense; his eyes could not penetrate it enough to pick up the outline of hedges.

"Lady."

"Initiate?" she had turned her face away and even now looked into the night.

"You aren't in the circle. Move back!"

Without turning, she said, "No, Darin. The circle is no longer for me."

"What do you mean?"

"What I said. Do not move. Keep the circle centered as it is; I choose to fend for myself."

"But you said you lost your power when you made your choice to wait here!"

"Did I?" Her voice grew distant, soft. "Yes. But Lernan's power is with me yet, in a fashion."

"Servant—"

"No. I have fulfilled my duty here. I have taught you what you must know; I have spoken with the Sarillorn, once of El-liath. I have seen the truth of some of the Lady's words. Let it be enough."

"Please . . ."

"Too late, Initiate."

And out of the shadows, into the periphery of the light shed by Bethany, stepped a shadow. He was dark, tall, unidentifiable in the anonymity of the darkness. With faltering steps, the old Servant walked into his path. She stopped there, folding her arms in a gesture that was familiar enough to evoke a hint of a smile from Darin.

To his great surprise, the shadow bowed.

"Keranya."

"Sargoth."

"It is odd, Seventh of the Sundered, to find you here. I would have thought that I would have had prior warning." He stepped closer still. "And it is odd that you choose so cumbersome a form. There is little enough of the light in it. Do you not come prepared for battle?"

"Always with your words and your games, Second of Malthan. Always." She did not move. "And as always, I decline to join you in them."

Two more shadows stepped out of the darkness to stand on either side of Sargoth.

"Yes," Sargoth said, without acknowledging them. "But the form? That question, at least, Keranya."

The last of the Servants of Lernan gave a weary sigh.

"It *is* as you see it. I no longer choose."

He advanced further still, but she made no move to retreat. "You do realize, Keranya, that you cannot hope to stand against even the least of us?"

"I realize it, Second."

"Yet you stand."

"Habit."

"And will you be destroyed for the sake of habit?"

She smiled. "We all will, Second of Malthan. Come; do your worst. I am quite ready."

He reached out to touch her with his cold, ebony fingers. Twin sparks, red and white, flared in the air, but the red lasted longer and burned the more brightly.

"How odd," he said, pulling away. His voice rose as his magic made clear to him all of her weaknesses. "Keranya—"

"Yes," she said, softly, as she met the gaze of her enemy. "What you feel is true. I am bound to the mortal plane. I shall never leave it."

"Then you cannot speak to your God."

She was silent a few moments, staring at him. When she answered, her voice was low with longing, pride, and the sound that only a pain dulled by time can have. "I have not spoken to God for almost four centuries, and I have lived through each minute."

"Why? Or has the use of Lernan become harsher in the time I have traveled outward?"

"No." She shook her head. "No. The choice was mine, in this."

"But—" His head shot up, then, and he looked directly upon the well. It was no longer glowing; the light had gone out of the water. But at its edge, shrouded in green brilliance, was the indistinct form of a woman. She did not move, although the light around her eddied.

And Sargoth laughed, the sound of it deep and laced with irony.

"How unexpected." He turned again to Keranya. "I believe I understand your game now." He laughed again with an edge of malice. "What else could force a Servant, even one of Lernan, to choose as you have chosen? The vision of the First of Lernan. We watched, Keranya; we spent much of our long time waiting for the danger she prophesied."

Laughter. Darin had never hated the sound quite so much.

"We could never have foreseen that one of our number—the First of our number—would be the one to harbor his future death." The laugh was softer now, more of a dry chuckle. "I shall have to tell him; I do not believe he knows. I am tempted, believe that I am tempted, to let this mortal continue what she tries. I have had some experience with the amount of power a mortal can contain. She will almost certainly be consumed."

The laughter stopped abruptly. Sargoth raised an arm and swung it in Sara's direction.

"Take her," he said to his companions. "Kill her if you must. I shall answer to our Lord should it become necessary."

Kirlan and Algrak moved silently forward, and Keranya raised both of her arms in a fluid motion that age could not deny. A coruscating wall of white and green, more solid than Darin's circle, sprang up in front of her.

"No, Sargoth," she said almost gently, "I am Lernan's Guardian still, and I cannot allow you to pass while I yet exist."

"Of course," Sargoth replied. His eyes flared red then, but not with the muted glow they had shown previously in the evening; they burned with a hot brilliance that encompassed the landscape. It was his gesture of respect for the last of Lernan's

Servants—true power called to obliterate what had once been a truly worthy foe.

Keranya watched, unperturbed, as the power rushed toward her. She didn't flinch as it struck home, enveloping the frailty of her body. She withered under its storm, falling slowly to her knees as the wall she held began to unravel.

Darin watched, pale with shock. He took a step forward and then a step back, to hold the position as she had commanded. It was all he could do; even speech deserted him as the clearing around the well took on an absolute and eerie silence.

"Sara!"

No answer. The last flicker of Keranya's light was dying. There was little left of her, and Darin averted his eyes—he had no wish to see the end of it.

Kirland and Algrak looked once at Sargoth, who ignored them for the moment.

"Sara!"

Sargoth walked over to the remains of the Seventh of Lernan and gingerly sifted through the ashes.

"Even in this, Keranya, your God could not aid you." Then he stood and turned to the others. "Take the woman now."

"And the boy?"

"As you wish; his fate is unimportant."

They started forward again, and Darin knew that Bethany's barrier would be little proof against them. Perhaps they would feel it, perhaps not—but that would not keep them out.

In desperation, he turned to face his Lady. His jaw slackened at the sight. She was burning brightly, too brightly to gaze upon without pain.

"Sara!"

If she heard him, she could not respond at all. The Hand of God had become a fist, and she was in its center. Like stone she stood, and like stone she was filled—too meager a vessel for the brilliance of Lernan to be contained in.

"Sara!"

*Darin.*

Shaking, he looked at the staff.

*Do not panic now if you value your Lady.*

He swallowed, nodded. *What's happened?*

*The power of God is too great; it will destroy her if she stands alone.*

He nodded again, seeing the red of Servants's eyes, the black of their shadow.

*Cut your hand, Initiate; cut it deeply and then step toward her.*

He did as she asked, propping the staff between his legs while his hands obeyed her commands.

*Take her hand from the blood of God. Do it now.*

He pulled, surprised at the ease with which it gave. But Sara still did not move or respond. It worried him until Bethany's voice cut across the thought.

*Now. The Lady's hand. The one not with God. Take it; cut it as deeply. But do not touch the water.*

Trembling, Darin reached for Sara's hand. It was still and rigid; he could feel it, but the light around it gave it no shape. Blade in hand, he thrust into the light. He felt flesh, or something, give way.

The knife fell; one way or another it would no longer be needed.

*Join blood, Initiate. Touch her hand to yours. Pray.*

Contact. If Darin closed his eyes he could pretend that they were alone, and that this was his initiation. He didn't dare.

But he felt a warmth suddenly shoot up his arm as Algrak approached and with one gesture removed Bethany's ward. Darin shuddered. The black hint of nightwalker mirth touched Algrak's shadowed countenance before he realized that fear had not caused that shiver. Not fear. The least of the Servants of the Dark Heart took one step back as Darin raised the symbol of his line. Algrak brought his arms up and quickly danced a red pattern across the air.

All of Darin's perceptions suddenly heightened as the staff glowed green against the night sky. He could see Algrak, inches away from the still form of Sara; could see Sargoth crossing the charred grass. Beyond them, in the distance, he could see the brilliant glow of a huge red dome that fell in a circle like burning blood. And somewhere, one dim red glow flickered in the background like the smallest of candles.

*Bethany!* he cried, holding the staff aloft in his free hand.

*Yes. Do not let go of your Lady's hand. Hold fast.*

Clutching the staff like a sword, he drew it across the air, each movement, each sweep and pass of arm, vibrant and decisive. He could see the trail that was left across the air like a signature—the signature of Line Culverne—or of God, burning brightly at the behest of His initiate.

Algrak cried out in surprise and pulled back quickly to avoid the spinning wheel of white-fire.

*Darin, watch the Sarillorn!*

He spun around as Kirlan's shadow encompassed Sara. The Servant's black hand rose to touch her face, but he did not look comfortable so close to so much light; his body was curved in an odd hunch.

Darin spun the staff gracefully, almost easily, toward Kirlan. White-fire surged outward, striking the Servant and flowing through him. Kirlan had no time to scream or struggle; he was blown away like ashes in a maelstrom. The staff flared bright again, and Algrak, retreating almost mindlessly, vanished in a brilliant halo.

A burst of dark, rich red struck the air in front of Darin's face and slid away like oil. It trembled, like the remnants of a living thing, before sinking into the grass. With a grimace of disgust, Darin aimed the staff downward and the white swallowed the red completely.

"Most impressive, mortal. I fear that I must grant you victory by leaving the arena."

Darin's head shot to the side, and for a moment he gazed upon the unhooded visage of Sargoth, Second of the Sundered. His eyes were caught and held by the ageless, unpredictable darkness in the red-rimmed eyes of the Servant. Those twin points focused clearly on him, as if absorbing every detail.

"We shall meet again. You have proven yourself worthy of such an exchange. I have been long without challenge to come to this pass."

The staff swung wildly, and Darin's arm lurched forward behind it. He staggered and felt his fingers slipping out of Sara's. He managed to hold on as a beacon spread outward and the power of Lernan stripped the clearing of darkness. Too late. Even though the white-fire lashed out, Darin knew that the Servant of the Dark Heart had vanished an eye-blink before the fire struck home.

He let the staff drop to his side, still clutched in tense fingers. His left hand trailed briefly across his forehead.

*Bethany?*

*Not yet, Initiate. Already the power of Lernan grows too brightly in you. There is another task.*

*Another?* He looked up to see the bright glow of the Enemy's barrier.

*Yes.*

*What do I have to do?*

*Release the power before it consumes you. That is all.*

*How?*

*As you have done: through me. Let it travel outward in an unbroken circle; let it meet the red wall that binds us here.*

An uncomfortable tingle had already started within his chest. He looked once again at the red, red wall; it stretched, impassive, over miles of land.

As he looked, a flicker caught the corner of his eye, one so dim in comparison that he had almost missed it. He turned toward it, saw the pale outline of its redness and its darkness.

*Lord Darclan.*

Because of Lord Darclan, they had come this far, to victory, to freedom.

*Darin, you have no time for this. Destroy the barrier or all you have done is for naught. You do not have the blood of the Sarillorn—you cannot contain His power for a fraction of the time that she has gathered it into herself.*

*But what of—*

*There is no time. Take the fire of Lernan.*

He was already in pain; the fires were burning.

But he had to ask. He had to know. *What will that do to my lord?*

*I do not know.*

The pain in his chest threatened to deprive him of even his hopeless indecision. In trembling hands the staff of Culverne was lifted. He had minutes to decide what to do. It didn't matter; if he'd had hours, the choice would become no clearer, and the action no easier.

For one stark moment he longed for a time when choices were not his to make; when decisions of life and death were the dreams of childhood. Even as slave, in the heart of Veriloth, with the twin companions of fear and pain, he had known a bitter peace—freedom from so harrowing a responsibility. He turned to look at Sara, his face an open plea for guidance or counsel. Her eyes were still turned inward, but he could see her now; the light that had held her was fading as he watched, although the clearing grew no less bright. She had no answer to give him, but even if she had, would the choice be any less his?

He looked down at the ground beneath him, and noticed that the light that shone round the well was within him now. Truly, then, the choice was his, and his alone, to make.

And would it be so wrong? Was this not what they had planned for, Lord Darclan, Gervin, and he? Lady Sara would at least escape the grounds, and with her the plans of the Church and

the Darkness. Was this not what they wanted? Hadn't Lord Darclan himself accepted the risk of Lernan's power so close to
home?

Was the present always to be so choiceless and he so helpless
against it?

His cry was lost as the power surged suddenly outward, rising
like a new sun. The light took his eyes, blinding them, but he
kept his grip on his Lady and his office and the painful strength
of his decision. As if the world were a lake, and he a pebble
carelessly tossed into it, power rippled outward in concentric
spheres. The least of his pains ended as Lernan's gift found its
release and drove into the barrier.

There were none who could witness it, Darin's sight tempo-
rarily gone, Sara's turned too far inward, and Lord Darclan
behind the stone walls of his castle. None to remark on the battle
of the hands of Twin Hearts as they met again, in force, and
joined.

What noise do the Gods make, without their servitors, mortal
and undying, to work through? What words do they speak, what
cry do they utter, what tongue do they have that can be fathomed
by the living? It matters little; only the end is visible; only the
result has meaning.

Power flowed to Darin, and through him to the staff of Culverne as it wavered in the air. He didn't know what happened
to it; he was a conduit only, not an ally. He didn't know how
long he stood, stiff and straight; nor could he pinpoint the exact
moment when the blood of Lernan ceased to flow into him. All
he could be certain of was this: The power within him was
fading quickly, ebbing away into sky and air and barrier.

Slowly the cold of the night air seeped in; he felt an over-
whelming weariness become the numbness of exhaustion as his
knees buckled. Still he kept the staff held high above his head,
ignoring the ache of muscles locked too long in the same position. Gradually he felt a hollowness grow within him, eating
away at the final reserves of his strength.

Then, emptiness.

The moonlight touched the twin trails of tears as they traveled, unheeded, down his upturned cheeks.

*It's over,* he thought, and the staff slid gently down to the
grass.

*Yes, Initiate,* Bethany replied gently. *Look.*

Ahead of him, as far as the eye could see, the sky was clear and blue; shades of morning painted their colors along the horizon. No sign of the Enemy's work remained.

*We've won.* He tried to infuse the thought with some sense of triumph, but felt only a dull ache.

*Yes.* Bethany spoke no more.

He turned once to look at the castle that had been his home for the past few months. The stone jutted out against the horizon, devoid of motion or life. He could see no flicker of red, no hint of familiar darkness. Somewhere in the bowels of that edifice lay the forms of two of the three who had completely changed his life.

And on the grass beside the gently glowing well lay the third. Her breath was even and untroubled, her brow smooth and relaxed. In the arms of sleep, beside the Gifting of God, she stirred without waking.

He was surprised at how young she looked. He rose stiffly and walked over to where she lay.

"Sara?"

She moved again, in response to his call.

Gingerly, he leaned over the smooth stone rim of the well. He drank some of the water, rubbed it into his eyes and along his face and neck. The he sprinkled it around the grass.

All around, where the droplets fell, small white flowers sprang up. Darin sat down beside Sara amid the eyes of God, and gently brushed the hair out of her face.

They would have to leave soon. He knew it, but felt no urgency. There would be little rest for them, wherever they chose to go, and little peace. Just for now he was determined to give himself, and his Lady, the peace of the moment.

But he continued to cry; for Gervin, for Lord Darclan, for Sara, and for himself.

He was still very young.

# epilogue

*Lord Darclan lay curled upon the stone floor, awaiting the coming of the night.* The night would not be a good one; it promised a full moon—with her bright glaring face, so much like the Lady of Elliath when she had watched over her mortal domain. He did not want the fullness of moonlight, but he'd not have the strength to call cloud cover; in his weakened state, he'd hardly have the strength to walk.

But he remembered. He did not have the strength not to. He was a Servant. Each circumstance of life was completely catalogued and could be recalled down to the slightest detail, at whim.

Lord Stefan Darclan had no wish for the memories that came unbidden.

He turned his head, scraping his cheek along the floor, until he could see, between the legs of the table, the bodies that lay against the west wall.

One in particular caught his attention.

*Gervin. Ah . . .*

He surprised himself in that; he felt some sorrow for the man's passing, although it was in no way untimely. In fact, considering the bodies of the Swords that lay about him, it was in some ways an accomplishment.

At least a portion of their plan had succeeded, and part of Gervin's command extended from the region of the dead to that of the living, for no slave had come into the hall, or even near it. He wondered, briefly, if there were any at all left on the castle's grounds—Gervin had planned an evacuation to start during the fight. He had no idea of how much time had passed, and that annoyed him.

*At least I now have the strength to be annoyed.* But it had been a close thing; the God of the Lernari had brought down the work of Malthan, freeing him and burning him both. Somehow, he had survived it. He would think on it later.

Yes, part of their plan had worked. But the important question remained unanswered, possibly unanswerable. He started to stand, then thought the better of it. Sunlight was streaming in through the large, stained-glass windows, and he had no desire to test himself against it; not now, when there was nothing to prove. His lady was gone.

He shook his head and rolled over onto his back to wait. But the question kept returning to him, hovering on the edge of his thoughts until he had no choice but to ask it.

*Sara, do you yet live?*

And again, he remembered. Sharply and clearly, each minute preserved in the immortality of a Servant's life. For so had he come to regard his existence, and if possible, regret it.

Nights beyond number—he could count them, but chose not to—he had lain at her sleeping side, tempted to call her too soon from enchantment into the world and know again the touch of her light—her love, as he understood it now. And that compulsion was strong in its way; as strong as the urge to feed that would eventually drive him from her protected, isolated room. But he had resisted, and found a cold pride in the action. That pride had sustained him then, with a future to look forward to.

It offered him nothing now.

*Sara, Lady, do you live?*

He rolled over before the open ceiling could see the expression on his face.

Through the years he had used his desire as the drive necessary to overcome his opponents and secure the Empire of Veriloth. He told himself, numerous times, that that was the only road he could take if he wished her eventually to be happy. He convinced himself that she would, over the years, forgive him for his crime—he acknowledged it now, when it would do no good—against her trust. Under his tutelage and guidance, with his protection and patronage, she would have enough to occupy her. Let her then change the law to cover the entire land; let her then save the lives that interested her or called her.

He built up a story surrounding her; called her the Lady of Mercy, so that the slaves might spread the story outward. He gave them the seed of the hope that she would ripen to fulfilment.

*Sara! Do you live?*

If he could have used his voice, he would have, but his throat was suddenly too tight and too full.

*I even gave myself a name you would have smiled at when all was finally revealed to you, Lady. Stefan Darclan. Do you recognize it now? Can you see how you named me?*

He knew that if she lived, she remembered all, as clearly as he did, for the memory was only two weeks in her life's past. He accepted the fact that she would hate him now, and possibly forever.

At one time he had felt that her death was better than the death of her light. Now, now it was different. He had lived without that light for centuries; had lived with the hope of it and the knowledge that it was perilously close. He could live with that hope again, even if he saw in her eyes the same rage, the same pain and the same hatred that had hurt him long ago. Anything if . . . *Sara Sara Sara*

*Please, please, do you live.*


Night came, cool fingers of shade and shadow. A welcome relief. His spirit drank it in, refreshing him. He stood, and found it relatively easy to do so.

Quietly and deliberately he walked over to the pile of bodies upon the floor. Vellen's was not among them.

*High Priest, you are stronger than you first seemed.*

With casual contempt, he kicked the bodies of the Swords aside. Then, carefully, he lifted the cold body of Gervin, the man who had stood by his side for the past forty years.

*Come, Gervin.*

Turning, he spoke a few words and the doors swung open. The two of them left the hall.

He was not sure exactly what he would do, but was not surprised when he found himself walking out, to the grounds of the castle, through the gate that led to the garden and beyond.

*You came here only rarely, friend, when you thought I was unaware. I believe you found it peaceful here.*

He continued to walk, a feeling of dread eating away at him. All paths led to the garden's center, and he walked a path, knowing what he would see there, but afraid to see more. He tightened his grip on Gervin's body, but refused to turn back.

And he approached the old well, the shield of his great Enemy. From afar he could see the way it glowed faintly against the backdrop of stars and moonlight.

Ah well, tonight he was strong enough to stand her gaze; let her watch what he might do. Sara had taught him, centuries ago, the lines of the moon's soft face, and the reason for her sorrowful expression.

*Lady Sara,* he had said, *your eyes cannot see the truth. It is only rock; it is not alive.*

But he let a human vision impose itself over his sight until he could see the shadowed eyes of a woman in mourning, the trembling, half-open mouth that uttered its eternal, silent cry.

*I am here, my Enemy. Will you not strike?*

The well made no reply, although its waters bubbled and swirled as he stepped into the clearing. All around his ankles, small white flowers seemed to twist to either side to avoid the touch of his step. He looked down at them, recognizing them, and gave a bitter smile. They covered the field.

And then he turned to look more closely at the ground. When he saw only flowers, he gave a sigh of relief before he could stop himself. He had dreaded finding a body.

*But if she could not contain the power,* he thought, the momentary joy passing, *there would be no body.*

Still, he knew she had made it at least this far; perhaps she had made it farther. He let that thought warm him, and gently laid Gervin's body down.

*You would have found it peaceful here, old friend.*

His hands shifted subtly to become the claws of his truest, oldest, form. Wordlessly he began to dig, tearing away huge chunks of earth and grass. It did not take long before he had cleared away what was necessary.

He straightened himself, letting the dirt cling to his fingers as he lifted Gervin for the last time.

*Find your peace here again. Keep it, knowing I can never take it away from you.*

And he laid the old man down in a bed of soft earth. He had no ceremony for the dead; his burial in the sight of the well was the closest he could come to a final gesture of respect—and against it, any human words he could utter would be meaningless.

He did not disturb the stillness with words. Instead, he bowed once, low and formal, and then put the dirt back, this time with care.

*Perhaps your spirit will guard what the Lernari lost to us centuries ago.*

"Stefanos."

He did not stop, nor turn, nor in any way acknowledge the spoken word.

"Very well, I shall wait. But I think it odd that you perform this human ceremony."

*Well you might.*

At last the grave was complete. *Gervin, I cannot gather flowers here, nor cause them to grow. I have done what is within my power to do. My thanks; you have served my lady well, and I shall remember.*

He bowed again, and that bow released him.

"Sargoth."

"I might have guessed that I would find you here; I did not expect to find you doing this. You still retain the capacity to surprise me. It is—refreshing."

"I see you escaped the Enemy's wrath."

"As did you. And which of the two is more unexpected?"

"Which of the two would be more hoped for?"

A dry chuckle.

"Come, Stefanos. I did what I had to do; the voice of Malthan is strong."

"As, it seems, are his First and Second."

"Indeed. But come. This place does not suit me. It is too—"

Stefanos knew well what Sargoth referred to; the light shed by the Lernari well was painful.

"Perhaps. But I have lived centuries with it; I would leave it as it is for the while."

"And I, First among us, would not make Algrak's mistake. If you wish to converse here, without seeing to the wound of the Enemy, I shall continue to do so. I was merely making my preferences known."

"Then come, I would not keep you in a setting that caused you discomfort. My home, at this time, is empty. I believe I can call my slaves home, but not until tomorrow, or perhaps a few days hence; their supplies will last them at least that long."

"You were prepared, then."

"Sargoth, I am always prepared."

"Yes. You did not seem surprised to see us. Even I, in your position, would have felt so. It troubles me, Stefanos. I can only think of one way—"

"Leave it, Second of Malthan. I will not speak of it." He began to lead the way out of the garden, walking both because it was natural and because it would irritate Sargoth. The Second of Malthan made no comment.

"But tell me, Sargoth. Why have you returned?"

"As always, because I am curious."

"Oh?"

"I wish to know what you will do now."

"As I have always done."

"Stefanos, you have not always mimicked a human life. I recall well the times that you led us in—"

"It was long ago. I have no desire to return to it."

"No, Stefanos? From what I have seen this night, there is now nothing to hold you to it."

Stefanos stopped moving abruptly.

"Explain."

"From what I can gather, it was the Lernari woman who held your interest."

The First Servant was completely silent.

After a moment, Sargoth continued.

"She is dead. The weak-blood, the boy, may have survived."

Stefanos did not hear the rest of Sargoth's words. He did not move, did not turn, did not blink.

*Dead?*

The words ate into him. Something began to build, a cry, perhaps a scream—but the Second of the Sundered was with him, and he was First. He wanted to run, then, to escape the full import of what had been said. But he was First Servant.

And with Sara gone, that was all he was.

Curtly, tightly, he said, "I see."

And the night took him, transforming the solid to the ethereal.

He could not surrender to his pain in Sargoth's presence, and so he surrendered the mortal plane for a time. Slowly but surely he willed himself into immortal regions, to find privacy, to find a space to let go of his emotion before it consumed him.

And Sargoth stood alone in the maze of the castle's garden, laughing with the voice of his God.

# about the author

Michelle Sagara was born. She spent a few months being an infant, and more than twenty years being a child. But she's grown up now—her life is owned by a house mortgage. She really hoped to have done something exotic within the last six months, but got sidetracked by usenet and Genie; valiant attempts at disconnecting the modem have stopped either from eating her brain.

She is still happily married, although many people have pointed out that Computer Nerd is not the correct term for her wonderful husband. Computer Geek is. She loves him very, very much.